GIRLS OF FATE AND FURY

Also by Natasha Ngan

Girls of Paper and Fire
Girls of Storm and Shadow

GIRLS OF FATE AND FURY

NATASHA NGAN

**HODDER &
STOUGHTON**

First published in Great Britain in 2021 by Hodder & Stoughton
An Hachette UK company

I

Copyright © Natasha Ngan 2021

Ikhara map by Tim Paul
Hidden Palace map by Maxime Plasse

A CIP catalogue record for this title is available from the British Library

Hardback ISBN 978 1 529 34264 2
Trade Paperback ISBN 978 1 529 34267 3
eBook ISBN 978 1 529 34265 9

Printed and bound in Great Britain by Clays Ltd, Elcograf S.p.A.

Hodder & Stoughton policy is to use papers that are natural, renewable and recyclable products
and made from wood grown in sustainable forests. The logging and manufacturing processes
are expected to conform to the environmental regulations of the country of origin.

Hodder & Stoughton Ltd
Carmelite House
50 Victoria Embankment
London EC4Y 0DZ

www.hodder.co.uk

*To all of you who've taken this journey with Lei, Wren, and me.
May you make your own choices and fight
your fears with fire forevermore.*

THE HIDDEN PALACE

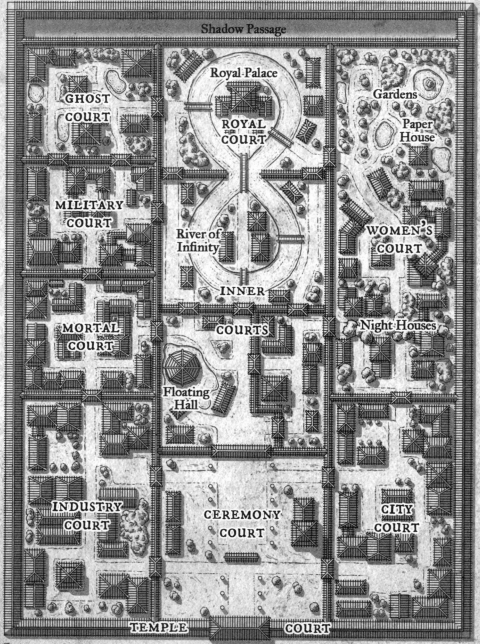

Shadow Passage

Royal Palace

GHOST COURT

Gardens

ROYAL COURT

Paper House

MILITARY COURT

River of Infinity

WOMEN'S COURT

INNER

MORTAL COURT

COURTS

Night Houses

Floating Hall

INDUSTRY COURT

CEREMONY COURT

CITY COURT

TEMPLE   COURT

Gates

PLASSE

The Great Bamboo Forest of Han

CASTES

At night, the heavenly rulers dreamed of colors, and into the day those colors bled onto the earth, raining down onto the paper people and blessing them with the gifts of the gods. But in their fear, some of the paper people hid from the rain and so were left untouched. And some basked in the storm, and so were blessed above all others with the strength and wisdom of the heavens.

—The Ikharan Mae Scripts

Paper caste—*Fully human, unadorned with any animal-demon features, and incapable of demon abilities such as flight.*

Steel caste—*Humans endowed with partial animal-demon qualities, both in physicality and abilities.*

Moon caste—*Fully demon, with whole animal-demon features such as horns, wings, or fur on a humanoid form, and complete demon capabilities.*

—the Demon King's postwar *Treaty on the Castes*

ONE

WREN

*T*HWACK!

The smack of a hundred oak staffs colliding at the same time reverberated through the training pavilion. It was ear-splittingly loud, echoing off the round walls, as though the pavilion were a giant drum and the warriors within it living batons, all beating to the same fierce rhythm.

Wren's muscles were on fire. Sand from the pit's floor whipped her cheeks as she danced and spun her bo with split-second precision, locked in formation with one of the Hanno warriors. Wren's father had ordered her to monitor the drill, not participate in it, but Wren craved distraction. She needed to move, to fight, to feel the reassuring, body-shocking crack of a weapon meeting another.

This she could do.

This she could control.

"Hyah! Kyah!"

Her sparring partner yelled with each movement while Wren parried in silence.

Sweat dripped from Wren's face. She didn't usually perspire so much when she fought, but she wasn't in her Xia state, her magic keeping her cool the same way normal shaman magic was warming. And it was hot in the pavilion. The circular wall was made of woven bamboo, and it trapped the midday heat. Light lanced in through the gaps, flickering over one hundred focused faces.

There'd always been drills and battle practice. Ketai Hanno, Wren's father and leader of the Hannos, Ikhara's most powerful Paper clan, liked to keep his army prepared. But since war had been declared, there was an extra sense of urgency.

An attack was imminent. What wasn't sure was who would strike the first blow. Ketai, or the King?

Locked in rhythm with the soldier, Wren was fully absorbed in each swing of her staff despite the pain of her month-old injury— or perhaps because of it. It roared in her lower back and hips, her own silent battle cry. The sensation was deep, more a weight than anything, as though her sacrum were made of steel instead of bone.

Pain wasn't new to Wren. She'd been forged with it through her father's and Shifu Caen's training sessions from as early as she could remember. And though she was healed each time afterward quickly enough, magic didn't erase memories, and the memories associated with this pain were infinitely worse than the pain itself.

They were memories of demon roars and blood on desert sands.

Of what was left once the screams and sword-clash faded to nothing.

Of a carpet of bodies—yet one even more terrible in its absence.

Lei.

Her name was the echo to Wren's every heartbeat. It was both bright and dark, both wonderful and unbearable, both Wren's strength and her deepest agony.

It was why she couldn't stand by watching this afternoon's drill and not *do something*. Watching only reminded her how useless she'd been that night in the Janese deserts a month ago, and she couldn't stand it. Her father and their doctors and shamans had ordered Wren to rest due to her injury. But rest and sleep were the last things Wren wanted. She knew who she'd find the moment she closed her eyes. And she knew the pain she'd feel once she woke to find the girl she was dreaming of not there.

Crammed in with one hundred moving bodies, Wren licked the sweat from her lips and pushed her partner on, losing herself in the rush of her staff. As the warriors turned, switching into a new formation, Wren caught sight of a figure watching from the viewing gallery—where she herself should currently be. She had just enough time to register her father's disapproval before his shout rang out.

"Halt!"

At once, the pit fell still. The soldiers dipped their heads respectfully, weapons lowered, panting hard. Only Wren kept her neck tall, locked onto her father's inimitable stare.

"Lady Wren," he called in a good-natured tone, leaning forward to grip the railing. "How is drill monitoring going? Well, I hope?"

A few tentative laughs rippled through the hall.

Wren swiped a rolled sleeve across her brow. She forced her expression to remain impassive, though now she'd stopped moving her injury was screaming more fiercely than ever, exhaustion rattling her bones. "Your warriors are so well trained my guidance is hardly needed, Father," she replied. "I thought I may as well get a little practice in myself."

Ketai gave a generous laugh. "A good idea, daughter. Might I join?"

He launched himself over the balcony without waiting for a reply. Then, tucking the hem of his long changpao shirt into the waist-band of his trousers, he strode forward through the sea of parting soldiers. Wren's sparring partner waited until Ketai reached them near the center of the pit before offering **her** training bo to him with a bow.

"Thank you, Amrati," he demurred, turning a twinkling smile upon her.

Wren had to hand it to him. No one could fault the way her father made his clan members feel seen. While the Demon King ruled with fear and intimidation, Ketai Hanno commanded with grace, charisma, and a warm, true affection that sometimes felt just like love.

Wren held her father's gaze as they moved into position. His smile, moments ago so easy, now had a twist to its edges. Ever since her broken group arrived back, he'd been tenser, anger and disappointment running under his calm, friendly surface.

It hadn't been the triumphant return any of them had wished for. In fact, the outcome of the journey with Lei, Caen, Merrin, Nitta, Bo, and Hiro to gather the allegiance of three of the most important demon clans in Ikhara had been worse than any of them could have ever predicted. Not only had they lost one of their most important alliances—the White Wing—after their clan leader Lady Dunya was usurped in a coup by her own daughter Qanna, but Qanna had then convinced Merrin to betray their group by giving the King their location.

None of them had expected it. Wren, who'd grown up with Merrin right here in the fort, wouldn't have believed it herself if she hadn't seen with her own eyes how his grief over Bo's death had twisted his heart, coupled with his repulsion at Wren's drive to win the war at any cost. All of which had led to that awful battle in Jana.

A bloodied desert.

Moonlight upon a sea of bodies.

Merrin, Nitta, Lei—vanished.

The White Wing had been integral to Ketai's war plans. Since the coup, its remaining clan members still loyal to Qanna's mother, Lady Dunya, were imprisoned in their own palace. Ketai was determined to free them. Yet no matter how many different ways they approached a rescue during their war councils, it always came down to one thing: they couldn't reach them without bird demons of their own. The Cloud Palace was almost impossible to access on foot, and with Merrin still missing, they had no means to reach it by air.

The White Wing's support in the war wasn't the worst of what they'd lost on that journey. Not by far. But at least alliances could be repaired—unlike hearts stopped by an arrow, or a young shaman's bloody sacrifice, or a girl disappeared into the night.

The soldiers packed to the walls to free up space in the pit. Directly across from Wren, Ketai adopted a defensive stance, lifting his oak staff. An invitation.

Wren lifted her own in acceptance.

Her father whirled into action so quickly she'd barely finished her breath before he was upon her. He struck with incredible strength. The impact jarred her teeth. She ground her heels into the dirt as he forced her back. But Wren had been trained by Ketai himself—she knew his fighting style inside out. She responded with a side-duck then a jump-kick, which he rebuffed with one arm before spinning low, aiming his bo at her feet.

Wren jumped. Launched into a flurry of fast jabs that Ketai parried with ferocious grace.

Caen once told Wren she fought like her father: elegant and unrelenting. A dangerous combination. But Wren had one key advantage. Her Xia blood.

As they continued to dance across the pit, drawing gasps of awe from the watching soldiers, Wren felt her magic calling. It tingled in her fingertips. It whispered in her blood. She held it back, narrowing her focus to her body and movements; the dark flash of her father's eyes and the grim line of his lips.

Because of the state she'd been in after returning from the desert, Ketai had forbidden her to use magic, ordering her to rest to recoup her strength. So far, Wren had followed his orders. Yet as she fought now, pain and determination pulsed more keenly through her with each passing moment, as it had done every minute she spent without Lei, not knowing where she was, if she were even *alive*, and with it grew Wren's craving for action, to be useful, to *do something*—

Magic burst from her in an ice-cold roar.

It tore through the pavilion, a powerful wave that threw the sand of the pit outward. There were cries from the watching warriors. They scrambled to take cover as sand dashed against the bamboo walls, showering them in grit and dust.

The magic sapped from Wren as abruptly as it had arrived. Before the Sickness, accessing her power was as easy as dipping a toe to a vast lake. Now, the lake's once-silky waters were thick as mud, and harnessing its might was a struggle. Yet another thing the King had stolen from her. Though they couldn't be certain, almost everyone suspected the depletion of qi across Ikhara was his doing.

Wren slumped to the floor. Shivers racked her body. Fighting to contain them, she lifted her head and saw her father being helped to his feet.

He met her concerned expression, his jet-dark eyes for once unreadable. Then, he smiled, brushing down his dust-covered clothes. "My daughter," he pronounced with a sweep of an arm. "What a warrior you have become."

He bowed, as was customary, congratulating her on her win. Wren returned it stiffly. When she straightened, her father was already striding forward. He clapped her on the shoulder as he passed, a little too hard.

"Come," he said. "I have as assignment for you."

The Jade Fort, the Hannos' homestead in central Ang-Khen, sat on a high viewpoint amid swaths of forested valleys. It had gotten its name from the sparkling jade of the pines that spread in all directions, shifting in the wind so it gave the appearance of an island in the center of a deep, golden-green sea. The sounds of the training pavilion faded as Ketai led Wren across the grounds and into the fort through its grand entranceway, banners with the Hanno insignia fluttering overhead.

Their clan members were quick to bow as they passed. This wasn't new, but their attitude toward Wren was. It had shifted after New Year's Eve, when she'd revealed herself as not the simple clan daughter they'd always thought her to be, but the sole descendent of the infamous warrior clan, the Xia.

Wren held in her question for her father until they were in a quiet hallway on one of the higher levels. It was the same one she'd asked him almost every time they spoke, and she saw him stiffen in irritation as she repeated it now.

"Wren, my answer has not and will not change. Our watchtowers are on high alert for an attack. We cannot spare any soldiers. Not to mention, you are still in recovery."

"I'm much better now," Wren countered. "I've had plenty of rest since Jana. And I don't need a big army. I could go alone, even—"

"Enough." Like all Ketai's commands, it carried weight. He stopped, facing her. "I know she was your closest friend. I know she meant a lot to you."

Is, Wren corrected in her head. *Means.*

"I can't imagine how hard it must be for you to not know what has happened to her—or to Nitta, or Merrin. It's been hard for all of us. But we need you, my daughter. *I* need you. Besides, Lei is the Moonchosen. If anyone is capable of surviving, it's her. I have no doubt she will find her way back to us."

Unspoken words hung in the air between them.

Survive *what*? Find her way back from *where*?

In the aftermath of the desert battle, Wren had hunted through the bodies for any sign of Lei. She'd tried using magic to speed up the process, but she was emptied of power by then. She'd only stopped when Caen physically restrained her, telling her he'd seen Merrin flying off with Lei and Nitta in the midst of battle.

"Where?" Wren had screamed. But none of them could answer her no matter how many times she shouted it.

She'd eventually passed out from fatigue. When she woke, she was in the back of a carriage. They were traveling northward from the border of Ang-Khen and Jana toward the Jade Fort. Lova explained everything that had happened, yet Wren hadn't been able to get her own voice out of her ears, that eternal scream: *Where where where where?*

She still was no closer to an answer.

Now, Ketai passed a rough palm over her cheek and gave her an encouraging smile. "Gods-willing, we will all be reunited in time. For now, though, we have work to do. I need your focus."

They were in a quiet wing of the fort, consisting mostly of spare rooms for guests and supplies, so Wren was surprised when they turned the corner to find a pair of guards standing by an unassuming wooden door. They bowed before letting Wren and Ketai inside.

It turned out the assignment was a boy.

A jackal Moon caste boy who looked barely old enough to be a soldier, though the red and black baju of the royal army he wore marked him as one. The clothes were too loose on his wiry frame. Blood had crusted his forehead where he'd been struck.

"We caught him close to the river watchtower," Ketai said.

They stood over the demon's unconscious form. The effects of the small room had been cleared and its shuttered window bolted tight. Unlike many clan homesteads, the Jade Fort didn't have cells, and in all her life Wren had never known her father to take anyone prisoner.

Perhaps he had, and this was the first time he was allowing her to see.

"He's so young," she said, disgust turning her stomach. Was the King recruiting children now to throw to slaughter? "He was alone?"

"A patrol is sweeping the area now, but I doubt they'll find any others. The boy claims he's a deserter, but refuses to talk."

"A deserter." Wren didn't sound convinced.

Neither did her father. "There are no deserters of the King's army. At least, none that live. They'd be captured and killed before making it five minutes from their station. You know, the King's generals make the youngest members of their battalions carry out the execution? Says it hardens them." After a pause, he placed a hand on Wren's shoulder. "Find out what he knows."

A cold lick traveled Wren's spine.

Before she could object, her father came around to face her, blocking the boy from her sight. He braced her with both hands. "Everything the King and his demons do breeds young, hard boys like this with hatred for Papers in their hearts. Young, hard boys who grow up to be cold, hard men, who have taken the lives of so many we care for. They are what we are fighting against." His eyes flashed. "You want to save Lei? This soldier might have information that could help us. If we have something more to go on, we can discuss her rescue seriously."

Lei's face burned in Wren's mind: those vivid molten eyes; her slight nose; the heart-shaped chin Wren spent so many stolen nights grazing her lips along.

Ketai squeezed her shoulders. "You told me you are tired of waiting. That you need something to do. Here is something."

Wren pushed out a breath, recalling how it felt to trawl through a sea of bodies, screaming Lei's name in vain until her throat was ripped raw. And all the days and nights since, her heart still screaming, not knowing whether or not it was all for nothing.

Her resolve hardened. "I'll do it."

Her father smiled grimly. "Good. Tonight," he said, "while everyone is at dinner." He didn't add why, though Wren knew. In case of sound. In case the boy needed a lot of...convincing to talk. He moved away, giving her full view of the jackal demon again.

He was so young.

But he was still their enemy.

Wren pictured Lei alone somewhere, possibly at the mercy of demons—and really, whenever were Papers *not*? And the pain that furrowed through her cemented her decision. Her father was right. Demon boys like this grew into demon men who wouldn't think twice before tearing their world apart. She knew; they'd done it to her and Lei.

There was no space for mercy in war.

Even though, as she gave the boy one last look before leaving, a small voice in her head reminded her Lei would say there was.

TWO

WREN

THAT NIGHT, WHILE HER CLAN MEMBERS headed to dinner, Wren went instead to the armory to choose a knife.

She settled on a simple gutting knife: small, jagged, not yet cleaned from its last encounter. She liked the way it felt in her hand. The way it was the opposite of her own twin blades, which were elegant and long and spotlessly polished. They were a true warrior's weapons. Honorable. Forgiving. Designed to let blood quickly and cleanly.

This weapon was for ugly deeds done in darkness. It was neither honorable nor forgiving, and when it tore skin it would *hurt*.

When she left the armory, Wren found Lova propped against the opposite wall.

The lion-girl's arms were crossed. Her golden tail twirled lazily, the lustrous fur that clung to her body almost an exact color match for the wide marigold trousers and wrap shirt she wore, the top's fastener loosely made so her generous curves spilled out. Lova was a perfect example of how striking Moon castes could be, her half lioness, half human features melded together in a way that brought out both beauty and power.

She cocked her head knowingly.

Wren strode past her.

"I know what you're doing," Lova said, following.

"I know what *you're* doing," Wren retorted. "You're General of the Amala, Lo. Babysitting isn't exactly befitting of your position."

"Aw, are you calling yourself a baby, now? How cute."

Wren gritted her teeth. "It was just a turn of phrase."

"*I* called you 'baby' once," Lova pointed out slyly, flicking her tail against Wren's side.

"A long time ago."

"Something that can be readily amended."

Wren cut her a sideways look. "A long, *long* time ago."

They were crossing the stone-floored atrium at the fortress's entrance. Members of the clan hung around, talking in groups or pairs. Some stopped mid-conversation to watch their Clan Lord's daughter and the beautiful General of the famous Cat Clan, the Amala, pass.

The pair had first met in this very spot. Wren's father had called a summit between clan heads to discuss the Sickness. Wren had been mesmerized by the strident young lioness from the moment she'd prowled into the fort as if her very presence claimed whatever space she was in as her own. One evening, Lova had stopped her in a deserted hallway. Wren was shocked; she thought at first the girl was attacking her. But Lova only brought her hand to Wren's cheek and announced boldly, without shame or hesitation, "You are the most beautiful girl I've ever seen. I can't wait any longer to kiss you."

"You—you've only been here three days," Wren had said, breathless.

Lova's lips sharpened into a hungry grin. "I'm not known for my patience," she said, before leaning in.

Two years, yet it felt like lifetimes ago.

It *was* lifetimes ago. To Wren, time would forevermore be divided into her life before Lei and her life after.

And this new, awful life *without* her.

She flexed her fingers, steadying herself. If the young jackal soldier had information on Lei's whereabouts, perhaps she'd soon be in a new lifetime—one where she and Lei were reunited. It was everything she longed for, yet it terrified her, too.

I thought the King was our only enemy. Now I realize there's been another one all this time—your father. The Hannos.

You.

It had been their last proper conversation, on Lova's ground-ship the night before the desert battle. And as much as Wren couldn't ignore the thousands of sweet memories of Lei, there was this one, too, a poison in their midst, threatening to sour them all.

She *would* find Lei. Wren didn't let any other option bleed in. But once she did, what Lei would she find? The girl that had loved her so tenderly and fiercely in midnight rooms and rushing countryside and under the starlight on a rolling sea? Or the Lei she'd lost in the body-strewn desert, who'd looked at her with such disgust, a roiling fury Wren never believed could be directed her way until the terrible moment it was?

Lova and Wren's footsteps rang off the high walls as they mounted the staircase that dominated the atrium. A canopy of banners fluttered overhead. There were hundreds of them, one for every member of the clan. It was an impressive sight, the mass of navy and white, like an upside-down sea softly swaying in the breeze brushing in through the fort's entranceway. Wren had practiced her magic here many times with Caen when she was younger, in the dead of night to ensure they weren't seen.

Following a sudden, childish urge, she snatched at some qi to whip up the wind, shooting a strong gust through the foyer and up into the banners, making them flap. There were shouts of surprise.

Wren bit back a hiss at the energy this frivolous bit of magic cost her. She was still hurting from her time in the training pit, every bit of her aching.

"It's the injury again, isn't it?" Lova said. "Let's go back to the armory. Or fight *me*, if you have to. I could do with some practice. Things have been rather boring around here lately."

"Boring isn't bad."

Lova huffed. "Says the sole survivor of Ikhara's legendary warrior clan, who will soon defeat the King's cruel rule to bring about a new age in our land's history." Her tone lost its teasing edge. "Boring wasn't in your past, Wren Hanno. And it isn't in your future." When Wren didn't respond, Lova caught her elbow. "This isn't like you," she said quietly.

"Isn't it?" Muscles tightened in Wren's jaw. She remembered again Lei's words: *enemy, you.* She sensed Lova wanting to continue the conversation, so she shot her a cutting look and they climbed the next few floors in silence.

When they arrived at the room her father had shown her to earlier, the guards bowed, opening the door.

"You don't have to come with me, Lo," Wren said. "Especially seeing how much you disapprove."

"Oh, honey," Lova purred, "as if I'm one for doing the good, sensible thing."

She strode in without waiting for a reply, and Wren followed, a little lighter knowing she wouldn't have to go through this alone. That was something Lei had taught her; burdens could be shared. Though Wren would never have wanted to share this with Lei. Lova, however...she, too, had been born with violence in her blood. She might not like what was about to happen, but she understood it.

The jackal demon was still asleep, curled on his side. Gangly limbs poked from too-wide hems.

Wren felt a surge of pity—which only reminded her how little mercy the King and his men had ever spared them.

She prodded him awake with her foot.

The boy was alert in an instant, scuttling back, awkward in his binds. His sharp ears pricked. He'd looked innocent in sleep, but now he fizzed with frantic energy. "Keeda scum," he snarled. His eyes shot to Lova. "Moon traitor." He scoffed. "I don't know which is worse."

Lova gasped dramatically. "How dare you! Of course I'm worse!" Her incisors flashed, and she leaned in. "Want me to show you just how much?"

Wren held out a hand. "Let me make this easy for you," she told the demon. "Tell me what you were really doing by our watchtower, or you can tell me in a few minutes—maybe even hours—from now. It'll be the same outcome, but one way will be far more pleasant for you."

"Far more pleasant for *all* of us," Lova added with a pout. "A lot of care goes into keeping this coat so glossy."

The jackal-boy bared his teeth at her. "I'm not gonna help *you* with anything, keeda-lover."

He was raspy with thirst. Wren considered getting him some water, but she didn't have the time. Not if the boy had information she could use to find Lei.

"So you're choosing the difficult way?" she asked him.

"Smart one, aren't you?" His eyes flicked over her. His lips curled. "Aren't you one of the King's little sluts? I'm sure I've seen you at the palace."

At his words, the room went dangerously silent. Wren sensed Lova bristling, clearly struggling to hold back her rage.

One of the King's little sluts.

Wren drew the gutting knife from the folds at her waist. She wanted this over with. She wanted *all* of this over with. This moment, this war, these children shaped by ugliness and malice.

The jackal-boy really was so young. And yet the contemptuous look on his face was as old and set as buried bones.

His eyes darted to the knife, then back to Wren. "Do your best, keeda," he sneered.

She crouched over him. "As you wish."

They rushed from the room as soon as the full picture of the demon's confession hit them.

Clan members gave Wren startled looks as she and Lova flew down the main staircase, and she knew what she must look like, blood-splattered and wild-eyed. But there wasn't any time to clean up. When they arrived at the atrium, Wren peeled off to find her father, while Lova paused, calling at her back, "I'll send up a doctor and a shaman. To help with his...pain."

Wren paused, breathless, turning. "Thank you," she said. She hated that she hadn't thought of doing the same.

Lei would have.

Then again, Lei wouldn't have done any of this in the first place.

How many more murders will you commit in the name of justice until you realize you're as bad as those we're meant to be fighting against?

Wren was thankful Lova's amber gaze held no judgment. "You did well, Wren," she said. "As well as that kind of thing can be done." Then she was off, the hems of her trousers rustling on the stone floor.

Wren hurried on to the dining hall. Wide eyes trailed her as she made her way through the vaulted room filled with noise and food smells, every table packed with Papers and demons. Wren's father was sat at his usual table at the head of the hall. Caen was beside him. The two of them were on their feet before she reached them.

"Our watchtowers have been compromised," Wren told them at once. "The King's soldiers have been taking control of them over the past week so we wouldn't be alerted to his army's movements. That's what the boy was doing by the river watchtower."

Caen tensed. He shook his head. "We should have known."

"How long do we have?" Ketai asked.

"Not we," Wren corrected. "Nantanna."

For a moment, the two men looked confused. Nantanna was their province's capital, and Ketai its steward. Though they'd heightened its security since the start of the war, it was the Jade Fort they'd been anticipating to come under attack. Naja, the King's personal guard, had even threatened Lei with it when she'd attacked them during their journey to secure allies. Nantanna was the third largest settlement in Ikhara. Alongside Papers, thousands of demons lived and worked there, and unlike other places there'd been little evidence of rebellion against the King's rule. Why would he attack one of his own cities?

Understanding darkened Ketai and Caen's faces.

They'd been tricked. It was foolish of them to have ever thought the King would be concerned about popularity among his citizens after the war. He was reckless. He was blood-hungry. The King would hurt Nantanna for the same reasons he'd hurt anything.

Power. Pleasure. Revenge.

"We leave at once," Ketai said, already ordering Caen away to assemble reinforcements, while he himself started for the foyer. A few curious-looking clan members had begun to gather nearby, and they startled as Ketai stormed past them. He shouted over his shoulder at Wren, "Stay here! In my and Caen's absence, you are responsible for the protection of the fort."

Wren started forward. "Father, wait—"

"There's no time! Hold the fort."

He disappeared in a sweep of dark robes.

The atmosphere of the hall was turning. Worried voices rose, clan members and allies crowding Wren, clamoring for her attention while she stood there, heart thumping. This was it. The attack they'd been waiting for. The first blow of the war—dealt by the King. But as terrible as that knowledge was, Wren's mind was stuck on the information she *hadn't* learned from the young demon boy.

Lei's whereabouts.

The question that had haunted her for one long month echoed in her ears, louder than those of the demons and humans clustered around her.

Where?

Where was she? *Where was Lei? Where where where—*

Stop, Wren ordered herself harshly, composing herself. From young, Caen had taught her there was a time and place for everything. She could sink into despair later, but right now, she had duties to uphold.

She was a warrior. A Clan Lord's daughter.

And she had a responsibility to act like one.

Wren took a deep breath before turning to address the anxious faces of her clan and allies, bracing for their reactions when they learned that the war had well and truly begun.

THREE

LEI

THIS TIME WHEN THE GUARDS COME to my door, I am ready.
I've been up all night, fashioning a loop of fabric from torn strips of my hanfu. Luckily it's still cold enough for more than one layer of clothes. Seeing as a brazier or lantern would be too much ammunition in my hands, the guards have been giving me fresh sets of double-layered robes every three days. Though it must be almost spring by now, it feels like winter in this window-less, marble room, and they can't have me catching a chill and freez-ing to death on their watch.

I am to die, but I am not theirs to kill.

When I hear movement in the hall, I scramble up. I snatch my makeshift weapon and press against the wall to the right of the door. I rub my finger over the braided fabric wound around my palm as the steps approach.

Demon steps. Not hooves, but heavy and dull and accompanied by clicking. Talons? Claws? After all this time locked up, I've grown adept at picking out the particularities of each guard's gait. The heavier steps mean bird or reptile, though it's more likely reptile since bird demons are rare. The other padded thuds sound as though they belong to a bear-form.

They always send the guards in pairs. After my first escape attempt a few days after Naja brought me here, they reduced my meals from two per day to one. After the second, they began putting soporific herbs in my food. After the third, they beat me until I passed out. When I woke, they'd removed the scant furnishings from my room—or cell, as I suppose it's more accurately called.

The Hidden Palace has always been my prison.

I wait in the darkness. *This* will be escape attempt number four.

In Ikharan cultures, four is an unlucky number because of how similar it sounds to our word for death. Babies born on the fourth day of the month are said to be ill-fated. We avoid lighting four joss sticks at a time so as not to taint our prayers. Tien—always the most suspicious out of my little herb shop family—would even skip *counting* the number. She'd push two of the bamboo beads of her abacus to jump from three to five, swift and precise, as if she'd be infected if she touched them too long.

Thud, click. Thud, click.

As the guards draw closer, I'm certain this attempt—unlucky number four—will be the one that works. After all, I want to bring death's attention to my door.

Crouched in the attacking stance Shifu Caen taught me, I twist my makeshift weapon and bounce on the balls of my feet.

There's the clunk of locks being undone. Then a crack of light slices into the room.

The first guard enters. I was right; it's a lizard demon. A flicker of puzzlement spreads across his scaled face when he doesn't see me in my usual sleeping spot, but before he's even had time to look around I leap at him and throw the noose high.

It slips over his head before I barrel into him.

He staggers back with a shout. Claw-tipped hands fly up. He scratches me, lands punches to my thighs and sides. But I cling on, half straddling his neck, pulling the noose with all my force.

The second guard barges into the room, saber drawn. She's an intimidating panda-woman bound with more muscles in one finger than I've got in my entire body. Yet instead of her sword, it's her weaponless hand that flies toward me.

I duck her reach, a manic grin twisting my lips.

They can't risk killing me.

I've known it since I was brought here—before, even, when Naja found me one month ago, alone and blood-soaked in the desert, and told me she was taking me home. I'm aware this protection is only temporary. The King wants to save all the damage, all the pain, all the *revenge* for himself.

But right now, I don't care. Right now, knees clamped about the lizard's struggling shoulders, I strain to keep the noose tight, sneering at the soldier brandishing her useless sword.

"The girl is escaping!" she yells into the corridor before trying again to grab me.

I'm saved by the lizard's knees giving way. We both go sprawling to the floor. I pin him down. His scaled hands flail. From behind, the panda-woman grabs a fistful of the back of my flimsy, half torn-apart robes, yet her force only draws the noose tighter.

The reptile guard splutters. It can't be long now.

Red pulses across my vision. A dark desire storms through my veins. More than desire: need. Need for *this*, for someone to take the fall for all that has happened. For some way to free the guilty anger that has been boiling inside me ever since that hopeless night at the desert. Ever since the last time I held *her* in my arms. Ever since we came across the burning wreckage in the middle of a paddy field. Ever since a laughing leopard-boy was set into the ground. Ever since...since *everything*.

And suddenly, as instantly as a match being struck, the rage and desperation and fire drop away. It's as though my soul has come untethered from my body. Floating outside of myself, hovering above the scene, I see it laid beneath me like a violence-soaked painting.

A soldier strains to break apart two struggling figures on the floor, one of them a demon near death, pinned to the floor by a crazed human girl with bloodlust in her eyes. The girl's head is tossed back. Her knuckles are white where they grip the noose she spent one long night making, all for this moment. Another death to notch to her list.

I stare down, and the girl's eyes lock with mine.

Framed in thick lashes and bloodied whites, her irises are golden: clear, liquid, New Year–moon gold. But that's all I recognize of them. Her feral look pierces me. She may as well be a stranger.

Then the moment breaks. Everything comes roaring back. The lizard's horrible sounds as he bucks beneath me. The panda-woman's yelling. Running footsteps thunder down the corridor— more guards.

I let go of the noose so suddenly it throws the panda soldier's weight off. She tumbles back with a grunt. I fall against her, and the next moment other guards are upon me, too many to fight, powerful hands twisting my arms behind me.

My mouth is prized open. Someone pushes the familiar bitterness of sedative herbs past my lips.

I swallow them, and when the darkness comes a few seconds later to drag me under, what I feel is gratitude.

*   *   *

For the first time since I was stolen back to the palace, I wake in a new room.

The warmth gives it away. Eyes still shut, I feel sunlight and the softness of bedding, both foreign after weeks of darkness and cold stone against my spine. The air is sweet: peonies and tea, with an undercurrent of muskiness the pleasant fragrances fail to mask. Something about the odor tugs at my memory. As I blink my eyes open, still groggy from the herbs, I brush the blanket draped across my body—only to realize I'm naked beneath it.

I jerk upright. Gripping the sheet to my chest, I look around wildly, teeth bared, primed to fight. But the room is empty.

Slowing my breaths, I push the hair back from my face with my free hand. I'm expecting tangles; long weeks in a cell and countless interrogation sessions haven't exactly done wonders for my beauty regime. But my fingers glide smoothly through.

I've been washed. My stomach knots at the thought of hands on my body while I lay unconscious. Then I huff a barbed laugh. Why should I expect anything less? This is the Hidden Palace. Here, my body is something for demons to do with as they please. This is what the court does best: taking things and scrubbing them blank. Paper isn't just a caste to them. It is a *state*, an expectation of what we should be. Weak. Blank. Something to tear. Something to use and discard without a second thought.

My heart pulses darkly. Because I learned long ago that Paper has its own power—the ability to ignite, re-form, evolve. And the young human girl they've brought back to the palace is not the same girl she was the first time around.

Focus, I tell myself. *Remember Caen's training. Assess your surroundings. Everything has the potential to be your undoing—or your route to victory.*

I take stock of the room. Though carved from the same cream-white marble of my cell, these walls and floors are softened with furnishings. Silks flutter over half drawn shutters. A rattan mat stretches from one end of the room to the other. I'm on a bed in one corner of the room. Across from me is a low table surrounded by cushions. The table has been set with two cups, one near empty, feathers of steam still rising from within.

Someone was here recently.

Under the tea, that sharp-musky odor jerks my recollection again. But I still can't place it, and instead of wasting time chasing old memories I turn my attention to the windows.

I'm on my feet in seconds, wrapping the blanket around my body as I move to the nearest window and shove the folding shutters aside. I scramble onto the ledge, almost crying out at the blast of cold spring air, gloriously soul-wakening with its birdsong and sunlight and the tantalizing promise of *freedom*—

Talons click behind me.

"Get down from there, Lei-zhi," orders a throaty voice.

I freeze, still contorted in an awkward jumble of limbs, the blanket twisted so much it's almost hiked up to my waist. But I don't turn. Now my eyes have adjusted to the light, I can't bring myself to look away from the view.

We're high up, at least three stories. Blocks of squat buildings stretch into the distance, punctured in places by green courtyards and wide squares. A river glitters under the noonday sun. My eyes are drawn to the far left, where a verdant landscape of gardens and forests rolls out. Birds wheel over the distant treetops in swirling formations, so familiar because of how many times I stared out of a different window in this same place, longing with all of my being that I could join them.

And there, far in the distance—the reason I never could.

Towering walls of midnight stone.

I'd known where I was all this time, of course, but it hits me afresh to actually see it. I'd once believed I'd never see these streets and courtyards again. I'd been so sure of it.

We'd been so sure of it.

"Lei-zhi!" The harsh voice barks at my back. "Get down from there at once! This is no way for a Paper Girl to behave."

Paper Girl.

The words carry an extra weight to their usual sting.

Wrestling my face into as neutral an expression as I can manage, I slide from the ledge. "Madam Himura," I say graciously, turning to face her. "How wonderful to see you again."

She glares, her yellow eagle eyes narrow. The feathers at her neck are ruffled—a telltale sign of anger—and she's gripping her bone-handled cane so tightly I'm amazed it hasn't cracked.

I hold myself tall, bracing for the inevitable attack, the violent force of Madam Himura we all grew so accustomed to. Though only a supervisor of courtesans, the old eagle-woman has always carried herself with the authority of an army general, able to keep us in order equally viciously with words or blows.

In the end, she only points a winged arm toward the table. "Sit," she says, almost tiredly. "And don't bother wasting any more of my time trying to escape. There are guards outside, and many more throughout the building."

"I could leave by the window," I suggest stubbornly.

"Can you fly?"

"I'm not sure. I've never tried."

Madam Himura waves an arm. "Go ahead, then, girl. It makes no difference to me." When I don't move, she snaps, "I didn't think so," before stomping to the table.

I don't join her. Still glaring, I start, "Where are—"

"We are in Royal Court, in the King's palace. This is the Moon Annexe."

The Moon Annexe. Dimly, I recall an early lesson as a Paper Girl in our other warden Mistress Eira's suite, where she described the various areas of the palace. The King's fortress in Royal Court is the largest building in the Hidden Palace, carved from the same dark rock as the perimeter wall. Conversely, the Moon Annexe is a ring in the eastern part of the building cut from white marble, as recommended by the architects for optimal prosperity. If I'm remembering correctly, it houses offices for high-ranking court members, along with rooms for entertaining and guest suites.

I shoot a look at the door, then the window, trying to conjure up escape routes. Yet now I've seen exactly where we are, I know any attempts would be futile.

At least, not without some proper planning.

Reluctantly, I join Madam Himura at the table. She reaches to fill my cup, and I arch a brow. "No maids?" I've never seen Madam Himura so much as lift a winged arm for anything—apart from to hit us with.

She sets the kettle down. "Not anymore."

My eyes flit over her. Under her drab hanfu, Madam Himura looks shrunken, her dark feathers flat and dull against her body instead of glossy with their usual oil and perfumes, and her movements are rigid, not quite as quick as before.

I've seen too many women who've had their spirit broken not to recognize it now. Still, whatever the King had done to Madam Himura, he was careful not to leave to any visible signs of abuse. Did shamans work on her body the way they did mine after my nights with him? Did they lay their magic on her skin to lift her bruises without allowing their enchantments to penetrate further, so the pain would live on, an invisible reminder to never again cross him?

My pity is short-lived. Madam Himura never showed any of us kindness when we were hurting. She tossed Mariko out as if she were garbage. *She* was the one who asked the shamans to leave me in my suffering when I'd been battered by the King.

Questions pour out of me in a rush. "Where's Mistress Eira? Are the other girls safe? Where's Kenzo? Lill? Why am I here?"

I don't say what I actually mean: why am I *alive*?

Madam Himura glares. "I am not here to answer your questions, Lei-zhi—even *if* you had the patience to ask them in the manner in which I trained you."

"Why *are* you here, then?" I say with a scowl.

She answers as though it's obvious. "What I have always been here for. To prepare you. You have an important dinner to attend tonight, and you must look your best for the King."

I laugh, the sound harsh. "You're joking." When Madam Himura doesn't say anything, I push to my knees, shaking the table so forcefully in the process that my cup tips, tea spilling across the lacquered wood. Madam Himura looks at the mess disapprovingly, but I don't tear my eyes from her. "You're disgusting," I spit. "All of you."

She clucks her tongue. "Calm yourself, Lei-zhi."

"Oh, my apologies for not being *dead inside*." My hands are trembling, a high-pitched ringing in my ears. "That's what you were always trying to beat out of us, wasn't it?" I press on bitterly. "Life. Passion. Any semblance of humanity. Paper—that's what you wanted us to be. Good little cut-out girls with nothing but reams of blank pages in place of hearts."

For the briefest moment, an almost hurt expression crosses the eagle-woman's features. Then she gets to her feet, her face once more a cold shell. "The King has called for you, Lei-zhi. You know what that means. Either you can let me prepare you, or we can drug you again and do it while you are unconscious. I shall let you decide."

"Fine," I reply icily. "I'll play along for now. But don't expect it to last."

I know what the King has in store for me. A demon like him would never let someone humiliate him and go unpunished. It's only a matter of time before an animal bores of playing with its food before devouring it.

Unfortunately for the King, the same goes for human girls.

The two of us have been toying with each other long enough. The last time I saw the King, I drove a knife into his throat. This time I know better.

This time, I'll aim for his heart.

FOUR

LEI

FOUR HOURS, TWO SHAMANS, SIX MAIDS, and three ruined sets of robes later—I wasn't going to make it easy for them, was I?—and I am new again. All signs of my interrogations have been enchanted away or are hidden beneath the gossamer-thin layers of my black and gold hanfu.

The King's colors. No doubt this is his way of reclaiming me, of reminding both me and any who doubt it that I have, and always will, belong to him.

Or so he likes to believe.

At least the court are smart enough to know better than to expect my insides to have been so easily cleansed as my skin. They prepare an escort of no fewer than eighteen guards to accompany me to the banquet hall. Metal clinks as they march me down the hallways of the King's fortress, weapons clasped in claws and talons and furred hands. I play the obedient prisoner, though when we pass other demons—shocked maids who grab their robes and press their backs to the walls, or court advisers who regard me openly with fear or disgust, or both—I can't resist flashing them a grin.

I even wave at a particularly nervous-looking councilor, who leaps back with a cry as though I sent a cursed dao his way.

I take stock of my whereabouts, committing every stairway and courtyard to memory. The more we walk, the more I remember. There: a curtained portico hiding a peaceful garden room filled with plants and bubbling fountains that I once took tea in with the other Paper Girls. Here: a long hallway we were led down on the evening of the Unveiling Ceremony.

We stop at a grand archway. Beyond is a high-ceilinged room, already filled with people, chatter spilling out. A red velvet carpet stretches beneath our feet, like the tongue of a beast laid open for its prey. As one of my guards talks to the servants welcoming guests, I suddenly recognize where we are; I've been here once before as a Paper Girl. Most of what I remember about that night involves Wren looking particularly striking in a deep plum-colored hanfu embroidered with winding bronze threads, the robes drawn apart at the chest to show off her glitter-dusted cleavage. I spent the whole night trying to sneak glances at her without being obvious.

I was probably *very* obvious.

Tears sting my eyes. Because tonight, there will be no Wren. There will be no raven-haired, hip-swaying, cat-eyed girl in gorgeous robes waiting beyond the archway for me to try, and fail spectacularly, to ignore.

Over the past few weeks, locked up with nothing but my dark imaginings for company, I dreamed a million scenarios as to where my cat-eyed girl might be. The last time I saw her, she'd been a tiny figure on blood-soaked sands, blades whirling as hordes of demon soldiers closed in. On good days, I'd envision those blades striking them down until not a single soldier is left. On bad days, I'd conjure up too many demons, a never-ending sea of fangs and spiked horns, until Wren would be swallowed by them, cut down or beaten, or simply drowned in their ceaseless wave.

On the worst days, she'd survive the onslaught but be too injured to make her way from the sands. She'd lie there—would still be lying there right now—the only living person in a sea of bodies, staring at the sky and wondering why I left her when I promised she'd never have to face the world alone again.

Outside the banquet hall, I steel myself. "She's alive," I whisper. "You *have* to be alive, Wren."

The guard at the head of my group comes over. He's a gazelle demon so tall he has to bend in half to grab my right hand. He shoves a bracelet onto my wrist, a heavy gold bangle. Though it's unadorned, a faint shiver of magic lets me know it's been enchanted.

"A little gift from the Heavenly Master himself," the guard says. "If you try to hurt anyone in this room, the bangle will shrink... and *keep* shrinking until it has cut off your hand."

One of the other guards mutters, "Should've made it a necklace."

"If she steps out of place," another says, "next time, it will be."

"And before you decide to get self-sacrificial," the gazelle demon continues over their rumbling laughter, "this bangle has a pair. Right this minute, someone you know—someone *we* know is important to you—is wearing it. So unless you want them to suffer, too, be a good little keeda and keep out of trouble."

Then, smirking at the shock on my face, he pushes me toward the archway.

I'm reeling from his revelation. It could be a bluff, but there are people within these walls I care about, and it wouldn't be too hard for the court to find out who. As much as I hate to admit it, they know me well. The first opportunity I saw to kill the King, I'd have taken it—if I only had myself to endanger. But now, with the knowledge I might be hurting someone I love...

I swallow my rage. I'm about to see the King for the first time in months. I will *not* let him see how much this move has shaken me. So, fixing a determined smile on my face, I step into the hall, back tall, chin tipped high.

All talk ceases. Laughter sputters to nothing. Somewhere, a glass splinters. The joyful song musicians had been playing stutters as every head in the room swings my way.

My smile trembles, but I hold it in place. It's been a long time since so many demon eyes were upon me at one time. The gazelle demon leads me between tables and groups of guests, drinks held halfway to open mouths.

"Is that—"

"It can't be—"

"Why is she still *alive*...?"

"Dirty little keeda—"

My hand twitches involuntarily toward my hip—but of course, I don't have my dagger. The knife Wren's father gifted me was taken by Naja when I was captured.

By now, the musicians have started up again, a singer accompanied by erhu strings and a bamboo drum. Beautiful Moon girls glide through the crowd, balancing carafes of sake and platters of crystallized figs. The hall has been decorated to the full. Reams of crimson, mustard, and royal blue adorn the walls. Lanterns hang from the ceiling, suspended on long ropes twined with blooming flowers, petals cascading down only to dissolve magically over the heads of the guests. At the center of each table sit spun-glass cases as delicate as spider silk, trapped fireflies glittering within.

Is it in demon nature to capture pretty things only to watch them shine through the bars of a cage? Then I think of Ketai Hanno and his hold on Wren.

No. This is something all castes have in common.

My heart drums a frantic rhythm, knowing I'll be coming face-to-face with the King any moment. At first, the hall is far too busy to see him. Then, as we reach the far side, the last of the guests move out of the way—

And there he is.

Risen from the dead.

The demon that will always haunt me, no matter how many times I kill him.

The King stands with his back to me, talking with a group of councilors. They're looking past him, aghast to see me, but the King doesn't turn. I take in those familiar sloping shoulders, the slim line of his waist and hips, surprisingly slender for a bull demon. Lantern light glints off his gilded horns as he takes a sip of his drink and murmurs something to the demon next to him. He would be the picture of composure, were it not for the fact we all know he's been waiting for me.

He can't have missed the reaction when I entered, the whispers of the crowd. The King of before would have wanted to watch me approach. The King of before would have taken pleasure in seeing me squirm.

A thrill runs down my spine. Because it seems that King is gone, and this one—the King of after I stuck a knife in his throat, after his world was shattered with the promise of war...

This King is scared.

My pulse spirals. He's not the only one. Still, my fear is diluted by revulsion and fury and grim satisfaction, all of which shine so vibrantly I'm suddenly giddy with a mad kind of confidence as, finally, the King turns.

This time, the smile that spreads across my lips is real. I take in the extent of the damage I dealt him months ago in one long, satisfied look.

"Hello, my King," I say.

He watches me with his one eye, and replies in a scraping, ruined voice, "Hello, Lei-zhi."

For a beat, we face each other in silence, almost as if each of us is daring the other to draw a blade or raise an arm, grab a neck and *squeeze*.

But we both know that's not how this can go.

Instead, the King offers a fake, lazy smile, gesturing to the table closest to us. "Please," he says. He angles his head, hiding the damaged side of his face. "Sit. You must be hungry, and we have so much to catch up on."

One of the councilors, a bison demon in rich fuchsia robes, splutters. "Heavenly Master, with all due respect, this—this *girl*—"

"Lei-zhi is our guest, Councilor Haru," the King cuts him off swiftly. "I expect you all to treat her as such."

The demon's cheeks color.

I keep my hands planted firmly in my lap as we take our places around the circular table to mask their trembling—and to stop myself from reaching for something to bash his skull in with. I regard a chopstick wryly. I could stab his second eye and be done with it. Yet while I'd willingly lose a hand to maim the King, I won't dare hurt one of my friends.

The gold band weighs on my wrist. Who did they force its twin upon? Aoki? Lill? Chenna? Mistress Eira? Kenzo? I'm almost hopeful it *is* one of them, because at least it would mean they're still alive.

As long as I'm well-behaved.

The King kneels to my left. His ink and gold hanfu, which mine has been designed to match, pools on the floor around him, overlapping my own.

I train my eyes on the table, heart hammering at his closeness. Under a glass covering, scenes from the *Mae Scripts* have been carved into the wood. Yet the King's face is what my mind is focused on. That single, piercing, ice-blue iris. Its pair a wreck of scar tissue, rough in shape but oddly smoothened from shaman work. Without the golden-brown of his bull's coat, it looks stark and raw, and I'm surprised he didn't cover it with something. Then again, I suppose that would show weakness. An acknowledgment he's ashamed of what one human girl did to him.

I sneak a glance at his neck. The King's robes have been placed in such a way they conceal the site of my attack without drawing attention to the fact, the gold trim high around his neck, almost like a collar, or the enchanted band circling my wrist.

I picture that collar constricting.

I want to jump up, shout loud enough for the whole hall, the whole palace, the whole *kingdom* to hear: *I did that! That was me!* They all know, of course. They must, given the way they reacted to my arrival. But to claim it publicly would be different. To look the King in the eye, bare my teeth, and remind him that for a few minutes at least, *I* ruled *him*. For the rest of his life he has to wear the marks of my hatred. My wrath.

My power.

We sit in taut silence as the final guests take their places. Naja is last to join us. A severe-looking young lizard maid helps her kneel to the King's other side. The white fox is draped in lapis robes woven through with silver thread, jewels dripping from her furred ears. She doesn't miss a chance to shoot me a scathing expression, though with the King between us she resists saying anything.

I glare right back. But as with Madam Himura earlier, I notice that something about Naja is off.

It takes me a moment to make the connection. The last time I'd seen Naja was during the journey with Wren and the others to gather allies. She'd ambushed us on our way back from the White Wing's palace. We'd fought. She'd almost killed me; I'd almost killed *her*.

There'd been burning grasslands. A flash of silver. Naja's wild, animal howl as Merrin's qiang passed cleanly through her arm.

She must have gotten to a shaman too late to save it. That's why a maid helped her sit, when Naja would usually slice a servant's hand off for touching her in public. I'd been too delirious to notice her injuries when she captured me weeks later in the desert, and I haven't seen her since we got back to the palace.

As with the King, I spare her no pity. In another life I might have admired Naja's ambition. Her singular focus. I even understand her behavior toward me and the other Paper Girls, even if I still think it ugly—she's a Moon, born already believing in her caste's superiority. She probably truly believes her treatment of us is fair. But I'll never forgive her for killing Zelle. Bold, smart, vivacious Zelle, the palace courtesan who taught me even before Wren did how much I am capable of.

Finish it.

Those had been Zelle's last words to me. And though she was talking about the King, as I take in the grand hall, filled with demons who built this beautiful, abysmal place on the backs of Papers they crushed without a second thought, I know that in order to truly finish it, I can't stop at taking the King's life.

I'm going to burn this whole godsdamned place to the ground.

As I'm about to turn back to the table, I spot another familiar face.

Mistress Azami, supervisor of the Night House concubines, where Zelle had worked. She's one table over. Graying umber hair covers her wiry frame, her features part human, part canine. She's deep in conversation with a demon at her side. Then one of her dog ears twitches, flicks my way.

She glances up. Inclining her head just the slightest, she catches my gaze from the corner of her eye.

And winks.

It's brief, but I know it's meant for me. Because in that instant I've remembered something else Zelle told me the last time I saw her alive—Mistress Azami is working for the rebellion, too. She's the one who helped Kenzo recruit Zelle in the first place.

I take in the glittering hall with fresh eyes. Mistress Azami. Kenzo. The maid who slipped a razor into my hands the night of the Moon Ball. Those in the court who were working with last year's failed assassins. Invisible as it may be, there's a whole network here of demons and humans who all want the same things I do and are working secretly with the Hannos to achieve them. If I can get to them, I can find a way to help.

Ever since I returned to the Hidden Palace, I've been trying to escape. But what if I could be of more help by fighting the King's regime from the inside? After all, more clan lords have been killed by poison than a blade. Sometimes, the easiest way to destroy something is to let it rot from within.

For the first time in weeks, I feel a spark of hope.

And with it, a plan.

FIVE

LEI

I'M ANXIOUS TO SPEAK TO MISTRESS AZAMI as soon as possible, but the banquet drags on, course after course brought to our tables without any sign of stopping. Not that I'm complaining. Food is one thing the court has always gotten right, and after one month of imprisonment I relish each delicious chopstickful: soy-marinated ginger root; tamarind duck slivers; oysters glistening in a rich rice-wine sauce. Even the King's presence barely sours each bite. Luckily, following his lead, none of the other guests at our table speak to me, despite their staring and pointed whispers. The King talks mostly with Naja. No matter how low he keeps his tone, the harsh rasp of his broken voice grates like wasp-buzz, and I hope it hurts him to speak as much as it sounds like it does.

A glass of sake rests untouched beside my bowl. I try to ignore it even as a dark twist of longing uncoils in my belly. What harm would a sip do? One glass, even? Traveling with Wren and the others, I used to drink much more. I know the burn the alcohol would make sliding down my throat. How the world would take on a warm, comforting fuzz that'd make all of this easier. Here, in the midst of all these demons, it's too tempting to dream about sinking down and away.

In the end, I deter myself by envisioning the cup filled not with sake but with my friends' and family's blood. Blood that will be spilled if I don't stay focused. If I choose to sink instead of to rise.

I *must* rise. My Birth-blessing word isn't *flight* for nothing.

My hand drifts to my neck, brushing bare skin. Naja took away my Birth-blessing pendant when they captured me. I'd woken in the cabin of a sand-ship rocking over the Janese dunes to find both my dagger and pendant gone. The Birth-blessing ritual is the most sacred tradition for all castes, and the thought of Naja's claws on something so precious to me made me sick. But I guess she waged it too much of a risk. The chain could have been used to strangle her or one of the soldiers—or myself.

Once the last of the plates have been cleared, the musicians finish their song and a pregnant hush falls over the hall.

Two servants rush over. Kneeling, they offer the King their bowed heads for support as he gets to his feet. The heavy drag of hooves on marble as he adjusts his position pricks my nerves. I try to steady my breathing, but it's difficult with hundreds of demon eyes on me and the King's shadow casting me in his dark silhouette. To his other side, Naja stares up at him, her silver eyes reverent.

It's then that I notice the King's hands. They hang at my eyeline, his furred fingers curled into fists. To demonstrate his power? Suppress his rage?

No, I realize, lips snaking into a gloating smile—to hide that his hands are shaking.

The Demon King of Ikhara is *scared*.

Triumph soars through my veins. *We* did that. Zelle, Wren, and me, and every other human and demon who's stood up to him since, tearing down his soldiers in battles or simply existing. Living, loving, laughing. Defying the darkness he and the court impose on us each day purely by pursuing happiness. By holding on to hope.

"Members of the court. My fellow demons."

The King's magnified voice echoes through the hall.

I flinch. Despite its raw scrape, his speech still carries authority— perhaps even more so. It gives him the gravitas of an old, battle-worn demon hardened by his scars. I'd overlooked the fact that men grow more respected the more marks and years they collect, while for women losing youth is a slow stripping away of our worth.

Well, our perceived worth, anyway. I think of Nor, Lova's second-in-command. Tien. Mistress Azami. All strong older women who defy others' expectations of them. Even Mistress Eira, who as weak as she was in many ways, showed me kindness when I needed it the most.

"Thank you all for being here tonight," the King begins. "I understand this has been a difficult period, what with the daily war councils and increased uptick in responsibilities given the, ah... *departure* of many of our members."

Judging by the side-looks a few demons share, the King means the executions or imprisonments of court members suspected of disloyalty he's been busy with ever since the Moon Ball. I'd caught snatches of talk of them from the guards as they came and went from my cell.

"I am thankful we are able to share tonight, and find a little respite during these trying times. Yet, first and foremost, I've brought us together—only you, the most trusted members of my court—to see to official business."

A hand lands on the top of my head. Claw-tipped. Forceful.

The King's hand, *on me.*

Whatever I was anticipating, this wasn't it. The King practically ignored me all night. To have his touch on my body so unexpectedly makes bile rise in my throat, bringing back memories I've worked so hard to keep at bay. With effort, I force my face to remain neutral, keeping my eyes trained on the table in front of me, where under a glass lid, dancing gods and goddesses lie frozen in wood. I spot the form of small, childish Mirini, Goddess of Secret Places, skipping between carved leaves. If only she could help me now, steal me to a safe place away from the eyes of demons and the King's—*the King's*—touch.

His hand slides to the back of my head. There's a slight tremor, but I'm not so confident now it was fear. What if it was anticipation for this moment, when he would finally claim me again? It would hardly take him any force to shove me forward, smash my forehead into the table. Is that what he's brought the court together for tonight? Killing the Moonchosen, right in front of them?

Defiance burns me.

I will *not* die this way.

I jerk my head back against his grip, eyes shooting up to meet his. His features are a mask of calmness, yet I alone am close enough to see the twisted mix of disgust and satisfaction in that single, ice-blue iris. The same look I gave him earlier.

The corner of his lips sharpen. He hisses so only I hear, "Get up, girl. Bow for your audience."

I rise, too anxious and aware of the dao-woven bangle on my wrist to disobey. The King's hand moves to the small of my back, making my insides roil.

"As you have seen by now," he tells the captivated room, "my former Paper Girl, Lei-zhi—or should I say, our little Moonchosen—

has returned to the palace. You may be surprised to see her. Surprised even more so to see her by my side, the two of us existing peacefully."

If peacefully means you had to restrain me with an enchanted band so I wouldn't scoop out your remaining eye with a soup spoon, I think sourly.

"The truth is," the King says, "one month ago we received a request from Lei-zhi for us to rescue her from the rebels."

"*What?*" I exclaim.

Thankfully my outcry is hidden beneath the tide of surprise that rushes through the hall.

The King's smirk widens. "Yes. As we long suspected, Ketai Hanno treats his followers with little care. His methods of rule are harsh and unjust. Remember, this is a man who was willing to sacrifice the life of his own daughter to hurt me." The King pauses for effect. "I am sure all of you know by now that it was Lei-zhi herself who attacked me at the Moon Ball. Who left me with these...souvenirs." He waves a hand at his face before laughing, a fraction too late and too loud.

Hardly anyone joins him.

This time, I'm certain. No matter how cavalier he acts, the King is haunted by what happened that night. As he has with me, I've left my mark upon him deeper than surface level. I have crawled underneath his skin to live there, a venom even shamans cannot draw out.

"What most of you do not know," he continues, "is that my poor Lei-zhi was brainwashed during her time here by Ketai Hanno's daughter. Under her father's instruction, it was Wren Hanno who encouraged Lei-zhi to turn her back on the riches and kindness we so generously showed her. Wren Hanno who tempted her with false promises. Who tainted her mind with the same wrongful accusations against myself Ketai Hanno is spreading throughout our kingdom this very moment. And though we cannot be sure, we suspect magic was involved to control Lei-zhi's behavior so effectively."

By now, the banquet hall is silent, every guest's attention rapt—mine included.

He gazes down, smiling tenderly at me, though the look in his eye is pure ice. "We have the gods to thank that Lei-zhi eventually escaped the bindings the Hannos held over her and realized what she had wrongly been a part of, leading her to reach out to us. Though I longed to share this information with you all, considering the caste traitors still being turned out among our ranks, I had no choice but to keep this news secret. General Naja and General Ndeze were tasked with rescuing Lei-zhi. Sadly, General Ndeze died a heroic death in battle one month ago with the rebels in the Janese deserts. And as you can see, General Naja did not escape this mission unscathed."

Naja stiffens at this, though whether with pride or shame, I can't tell.

"Yet thanks to their bravery," the King says, "General Naja and her soldiers successfully extracted Lei-zhi from the rebels to return her to her rightful home—here in the Hidden Palace. And while we've nursed her back to health over the past weeks, she has been feeding us with information on the rebels and their movements."

I bristle, biting my tongue to stop from shouting out at his lies.

"There was little doubt we would win the war before," the King growls, "but now we know exactly what Ketai Hanno is planning. It was partly thanks to Lei-zhi's information that we were able to execute our attack on Nantanna so impressively—not to mention we planned a little surprise for Ketai Hanno when he tries to return to his fort tomorrow."

My heart skips. An attack on Nantanna? Some "surprise" for Ketai Hanno tomorrow? I didn't know about any of this, but the King smiles down at me as though it was all my doing.

He snatches up his glass of sake and holds it high. "The Hannos' ragtag army stand no chance against the might of our court! Let us continue to show them how foolish they were to ever turn against us!" The guests cheer, lifting their own glasses, and the King finishes, triumphant, "Let us remind them whose sides the gods are on! Now she is once more at full strength, let me present to you— Lei-zhi, my returned Paper Girl. *Our* Moonchosen!"

The crowd erupts.

I want to tear myself from the King's grip, scream that none of it's true. But what demon would believe me over their King? All this time, I thought I'd been waiting for an execution. But the King's speech intensifies my dread. Because if he isn't planning to kill me as a traitor, what *does* he want me here for? Surely my symbolism as a good-luck charm and anti-rebel icon isn't enough.

No one betrays the Demon King of Ikhara and escapes unpunished.

The music swells back up, and the guests rise with it, hurrying to congratulate the King. The sake girls reappear, this time with a sparkling kind, the pop and fizz of bottles punctuating the excitement.

Naja turns her cold silver eyes on me. Her smile is victorious.

Our contact breaks as a councilor bumps into me in their rush to get to the King. Smirking, Naja turns to toast with a nearby court member, while I stand trembling from head to toe, trying not to vomit.

The King is to use me as a puppet in the palace from now on, and Ang-Khen's capital, Nantanna, has been destroyed, marking the King's first win against the Hannos and their allies.

What a night for good news.

Suddenly, I can't stand to be here anymore, listening to the King's gloating and his court members' ingratiating praise. I stumble in a random direction. The hall is charged, its atmosphere fever pitch. I'm bumped this way and that, addressed by demons with words I block out, too on edge, too close to unraveling—and I *won't* unravel, not in front of them.

I expect someone to stop me. For Naja or one of the guards to drag me back to the King's side. But it seems I've been forgotten in the euphoria, or—more likely—the court isn't worried about me escaping. They know I won't do anything with the enchanted bracelet threatening someone I love.

"Sparkling sake, Mistress?" One of the demon girls proffers a tray of crystal glasses. The instant she recognizes me, she shrinks back. "I—I mean, M-Moonchosen…"

I stop. Not because I'm considering taking one—because, past the girl's glitter-dusted shoulder, I've spotted the only demon in this room I can trust.

I stride forward and grab Mistress Azami's arm. "We need to talk," I hiss.

The dog-woman's expression doesn't change, though a warning flashes in her eyes. "Lei-zhi. How wonderful to see you. I'm glad you returned to us."

She grimaces in apology at the demon she was talking to before leading me to a quiet spot near the wall. She plucks a half empty glass from the closest table and hands it to me.

"I don't want it," I snap, pushing it away.

"You'll contain your emotions better with something to hold," she says sternly. "Didn't Mistress Eira or Madam Himura teach you girls that?"

"Probably. But Shifu Caen also taught me how to turn anything into a weapon, and right now all I can think about is smashing this glass and slicing it across the King's throat."

There's a glint of something approving in her flint-colored eyes.

"What the King said—" I start.

"Oh, that didn't fool any of us," Mistress Azami cuts in. "At least, none of us with half a brain. I know where your loyalties lie, Lei. None of us who are working with Ketai will doubt it. Still," she mutters, "it wasn't a bad move on their part. Unseat you from an emblem of the rebellion to a symbol of repentance. Spread rumors through the clans' spies you've changed allegiances. Reassert his own power within the court. The King might be a monster, but he isn't an idiot—and when it comes to kiasu, he's a master." She takes a sip of her drink, her furrow deepening. "This could change things. Ketai won't be happy the King landed the first blow." She huffs. "At least *try* to look happy. You've just helped your beloved King take down one of his opposition's greatest strongholds, after all."

"I don't want any part in his games," I snarl.

"You have no choice, Lei. We must all play along. No matter how much it pains us to."

I hide my scowl in my glass. Though I want the alcohol—more badly than ever before—I don't let a drop touch my lips. I can't lose an ounce of focus. "Mistress Azami, I need to know how the others are doing. If you have any information at all. Kenzo, Lill, the other Paper Girls…"

"Everyone is alive and safe. You don't need to worry about them."

"But—where are they?"

"Lill and Kenzo are with me, and are being well looked after by my girls." The dog-woman softens slightly, something affectionate entering her tone; the same fondness I heard from her before with

Zelle. "Your young maid is a sweet girl. No harm will come to her while she's under my roof, I promise. She asks about you often."

Tears blur my eyes.

"As for the remaining Paper Girls," Mistress Azami goes on, "they are being held in Paper House. They're being left to their own resources for the most part, which is much better than the alternatives. My allies help when they can—mostly to bring food, or medical supplies. And yes," she says quickly when I begin to interrupt, "I've thought about freeing them, but it'd be too suspicious, especially after we freed Kenzo from the Lunar Lake prison. The King knows there are those that work against him within the court. He's out for blood. I'm not scared to die, but I have too much work before I do." She doesn't laugh; she's entirely serious. "For now, the girls are safe enough at Paper House. Blue was quite badly injured at the Moon Ball, but I'm told she's making a good recovery."

My relief flowers. Kenzo, Lill, and the Paper Girls. Alive and well. It's more than I dared hope.

"Mistress Eira will be looking after the girls," I say. "I'm glad."

Mistress Azami's jaw stiffens. She looks as though she's about to say something, but I go on before she can speak.

"I want to help—with the rebellion. What can I do?"

"Oh, Lei, you've already done enough."

"No. I haven't." I move closer. "If you won't help me, I'll just have to do my best on my own—and it could put all of us in danger if I make a wrong move. Isn't there something...some way you and the other allies communicate?"

Mistress Azami hesitates. Then she sighs. "*The small bird flies on the wings of the golden-eyed girl,*" she says. When I frown at her, bemused, she explains, "It's the code we use to know who we can trust—"

Laughter from a nearby group of demons startles us. Beyond

them, I spy my guards pushing through the crowd, Naja leading them. The same maid who helped her earlier—a dull-scaled wiry lizard-girl—supports her as she walks. Naja's snowy face is set with its usual ferocious determination.

I turn back to Mistress Azami, wanting to ask for news from outside the palace, but she speaks first, low and urgent. "Lei, listen. I can't be sure of the King's plans—he has a habit of changing his mind last minute. But from what my informants tell me, things are about to get a lot more difficult for you. Promise me you'll stay strong. Play your part. Be patient. Whatever happens, you must go along with the King's games. It'll be too dangerous not to—"

"Mistress Azami."

The dog-woman's features slip into a neutral look. She turns, greeting the white fox with a bow. "General Naja."

"How nice to see you spending time with your old student. I trust you had a lot to catch up on. The last time you saw each other was quite an eventful evening."

Naja's suspicion is evident. But Mistress Azami gives her a thin smile, unflustered. "And how good it is to see you looking so well, General. The gods have blessed your recovery. Another reason to celebrate tonight." She puts a hand on my shoulder. "Lei-zhi, I do hope to see you again soon."

As she walks briskly away on her haunched legs, Naja jerks her chin toward me. The guards take formation around us.

"Careful, Lei-zhi," she whispers, as I'm marched back to the King. "There are those in the court who cannot be trusted. It would be a terrible shame if the King were to find out you've fallen in with the wrong crowd under his watch for a second time."

"Yes," I reply coolly. "And with *you* keeping such a close eye on me. How disappointed he'd be." Then I turn away, resisting the urge to laugh at the look on her face.

If I am to be the King's Moonchosen, I will play my part for now, just as Mistress Azami asked.

But I never said I wouldn't cause a little trouble.

The demons celebrate long into the night.

The King keeps me close. I greet sycophantic court members with a flat smile plastered across my face. I force myself to appear interested as they fawn over him: *What a brilliant maneuver, Heavenly Master! Only a month into war and we have dealt the traitors such a blow! Ketai Hanno's pitiful alliance will surely not recover from this!* Instead of their words, however, it's Mistress Azami's I am focused on. What does she know? What is coming that's about to make my life more difficult—as if being back in the King's palace isn't enough? And who among these awful demons might be a secret ally?

When the party finally winds down, the King bids his guests farewell before—angling us carefully so they all see—he draws me close. After a second's hesitation only the two of us notice, he plants a kiss to my forehead. There's the rustle of clothes as the remaining demons lower into reverent bows.

I follow suit the second the King releases me. My hands to the marble, I grind my forehead against it even harder, trying to scrape away the feel of his lips on my skin. None of us move until the familiar heft of his hoof-beats fade. Then my guards wrench me to my feet, leading me back to the room I woke in earlier, which I suppose is mine from now on. At least it's more comfortable than the last. Best of all, I have a window, which means I might well be able to figure out a way to climb down. And if not, I'll always be able to look out at the sky and remember what it is I am fighting for.

My wings. Flight.

Freedom.

Not only for me, like the last time I was here in the palace. But for all those *like* me—girls and Papers and even demons. Anyone in Ikhara who has felt the brutal force of the King and his court.

Before my guards leave, the gazelle demon grabs my arm. "We'll be right outside," he snarls, then shoves me through.

The door slams. In an instant, I fall to my knees and retch. Tears leak down my cheeks as I throw up everything I ate so eagerly a few hours before. I know the guards can hear, but I can't help it. I've spent all my force to get through the evening. To be able to be so close to *him* and not fall apart.

When I'm done, I wipe my sleeve across my mouth and crawl to bed. I burrow beneath its silks, still fully dressed, and hug my knees tight. The bangle strapped to my right wrist digs into my skin. It strikes me that the last time I was in a proper bed was in the White Wing's Cloud Palace. To think that was months ago, right at the beginning of my journey with Wren and the others.

Wren and I shared a bed in the bird demons' palace for two nights. The first, she snuck out and murdered one of Lady Dunya's daughters. Yet just hours before, I embraced her in the bathing room as she broke down at the news the King was still alive. As she admitted what had happened to her at his hands. As, finally, for the first time, she gave her trauma a voice.

I huddle under the covers, holding myself because the girl I love isn't here to do it, recalling Wren's assessment of us based on the dresses we wore the night of our Unveiling Ceremony when we were first presented to the King.

The dresses were made to represent us based on the results of our assessments. Mine was everything I've been trained to be. Strong, without compromise. Unforgiving. I knew what yours meant the minute I saw you. Your dress showed me that you had strength, but softness, too. A sense of loyalty, but not without fairness. Fight, and mercy. Things I wasn't allowed to feel. Things I didn't know how badly I needed.

Wren's words sting. Because life is not as simple as two dresses, cut to be the opposite of each other. If I have learned anything since this war began, it is that souls are messy, imperfect things. Even the most beautiful of them have the capacity to be cruel.

Uncompromising and unforgiving.

Fair and merciful.

Hearts are all of these things, and more. And no matter how complex, how contradictory they might be, that doesn't mean they do not deserve love, or forgiveness.

Or a second chance.

SIX

WREN

WREN WAS PACING HER ROOMS when the shouting began. She snatched the gutting knife from her side cabinet without a second's hesitation and sprinted into the hallway. It had been a few days since her father and Caen left for Nantanna with a contingent of their army and allies. Lova had stayed behind to help protect the Jade Fort with her, sending her second-in-command Nor in her place as the Cat Clan's representative. Wren was doing her best to keep the fort running smoothly, constantly on high alert. She hadn't been sleeping much before. Now she barely closed her eyes, tracing the same pattern across the floorboards of her bedroom as she braced herself for something that seemed to have finally arrived.

By the time she was on the stone staircase, leaping them three at a time, the yells had grown, accompanied by running footsteps. The foyer was teeming.

Wren spotted Lova's gleaming blond fur. She was barking at one of her warriors. "Bring me my cannon! I won't let that beaked bastard get away this time."

Wren pushed toward her. Lova was already striding outside. It had been raining all day. Wren was soaked through in an instant. Around the grounds, the Hannos' remaining soldiers sprinted about. A few spotted Wren and came over, requesting orders.

She ignored them. Catching up with Lova, she asked, "What is it? An attack?"

"I wish."

"Is my father back?"

"Someone else," the lion-girl spat, and pointed to the sky.

Wren blinked the rain from her lashes. The sky was dark. It took her a few moments before she saw what Lova was indicating: the familiar outline of widespread wings. A bird demon—soaring straight toward them.

A growl rumbled in Lova's throat. To Wren's other side, one of the archers her father had left under her supervision, a teenage Paper boy called Khuen, strolled up lazily, as if coming out to admire the view. Twirling an arrow between his fingers, he drawled nonchalantly, rain slicking his dark curls, "Want me to shoot them down?"

Wren didn't answer. Her eyes were locked on the fast-approaching figure. There was a rumble of thunder. A flash of lightning. But Wren didn't need it to know who it was. She'd seen this particular bird demon flying enough times to recognize him from his silhouette alone.

Merrin was back.

They brought him to a windowless room off the foyer, her soldiers throwing him inside with a roughness Wren didn't reprimand.

"Guard the doorway," she ordered.

A few hesitated. Like Wren, they knew who Merrin was, had lived with him and liked him for so many years—and they knew of his betrayal. Most of the guards stood with their weapons still pointed where Merrin sagged on the floor, water dripping from his feathers. His head was bowed, as if he knew one look at his guilty face would be all it would take to break their self-control.

"*Leave,*" Wren commanded the guards, harder this time, imitating her father's authoritative tone. They moved away. When Khuen made to go with them, she stopped him. "Not you."

The boy shrugged. He reset his position at her side, a notched arrow trained on Merrin.

Lova huffed. "Baby archer gets his bow, but I'm not allowed my cannon?"

"Your cannon would blast half this building to rubble, demon," Khuen retorted. "My bow and arrow might not be as *flashy*, but they're efficient. Far less cleanup."

"That's half the fun."

"Anyway," the boy added, "the way the old owl is looking, I could probably take him down with a child's slingshot." He cocked his head toward Wren. "Want me to try?"

"I'll do it," Lova offered quickly.

Wren shut them both down. "The bird is to be kept alive."

For the first time since he'd landed, Merrin made a sound. It was a laugh, a rough noise at the back of his throat. "The bird?" He raised his head, and his molten orange owl eyes, just as piercing as Wren remembered, finally met hers. "You've never called me that before."

"And you've never betrayed us before," she shot back. "At least, I assume so." Her anger was rising. "My father trusted you with our lives. He took you in when you were six years old, when your clan was slain by soldiers for refusing to join the King's army. You helped him find me when those same soldiers came for my own clan. I grew up with you. And after all of that, everything we went through, what you *did*..."

Merrin looked gutted by her words. His soaked robes clung to his thin frame. A puddle of rainwater pooled around him.

"Lei," Wren said. "Nitta. Where are they?"

Merrin didn't answer, gazing at the floor with sad eyes. In turn, Wren glared down at the demon she'd known all her life. He'd once been a gangly limbed, keen-to-please, careful, sweet bird-boy her father trusted enough to leave her alone with when she was just a toddler. She'd even thought once that he was her actual brother, because of how much time they spent together. And he'd cared for her like one. Just like Kenzo. The only people her parents had trusted with her true identity, along with Caen. Merrin and Kenzo's feathers and fur and her own paper-thin skin hadn't mattered. They'd been family. They'd taught her what trust looked and felt like. What it meant to have someone's back, no matter what.

Now, one of them had also taught her how terrible it felt when that kind of trust was broken.

"Where are they, Merrin?" Wren repeated coldly.

"Nitta is safe," he started, speaking quietly. "Her back...it was broken in the battle. I brought her to a renowned healer in the Red Sand Valley I'd heard about. I worked as a hunter for the healer's clan to pay for her care, and as soon as Nitta was well enough to leave, we came here—"

"Where is she?" Wren interrupted.

"She's hidden nearby. I—I wasn't sure if you would shoot me directly upon sight, and if you did, I didn't want her to be injured in the fall."

"You left her alone?" Lova spat, advancing on him. Outside, rain was still lashing down. "In *this*?" She sounded more indignant about a cat demon being left out in the rain than alone and possibly defenseless after a serious injury. "Directions," she demanded. *"Now."*

The second she had Nitta's location, Lova turned to Wren. Though her face burned with determination, she hesitated. "I can send one of my cats instead if you want me to stay."

Wren shook her head. "Go. Nitta should see a familiar face. Take a horse from the stables and ask the maids to prepare a room—"

Lova was already stomping off. They heard her barking orders from the atrium.

Wren returned her attention to Merrin. Slowly, carefully, she said, "What about Lei?"

Merrin went to say something, faltered, and suddenly Wren found herself shouting.

"Lei! You remember her, don't you? The girl we rescued from the Hidden Palace after she stuck a knife in the King's throat? The girl you traveled with for months? Who helped us gain the White Wing's allegiance—which you went on to lose? The brave, beautiful girl who hurt so much for you when Bo died, who would've done anything, *anything* to help you, to help any of us—"

She fisted her hands, controlling herself in an instant.

When she spoke next, it was through clenched teeth. "Where is she, Merrin?"

He looked more miserable than ever.

Wren hissed at Khuen, "Take out a wing."

As the boy drew back his arm, Merrin muttered something.

Wren held out a hand. Khuen halted.

"Louder!" she snarled.

Merrin cleared his throat. "She—she left to try and get back to the battle. She left, and with Nitta, I—I couldn't follow her. She made me promise to stay…"

For one wild instant, relief staggered through Wren. Lei was still in the Janese deserts? Then she was alive! Lei was resourceful. She was a fighter. Wren could picture it now: she'd have made it to one of the desert villages or roaming clans, gathered supplies to make it to the Demon Ridge mountains, then on into Ang-Khen. Maybe she was close by even now, and any minute she'd run in through the fort's entranceway with her perfect face and dazzling, hopeful eyes and a smile that would light Wren's heart on fire, and everything would be all right because they would be together again—

Merrin's voice crushed her daydreaming.

"News reached us while Nitta and I were in the Red Sand Valley. A royal carriage passed through the One Thousand Mile Road. Naja was spotted speaking to the road guards. Rumor has it she captured Lei in Jana and has since…" He seemed to deflate. "Has since brought her back to the Hidden Palace."

The room was deathly still.

Wren's body flooded with ice. It felt like when she was in a Xia trance, except this was not magic. This was not power.

This was the very opposite of it.

Drawing a blank mask over her features, Wren closed her eyes. Her right hand moved to the knife in her robes, a familiar song calling to something deep within her, a place first born from her warrior blood then honed by Ketai. An ugly, wrathful core she both loved and hated, because it was her strength yet was also what had caused Lei to look at her and see an enemy.

Wren pulled the knife free.

Khuen, sensing danger, said, "Lord Hanno will be back any day now. Perhaps we should wait until he speaks to Merrin? He may have more information that could be useful to us."

Wren held her rage in with all she had. She finally had the answer to the question she'd been waiting over a month for, but it didn't bring relief, or peace. And while she would give anything to be able to force Merrin to fly her right then and there to the palace, she had been left in charge of the fort. She had to wait for her father. She was, once again, useless to help Lei.

She turned on her heels before her self-control snapped. "I'm going to get things ready for Nitta," she told Khuen. "Keep him here. I want to hear Nitta's side of the story before we question him more."

"Wren. I am so sorry for what I did."

Her back stiffened. Merrin held her name so tentatively, so lovingly on his tongue, and it *pierced* her.

She drew herself tall, composing herself. Then, like Lova minutes before, she stalked off without a backward glance. Outside, she gave orders to the waiting guards and maids, and the rain-hushed fort filled with sounds of activity.

It wasn't until five minutes later that Wren realized she'd broken the handle of the small knife beyond repair. It was crushed beneath her fingers. She opened her hand and tipped her palm, watching the shattered pieces fall to the floor with empty eyes and a darkly raging heart.

She didn't recognize Nitta at first.

When the guards alerted Wren that Lova had returned, she went to stand by the foot of the stairs under the ruffling banners of her clan, waiting, ready, wanting, *needing* Nitta's big smile and playful confidence, the echo of her brother's cheek. She clung to the idea that it'd be almost like having a part of Lei back. A flicker of light in the darkness that had been these terrible past weeks.

At the sound of hooves, the foyer grew quiet. There'd been an air of anxiety ever since Ketai left for Nantanna, and Merrin's return had done nothing to ease the tension among the remaining clan members.

Past the entranceway, the grounds were dark and rain-lashed. Hoof-beats drew closer. Wren expected them to stop when the horse's bulky silhouette came into view, wet coat shining under the atrium's lanterns. But the horse continued right up to the palace entrance—and then inside.

Lova, just as rain-sodden, jumped from the horse's back and strode into the foyer with a look of pure, thunderous hatred. "I'll kill him!" she snarled, drawing her cutlass with such force many of the watching clan members scurried back. She made a beeline for the room Merrin was being held in.

Wren blocked her. There was the clink of weapons as the guards outside his door readjusted their stances, readying this time not to keep their prisoner in but to keep Lova out.

The lion-girl laughed in their faces. "As if."

"Lo," Wren warned.

Lova growled and jerked her neck, raindrops flying from her fur. "Look at what he did to her!" she yelled, throwing an arm out. *"Look!"*

Even in the impressive foyer, the horse looked huge, a towering black-and-white stallion bred big enough to seat demons. A sodden lump of fabric was heaped on his back. Wren looked past the horse, confused. Where was Nitta? And what was Lova thinking, bringing a horse into the atrium?

Understanding struck her.

Ignoring her father's aides, who were yet again bustling about, requesting instructions, Wren went to the sorry-looking mound of wet clothes on the horse's back—which was not a pile of clothes at all but Nitta.

Nitta. Collapsed, bedraggled, broken.

The leopard demon was slumped over the horse's neck, head resting on one arm. The other dangled limply at her side.

Wren took her drooping hand. "Nitta," she whispered.

Nitta looked exhausted. Her fur lay soggy and matted against her. The coat she was wrapped in dwarfed her meager frame, the ridges of her spine sharp beneath it, her exposed collarbones delicate as wishbones. The leopard-girl had always been wiry, but this was a different kind of thin.

Slowly, Nitta lifted her head. She looked at Wren with her lovely green eyes, the faintest sparkle in them. "Wren," she said in a low croak. One corner of her lips tucked. "You're looking well, considering, you know..." Her lashes fluttered. "Last time we saw each other. Fight to the death, and all that..."

Then her head slumped.

Wren caught her as she slid from the stallion's back, drawing her smoothly into her arms. "Take the horse to the stables," she ordered the milling clan members. "And show me to Nitta's room. *Lo*," she added sharply over her shoulder.

Lova had been edging toward Merrin's room while everyone's attention was averted. Looking frustrated, she joined Wren. "You have to let me do it at some point," she grumbled. "Unless you want the honors yourself?"

Wren didn't answer. She wasn't sure what she wanted. She wanted to tear Merrin apart. To storm into the Hidden Palace and cut down every demon until she found Lei. She wanted to hurt, to destroy...and she wanted to lie in a quiet room with a girl in her arms and know that no one would ever hurt either of them again. Oh, how much she wanted that.

Wren wanted it all, but she wasn't sure if she could have any of it, and she especially wasn't sure she deserved to.

There was a crunch as she stepped on the broken pieces of her knife.

No wonder she'd been so drawn to it, she thought dully. She was everything the knife was. Jagged. Cold. Bloodstained.

Broken.

SEVEN

WREN

NITTA SLEPT PAST NOON THE FOLLOWING DAY.
Wren stayed with her all night, alternating between sitting in a chair by the bed and pacing the windows, hoping to see her father and their army returning. Lova had insisted on keeping her company. The Amala General sat on the floor, cleaning her cutlass or turning it in slow swishes to catch the lantern light.

At the ring of the bells signaling lunchtime, Wren got to her feet. "I'm going to check on the clan. I'll have some food brought up for us. Keep an eye on her."

In the dining hall, Wren moved between the tables, talking with her father's councilors and various leaders of their allied clans, answering questions and receiving updates. Merrin was still being kept under guard. She ordered some food and water to be sent to him.

"No poison," she said, only half jokingly.

On her way back upstairs, a pair of maids trailed her, delicious scents wafting from the trays they carried. Wren was nearing Nitta's room when she heard voices drifting from the crack in the doorway.

They were low, secretive. She held up a hand, stopping still. The maids followed suit.

"We never told her—"

"I know that! Do you think she'd still be talking to me if she knew? I know she doesn't know, cub. What I don't understand is why."

"If you *still* don't understand, Lova, you never will."

"You owe me no allegiance, Nitta. Neither you nor Bo. You could have told Wren right away what I'd done."

Nitta sounded hurt. "Do you think we ever stopped being Amala? You exiled us, Lova. But it didn't stop us from loving you. From loving our family—"

A sneeze broke the quiet.

One of the maids was wobbling, desperately resetting her balance after almost spilling the bowls of goji soup on her tray.

The door to Nitta's room slid back. Lova stepped out. "We didn't hear you coming," she said, before adding, "Nitta's awake."

Wren was too tired to try and make sense of what she'd overhead—clan squabbling was the least of her concerns. And anyway, the moment she saw Nitta sitting up in bed, a weak grin on her sweet face, the conversation flew from her mind.

Nitta was here, and she was awake, and she was *smiling*.

"Miss me?" she asked as Wren sat next to her.

For what felt like the first time in years, Wren smiled. Not a smirk or wry curl of her lip, or a fleeting, amused twist. A real smile. It was small but true.

"Yes," she replied. "Oh, Nitta, *yes*."

Their hands found each other's.

"I didn't think I'd ever see any of you again," Nitta said, her large emerald eyes imploring. "Lova told me you're holding Merrin prisoner. Wren, you *have* to listen to his story. I'd be dead if it weren't for him."

"You almost died *because* of him," Wren said. "All of us did. And Lei—"

She cut off. She couldn't talk about what she'd learned last night about Lei's whereabouts. Not yet. Just thinking it was a punch to her gut.

"He made a mistake," Nitta said. "He's learned from it. He's trying to redeem himself." As Lova made a scoffing sound in the corner of the room where the maids were setting up the table, Nitta added patiently, "He lost someone he loved, and it obscured his judgment. That's something all of us can relate to."

Wren thought of the bloodied jackal-boy in a room nearby. Her gaze lowered to where her fingers were entwined with Nitta's. For an instant, it was Lei's hand she saw, shorter and paler and un-furred. She ached to feel them again, so soft and warm against her skin.

Nitta squeezed her hand. "We've all done things we're not proud of," she said. Her eyes moved to Lova. "We've all betrayed those we love in some way or other. Merrin did a horrible thing, but he has a good heart. He deserves our forgiveness."

"Lei is..." Wren forced the words out. "Lei is back in the Hidden Palace. How could I ever forgive him for that?"

"Because," Nitta replied, "he wants to help get her out."

With a growl, Lova immediately shooed the maids from the room. She watched from the doorway until they were out of earshot, then slid it shut. "What do you mean?" she snarled, rounding on Nitta. "He's found a safe way in?"

"Well, no," Nitta admitted, making Lova toss her arms up in frustration. "But he's a bird demon. He's willing to try, if that's what we want. Why don't we talk to him?"

"I will *kill* that Bird if I have to spend one more second in his undeserving presence!" Lova erupted. She prowled forward, face hovering an inch from Nitta's. "Have you forgotten what he did to you? What he took from you? What he *made* you?"

It was a topic Wren had been waiting for Nitta to bring up herself. Of course, Lova wasn't quite as sensitive.

Nitta lifted her chin, staring Lova straight in the eyes. "Yes, I am paralyzed from the waist down. But that doesn't make me any less than I was before. I am still a warrior. I am still myself."

Lova lurched away, a disbelieving sound in her throat.

"My back was already broken at the battlefield," Nitta declared calmly. "I'd have been trampled to death if Merrin hadn't gotten me out of there. That's why he took us away—to protect us. Lei asked him to take me somewhere safe. And he took her because he wanted *her* to be safe, too. Merrin hadn't been able to go after her later because he couldn't leave me alone in my state. I *begged* him to find her. But he wouldn't leave me."

"Coward," Lova scoffed.

Nitta ignored her. "I kept passing out from the pain. Every time I came to, we were somewhere new. I could tell it was still Jana, still the desert. Then mountains appeared in the distance. The next time I woke, the color of the sand was this rusty red and Merrin was pulling me in some cart he must have found. The next time, I woke inside the healer's hut. She told me about my injuries. That I'd never walk again. But she managed to save feeling from my waist up, and I would live—"

Nitta stopped abruptly. Her eyes were glassy. She scrubbed a hand over her face. She looked between them, then let out a burst of laughter that made Wren flinch.

"I'm crying because I'm *happy*, you idiots!" she exclaimed, grinning her crooked smile, so like her brother's. "Because I'm alive! Merrin saved my life, then the Red Sand healer saved what she could of my body. It took a long time to be in a stable-enough condition to travel, but we're here and we're ready to work." She grasped Wren's fingers. "Come on. Don't you want to save our girl?"

Wren stood, turning her back to the bed.

Nitta snorted. "Sweet Samsi. You two are so dramatic."

"I'll take that as a compliment, thank you." Lova sniffed.

"Maybe after all this is over," Nitta suggested, "you should consider hanging up those giant swords that are going to cause some *serious* backache and starting up a theater group. A little bit of makyong, maybe? Or how about some good old-fashioned opera? Your singing never was that good, General, but Nor has some impressive pipes from what I remember, and Osa—"

"Is dead," Lova finished bluntly.

The light atmosphere Nitta had been attempting to build vanished in an instant.

"I'm sorry." She was quiet. "At the sands?"

Lova didn't reply, but Wren imagined she'd nodded. After a long pause, Lova said, "He *was* great on the sitar."

Wren turned in time to see a smile lift the corner of Nitta's mouth. Then their eyes met, and Nitta's expression sobered.

"Talk to him," she urged.

Lei's face came to Wren—and she knew in an instant what she had to do. It was what Lei would do. What she hoped one day, Lei would do for *her*.

"All right," Wren said. As Nitta beamed, she added, "But I make no promises as to whether we'll agree with what he says."

"Speak for yourself," Lova muttered. "I doubt whatever Feathers says is going to stop me from wanting to stamp on his stupid neck—"

Running footsteps thudded outside.

In an instant, both Wren and Lova backed to shield Nitta, Lova drawing her cutlass. The door slid open with so much force it almost shut itself again—though not before a blur of graying russet fur streaked into the room.

"Where is he!" the blur demanded, whirling around like a furry tornado, poking into every corner of the room. *"Where—is—he!"*

Lova lowered her cutlass with a sigh.

"Tien," Wren said, straightening from her defensive stance. "If you're talking about Merrin, he's not here. And could you please quiet down? Our friend is trying to rest."

"No, I'm not," Nitta said brightly.

The whirr of fur finally came to a stop, revealing it to be an aging Steel lynx-woman. Though she was short for a demon, she held herself tall, her chin jutted proudly, the ruff of fur protruding from her collar bristling.

"It is the afternoon," the demon snapped, "and we are at war. No one should be resting at this hour." Her feline eyes narrowed at Wren. "And watch how you speak to your elders, young girl. I don't care if you *are* a Clan Lord's daughter. I am still your superior, and you shall address me as such."

Nitta burst into gales of laughter. "I *like* her!" When Tien swung her glare her way, Nitta amended hastily, "I mean, I like your attitude, Auntie. No disrespect intended."

Tien considered her. "Who are you?"

Before Nitta could answer, more dashing footsteps sounded. A Paper man appeared. He clutched at the doorframe, red-faced. "Eight... thousand...apologies," he panted. "Tien, this is not our home! You can't go bursting into any room you please!" He wiped the sweat from his brow, still doubled over. "Dear *gods*, that old demon moves fast."

Tien prickled. "Watch who you're calling old, old man! You could use the exercise anyway. And tell your daughter's lover to show more respect to her elders!" She waved an irritable hand. "The things I have to put up with. These modern provinces. I tell you, back in Xienzo…"

As she babbled on, the man's face snapped up. He gaped for a moment when he caught sight of Wren before hurriedly sinking to his knees. "Lady Wren, I apologize—"

Wren came forward. "Please, Jinn." She bent to help him up, uncomfortable—both at Tien calling her Lei's lover in front of Lei's father and his embarrassment at his accidentally casual behavior in front of her. "We've discussed this. Wren is fine."

Jinn nodded, though he still looked flustered.

Wren battled her own discomfort. While she couldn't speak for Jinn, she knew she'd been purposefully evading him. Part of it was guilt. She still remembered so clearly the day she and the others returned from Jana. They were dirty and exhausted, their moods dark. Wren had seen the expectant hope on Lei's father's face as he scanned their group for his daughter's face. How that hope quickly turned to confusion—then despair.

"Wren, then." Jinn gave her a tentative smile, so familiar it hurt. And here was perhaps the primary reason Wren had been avoiding him: he reminded her too much of Lei. They even had the same mannerisms. Like now: with hands weathered from a lifetime of physical work—presumably what had prematurely thinned his dark hair—Jinn smoothed down his rumpled hanfu in the same way Wren had seen Lei do countless times.

His robes were simple tan-colored cotton. Ketai had offered Jinn use of the Hannos' tailors and free pick of the luxurious fabrics in their stores, but Lei's father had insisted upon only a few modest garments. Tien, however, had gladly taken Ketai up on this offer—and *how*.

Today she was dressed in sweeping gold and magenta robes whose many layers padded out her bony frame. A jade pendant hung at her throat. It was an outfit more suited to an elegant dinner than working in the kitchens, which is where she was to be found most of the time. But Tien wore it with complete confidence, and each day she paraded around in some wonderful new outfit, acting as if she owned the place. Wren even caught her scolding *Lova* a few times, complaining about mud she'd tracked in when coming back from a patrol or after stealing rhum from Ketai's personal drinks cabinet.

Lei had told Wren countless stories about her fussy old shop hand. Clearly, she hadn't been exaggerating.

"Well?" Tien demanded. "I'm still waiting! Where is he? Where is the bird demon who kidnapped my niece?"

Lova smirked. "He's downstairs. I can take you to him, Auntie, just me and you—"

"No, *thank you*, Lo." Wren shot her a pointed look, knowing full well Lova's intentions. Presumably she didn't expect Wren to punish one of Lei's family if it was they who hurt Merrin. "Tien," she began—then, at finding *herself* on the receiving end of a dangerous look, corrected swiftly with the respectful suffix for an older woman, "Tien-ayi, Nitta is the leopard-girl Merrin took from the battlefield along with . . . with Lei."

Saying her name was like pulling teeth, especially with her father and Tien staring right at her.

"Nitta's just told us what happened," Wren said, "and that Merrin would like to help us save Lei."

"She wouldn't need saving if he hadn't flown her away in the first place!" Tien retorted.

"Exactly my sentiments!" Lova grinned darkly. "Now, as I was saying, Auntie, why don't you and I—"

"*I* am the General of this clan, Lova. Not you."

Wren's cutting tone surprised even her.

Lova crossed her arms, head tilting. "What do you propose, then, *General?*"

"We'll hear Merrin out together," Wren decided. "But first, Nitta needs to eat. Why don't we have lunch, and we can share Nitta's story with Tien-ayi and Jinn, so when we speak to Merrin we're all a bit more...level-headed."

Both Tien and Lova scoffed at this. To avoid any more argument, Wren went to pick Nitta up. The others busied themselves adjusting the table setting to accommodate Jinn and Tien.

Like last night, Nitta was shockingly light when Wren held her, yet the smile she flashed was exactly as it was before her accident: bright and sharp and teasing. It ached something deep beneath Wren's ribs.

"How much do you wanna bet that by the end of the meal Lova is begging Tien to join the Cat Clan?" Nitta asked in a whisper. "Oh! How much on Tien usurping Lova within a week?"

And, just as she'd smiled for the first time in weeks, Wren let out a burst of laughter. It was honest and unexpected, devoid of any bite, and came from a genuine place of happiness—a place that had been ripped from her with the loss of Lei.

The feeling didn't last long. Wren maneuvered Nitta into position at the table when a sound reverberated through the fort. It was the song of the three immense bells mounted in the east wing's tower. An alert that clan members were approaching.

Lova rose at once. "They're back. I'm going to see how my cats

are doing." And she marched from the room without waiting for a
response.

"Aiyah," Tien complained, picking up her chopsticks. "Why does
everything have to be so *loud* in this place. Can't an old woman eat
in peace?"

Wren touched Nitta's shoulder. "I should welcome them. Will
you be all right here?"

"Sure! I'm famished. Besides, I bet Jinn-ahgu and Tien-ayi would
love to hear stories from our mission. I've got loads of good Lei
ones—that girl is one daring little Paper." Nitta waggled her eyebrows at them, and Jinn's lips quirked.

"My daughter is just like her mother," he said. "Brave."

Tien huffed, her mouth full of food. "You mean reckless."

"And smart—"

"Smart-*mouthed*."

Nitta beamed at Wren. "See? We'll be fine here. Go check on
Ketai and Caen." Her face softened. "I hope it wasn't too hard on
them."

As Wren descended the stairs, she prepared herself. She wasn't
quite sure what they'd find; they'd not sent a messenger with news
in the days they'd been away, so clearly they'd been busy. From what
the young jackal-boy said during Wren's interrogation, it seemed
unlikely they'd arrive in time to save the city, though Wren had
clung to the hope they somehow had. Yet when she strode out into
the rain-sodden grounds, she saw she'd been foolish to do so.

Clan members spilled out around her, less controlled in their
reactions. There were cries and wails. Individuals sprinted off
toward the bedraggled group riding slowly up the hill, shouting out
names of friends, lovers, family members who'd been a part of the
army Ketai had taken with him to Nantanna.

An army that was now a fraction of its original size.

Wren stood rigid, forcing herself to be the calm clan leader her father expected of her, as his broken army advanced, and steeled herself for whatever awful news they were most certainly bringing with them.

EIGHT

LEI

MY NEW ROUTINE IN THE PALACE is so similar to when I was a Paper Girl it's as though I've slipped back in time, gotten caught in some twisted loop, forced to replay some of the worst months of my life.

Each morning, Madam Himura tramps into my room with a group of blank-faced demon maids. I'm fed the same, simple breakfast—tea and two slices of kaya toast—before being washed, dressed, then ushered out the door to my next chaperones, these ones far less dainty: my guards. They're the same eighteen guards who accompanied me the night of the banquet when the King announced my return to the court, led by the towering gazelle demon I've since learned is Commander Razib. They march me to and from whatever events the King bids me to that day, which often run so late into the night that when I'm finally brought back to my room, I crawl into bed fully dressed and fall head-first into nightmares.

Despite their similarities, though, my new routine comes with some major differences—the biggest of which is that I'm never left alone with the King.

Not much more is asked of me than to sit dutifully at his side, draped in my Moonchosen uniform of black and gold. Through lunches in pretty gardens blossoming with spring's arrival, intimate tea ceremonies, and lavish, lively banquets with court officials, I keep my mouth shut and my ears open. I'm even brought to watch a couple of military demonstrations, though I notice I'm never allowed to be close when court officials come to discuss the war with the King. No matter how frustrating this is, I treat it as a victory.

It means the King is scared—of me. Of the enemies he clearly worries still lurk within the palace. And while I doubt he believes I'll be able to connect with them, given our packed schedule and how close an eye he's keeping on me, it shows he understands that any piece of information in my hands might be used against him, no matter how small. How, with the right intent, words can be sharpened into blades.

Yet what makes me most sure of the King's fear is that he never once brings me to his chambers. The King of before would have brought me to his bed, just to enjoy breaking me. But this subtly new King, who hides his nerves behind too-hard laughter and grandiose proclamations of power...this King knows that if he brings me to his chambers, it might instead be *me* who breaks *him*.

Whenever I'm on the brink of crumbling, the King's nearness too much one particular day, or I lurch awake in the middle of the night from a nightmare in which Wren's dismembered head rolls across the bloodied ground at my feet, I remind myself of this: The Demon King of Ikhara is scared of *me*. I repeat Zelle's words to me the first time we met, until they become a mantra, a comforting refrain that stokes the fire in my core.

They can take and steal and break all they want, but there is one thing they have no control over. Our emotions. Our feelings. Our thoughts.... Our minds and hearts are our own. That is our power, Nine.

Never forget it.

*   *   *

Days slide by, each following the same grim pattern, until one morning I wake and know this one will be different.

Nothing is out of the ordinary—yet. The dawn light filtering in through the windows is just as it was yesterday. The birds outside sing the same shrill song as they skate through the pale sky. Throughout the morning, Madam Himura barks orders at the maids while they dress me in a fresh set of hanfu, careful never to catch my eyes, even when they're coloring my face with powders and paints.

But I can feel it. Like the electric shiver before a monsoon deluge, or the sharpness of air before snow; the sense of change to come.

Usually when we leave the room, Madam Himura hands me over to the guards. Today, she accompanies us. Her cane and talons click out of time with the other demons' heavier, sturdier footfall.

Here it is. The first difference.

As we travel down the marble halls of the King's fortress, my senses fire, hunting for more clues. A second change: the guards seem to be anticipating something; Commander Razib throws me more than one knowing look over his shoulder. A third: I'm led into a part of the building I've never been in before.

With each step, my apprehension grows. I thought I was beginning to know the King's fortress well, but to be surprised with an entirely new wing shakes my confidence. We pass through a series of archways each framed by a pair of guards, until they end abruptly in a small circular room. Because my view is blocked by the guards in front of me, I don't see what's inside until I'm right upon it.

The top of a spiral stairway.

Its steps twist out of sight. Commander Razib starts down them, while I hesitate.

One of the guards behind shoves me. "Down," he orders.

"Well, I wasn't exactly going to go *up*," I hiss.

"What was that, keeda?" the Commander growls.

"Oh," I say, flashing him a mocking smile. "You know. Just admiring the view."

Anger flares across his face. I ready myself for a slap or a punch to the gut, but none come, and I gain a fickle sense of triumph. I'm the King's Moonchosen now. Even the guards have to be careful how they treat me in public. Being here is supposed to be my choice, after all. My *privilege*.

We trudge down the staircase. The steps are narrow and winding, only fitting two demons abreast. It gets dark quickly, and a few of the guards light lanterns, flames flickering off the stone walls. When I'm wondering if we'll ever reach the end of this infernal stairway, we emerge into a long, lantern-lit corridor. And at the end of that—

The sight arrests me, snatching my breath away.

The chamber is not much bigger than my room in the Moon Annexe, but its walls curve up to a high domed ceiling, making our footsteps ring out and giving the impression we're in some sort of cave. The walls and floor are rough, hewn like the stairs and passageway from the earth's rock. Lantern light glimmers off the dully glittering granite, reminding me unpleasantly of the King's mirrored bedroom.

Yet that isn't what has made me reel. And even though the King *is* here—along with Naja and a group of shamans working the magic sending waves of static over me—none of this is the worst thing about this horrible place.

In any other situation, I would have been happy to see a friend's face. But not here. Not like this.

Not hanging from the ceiling on a metal chain, a curved hook embedded in their back, holding them a foot off the ground.

The dripping of blood is loud.

"My dear Moonchosen. We're so pleased you could join us."

The King's voice sounds from where he is seated beside Naja in a ring of stone benches that circle the chain and its suspended prisoner. He rises, opening his arms in welcome.

"I thought you might like to see an old friend of yours. Why don't you say hello?"

The King waits, smiling, but I don't move. Every inch of me has turned to ice despite the uncanny warmth of the shaman's magic where they face the prisoner—*my friend*—weaving daos over him. And I realize their magic isn't harming him—it's *healing* him.

Just enough to keep him alive.

Magic has no effect on dead things, despite countless efforts by shamans over the ages. And the King does not want this prisoner to die.

Not just yet.

The King's smile sharpens. "Don't be shy," he says, his arctic eye fixed on me. "Come closer, Lei-zhi."

When I make no move, Commander Razib pushes me. I stumble, my uneven steps echoing off the walls. But the drip of my friend's blood is louder. It is everywhere, pounding in my ears and beating in time with my frantic pulse and ragged breaths.

I don't want to go on, but the Commander shoves me again, and again, until my slippered feet slap into the pool of widening red with a sickening splatter.

Jeers rise from the guards.

The King and Naja watch, quiet, intent.

Blood seeps up my robes. I wish I could scream, run away, tear off my soiled clothes—but it wouldn't be fair. I owe it to my friend to stay in this with him.

Horror clenches my gut as my gaze meets his: those small, crinkle-edged gray eyes, so familiar to me after months of traveling and laughing and arguing and fighting together. Even after the way we left things between us, they were eyes I'd one day hoped to see again.

How cruelly the gods have granted my wish.

"Shifu Caen," I choke out, unable to stop a sob escaping.

My old friend and ally—Wren's lifelong mentor, her father's lover—looks down at me, turning slightly where he hangs from the chain. His long hair, usually tied in a half knot, is ragged and loose, tangling in sticky clumps. Bruises bloom across his skin. One of his cheekbones looks wrong, unnaturally sunken. A ragged thread of air rasps through his cracked lips, and though there is pain in his expression, and fear, and sorrow, the thing that burns most brightly is determination.

A warrior, to the end.

"Caen," I breathe, softer, so only he can hear.

Another name hovers in the small space of our silence.

His eyes soften. "She is safe," he croaks, hardly moving his lips so the demons can't read them. "They are all safe." And as relief floods me, his eyes harden.

I know instinctively what is coming.

His voice is calm. "Do it."

Without even pausing to consider—because I know it is right, because I know whatever waiting for him is worse, and that the end is better at the hands of a friend than an enemy—I whisper in a rush, tears rising, "Thank you. I'm sorry. I'm so sorry." And as roars surge from the watching demons as they comprehend what I'm about to do, I bend my knees and launch into a high, powerful

jump—just as Caen himself taught me—and, using the momentum and all my weight, I grab his head.

And thrust it backward.

Straight onto the sharp end of the hook protruding from the top
of his back.

NINE

LEI

IT'S NOT UNTIL LATER—LONG AFTER the guards wrestled me to the floor, the dungeon alive with snarled orders as the King stood over me, nearly too incensed to speak, Commander Razib's cloven foot digging into my back; after I've been dragged back to my room and flung inside with no hint at what punishment awaits me—not until I'm lying on the rattan mat of my room, shivering and shaking and still red, dark red all over from Shifu Caen's blood, that I realize I pushed his head so hard the hook's tip dug halfway into my palm.

I stare at the wound—and that draws my attention to the cuff at my wrist.

Caen's blood has dimmed its gold. My own blood drips down from the still-oozing tear in my hand, mingling with his. With a dull heart, I wonder who else of my friends' blood I may have drawn today. Yet even though the thought of it is awful—too awful yet to comprehend—the worry doesn't quite latch.

I'm too full of what just happened.

What I just *did*.

From the instant I entered the chamber and saw Caen hanging there, I knew how it was going to end. Before he'd looked at me and told me what to do, simply and clearly, without fanfare, as had always been his way. The decision was foregone. I would not allow them to torture him in front of me. I wouldn't see him suffer any longer. Him asking me only gave me the confidence to do it.

Escape for him could take only one form.

Do it.

His words shiver over me, so similar to Zelle's the night of the Moon Ball. I failed her then. I wasn't going to fail Caen today. Especially not after his parting gift, one I'd been aching for every second of my imprisonment, ever since I watched silver blades flash in a storm of ruby and black.

She is safe. They are all safe.

I lie on the floor of my room for hours, not moving from where Commander Razib flung me. Before leaving the underground chamber, the King's shamans wove a dao to vanish me from view so the rest of the palace wouldn't see the state I was in. I must have looked like the stuff of nightmares. A limp, dead-eyed girl covered head to toe in blood. Though the enchantment is long gone, I envision it strengthening instead, so I fade away a little more with each passing moment until eventually there'll be nothing of me left at all.

If only it were that easy to disappear. To hide from yourself.

I've killed before—but only in defense, in times of battle or danger. Demons I'd hated, or who hated me. This was different. More necessary, more important perhaps than any of those, but a thousand times more terrible. No matter how much I tell myself it was a mercy, I can't shed the sickening blame that makes me want to plunge a hand inside my chest and rip out my traitorous heart.

The light drains from the room until I'm left in darkness, broken only by shafts of moonlight from the open windows. I still don't move, lying in a jumble of limbs, spent, emptied, alone.

I've passed so many nights this way since my return to the palace, yet tonight more than ever I long for Wren. To have her strong arms wrap around me. The touch of her steady hands. Her comforting words. The ocean scent of her skin never fails to calm me, or light me on fire in the best possible way.

Mostly, I crave her understanding—even though I wouldn't give her my own.

A memory hits, powerfully vivid. The desert night. The Amala's ground-ship skating over the dark dunes, its whooshing burr filling the quiet. Stars sparkling overhead. Kneeling face-to-face with Wren at the back of the ship, Hiro's Birth-blessing pendant clutched in her hands, its golden casing catching the moonlight.

We had the same word. Hiro and I were kinyu.

What is it? Your word?

Sacrifice.

"Wren," I whisper now, tilting my face toward the window where silver light drapes over the rattan mat like the silk of a mourning shroud. Knowing she is alive has calmed one part of me but awoken another. Replaced the pain of not knowing with the pain of knowing and not being able to do anything about it.

I don't know which is worse.

"Wren? Is this what it feels like? Sacrifice?"

She doesn't answer. No one does.

My arm falls to the floor, bloodied palm up, fingers open. Waiting, waiting for something.

Someone.

I watch the moonlight glide slowly across the floor until it's eventually replaced by the soft light of another spring morning. Outside, birds begin to sing.

My palm remains empty.

My question unanswered.

The room is warm and filled with noonday sunshine when I'm jerked alert by a burst of noise.

I scrabble away from the door where it's slid open. It's the first time I've moved since we got back from the dungeon, and I sway, head swimming as people file into the room. From my low position, all I see are swishing skirts; the flash of a bare calf from ragged robes. Hushed voices murmur above me.

Hushed, *familiar* voices.

I rub my eyes—forgetting my hand is caked in dried blood. I blink frantically to clear them, and as if from within a dream I hear a girl's gasp and more muttering, agitated now rather than nervous.

"Is she—"

"What *happened*—"

"Oh, *Lei*..."

"Look at this mess!" Madam Himura cries shrilly. "Blood everywhere! As if I didn't have enough work, now I'll have to get the mat replaced, too. Girls—fetch the tub. This abomination is going to take all afternoon to clean. You'd better get started."

"But M-Madam Himura." The girl's voice is barely a whisper, but I'd recognize it anywhere. My heart lurches. "Sh-she's hurt. Shouldn't she see a doctor...?"

There's a flurry of movement. The sound of a cane-crack ricochets through the air.

"Do not talk back to me, stupid girl! You're not a Paper Girl anymore. Gods know why the King has decided to keep the five of you around, but do not forget your new status. Lei-zhi here"—disgust etches her voice to speak my name with respect—"is the Moon-chosen, and you are her maids. You are to look after her and ensure this kind of mess *never happens again.*"

Past Madam Himura, I spot the glint of gold on pale skin. She's grabbed one of the girls' wrists. She turns it, and the girl it belongs to inhales sharply.

"Isn't this enough of a reminder? Your fate is tied to Lei-zhi, Aoki. So you'd better remind her to be more considerate of others before she acts so recklessly, or next time you won't only injure your hand. You'll lose the whole thing."

She tosses the girl aside. Then she's upon me, dragging me to my feet. Piercing yellow eyes fill my vision as she draws me close.

"Let us be clear about this, Lei-zhi. None of us are happy you are still alive after that stunt you pulled yesterday—least of all the King. But it's too late to turn back now. Your path at his side has been set by the gods, and we must follow its course through to the end. No matter how reluctantly." She studies me, feathers bridling with scorn. "*Keeda* really *is* the right word for your kind. Only worms continue to persist in the face of such odds and despite such a repugnant lack of talent or power. Yet even parasites cannot survive forever. One day, you'll return to the ground from which you came, and we shall finally be free of you."

She lets me go, and I stagger, reeling from her malice.

"Shamans will come by in an hour to heal Lei-zhi's wound," Madam Himura barks at the ragged-clothed girls standing in a huddle. "Have her ready by then. She must look flawless. The rest of the court is not to know what happened yesterday." Then, with one final sneer, she sweeps from the room.

After the door slams shut, none of us move or speak—not me,

nor the five girls still gaping at me. Madam Himura's musky scent hangs in the air, making this feel even more like we've been thrown back in time, though it's clear we've all changed, each one of us marked by the months since we last saw each other.

Finally, one of the girls comes forward. Lank locks hang around knifelike cheekbones, the deep azure tint of her hair noticeable when she jerks her chin and it catches the light.

"No hug?" she says. "No kisses? This isn't the sort of warm reunion I was expecting from you, Nine."

"Blue."

My voice is raw. But it breaks the spell, and suddenly Blue is rolling her eyes as with one collective shout of "Lei!" three of the other girls push past her and I'm bundled into a fierce embrace, so tight I can barely breathe, but I don't care, how could I care when it's Chenna, Zhen, and Zhin, alive and safe and *here*.

When we break apart, I sniff my tears back, taking in their beautiful faces. The twins are grinning. Chenna gives me her smart, wry smile, my hands in hers. Then, over their heads, my eyes meet those of the last girl.

Big green eyes: green like forests under rain, like the deep of the sea.

Rust-colored hair that's grown out from its short chop.

A face as round and sweet as I remember it, even if its cheeks have hollowed and her skin is waxen.

Aoki hangs back from us—from *me*. I want to run to her, grab her lovely face, her whole lovely self. But her expression locks me in place.

Unlike the others, she doesn't look remotely happy to see me. At least Blue managed a sneer and a barbed comment. In her books, that's practically a jubilant welcome. But Aoki's lips remain flat.

"Aoki," I breathe, my tears coming hard again, though from more than relief and happiness this time. I start forward.

She edges away. "M-Madam Himura said to get to work," she stammers. "We have a lot to do." And though she's swift to slip her sleeves back over her wrists where they've bunched up, it's not quick enough to stop me from spotting the band circling her left arm. It's the exact replica of mine, only hers is tighter. So tight it must be digging into bone. The skin around it looks newly bruised, crusted with blood.

I choke down a sob. Like the wound in my palm, and who I killed to get it, Aoki's injury—her pain—is of my own creation.

TEN

WREN

"WE SHOULD STORM THE PALACE!"

"And invite another ambush? Ridiculous!"

"If we wait, we give them time to regroup—"

"There are ways to weaken them without having to engage in battle. As I proposed yesterday—"

"Yes, Zahar, we remember your fancy maps and diagrams. But it's far too late for any of that. What if they storm another of our cities? Or one of their own, and blame it on us?"

"It worked well enough when we did it with the raids, didn't it?"

"And it'll work even better for the court, who have half the kingdom on their side and are eager for any excuse to tear us Papers down!"

Wren was only half listening to the debate. For what felt like the hundredth day in a row, though it had been just over two weeks, she was at her father's daily war council. It was the same arguments over and over. From when Ketai and the ragged remains of his army returned to the Jade Fort, the council had been divided. Half wanted to launch an all-out retaliation, while the rest thought it more important to take time to recover and reestablish tactics. And of course, none of them agreed on how to go about any of it.

"You are still not getting it!" a voice boomed. Commander Chang was the Hannos' military leader, a Paper man whose stature—and mustache—was as imposing as his voice. "The time for tentative tactics is past! As the great Yu-zhe said, water is only strong against fire when its flames have no more kindling to feed upon. We have played soft like water for too long. It has let the King's flames run wild." He slammed his fists on the table. "We must be decisive!" Another bang. "Swift!"

From a few seats away, a sardonic voice said, "Hence two weeks of *this*."

"Thank you, General Lova. We are quite aware of your opinions."

A hush fell at Ketai Hanno's reprimand.

To Wren's left, at the head of the table, her father was silhouetted in early evening light from the open balcony doors at his back. Violet shadows clung to his eyes. He'd let his usual peppered stubble grow out longer than usual, the tips beginning to curl.

Wren's eyes shifted to the empty seat directly across from her, to her father's other side. Somehow, each time she looked, she held a small glimmer of hope that some unknown magic would bring back its occupant. But Wren knew magic. You couldn't heal that which was already dead.

Pain pierced her, almost as physical as the constant ache in her hips.

Around the table, the discussion sprung back into life.

"Well, I agree with Chang. We saw what happened to Nantanna! Such destruction in such little time. They must have discovered the secret to some new weapon or magic."

"All the more reason to be cautious with our approach. If the

King truly has such devastating power on his hands, we must take our time to understand it. Study it, even."

"How?" Lova's words dripped with sarcasm. "Should we send a friendly envoy to the Hidden Palace? Pop over and ask? *Excuse me, Heavenly Master, a quick question before we try and obliviate you. Do hope you don't mind.*"

Ketai stared her down. "Enough with the jokes, Lova."

"She has a point, though." It was Nitta's turn to speak up. "Now that we have Merrin, we can rescue the White Wing loyalists, then use them to keep the Tsume and other guards busy while he enters the palace to rescue Lei. Maybe there's a way to work in some reconnaissance work at the same time."

"Of course you would side with your own kind, Cat," Commander Chang retorted.

"And of course *you* won't listen to sound advice, little man," Nitta returned. "How many battles have you actually been in? I bet you wouldn't last eight minutes in real warfare."

"And how well do you think *you* would last, immobile and chairbound?"

At this, there was a shift in the air, as if the room had dropped in temperature.

Nitta lifted her head proudly. "This *immobile, chairbound* cat could still wipe the floor with the King's men and have enough energy to drag *your* useless corpse all the way home!" Her emerald eyes flashed. "Why don't we step outside, Chang, so I can give you a demonstration?"

"Yes, thank you, Nitta," Ketai Hanno interjected as Chang began to rise from his seat, his face purpling. "Let's stay focused."

Another councilor immediately piped up. "Lord Hanno, if I may, I'd like to revisit the idea of Merrin infiltrating the palace. What about a flyover? If we could just *see* what the King is doing with his army…"

"The whole place is on highest security!" another adviser exclaimed. "It'd be a suicide mission!"

"Personally," Lova said, "I'm all for that traitorous chicken getting himself caught and roasted alive for the King's lunch. But how would he get the information back to us once he's chewed up meat digesting in the King's stomach? Or being ejected in a pile of steaming—"

"That's *enough!*" Ketai slapped his palms on the table. "Whatever his faults, Merrin is still a member of our clan. I will not have him spoken of this way."

"No," Lova seethed, "but you *will* let him betray us all, getting hundreds of my Cats killed and a young girl sent back to her rapist!"

Ketai was on his feet in a second. He pointed at the door. *"Out."*

Lova pushed back from the table. "My pleasure," she snarled. Her honey fur was ruffled, and she tossed her head, surveying the room with disdain. "I've had enough of this useless posturing anyway. Our cautiousness is what led to both our seconds-in-command being killed in an ambush we should've seen coming eight thousand miles off. And I, for one, am fluent in only one language of revenge."

She drew free the cutlass from her back and swirled it so ferociously the council members sitting closest to her cringed back.

Lova leveled her weapon at Ketai. "Let me know when you're ready to join me in speaking it."

Then she spun on her heels and stormed out.

Nitta rolled her eyes at Wren and mouthed, *Drama queen.*

Lova had left the double doors ajar. While two servants hurried to slide the doors back into place, Ketai sighed. He wore a weariness in his expression Wren had rarely seen before.

She glanced again to the chair across from her and its emptiness speared straight through her. Wren was so accustomed to the presence of the man who occupied it. Not within this room—she'd only been allowed to join the council after the Moon Ball when all pretense of her not being a warrior had been dashed. But within the Jade Fort. By her father's side.

By *her* side.

Second-in-command. It wasn't adequate to express all Caen had been—and neither for Nor to Lova.

When they'd been lovers, Lova told Wren how Nor had practically raised her after her parents passed. That the old tiger-woman had saved her life on more than one occasion. And though decades her senior and far more experienced in leadership, Nor followed Lova's command when she inherited the clan at just sixteen years old without question.

Since receiving the news of Nor's death, Lova had kept her grieving for Nor private, even from Wren. Wren knew her father had been trying to do the same, but he wasn't doing quite as convincing a job. She could read his loss in the slight slump of his shoulders. The way he turned every so often to the doors, as if expecting Caen to walk in, rumpled and battle-tired, but alive. Caen had been more than Ketai's second-in-command. He'd been her father's closest friend. His lover.

Caen's loss was in Wren, too, that weighted pit right beside the one Lei had left. It was different, but no less significant. While Lei had always felt linked to Wren's future and hopes, Caen was tied inextricably to her past. He'd been a constant in her life, the anchor of her small family in so many ways that she'd hardly believed it when her father returned from Nantanna without him.

It had been a terrible moment. Ketai's forces had been ambushed on their way back from Nantanna, and though they fought so hard the King's soldiers eventually retreated, the Hannos lost more than half their soldiers in the process. Ketai hadn't seen Caen's death himself, but one of his warriors told him they'd seen him dragged into a group of demons—and he hadn't emerged. The King's army had set fire to the forest they were fighting in, so Ketai and the others had been forced to flee. It was an extra blow, not being able to bring back the bodies of those they'd lost and give them the proper send-offs they deserved.

Standing now at the head of the table, Ketai seemed to collect himself. The spring twilight was drawing in, a purple-pink glow tinting his frame. "I might not like her phrasing," he said, "but Lova is right. We *have* been too cautious. Naive, even. We cannot underestimate the King's forces again."

He released a heavy sigh. After a glance at the empty chair to his left, he drew to full height, facing each person at the table in turn with those darkly shining eyes Wren knew so well. It was a look that meant her father was angry. That he was determined. That he had a plan.

And he'd burn down anyone who stood in its way.

"Zahar, Ijuma." He gestured at two of the councilors. "Assemble the plans of the operation to choke off the Golden Triangle, as discussed. You were right. It's our strongest chance at blocking the court's main transport routes and will allow us to hold off reinforcements from reaching the Hidden Palace. We'll launch our siege on the palace from there."

"Already?" Zahar gasped.

Ketai's face was grim. "What are we waiting for? More allies? So is the King. Time to recuperate? As we have seen, they won't let us have it. It is either our palace which'll be under siege, or theirs. It will already take us at least two weeks to prepare. We must not delay any longer. We must strike soon, and hard." He looked around the table. "Anyone else wish to express their doubts?"

No one spoke.

"Good. Then we are finally in agreement." Ketai turned. "Chang, I'll leave it to you to prepare our soldiers for the operation, along with each clan head. They know best how to organize their warriors."

He went on, directing the remaining members until it was Wren and Jinn's turn.

Jinn, like Nitta and Lova, had been asked to join the council as honorary members. Though most of the others weren't keen on the cat demons' presence, Jinn had been welcomed more warmly given who his daughter was. Everyone knew what Lei had done. Any Paper who stuck a knife in the King would be welcome at the Jade Fort.

Ketai had also invited Tien to the meetings, but after the first one she'd stormed out in a huff, much like Lova today. "This war council is worse than my old mahjong group!" she'd complained. "Alamak, what a bunch of whiny, argumentative old farts! Let me get back to my kitchens. At least I'm listened to there!"

Nitta and Lova had rejoiced so loudly at the lynx-woman's dramatic departure that Ketai had ordered a five-minute recess to allow them to calm down.

Now, Ketai set his hands back on the tabletop, the line of his mouth tightening. His shadowed eyes flitted over Wren and Jinn. "It is time to decide what to do regarding Lei. I know what I think, but there is only one person in this room who the decision should fall to."

Wren stiffened. Was her father really about to single her out? Had he suspected all along what Lei truly meant to her? A well of gratitude rose up in a rush, and she was about to speak out, a resounding *Yes, of course we must save her, yes,* when—

"Jinn?" Ketai prompted.

A cold pit hardened in Wren's gut.

Lei's father blinked, seemingly taken aback at being addressed. For the past two weeks, he alone had sat quietly at the table. Wren couldn't tell if it was because he was intimidated or if he didn't think he'd be listened to.

"As Lei's father," Ketai said, "you should have final say as to whether we rescue her." Voices rose up in contestation, but Ketai held up a hand.

Even as the council members scrutinized him, most not bothering to hide their unconvinced expressions, Jinn straightened, his jaw set in the same prideful hold his daughter so often wore. He met the waiting faces. "I trust Merrin," he declared. "And I want to save my daughter."

Wren's heart soared. Finally, the moment she'd been waiting for ever since returning to the fort. What Wren argued so fiercely for in these meetings, what she'd asked her father for every day. If there was a way to save Lei, they should take it, at any cost.

She was worth it. She was worth anything.

Everything.

Jinn swallowed. "But I know it's not what Lei would want."

A few of the councilors clapped, speaking out in assent and relief. Nitta's face swung toward Wren in horror.

"She risked her life to start this war." Wren heard Lei's father speaking as if from far away. "She'd want us to do everything to win it. Even if she were here with us, she'd be in danger. Nowhere will be safe for Papers until the King is off the throne. That is exactly why she fought"—he caught himself—"*is* fighting. And she would want us to respect that."

No! Wren wanted to scream. She wanted to leap from her seat, grab Jinn by the collar, and shake him. *Lei is with the King. Don't you understand what that means? If you love her, how could you leave her with him again?*

"All right," Ketai agreed, over the murmuring council members. "We will have to trust in Lei's strength for now—and what strength it is. Taking away her rescue, I propose we instead use Merrin to free the imprisoned White Wing loyalists. We have desperate need of bird demons in our upcoming battles. Wren and I will work with Merrin to refine the details. Thank you, everyone. I know these deliberations were anything but easy. I appreciate your patience."

As the scrape of chairs and rustling of papers and robes filled the room, Jinn caught Wren's gaze. There was an apology in his eyes. More than an apology: a request for forgiveness.

Wren turned abruptly away. Because what she saw in his expression was too familiar. It was a mirror to her own desperate plea for Lei's forgiveness after everything she'd done those months traveling Ikhara: killing Lady Dunya's daughter Eolah at the White Wing's palace; being complicit in the deaths of Aoki's family; using Hiro's life to save them on the Czos' island; not healing Bo when there might still have been time. And if this is how Wren was feeling toward Lei's father for one painful decision, how could Lei ever forgive Wren for the hundreds of terrible ones she had made?

She risked her life to start this war. She'd want us to do everything to win it.

Even though he wasn't a warrior, Jinn seemed to understand that sacrifice was necessary in war. Even when it was personal. Even when it was the last thing you wanted to do.

Even when it carved your heart in two.

ELEVEN

LEI

"GIVE HER TIME. SHE'LL COME AROUND."

"She hates me, Chenna. I know it."

"She doesn't hate you, Lei."

"The way she looks at me..."

"She's conflicted."

"Because of me. Because of *him*."

"Because of the whole situation. It's complicated. Things changed after the Moon Ball."

With a guilty sigh, my eyes drift past Chenna's shoulder across the room, where Aoki is curled on her sleeping mat, picking absently at her toes. Two weeks since the girls arrived, and Aoki still won't meet my eyes. She's been like the demon maids that tended me before—working over me, polishing me, painting me, without ever truly looking *at* me until the last instant. When, just as I'm being led from the room by Madam Himura, she finally regards me, unable to keep the hurt from her face that *I* am the one going to sit by his side and not her.

"Yes," I mutter. "The night I tried to kill the demon she loves."

"Not the best of things for a friendship," Chenna quips, and we swap a look, part amusement, mostly sad understanding.

As if sensing our attention, Aoki glances our way. Her eyes skitter from mine before she quickly snuffs the lantern hanging by her head and twists to face the wall. To her other side, the twins are already asleep, each with an arm around the other.

I've learned that Zhen talks in her sleep. She seems to be speaking to her brother and her parents. She often laughs with them; once, she cried. The twins' family live in Han's capital, Marazi. When we were Paper Girls, they came almost every month to visit. Due to their family's status, Madam Himura would allow Zhen and Zhin the afternoon off to spend with them. Each time they came back bearing armfuls of stories and presents and were rosy with love, I'd feel so sorry for Blue, whose own parents live here in the palace and yet didn't visit her once.

Like usual, Blue is lying on the opposite side of the room from the other girls. Chenna elaborated on what Mistress Azami had told me, that one of her legs was injured during the battle at the Moon Ball when she came between fighting warriors, and it never healed properly. Though she does her best to hide it, she walks now with a limp. I want to tell her not to spend the energy on masking it—no one would, or should, fault her for it. But like Aoki, Blue isn't exactly my biggest fan.

At least that's nothing new.

"Aoki'll come around, Lei," Chenna reassures me. The two of us sit close on my bed, speaking in whispers. "She's still in shock. We all are. I mean, you're here. Alive."

I smile. "So are all of you."

The line of her mouth is tight. "Just about."

"I'm so sorry, Chenna. I never meant—I never wanted *any* of this—"

"I'm not blaming you, Lei. Nor Wren. It's just the reality of the situation. We barely hung on. Some of us are still grasping." Her dark-brown eyes search my face. "From everything you've told us, it sounds as though you and Wren barely made it through, too. All that traveling and fighting...and Wren still out there, in the midst of the war."

Wren. Every time, her name hits me like a thunderclap.

Chenna presses her shoulder to mine. "She's a fighter, Lei, and a good person. The gods will look after her." With a stretch, Chenna slides off my bed. She gives me an encouraging smile before sloping off to join Aoki, Zhen, and Zhin.

I want to ask her to stay. To lie beside me in my too-empty bed, in the haunted space where another girl's body should be. Instead, I watch Chenna kneel on her sleeping mat. She prays before settling in beside the twins. I'm still amazed we are all together again. It's selfish of me, I know, but I'm glad for their presence, even if something indelible has changed between us, a line drawn between me and the five of them I'm worried neither effort nor time will dissolve.

Perhaps, if I can find a way to free us, I might be able to give us the time and space from the palace we need to heal. It's my goal now, part of my plan: make allies, find a way to get these bands off Aoki and me, get the girls safely out of here—and kill the King. I still have no idea how to do most of those, let alone all of them together. But I'll try. I have to.

Because if I don't, the chances for my second, even more impossible plan will be zero. And while that one only has one step, it's almost too huge to hold in my heart.

Reunite with Wren.

I put out the lamp beside my bed and slip under the covers.

As usual, rest doesn't come easily.

But the nightmares do.

I'm submerged deep, mired in blood and screams while the shadow of a monstrous demon looms over me, when something stirs me awake. In the gloomy echo of the dream, I'm disorientated—because something from my nightmare is here.

A monstrous demon, in this room. Leaning over me.

The King presses a finger to my lips. "Shh," he whispers. His smile is a cut of jagged white in the darkness. "Let's not wake the others."

Shock locks me in place. I want to alert the other girls. *We've got to run! Fight! Grab something, anything—the King is here, alone, unguarded. This is our chance!* Yet my lips remain sealed. I only move when the King jerks down my rumpled sheets and seizes my forearm, yanking me out of bed.

His grip is painfully tight. He pulls me with him, the tips of his gold-inlaid horns almost touching the ceiling. A frisson of magic blankets us, and I realize this is what must be muffling his hoof-fall and keeping the other girls asleep. I could scream as loud as I want and they'd still not wake.

Maybe the King told me to stay quiet just to see if I'm still afraid of what he'll do if I don't.

Loathing boils within me—because I am. Especially now after Caen's awful death and Aoki's damaged arm. Yet like my voice, my anger is bottled, stoppered by my fear.

I grasp at my mantra. *Fire in, fear out.*

Ever since I saw the obsidian rock of the palace walls through the window of the carriage Naja and I shared on the way back from the southern deserts, I'd anticipated the moment I'd finally be alone with the King. Yet night after night passed, and the call never came. I'd felt powerful. Believed him too afraid to be alone with me. Now, horror shimmers in my veins. Because what if, just like when I was his Paper Girl, he was only biding his time? Giving me a false sense of security to make it all the more awful when he finally tears it away?

On our way to the door, we pass the corner where Chenna, Aoki, and the twins lie in a huddle. The King pauses. Aoki's fists are pressed between her mouth and the wall, as if she, too, is holding in a cry. She stirs, and I can't help but glance up to see the King's expression.

He's smiling, but his eyes are cold. "They're so much more beautiful in their sleep, don't you agree? If only they could be this silent and sweet all the time. But you never were silent and sweet, even in your sleep, were you, Lei-zhi? You have always been haunted." He jerks me closer. His wicked grin cuts wide. "*You* live your nightmares, every moment of your life. You, Lei-zhi, will never be free."

Then he leads us out the room, and it's only then that I let myself breathe.

He marches me down the deserted, starlit halls of the palace. Dao-woven silence swallows our footsteps. I note with relief the direction we're heading in doesn't lead to the King's bedchambers. Though we don't cross anyone, I catch glimpses of moving shadows at the corners of my vision. The tail end of swishing robes. Glints of light that might be eyes. Shamans? Guards?

Probably both. The court wouldn't let the King walk around alone with the girl who once stole his eye and drove a knife into his throat.

When we emerge through the fortress's vaulted entranceway, the night is startling, fresh-aired and moon-glazed. Starlight glints off the royal palanquin waiting at the bottom of the stairs.

The usual four ox demons that carry it are absent. As we approach, the velvet curtain draped over its sides flaps open of its own accord. The King lets go of me to step inside. Before I can bolt, invisible hands wrap around my waist and legs, pushing me up after him.

I land inside the carriage sprawled on my front. It rises, gliding into movement.

"Sit," the King demands from the bench. His eye slides to where my thin nightdress has ridden up, exposing my thighs.

I fumble to pull it down, even though there's no desire in his look. Only derision. And something else, that same leashed fear that's dogged his interactions with me ever since my return—the King doesn't want me near him.

The knowledge emboldens me.

I climb onto the seat. We ride in silence, both of us watching the moonlit grounds glide by. The streets and courtyards lie still. Even the flowers seem frozen, hard, lifeless things silvered by the night. Before I tried to kill him at the Moon Ball, the King called me a beautiful lie. That's how I see the palace. It would be so lovely, did I not know the darkness lurking under it. The cruel, numb heart beating malice through its veins.

"Are you happy to have them back?"

The King's chafing voice breaks the quiet.

There's a challenge in his words. I reply monotonously, "Yes, my King."

"Wondering why I sent them back to you, perhaps?"

"Yes, my King."

"Don't worry. You will find out soon enough." His tone is gloating, as it is anytime he holds a secret he knows I won't enjoy learning.

Without warning, the King wrenches my hand into the air, the bracelet digging into my wrist.

"Clever, hmm?" he says. "It was Naja's idea. She must have been inspired after losing her own arm to you. But it was my idea to make a twin. I know you, Lei-zhi. I know you fight harder for those you love than you do for yourself." He makes a disparaging noise.

"Such a naive way to live. Any smart demon knows love makes you weak. It's the easiest emotion to exploit."

"I disagree," I say.

"Oh?"

"The easiest emotion to exploit is fear." I go on, bolstered by the recklessness the King's presence has always brought out in me. "The girls told me you stopped Aoki's bracelet from cutting off her hand. At least they guessed it was you."

He considers me. "Is that what you heard."

"They were surprised. But *I* wasn't. Because whatever you say, I know Aoki means something to you. Maybe not her herself, but her loyalty. Her adoration. No one else gives you what she does. Naja, perhaps, but that's different. She doesn't get to see the vulnerable side of you the way we do." My words spill out in a bitter stream. "Aoki could've been just like the rest of us, disgusted anytime you touch us. Instead, she showed you kindness. Affection. True, selfless affection. And it threw you—just as much as my rejection of you. And you're scared that if you really hurt her, she'd turn against you. Even if it was my fault it happened, it was you who ordered the punishment, and she knows it, and that *terrifies* you, you're *petrified* to lose her love—"

"*ENOUGH!*"

The back of my head smacks against the wall as the King pins me there. The palanquin has tipped with the force of his movement. It takes a second for our invisible carriers to right it.

The King clasps my jaw. My heartbeat flutters under his fingertips, frantic, like a trapped hummingbird.

"You don't know me, Lei-zhi," he sneers. "You're not as clever as you think. None of your kind are. No matter how hard you fight, it will be in vain. Paper can never triumph over Steel and Moon—you are too easily broken. You are weak, and we... *I* am strong. You will see. I will burn all your hopes and dreams to ashes, Lei-zhi—along with everything you so proudly, foolishly *love.*"

He spits the word like venom.

The palanquin has come to a stop. The curtains open, a breeze riffling the hairs on my neck where they're standing on end.

Abruptly, the King lets me go. He leaves the carriage, that same unseen force pulling me in his wake.

We're in a part of the palace I've only passed through a couple of times and never visited. A small collection of single-story buildings and manicured grounds are encircled in the distance by the shimmering loop of the river that winds through the Inner Courts. It's quieter here than back at the King's fortress, and the hush feels reverent, like at a temple. The River of Infinity was designed to attract luck from the gods. The King's palace sits within the upper loop; this place is within its lower one. I'd always wondered what it's home to. Due to its auspicious placement, it must be important.

Wind murmurs through the trees, thumbing loose petals and leaves through the air. One catches in my hair. It's a gingko leaf, warm green. A painful yearning spikes through me, the color reminding me of Nitta's and Bo's eyes. Then the King's voice whisks the sentiment away.

"Bring that with you. It will make a good offering."

Offering. The word hums with its unspoken shadow.

Sacrifice.

Even if I didn't have a personal reason to detest the word, I wouldn't be easy sensing it now. We head to the central building. A ring of trees encircle it like a wall. As we pass between their close-knit trunks, I make out the shadowed figures of guards positioned under the trees and the house's red-painted eaves.

"Heavenly Master. Eight thousand blessings on this sacred night."

Two female demons are bowed low, one to each side of a short flight of steps up to a veranda ringing the house. The door at the top is open, waiting.

My heart was already beating with trepidation, suspicious as to where we are. It grows stronger as the King sweeps up the steps and through the doorway. I stumble behind him, not sure whether magic or compulsion makes me follow. The air inside is thick with incense: smoky lavender and pine. Relaxing scents that do nothing to calm me.

The King crosses the elegant living space, sliding open the paper door on the far side of the room. Warm light gleams within. I walk dazedly toward it. Below the incense, my nose picks up another scent, both familiar and not at all. There is musk and earthiness, laced through with sweet, rosy notes.

I hear her before I see her.

"Heavenly Master. This is a surprise."

Her voice is nothing like how I'd imagined. The bull demons I've known have been men or soldiers, all roped muscles and thundering hooves and horns as long as my arm.

The Demon Queen's voice is light. Musical.

Then the King moves aside and I see her. I'm struck first by her beauty—then by the blazing look she gives me as she realizes who *I* am.

She rears back, clutching her sheets to her chin. The lamplight beside her bed accentuates the pretty chestnut shade of the fur that envelops her body, gleaming with russet-red accents. Dark, long-lashed eyes flick between me and the King. "What is *she* doing here?"

The Queen's head is dipped. Her horns—not as long as the King's but grooved in identical patterns decorated with gold—point accusatorily at me. The strap of her nightgown has slipped from one shoulder, and she sweeps it back into place, chest heaving.

"I thought it was time the two of you meet," the King says. "Gods know you have a lot in common."

He doesn't say it kindly. But something in the Demon Queen's stare shifts and a kindred current of understanding passes between us.

A critique from him is a compliment for *us*.

"And," the King continues, "I thought I'd show her the good news in person. As my fortune-tellers have reminded me, it is thanks to the Moonchosen the gods have finally blessed us with what I've waited so patiently for all this time, so it seems only fair for Lei-zhi to see the results her luck has brought me."

Despite the warmth of the room, my blood chills.

It can't be. Surely, not *that*.

As the King turns his attention to me, something flashes in the Queen's deep-brown eyes, her expression shifting. A warning of some kind.

With an impatient growl, the King drags me forward. "The offering," he snaps.

Up close, the Queen is even more beautiful. She looks quite a bit older than the King, but perhaps it's the intensity in her expression, the way she seems to carry the heft of a hundred of years upon her slender shoulders. I wonder if I look like that. If anyone ever looks into my eyes and sees the things that have been done to me, senses the weight of the horrors I have endured.

Like all Moon castes, the Queen's features are a blend of animal and human. On her, the mix is sublime. Her face is slim like the King's, nose more delicate than the usual bull demon's, with deep, wide-set eyes framed by heavy lashes. Reddish-bronze hair wraps her body, with pale patches at the base of her neck and circling her left horn, as if those spots have been painted by a brush dipped in moonlight. No doubt the royal diviners read auspicious signs in them when they chose her for the King, the same way humans and demons for so long have wondered at my golden eyes.

The Queen doesn't smile, but her expression is not unwelcoming as she watches me take her in.

"The offering, Lei-zhi!" the King barks.

The Queen adjusts her position, sitting straighter where she's leaning against the bed's headboard—and that's when I notice it.

The low swell of her belly.

It is small but unmistakable. Her sheets stretch neatly over it like a cocoon.

The results her luck has brought me.

My eyes flick back to the Queen's face, my own stomach turning. Feeling stupid and slow, I thrust my right palm out. "It's—it's—" I can barely speak.

"A gingko leaf," she finishes. "Thank you." She reaches for it, but the King stops her.

"It is not for you."

Both of us hesitate. Then my eyes go back to the bump the Queen is cradling protectively with one hand.

"Give it to him," the King commands.

And as I have done countless times, the Queen obeys him.

She slips her nightdress to her waist, then takes my hand. Unlike the King's touch, hers is gentle. She guides my fingers to her belly. Knowing the King is watching closely, and anticipating what's expected of us, I turn my hand to press the gingko leaf to her bump. The Queen lays her hand atop mine. I feel a heartbeat, but I don't know if it's the Queen's own pulse or that of the child. Judging by the size of her bump, she can't be much more than three or four months along. Surely it'd be too soon to notice anything?

The thought brings the reality of the situation crashing down on me.

A child.

The King's *heir*.

"You will bless this child, Moonchosen," the King says over the rush of blood in my ears. "Bless my *son*. Bless him to be healthy, and strong, and powerful, so he will grow up to be just like his father."

I meet the Queen's eyes, which still burn with a look I'm struggling to read. I force out a few mumbled prayers. When I draw away, the leaf remains pressed to the Queen's belly. The King reaches out, and it disappears beneath his own, much larger hand. He tells me that from the angle of the Queen's swell, the doctors are sure it's a boy.

"My heir," the King breathes, reverent.

The Queen and I wince.

The King gives a resentful snort. "My fortune-tellers and diviners attribute this luck to you, Lei-zhi. Well, if this is what the gods needed to be appeased, so be it. They've seen how hard I've been trying to do right by Ikhara. They have finally been moved by my fealty—and this is only the beginning. More rewards for my hard work and sacrifice are to come. I am certain." His stare is piercing. "Well, Lei-zhi? What do you say to an expecting parent?"

Parent. Not parent*s*.

Something flares across the Demon Queen's face, and I understand perfectly then what she's been trying to tell me.

The King must not have his heir.

I keep my eyes on the Queen as I clear my throat and say, "Eight thousand congratulations."

My pulse doesn't stop racing even once we're back in the palanquin. The King sits closer this time, and I sense the confidence rolling off him, his old swagger restored by our visit. On the way to the Queen's quarters, he only touched me in ire or force. Now, as the carriage glides on invisible shoulders back to Royal Court, he leans in, brushing a finger along my cheekbone.

"You think you are so strong," he drawls. His tone and touch ignite my memory, making me recall all the times he was easy and calm around me, sure I could never hurt him. "You think your lover and her pitiful father are going to rescue you again, don't you? That they'll overcome my demons and take this land from me."

The King goes to laugh, but the noise hitches in his ruined throat.

"I warned you, Lei-zhi," he continues after a pause. "You are powerless—and so are they. I have already crushed Nantanna and taken Ketai Hanno's right-hand man down, along with half his strongest warriors and allies. The White Wing have pledged their allegiance to me. It's only a matter of time before the rest of the Hannos' pathetic uprising falls. Once it does, I will restore this king-dom to its former glory and rule over it with my son at my side."

I want to scream. Thrash out and smother him right here and now. I could—and maybe I would, were it not for the band on Aoki's wrist and the rest of the Paper Girls, sleeping soundly in my room, and the message in the Demon Queen's eyes.

Killing the King is not enough. Not now that I have the girls to save—and *especially* not now that he has an heir to take on his poi-soned throne.

Love. Fear. Maybe both the King and I are right: they are the two most powerful emotions for your enemy to exploit.

I think of the Queen's burgeoning bump beneath my fingers and the pulse I felt there. I know what Wren would do in this situation. What her father would have prepared her for. What they would tell me now to do. But the Demon Queen's look bared what *she* wants, and regarding this, hers is the only opinion that counts.

She was telling me the King must not have his heir.

So instead, I need to make sure the Queen will have hers.

TWELVE

LEI

THE NEXT MORNING, THE KING holds an announcement ceremony for court officials. By sunset, the news is all over the palace. Though no Demon King has ever officially broadcast a Queen's pregnancy, rumors—like blood—have always run easily within these walls. I didn't tell the girls about my midnight excursion, yet by the time I return from the celebratory meetings and banquets I was forced to attend, they'd overheard the news from loose-tongued demons gossiping in the corridor outside. The instant I walked into our room, I knew that they knew.

They only looked at me, all of us silent for a long while. Then Blue barked, with an impatient flap of a hand, "Well? Is it true?"

"Yes."

Though all the girls were staring at me, it was Aoki my eyes locked on. Her hair was mussed, her eyes red from crying. At my answer, anguish wrecked her face. She crumpled to the floor and burst into wails.

I moved, wanting to comfort her, to reassure my best friend in the way I used to. In the way *she* used to do for *me*. But Chenna stopped me. So I hung back as Zhen and Zhin went to her instead.

Not now, Chenna's look told me.

Not ever, a dark voice in my mind amended.

Later, when the room is finally quiet, Zhen and Zhin cradling a spent, blank-eyed Aoki and Blue picking at the frayed rattan mat in her usual corner, Chenna finally broaches the subject.

"You knew, didn't you?"

We're perched on my bed. It's become a nightly routine. After the others retire to their mats, Chenna keeps me company, and together we pick apart fragments of conversations for clues as to what's going on in the war.

I'm not surprised by Chenna's astuteness. She's always been shrewd, understanding more than she lets on.

She gives me her trademark dry smile. "Your clothes and hair and makeup," she explains. "Everything is still perfect. If you'd only just found out, you'd never remain so calm as to not get even *one* wrinkle in your hanfu."

I almost laugh. "The King brought me to the Demon Queen last night," I reveal in a whisper.

Chenna's face blanches.

"I know," I say. "I still can't quite believe she's real."

"Where?"

"A building in the southern loop of the river."

She sucks in a breath. "So close. All this time, she's been so close, and we never knew." Her eyes are wide. "What is she like?"

"Incredible. She's *incredible,* Chenna. Strong. Resolute. Kind. Even after all these years, cooped up in that house, basically alone apart from when the King——" I shake my head. "She's incredible."

"Did you get a chance to talk to her?"

"The King didn't let me out of his sight for a second. But..." I hesitate, knowing the weight of what I'm leading to. I choose my words carefully. "We touched. The King made me place a gingko leaf to her belly to bless the baby, and the Queen held my hand. I think it's a Han tradition."

Chenna doesn't interrupt, still incredulous—and, now, something more. Emotion hums beneath her collected manner, and I lean in closer, wanting to confide in her further as I sense her silently encouraging me to.

"And the look she gave me...Chenna, she was telling me something. About the baby."

I'm breathless now. After Wren and Aoki, Chenna's always been the Paper Girl I've felt the strongest bond with, and unlike the others, she's always taken an active interest in the politics of our kingdom. I want to trust her—and she's never given me reason not to. I scan her features: those big, treacle-dark eyes, shimmering with intelligence; her tightly set jaw; slim brown lips slow to smile.

I glance about to make sure the others are still out of earshot. Then I say in an undertone, "The Queen doesn't want the King to have his heir. She knows what it'll mean for Ikhara. I think she's on our side."

Our side.

I let the words speak for me, and watch as understanding passes over Chenna's features. Her eyes blaze. "Then we have to get her out."

"Yes," I reply, my pulse racing. "We do."

Over the next fortnight, spring comes into full bloom across the palace, a wave of pastel hues and spilling petals, and greens so rich they make my eyes water. Days dawn warm and sunny before winds bluster in clouds, bringing flurries of rain that are blown away to make way for bright, star-flourished nights. In Xienzo, spring has always been good to us, nourishing our plants and clearing winter's grip on the land. When my mother was still alive, my father would come home with armfuls of meadow flowers, knowing how she loved their colors and honeyed scents. I still recall the sound of her delighted laughter. How she'd weave the smaller blossoms through my hair. Once, she made me a crown of peonies and pronounced me Ikhara's first Paper Queen, and we all grinned, as if we truly believed there could ever be such a thing.

In the Hidden Palace, the season that once brought me so much joy only taunts me. The prettier the palace grows, the crueler my life here becomes.

I'd thought things would get easier with the other Paper Girls around. That it might be a bit like last time, when, despite the trepidation a delivery of a bamboo chip with red calligraphy carried, I had friends. A makeshift family in these girls. The lightness at the end of the day when we got back to Paper House and I knew a few stolen moments joking with Aoki or chatting with Lill or—best of all—loving Wren awaited.

Now, Wren and Lill are gone. And when I return to the room in the Moon Annexe, there is no laughter to share with Aoki. Only her hurt, jealous eyes, and the slow breaking of my heart.

"Give her time," Chenna keeps reminding me, and I do; the way she avoids me, I don't have much choice. But I worry if I wait too long, the wounds I've inflicted upon her will heal over, trapping our friendship beneath hardened skin.

Still, I don't lose sight of my plan. It's expanded now to include saving the Queen and her child, but even the simpler things—how to remove my and Aoki's bands, or connect with allies—seem impossible. The King keeps a close eye on me when we're together, and though I pay attention to everything that goes on at each seemingly vapid banquet and dance recital, I fail to find anything useful.

Until this afternoon.

I'm at a parade in Military Court, watching from beside the King's throne as different battalions showcase their skills. There are archers who shoot fire arrows into the sky to spell out the King's title. Sword-wielding soldiers who perform a complex drill in such tight quarters I'm amazed their blades never catch. Muscled silat cekak warriors grapple and throw their enemies with astonishing speed, one warrior for every ten opponents. A duel between two of the court's most skilled fighters has even Naja offering her praise when it ends after thirty minutes of breathless action.

We're set up on a viewing platform overlooking one of the training grounds. Silks flutter overhead, offering shade. Below, warriors fight in the exposed pit, the stench of sweat strong even from here. Still, by the time the last presentation is announced, we're all sweating, too, and Naja orders her maid over to fan her.

A lizard-girl who looks a few years older than me kneels right behind me, angled to direct the large leaf at Naja, who sits to my other side. I glance over my shoulder and recognize the demon's angular face tipped in russet scales. She's Naja's primary maid—Kiroku, if I'm remembering the times I've heard Naja berating her correctly.

Kiroku begins wafting the leaf, making a gentle rustle. I'm turning away, appreciating the breeze on the back of my neck, when her gaze meets mine.

I've learned every look the demons of the court give me, and hers is one I rarely see: something intent, knowing, and urgent.

Just like the one the Demon Queen gave me that night in her room.

The air is bright with battle cries as the final regiment showcase their skills—but it's still not enough to hide my voice if I tried to talk to Naja's maid now. Then an idea springs to mind.

I pretend to watch the show while sliding my hand on the rug spread beneath us, making sure I move slowly enough to avoid attracting either the King's or Naja's attention. I grasp a stone that was kicked up earlier by one of the warriors and hide it in my palm. As soon as there's an extra surge in noise from the pit, I launch the stone with a flick of my wrist—right at Naja.

The white fox hisses with surprise as it pings into the side of her face. The rock is so tiny it can't have hurt, but it's had the effect I wanted. A few court members pitch forward to help her, including Kiroku.

"Oh, my gods!" I cry dramatically, throwing my hands out. "General Naja! Are you all right? I think you're bleeding!"

"Get off me, stupid girl!" she snarls, batting me away.

"What in the gods is going on?" the King growls.

"Naja's been injured!" I shout.

Murmurs rise, councilors farther away shuffling to see what the hubbub is. As Naja turns to hiss at a demon who's come to check on her, I shift back, hands over my mouth in fake shock, and murmur to Kiroku where she's kneeling forward, her face right beside mine.

"The small bird flies."

I don't dare look at her. There's a split second where I wonder if I'm making a huge mistake. Maybe what I took for a meaningful look was simply more demon repulsion.

Then I hear her whispered response.

"On the wings of the golden-eyed girl."

Excitement rushes through me. I inch my head just the slightest to meet her striped reptilian eyes and say, "I need help."

"It's coming," she replies swiftly. "We're getting you out."

I flinch—because that isn't what I wanted to hear. I can't leave yet. I still have the girls and the Queen and her baby to protect.

"No!" I hiss back under the commotion. "I don't want—that's not what I mean—"

"It will happen soon. Wait until you hear the blast. Go to the Temple Court entrance opposite Madam Kim's Seafood Palace—"

Before either of us can say anything more—or I can make sense of Kiroku's bizarre directions—Naja finally extricates herself from the fussing council members and turns to me, silver eyes murderous, snarling under her breath about how if it weren't for me being the Moonchosen, she'd toss me into the pit right now to see how I fare against the soldiers.

"Funny," I shoot back, "I'd like to do the same to you."

And I turn my attention back to the training ground with an icy smile on my lips.

Like Naja said, I'm the Moonchosen, and the King is watching us. She wouldn't dare disobey his orders. And for now, he wants me alive. Still, I sense her cutting glare on me the rest of the performance, and I have to admit that whenever he changes his mind, I'd rather Naja not be anywhere nearby.

Later that night, once the other girls are asleep, I tell Chenna what I learned from Kiroku.

"So, you're escaping." Though she gives me a smile, her voice is weighted by bitterness. "Again."

I blink, taken aback. Chenna isn't one to sugarcoat things, but she's also been nothing but supportive since our reunion, and I realize how much I've counted on her, needing her kind words and company to balance out Blue's scowls and Aoki acting as if I barely exist, and Zhen and Zhin's protectiveness over Aoki. Even if the twins laugh and chat with me, I can't be open with them the way I am with Chenna.

"I deserve that," I say. "Last time, I wasn't thinking any further than killing the King and getting out of the palace. I didn't have any plans to protect the rest of you, and now you're all suffering because of it."

"Lei, I didn't mean—"

"No." I brush her arm. "Let me apologize. I was careless, and thoughtless. But that's not the way things are going to be this time around."

Chenna frowns. "But what the allies have risked for you... You can't give up an opportunity like that."

"I won't." Her frown deepens, and I go on, "Their escape route must be somewhere in Temple Court, right? That's why they told me to go there. So what else is in Temple Court?"

After a beat, Chenna's brow unknots. "Shamans."

"Exactly. And if this means there are shamans working on our side, maybe I can get them to help me in a different way."

Both of us look down at the gold band at my wrist. Then Chenna glances back up. Though there's eagerness in her eyes, there's concern, too.

"It's too risky," she says. "You'd not only have to get there and find the rebel shamans, you'd also have to make it back to wherever you've come from. The allies haven't planned for that."

I shake my head. "Kiroku said 'blast.' If there's an explosion, or something similar, it should create enough of a diversion for me to get there, find the shamans, and get back." Chenna looks unconvinced. I take her hand. "I've got too much to do here," I say, squeezing it. "I can't leave yet. And if I can get help with these stupid things"—I nod at the bangle—"it'll be worth the risk."

Chenna hesitates. But I stare her down, and eventually she gives me her familiar wry smile. "Thank you," she says, squeezing my fingers in return.

I grin. "Thank me once we're out of here. Deal?"

For the briefest of moments, her smile widens just enough to crinkle the edges of her tawny eyes.

"Deal."

THIRTEEN

WREN

IT TOOK THEM A FORTNIGHT TO make it to the Cloud Palace. It would have been quicker, but they'd had to be careful not to fly over areas infested with the King's soldiers or where they might make camp too close to one of his allies' strongholds.

Only Wren, Khuen, and Merrin made the journey, as there hadn't been space for anyone else on Merrin's back. Since Lova wouldn't have anything to do with him, and Nitta's chair would make it difficult for her to navigate the Cloud Palace, Khuen had been chosen to help with the rescue of the imprisoned White Wing. After the two cats, he was the Hannos' strongest shooter. If they encountered bird demons in the air, he'd do with his arrows what Wren's blades didn't have the reach for.

When she saw the glittering facade of the White Wing's palace sparkling amid the jagged spikes of the Goa-Zhen foothills, amethyst-black in the setting light, Wren couldn't help recall the last time she'd been there. She wished she could scrub it from her memory. Killing Eolah, Lady Dunya's daughter, had been the beginning of her downward spiral. Merrin was taking the brunt of the blame for what had happened at the deserts and their loss of the White

Wing's allegiance, but it had been Wren's actions that ignited Qanna's coup and Merrin's betrayal.

Like its name suggested, clouds wreathed the building's gilded spires. Wren spotted the tiny flecks of guards circling. Merrin flew lower, using the cliffs for cover. He brought them down on a rocky escarpment hidden from view by a crag that jutted overhead.

Khuen slid off Merrin's back like a wilting flower. He slumped against the rock wall, glowering. "As soon as all of this is over," he grumbled, "I'm retiring and taking up a less stressful vocation."

Merrin was rolling out the kinks in his neck. "How about gardening? Or cooking? I've heard both are relaxing."

"Anything close to the ground will do."

Wren surveyed the skies. "Six—no, seven guards," she counted. "That doesn't seem like enough."

"No doubt there'll be more inside." Merrin came up beside her. "See that entrance? From there, it's almost a straight shot to the central staircase."

Wren nodded.

"What do you want to do about this lot?" he asked, gesturing at the flying guards.

She considered. "Let's make one full lap of the palace. We can take them down from the air. It'll raise less attention."

"Want to wait for full darkness? It's not long now."

"No. Better to use the cover of dark for when we make our escape."

Merrin crooked his head. "You got it, darling."

Wren bristled at the term of endearment. And because she sensed he was about to try and engage her more, as he'd been attempting unsuccessfully throughout the journey, she moved away. "We leave in five," she announced. "Leave all nonessential items."

Khuen sighed. "I'd *just* found a good napping position."

Wren raised her brows at him; the boy was sprawled over rocky ground, a stone for a cushion. How anyone could sleep like that defied belief. She stared him down, and he and Merrin followed Wren's lead, adding weapon belts and harnesses to their robes and taking a few last swigs of water before casting their traveling gear aside.

The instant the weight of her swords hit her shoulders, Wren felt the familiar focus settling in her veins.

"Let's get this over with," Khuen said, as Merrin knelt to allow them onto his back.

Wren climbed up. "Don't forget about the trip back."

Khuen's arms cinched around her waist. "Maybe I'll hang out here. Place looks pretty fancy. It could be comfortable enough."

"If you enjoy the company of dead corpses," Merrin said darkly.

"They're still probably more fun than the two of you," Khuen said—then let out a shriek as Merrin launched them from the cliff edge.

They flew low and fast, coming at the palace from an angle so they'd only be seen by the closest two guards. Mist swirled. Cold wind lashed Wren's cheeks.

"Khuen!" she yelled. "Get ready!"

Despite his trembling, the boy let go, leaning into her to draw his bow and notch an arrow as Wren reached around, securing him to her with one hand. Her other gripped a fistful of Merrin's feathers. The tip of Khuen's arrow hovered by her ear, bobbing with each beat of Merrin's powerful wings.

The guards hadn't spotted them yet. As they came into their shadow, Merrin lifted his nose. They shot up with astonishing speed, right beneath the guards, until they were so close Wren could see the white paint of their feathers and the tarnished silver of their armor.

Khuen fired.

The first shot hit true, right between the joints of the demon's armor. She tumbled from the sky with a cry. The second guard— a kestrel-woman—banked in time to avoid a clean shot, though Khuen's arrow caught her in her right arm.

"Commander!" she screeched as she listed, dropping into a messy landing on one of the palace's platforms.

Commander. Did that mean Commander Teoh was nearby? Wren had been hoping the inimitable hawk demon, leader of the White Wing's army, wouldn't be here. But sure enough, as Merrin flew on, Khuen taking down two more guards, a large figure appeared past one of the palace's towers.

Wren recognized her at once. Trailed by a pair of smaller demons, the Commander flew with ferocity, zeroing in on them without hesitation. The setting sunlight caught the tip of her qiang.

She raised it, aiming straight for Merrin.

He dove, anticipating her attack. But there was no whistle of a spear cutting the air. No flash of silver. Commander Teoh had feinted—and in doing so, pushed them right into a trio of new guards who'd appeared below, bursting from a thick squall of mist.

Khuen's yell was earsplitting as Merrin tucked his wings to roll past them. As they dropped, they brushed so close to one of the guards Wren felt a taloned hand scrape her robes. She'd have been pulled straight off Merrin's back were it not for Khuen's viselike grip—even if it was only an accidental side effect of his terror.

Merrin flattened out. He sped lightning fast through the icy air, all six birds in pursuit. Two were right upon them, jostling at their sides. Still gripping Khuen with one arm, Wren clamped her legs tighter and let go of Merrin's feathers to draw a sword. She lanced out in one powerful slice. With a rattling scream, the guard fell from the sky.

"Khuen!" Wren roared. "Shoot!"

For a moment, it seemed like the petrified boy had finally reached his limits. Then he was drawing a fresh arrow, twisting around.

A buzzard demon plummeted in a tangle of limp wings. There was another burst of red as Khuen's following arrow met its mark.

Now there were only two guards and Commander Teoh left.

As Merrin sped through the air, following a wide loop around the palace, the Commander yelled, "SOUND THE ALARM!"

One of the guards flanking her peeled away—only to plunge a second later, crumpling around the feathered tip of Khuen's arrow.

"Wren!" Merrin shouted.

He jerked his head. She followed his movement and saw the veranda they'd picked for their landing spot.

"Should I—"

"Yes!"

He veered so steeply poor Khuen let out another wail. Wren felt him slip. She wrenched her left arm back even farther, pinning him to her, muscles straining to keep them both in place. The pain from her old injury was a starburst, radiating from her hips, and she growled, forcing back the nausea it wrought.

Merrin canted. Khuen's bow cracked into Wren's cheekbone. An arrow tumbled from his grip. But they were almost there now, the terrace rushing closer, its white marble sparkling as the sun dipped behind the line of mountains—

"Argh!"

Khuen slipped from Wren's grasp. A second later she was thrown from Merrin's back as they landed heavily, tumbling across the polished tiles.

The world whirled by in flashes of white and sunset gold. Wren tried to curl into a ball, but the momentum was too great. All she could do was brace herself against the pain until finally she was sliding slower, slower...

She bounced to her feet. Merrin was clambering to his own a few meters away. Wren scanned the veranda for Khuen. Before she could find him, Commander Teoh and the remaining guard—a kite demon, sharp-eyed and sleek—landed in front of her.

Wren drew her second blade and charged.

The Commander came at her first, but Wren ducked, using the slippery surface of the tiles to skid under her outstretched arm. She arced one sword across the throat of the kite guard before she even had a chance to draw her own. Blood sprayed, hot and stinking. At the same time, Wren thrust her second blade behind her, feeling the satisfying *snick* as it caught the Commander's armor.

She swirled. Commander Teoh backed up, spear pointed like an accusatory finger. Out the corner of her eye, Wren saw more guards running onto the terrace. Merrin met them. The clash of weapons rent the air.

"I don't want to kill you, Commander," Wren said, panting for breath.

The hawk-woman's black eyes flashed. "I am loyal to Lady Qanna, Wren Hanno. I will follow her to my grave."

"Luckily for you, then, it's not far."

The voice that spoke wasn't Wren's. It took her—and the Commander—a moment to notice the arrow tip protruding from her throat.

The Commander's face went slack. She reached a talon to her neck, where liquid red gushed, vivid against the white clan paint of her feathers. Blood gurgled out from her beak. With a soft sigh, she slumped to her knees and fell to the marble tiles.

A garnet pool crept out around her head, a macabre halo.

Khuen knelt to prize the arrow from her neck. Then he was off, joining Merrin to face the new guards.

Wren stepped forward to make the sky salute over Commander Teoh's body. She stared down at the bird-woman's lifeless form. Nearby lay the kite guard's body, whose opened throat looked like a gory smile. Here it was. The first blood she'd spilled since the battle in Jana. After a month and a half of desiring it, yearning for it—the slice of her blade, the give of demon flesh—after being so desperate to do something that'd help her feel useful and powerful again, she was no longer cooped up in the Jade Fort with only her failure and guilt for company. She waited for the surge of strength and *rightness* the dance of weapons usually brought.

Instead, something deep within her seethed, dark and disgusted, and just so, *so* tired.

Lei's voice rang in her head.

How many more murders will you commit in the name of justice until you real- ize you're as bad as those we're meant to be fighting against?

Wren moved away before the spreading pool of the Commander's blood reached her boots.

Across the terrace, Merrin and Khuen had almost finished with the guards. An alarm rang within the palace—the same one Wren had set off half a year ago. The sound spilled from every archway and window to mix with the howl of the wind, so it seemed as though the whole mountain was alive.

Merrin cut down the last of the guards. He waved Wren over, feathers splashed in blood, before disappearing with Khuen inside the palace. After a beat, Wren followed, stepping around the pile of bodies they'd left in their wake. Her blades dripped red.

She didn't bother wiping them. They'd only be dirtied again all too soon.

*   *   *

"Let me help you with that."

Wren flinched as Lady Dunya knelt on the rocks beside her, taking the bloodied scrap of cloth Wren had been washing the gash on her arm with. "You don't have to do that, my Lady," she protested, but the swan-woman didn't stop.

"I always tended to my children's bumps and bruises." She laid Wren's arm in her lap and dipped the cloth into the cool river water before dabbing it carefully along the ragged edge of her wound. "It frustrated their nurses no end, and Hidei never understood why I'd waste my time doing something they were paid to do. But as much as I am a Clan Lady, I am also a mother." A pause. "Not that my children are around to take care of, now."

Guilt turned Wren's stomach. One of those children had died at her hands—and now, on her father's orders, she had to pretend to the Clan Lady's face she was innocent.

As if her shame wasn't enough already.

Hours earlier, Wren, Merrin, and Khuen had fought their way through the Cloud Palace. They'd spilled blood all the way down to the building's bowels where they found the thirty clan members who'd refused to join Qanna's coup—and not been killed in the ensuing struggle—crammed together in a few small cells. Even drenched in blood, Wren was almost overcome by the odor of demons trapped in such cramped quarters for so long.

Given their condition, she'd been impressed how not one of them wavered when she'd ordered they leave immediately in case a guard had managed to slip away for reinforcements. The secure location Ketai had picked for them to spend the night was a couple of hours' flight away in the forested foothills of the mountains southeast of the White Wing's palace. They set up camp, and over a dinner of stale roti, Wren explained all that had happened since Qanna's coup.

It was late now. Most of the wearied bird demons had fallen asleep, huddled together against the crisp night air. A few were still up. A couple of older birds were deep in conversation with Merrin. Where Khuen was perched on a tree stump near the back of the camp on lookout duty, a pretty Steel hawk-girl sat with him. The pair of them were comparing bows.

Wren had gone to the rocky banks of the stream to clean the nasty cut in her arm one of the guards had given her. Lady Dunya was the last person she'd have wanted to be alone with, yet as the regal swan-woman tended to her wound, Wren found her presence comforting.

"There." Lady Dunya finished tying a strip of cloth around Wren's arm.

Wren murmured a thanks, dipping her head respectfully.

Even in the grimy dark of the Cloud Palace prison, it had been clear how cruelly three months of captivity had treated the formerly opulent Clan Lady. Up close, though, it was etched upon every inch of her. Her feathers, once pearl-white, were ragged and dirty. Where diamonds and opals used to adorn her neck and wrists, there were cuts and chafes and oozing scabs. In place of a crown and silver-white robes, she wore a tattered hanfu turned brown-black with grime. And where her husband once sat at her side, now there was only empty space.

Lord Hidei had died early on into their imprisonment. No one was quite sure what of—an infection, perhaps, or a weak heart. His body had been disposed of by the guards because it had started to smell.

Wren was about to offer her condolences when Lady Dunya said, "I'm surprised you didn't heal it already." She motioned at Wren's freshly bandaged arm. "The Sickness, I suppose?"

Wren dipped her hands into the water, scrubbing at the blood under her nails. "It's worse than ever," she admitted. "I could have done it, but I'd prefer to save my energy." She didn't add that before she'd left on the rescue mission, her father had expressly forbidden her to use magic unless it was absolutely essential.

In fact, she'd been surprised he'd even assigned her the mission, given how much he'd insisted on her resting after Jana. Knowing her father, there were probably a multitude of motivations. She didn't have care to untangle them.

"A good idea," Lady Dunya said. "We still aren't in the clear yet."

"Will we ever be?"

The words slipped out. Wren was embarrassed by her own candor. She was a Clan Lord's daughter. Leaders were supposed to be confident and optimistic ... or should at least present themselves so.

Yet Lady Dunya nodded. "A Clan Lady's life isn't easy," she said.

I don't want an easy life. I want a meaningful one.

The words rushed at Wren with such force it shocked tears to her eyes. Had she really once spoken them?

Did she believe them still?

"Thank you," she said. "For agreeing to help us in the rest of the war."

"Of course. We made a pact with your clan. I do not intend to renege on it now. Especially not after you saved our lives."

The shame. Wren thought she'd burst into flames from it.

She hurried to stand. As she brushed down her clothes, she saw how bloodstained they were—blood that belonged to Lady Dunya's kin. Wren cursed herself that she hadn't thought of washing when they landed. She'd gotten so used to the feel of blood on her skin.

"Are we meeting any of your clan or allies here?" the Clan Lady asked suddenly.

"No. We're to join them once they've made camp outside of Marazi in four days' time."

"Then who are *they*?"

Everything in Wren went tense. She followed Lady Dunya's stare across the stream. At first, there was only forest, tangled shadows. Glints of moonlight winked like beetle shells. Then she made out the silhouettes of three human figures. They stood so still they'd melted into the darkness.

Wren blocked Lady Dunya, boots splashing in the shallows as she sank into a defensive stance and raised her fists. "Show yourselves," she growled, "or I will attack."

To her surprise, one of the figures laughed. It was an old, wheezing laugh. "Your kind always were so sure of themselves. Lower your fists, Wren Hanno. We are not here to harm you, nor your friends."

Icy fingers trailed Wren's spine. She said sharply, "What do you mean, *my kind?*"

The woman glided forward, so smoothly she could only be a shaman. Even though she wasn't using magic, the echoes of it clung to her, an ethereal glimmer in the air. As she came closer, Wren saw a bald head and weathered skin riddled with tattoos. Bright eyes shone from heavy-lidded sockets.

The ancient shaman wore a wide, toothless grin. "Your blood relatives, of course," she replied, opening her arms. "Your clan. Welcome back, little Xialing."

FOURTEEN

WREN

MORNING SUN SPARKLED THROUGH THE BOUGHS, dappling the forest floor where Wren and Ahma Goh walked. The forest had seemed cold in the dark; in the daylight, spring burst from every spore. Flowers blossomed in the cracks of rocks. The stream, rushing happily by to their right, twisted and twirled like a dancer's ribbons. Overhead, gold-green leaves flashed like tiger eyes. Wren felt drunk from the sweet air, from the colors and beauty. And, best of all, from old Ahma Goh's words—her wonderful, impossible words, punctuated by a gap-toothed grin and generous laugh.

None of it felt real. Here she was, walking in the mountain forests her birth clan—her lost clan, her lost *family*—had once walked, too, in the company of a shaman who knew their stories.

Who had known *them*.

Ahma Goh chuckled. "Your sister Leore, now she was a real firecracker. From the instant she could walk, she was running, forever trying to outdo the others. Oh, and Kucho, what a little troublemaker! He was your cousin on your mother's side. Aiyah, how he used to menace your grandfather. Always getting into scrapes and relying on others to get him out of them."

Wren laughed with her. "And my grandmother?"

"Yakuta—a brave woman. The way she'd scold your grandfather! He called her his Ox for how strong-willed she was. Always the first to grab her weapons anytime the clan was threatened." Her smile flickered. "And the last to drop them."

They had walked in a full circle. They were almost back at the compound where Ahma Goh and the rest of the mountain shamans lived—and where they'd invited Wren and the others to stay.

Earlier, when Ahma Goh led Wren away at sunrise to show her around the forest and connect the stories of her clan with the places they'd played out, the settlement had been quiet. Now there was chatter and the clatter of pots and pans. Incense lifted from where shrines lay nestled among the leaves. The fragrance of simmering herbs drifted on the breeze. A hazy glow lay over everything: protection daos to keep the settlement safe.

Magic crackled in the air, but more than feeling like magic, the place simply *was* magic. A sanctuary not just from the war but the rest of Ikhara; even from time itself, the echoes of her Xia family weaving in and out of the trees. Her sister Leore, speeding over the stony grass. Kucho trying—and failing—to trip her. The elder clan members, shaking their heads in that fond, weary way of the old watching the young.

Wren couldn't believe her luck that their rest stop had been so close. Half a mile away and she'd never have known this place existed.

Her ears popped as they passed the perimeter enchantment. Within its protective bubble, the sounds they'd heard from outside were instantly louder. Even the air was clearer, sunlight winking off the varnished eaves of shrines and sparkling off the river's surface. Cherry blossom drifted through the air. A petal landed on Wren's brow.

Picking it off and holding it delicately, she was reminded of another secret temple—the one within the Hidden Palace's Ghost Court. She'd taken Lei there to see the paper tree with its lost women's names.

Wren let the petal loose. The breeze danced it away. She hadn't yet brought herself to ask Ahma Goh about her parents. It wasn't that she didn't long to know what they'd been like. It was that she was too nervous. Would Ahma Goh think they'd have liked her? Been happy with the young woman they'd brought into the world?

Ahma Goh smiled fondly at the bustling encampment. "This is the Southern Zebe Sanctuary," she explained. "We've been around for as long as the provinces themselves. The four Sanctuaries were set up throughout the mountains as a safe haven for travelers." They followed the stream. Trees hid the lake it led to from sight, where the splashing of morning bathers rose. "This is one of the tributaries that feeds the River Zebe. Its source is deep in the mountains. Many shamans make pilgrimages there. The Sanctuaries became known as places for them to seek refuge during their trips. And as more and more shamans visited..." She slid her eyes sideways, her wrinkled face mischievous. "Can't you feel it?"

Wren frowned. "Magic? The protective enchantments—"

"More than that, child." Ahma Goh grabbed her hands. "*Feel* it."

Wren closed her eyes, breathed deeply—and *felt*. There it was, what she'd been sensing all along. She thought it came from being in a place linked to the Xia. But it was more literal than that.

Magic *lived* here.

It was why colors seemed sharper, each smell and sound keener. Why the constant pain she'd been in from her injury had dimmed. The earth's qi was open and bountiful here, nourished by constant shaman care. The Sickness hadn't touched this place.

It must be one of the only places in Ikhara where the rotten heart of the King and his demons hadn't poisoned.

Wren wished Lei was here. Not only for the wonder of it all, but to show Lei that magic could be beautiful, too. As much as it took life, it could breathe life back into the world. It could be a source of good.

She could be good. At least, that's how being here made her feel.

Ahma Goh led Wren toward a small temple. "The Xia spent much time here. Like all who have passed through the Sanctuaries, we share their histories from shaman to shaman." She beamed up at Wren. "Storytelling is a wonderful kind of magic, don't you think? It is how we keep people alive in our hearts long after they are gone."

Wren replied quietly, "And even when they're not."

Ahma Goh squeezed her hand. "And even when they are not."

They approached the shrine, idols adorning the walls, with just enough floor space for a prayer mat and incense pot.

"Why didn't the Xia stay here, if it's so safe?" Wren asked. "When they knew the Demon King's men were coming for them?"

"But they did." Ahma Goh's face creased. "Oh, child. I thought Ketai Hanno would have told you. The day of their massacre, your clan was in the Northern Sanctuary, deep in the mountains of Rain. The Northern Sanctuary is the most remote of the four. We thought they'd be best hidden there—and they would have been, had the King not chosen the one day he knew they'd be defenseless." Her head drooped. "No one has set foot in the Northern Sanctuary since. It is not a place for the living. Not anymore." Abruptly, the old woman clapped Wren on the back, brightening. "Come now, child. All is not lost. Look! The Xia clan remains alive—in *you.*"

Wren tried to return her smile, but at the reminder of the Xia's power, something dark nagged at her. "My father—he thinks the King has been trying to replicate the Xia's methods. That it's what's causing the Sickness."

Ahma Goh sobered. She waited for Wren to continue.

"And we're pretty sure the Xia's magic has something to do with...with death."

"Hmm."

"I used it, once. A shaman friend. He sacrificed himself to strengthen my magic."

Ahma Goh's face was still unreadable. "And did it?"

Wren nodded, even as the admission sickened her. "But I've been wondering...this place. The way you talk about the Xia? It's all so—so vibrant. Full of warmth and laughter. But if the King is using their methods and it's causing the Sickness, and their methods use *death*, then how is this place the way it is? Why isn't it crippled by the Sickness, too?"

"What is magic at its roots?" Ahma Goh asked.

Wren hesitated. "An exchange of qi. Of energy."

"From who?"

"From...ourselves."

"And so if death was to be used as an exchange, *whose* death should it be?"

"I don't follow, Ahma Goh."

The old shaman waved her papery hands. "We offer the earth our *own* pain—or our own beauty. It depends upon the clan as to which method is preferred. Still, both amount to the same thing: in needing something from the earth, we shamans give it something of ours in return. Death could be an offering, certainly. But death of another is not death—it is murder. And murder is not an offering. It is *taking* that vitality from someone else. Qi draining in its purest form. That was why your shaman friend's death offered you such intense power. You didn't take his life—he *gave* it to you."

A gift. Wren hated the thought.

Hiro's sweet young face came to her mind. The memory of him carving a line down his arm and offering his blood up to her as simply as if he were handing her a flower. She thought of her Birth-blessing word. She'd always thought *sacrifice* meant her own—but what if this was its true meaning?

Lei's prediction on Lova's ground-ship came back to her. The words had been eclipsed by all that came after. But Wren was struck then by the earlier part of their conversation.

So Ketai doesn't know about your power yet.

No.

Are you planning on telling him? You know what he'll do with this information, Wren. He'll find others to pledge themselves to your power. Other broken boys like Hiro who have every reason to hate the King and don't value their own lives enough. You'll have a whole army of willing sacrifices.

Her father *did* know about what had happened to Hiro. Caen must have told him, because early on into their return to the Jade Fort, Ketai had approached her and congratulated her on what she'd done on the Czos' island. She'd saved them, he'd said. But that wasn't exactly true. She'd used her magic, yes, but it had been Hiro who'd bolstered it. Without his sacrifice, they'd have been overcome.

Was this the true meaning of her Birth-blessing pendant, then? Was Wren's father hoping she'd lead their clan to victory along a path of corpses built from the bloody bodies of her own allies? Her own kin?

Her *friends*?

Ahma Goh seemed to sense her spiraling thoughts. She took Wren's hands and smiled up at her, her milky-black eyes shining. "Put this from your mind, child," she urged. "Whatever you are worrying about, it is not with us right this moment. If you carry the full weight of your responsibilities all the time, even the strongest person would be crushed." She waved at the shrine. "How about you pay your respects to the gods and your ancestors. They'd like that." Her nose wrinkled. "And when you're done, it's about time for a wash, wouldn't you agree?"

Wren forced a smile. "Thank you, Ahma Goh," she said. "For everything. You and your shamans have been so generous. I wish we didn't have to leave so soon."

"Leave?"

"We have to keep moving. My father gave me clear instructions. In fact, we should be setting off for the next secure location within the hour—"

She broke off as Ahma Goh dissolved into rasping laughter. "Sorry, my child. It's just, you *still* haven't understood."

"Understood?"

"You are safe here, my child." The old shaman smiled sadly. "You have spent your life fighting. I can feel that. And it has made you strong. But do not speed through life so fast you miss all the joy as well as the pain." She clasped her fingers, leaning in. "Stop *running*, child. Set down your blades. We both know too well how soon you'll have to pick them up again. For the next few days, I do not want to even see you *close* to a weapon, do you understand me, Wren Xia Hanno? Here at the sanctuary, you are not a clan leader at war. You are a young girl in need of rest and care. Let us give that to you."

I don't deserve it, Wren wanted to say.

Perhaps Ahma Goh sensed so, because, eyes twinkling, she said kindly, "We all deserve a break, child. Your ghosts shall not haunt you here." And flashing one last, toothless grin, the ancient shaman shuffled away, leaving Wren alone with wet eyes and a quietly expanding heart.

FIFTEEN

LEI

AFTER MY EXCHANGE WITH NAJA'S MAID Kiroku, I spend every moment alert for a sign that whatever my allies have planned is on its way. Yet days pass without incident. I even stay up throughout the nights, just in case the "blast" Kiroku mentioned happens then, leading Blue to grumble about how much extra effort she has to expend in order to hide my under-eye circles when she does my makeup.

When four days have gone by without incident, I'm ragged from fatigue and frayed nerves. That evening, when Madam Himura and I head home after a banquet in City Court, I doze off only a minute after climbing into the carriage. When we jolt to a stop, it takes me a moment to remember where I am. Then Kiroku's words snap into my mind.

It will happen soon. Wait until you hear the blast.

I sit up straight, wiping drool from my chin. My dangling earrings chime.

Madam Himura slaps her cane across my chest. "Do not move."

The faint hum of the shamans in Temple Court purrs under the sounds of the bustling street, and my ears latch on to it, remembering the opportunity I'm being given.

Cloven steps approach. Commander Razib flings the curtain aside.

As usual, the Commander and my other guards have been riding alongside our carriage on hulking horses bred big enough to carry even the largest of demons. On wider roads, they surround us on all sides, but here in City Court most of the streets are narrow. The one we've stopped in is a popular drinking spot. Covered paths double as terraces for the busy bars and late-night restaurants, colorful banners flapping from the walkway eaves.

"Commander," Madam Himura croaks. "What is the holdup? It's late, and Lei-zhi has an early appointment with a diviner tomorrow."

"There is some sort of commotion a few streets away," he says. "Half the guards are to remain here with you while I bring the others to investigate. Do *not* leave the carriage—"

A light erupts beyond his head; an unreal, blue-white flare.

It blooms in the sky. Then—

Whoomph!

I've just enough time to throw myself down before the blast of air hits.

The carriage quakes. We tip to one side. There's crashing and the drumbeat of things beating the walls, the wood rattling under their force. Something strikes my hands where I'm cradling my head, igniting a spark of pain. The air is thick. I gasp, huddled in a ball, feeling the world shudder and shake, until, as abruptly as it began, everything falls still.

Trembling, I lift my head. Palls of dust swirl all around. After the violence of the blast, the sudden stillness is jarring. I cough, dust stinging my throat and eyes. The carriage has completely tipped on its side, the open doorway now above me. The curtain Commander Razib drew aside has been torn away—along with the Commander.

As I move to get up, my hands press into something warm.

Madam Himura.

I jerk back. Through hazy eyes, I notice the subtle rise and fall of her torso where she's been tossed onto her side, one wing spread across her like a blanket. She's alive, then.

The realization gives me pause.

If I ever wanted to get rid of her without implicating myself, here is my chance. I could slip my hands around Madam Himura's neck and that would be it. An unfortunate accident. Another casualty from the explosion.

Long seconds pass as I survey her prone form, debris drifting down like pyre ash, the gods seeming to sense my intent. But I don't move. Where I was expecting fire to light my core, all that rises is a sad, empty feeling. Maybe it's because it doesn't seem right to murder someone in such a vulnerable moment. Or maybe it's because, no matter how much Madam Himura has hurt me and those I love, I know how trapped she herself is by the King and the palace. Even though she wouldn't offer me any, I can't help but pity her for it.

With a frustrated growl—and a prayer that my decision to spare her doesn't come back to haunt me—I get to my feet.

Spitting out the dust that swirls into my mouth, I reach for the opening overhead. It takes me a few unsteady tries before I lift myself through. I clamber over the side of the carriage and drop to the ground.

What had been a bustling street now resembles a battlefield. Beneath drifts of ash, bodies and debris are strewn everywhere. One of the guards' horses lies behind our carriage, its eyes wide and white, its chest pumping quick. A second later, the poor thing falls still. I lurch away. My heel hits something. I catch myself before I fall and look around to find a human leg on the floor. No sign of the rest of its owner.

I stagger on. Garnet splatters of blood mark the road and previously busy walkways. Everything is lit in an eerie orange glow, half the buildings on fire. A few streets away, a great plume of smoke mushrooms into the sky. The blast site—and my diversion.

Wait until you hear the blast. Go to the Temple Court entrance opposite Madam Kim's Seafood Palace.

I stumble into action.

Figures flow past me, some silent, some wailing, others muttering blankly to themselves. I push through them, bundling aside the skirt of my hanfu to free my legs.

It doesn't take me long to orient myself. I've been enhancing my mental map of the palace with each outing. Once I'm far enough from the blast, the dust starts to clear, and I move faster, gulping down lungfuls of fresh air. I have no idea where Madam Kim's Seafood Palace is—which I'm guessing is a restaurant—but I start by heading toward Temple Court. Tonight's dinner was held in a sake house on the far east side of City Court, placing me close by. Though I've never been inside, Temple Court is impossible to miss, being housed within the perimeter walls of the palace themselves. All I have to do is run straight for the towering slabs of onyx rock I've come to know so well.

I wind my way through the snug streets. Shop and bar owners have emerged from their buildings, many more hanging out of windows, pointing at the roiling smoke and exclaiming to one another.

Soon, I'm only one street away from the walls. They climb so high the buildings around are cast in perpetual shadow. Not even a single glint of moonlight reflects off a metal idol or ornamental pond. I take note of the name of the kopitiam in front of me, then move right, scanning for Madam Kim's Seafood Palace. If I don't find it, I'll head back to the kopitiam and try the other way. But not even a minute later, I see it: a large restaurant with gaudy red signs and fish-shaped lanterns dangling over its door.

"Hello, Madam Kim," I say, and slip down the dark alley beside it.

I crouch in the cover of the shadowed eaves of the back of the restaurant, positioning myself right across the closest entranceway leading inside the walls. Apart from when I've entered and left the palace, I've never been this close to its walls before. Their black stone moves with a liquid sheen, bronze characters from the shamans' never-ending daos infusing it with its unbreakable protection. Yet while the magical light shimmers within the rock, it doesn't illuminate anything beyond.

Thank gods. I'll need the darkness if I'm to approach unseen. Because, just like the outer side of the wall, there are guards *everywhere*.

There must be a hundred of them in my line of sight. Due to the explosion, they've scattered from their usual posts, most standing in clumps, no doubt speculating about what happened. A few of the commanders call guards over, sending them off in groups toward the blast site.

My allies have done well. On a normal night, I'd never make it past them. Tonight, I might just have a chance.

Just like at the military parade, a stray pebble comes to my aid. This one is larger. I heft it toward the wall as hard as I can.

By sheer luck, I strike one of the guards in the back. His yell of surprise draws the attention of the nearby guards—including those outside the entrance I need to get to. Heart hammering, I dart from the cover of the building and dash to the wall.

The instant I make it through, I press my back to the passageway within, anticipating guards to come rushing. But none do, and as I soften with relief, I'm suddenly aware of the charged shivers brushing up and down my skin.

Magic. So much of it I feel it with every ounce of my body, alert to the fact I am *inside* magic itself, the air alight with powerful daos. Ghostly chanting reverberates in the tunnel.

The royal shamans. Thousands upon thousands of them, within these walls.

A movement outside makes me skitter from the entrance. Hugging the wall, I head down the corridor I've found myself in, moving warily. The chanting grows louder. Static glances off my skin. I pick up my pace, a rich glow spilling from the opening ahead, and then I'm stepping through—

A shockwave of magic knocks me so hard I reel back.

By now, I've seen shamans at work countless times. The ones in the palace who either healed or bound me. Sweet Hiro, so steady in the face of death. Wren in her Xia trance, the most awe-inspiring of them all. But this is beyond anything I could have imagined.

A vast, high-ceilinged cavern stretches to either side of the archway I'm standing within. And almost inch of it is occupied by shamans.

Ebony-robed, tattoo-riddled shamans, kneeling with bowed heads, power crackling off their bodies like lightning in a thundercloud. They are packed so tightly their robes lap over one another, creating a rippling black sea. More golden marks—the words of their daos—shimmer in the air before latching to the walls, sinking beneath the stone. Unlike outside, here the characters come so fast and thick the air glows with a swirling, molten-bronze wind.

Past the passageway, a narrow walkway lines the chamber. I step into it, glancing for guards. All I see in either direction are more shamans.

Then I notice the chains.

I'd missed them at first with the squalls of magic spinning through the air. My blood runs cold as I follow the line of the chains down from hooks in the ceiling to where they are attached to each shaman's neck with a heavy gold collar.

Just then, voices sound over the chanting.

"How many did the General say?"

"Three hundred. For now."

"You think we'll need *more?*"

"You saw the size of the blast, Mofa. We'll be lucky if half this side of the wall isn't cleared out to deal with the damage."

"Gods. Whoever did this is going to wish they'd died in the explosion themselves. The King has been on the rampage ever since the Moon Ball."

I drop to the floor, shoving my back to the wall. Luckily the guards have come from an entranceway farther up to the left, and the pair of them busy themselves with unlocking the chains of the tightly crammed shamans, hefting them to their feet before making them file out one by one.

I'm wondering what to do next—Kiroku didn't have time to give me any further instructions—when a hand grasps my ankle.

I stifle a scream.

A young shaman leans from the pack, red-faced as he strains against his binds, but his expression is composed as he addresses me, a quickness in his hazel eyes.

"Moonchosen," he says. "We've been waiting for you to come."

Breathless, I look back at the guards, but by chance they're moving in the opposite direction, their backs to us.

"Don't worry about them." The shaman sits back so his chain isn't pulling so tight and gives me a small smile. "I'm Ruza."

"L-Lei," I stammer.

"I know that. The small bird flies."

"On the wings of the golden-eyed girl," I finish.

His face sharpens. "Ready to spread those wings, golden-eyed girl?"

My nerves flicker brighter under the waves of enchantments. The chanting reverberating through the hall hides our voices, but Ruza doesn't look concerned about the shamans nearby overhearing.

I glance around pointedly. "Are we—is it safe..."

"We're all on your side here, Lei." Ruza spreads an arm, and I notice painful-looking welts and slashes covering his skin as the sleeve of his robe slips. "It took a long time, but our network in the palace managed to move all rebel shamans into one place, and we've been working on creating an opening in the wall." As I crick my neck to look, he says, "You won't see it. We're using daos to hide it from the guards. So you'll forgive the others if this isn't the warm welcome you were imagining. We're a little tired."

Guilt cinches my throat. All this magic and pain...

For me.

"You shouldn't have done this," I say.

Ruza frowns. "Do you know *why* we're doing it?" When I shake my head, he says, "The same reason *you* fight. We want to see the King and his court brought to their knees." The boy winces, adjusting the collar at his neck. The skin around it is purpled and crusted with dried blood. "My entire clan was imprisoned by the King— only one of us escaped. My best friend. Hiro."

I freeze. "You mean..."

Ruza nods. "The same Hiro you knew. Kiroku was the one who

recruited me a few months ago. She brought me and my clan members news of your friendship with Hiro. How he'd sacrificed himself to help you and the Hannos. Even if we hadn't spent over a year in these conditions, that would have been enough to convince us. We've been working with her since, along with many other shamans. There are hundreds of us, Lei."

He spreads an arm again, and I follow it, taking in the cowed, black-robed figures with a swelling wonder. Hundreds of royal shamans, working against the King. It's more than I'd dared to believe.

When I return my gaze to Ruza, the young boy's expression is determined and proud. But it strikes fresh shame through me.

"Ruza," I start, "Hiro died because of us—"

"He *chose* to die for you. That's all we ask. To have the choice—"

Shouting comes from where the guards are unshackling the weary shamans. One of them keeps falling when they try and get him to walk. A whipcrack echoes out, and I wince.

"We should hurry," Ruza says. "I can't come with you, or it'll look too suspicious, but I'll free myself with magic to take you to the spot—"

"I'm not going."

Ruza stares.

"If I go," I say, "I'm putting too many people at risk. There are things I need to do here. People I need to protect. I've made promises, and I don't intend on breaking them."

"You could be free," he says.

"But they wouldn't. Please, Ruza. I'm so grateful for everything you've all done to arrange this for me, but I can't leave. And I—I'm sorry, but I need to ask even more of you."

He smiles. "Anything for a friend of Hiro's."

That guts me, but I press on before I lose courage—because

the last thing I want to do is ask this young shaman who's clearly drained and in pain to hurt himself further for me. I extend my arm, showing him the band strapped around my wrist.

He brushes a finger over it and flinches. "A cruel magic," he says.

"I can't take it off, or they'll notice, and my friend Aoki—"

"I know. I can read the daos woven into it. The bands are linked. Whatever is done to this one will be done to hers."

My heart races. "Is there any way…"

But Ruza's already wrapped both hands around the bangle. His eyes close, magic shivering into life as he whispers in the strange language of the shamans. His brow is drawn, face tight with concentration. The tendons of his neck tense. I can feel him trembling, his fingers white where they grip my wrist. Just when I think I can't take it anymore, reminded too much of Hiro, Ruza gasps, sagging.

He can't even fall to the floor because of the chain.

I hold him, doing what I can to steady him. It takes him a while to compose himself. But he does, and without any fuss and brushing away my apologies.

"It's done." He drags in a labored breath. "I've countered the enchantment, so the band will not shrink—and since the bands are linked, neither will its partner. But the original enchantment is woven deep within the material. My magic will only hold it off so long."

"I understand. Thank you, Ruza. I'm so grateful for everything." I bite my lip, unable to stop my eyes from wandering to the raw skin at his neck, the heavy chain locking him in place. "Couldn't you… couldn't you all leave?" I ask. "If you've made an opening, can't you use magic to free the chains and go?"

"You are not the only one choosing to stay and fight," he replies.

Before I can say anything, new voices come from down the hall. More guards.

"Go," Ruza tells me, and I scrabble back to the passage before they can spot me. "Lei?"

I turn back, couched in shadows. Ruza's hazel eyes are determined.

"We'll keep the passage through the wall open," he tells me. He gives me the same inscrutable smile. "Just in case."

SIXTEEN

LEI

"L EI-ZHI!" MISTRESS AZAMI'S VOICE RICOCHETS OFF the marble walls. "Stop dragging your heels! That is not how the Moon-chosen should walk."

I roll my eyes, resisting a smirk. The Night House mistress sure knows how to play her part. Her glower prickles the back of my neck as I follow Commander Razib and my guards back to my room after a lunch with the King.

It's been four days since the blast. While Madam Himura recovers from her injuries, Mistress Azami has been chosen by the King to watch over us. Though we've not had time alone to discuss what happened that night, it's comforting to have her around, a reminder of how unaware the King is to how deeply the rebellion has rooted itself within the court. And with our bracelets free from his influence, I'm no longer shackled by my fear of hurting Aoki—any more than I already have, that is. Still, I haven't worked out the rest of my plan. I've made allies and nullified the bands, but I have yet to figure out how to get the girls and the Demon Queen safely out of here.

Then of course, there's the tiny matter of killing the King.

We hear the commotion before we turn the corner.

"You all saw!"

"I was cleaning it, which was your chore to do in the first place, in case you'd forgotten."

"I don't take orders from *you*."

"Blue, calm down, I'm sure Chenna didn't mean—"

Commander Razib's hand moves to the hilt of his sword. He hastens us on, toward where the pair of guards outside our door are looking uncomfortable, clearly unsure whether they should be intervening. The arguing voices grow louder. Commander Razib throws the door open and waves at Mistress Azami.

"Control them!" he barks.

Mistress Azami folds her arms, leaning casually in the doorway. "Oh, this? Just a frivolous dispute, you know how women are. Better to let it blow over. My girls do it all the time. The Night Houses are a constant battlefield, I swear my girls do more arguing than—"

"*Mistress Azami.*"

Though her gray canine eyes narrow, she says in a clipped tone, "Yes, Commander." Then, with an almost imperceptible wink in my direction, she pushes off the wall and strides inside. "Girls! Silence, now!"

With an impatient growl, Commander Razib shoves me after her.

It doesn't take long to see what the girls have been fighting over. A pool of water has spread into the rattan mat from the bathing tub in the far corner of our room, where a large crack has split its side. Chenna and Blue are standing off, Chenna calm, Blue hunched over and bristling with indignation. Aoki and the twins hover close to her, as if ready to grab her if she decides to launch at Chenna— which she looks likely to do any second.

Though Chenna, Zhen, Zhin, and Aoki dip their heads

respectfully as Mistress Azami approaches, Blue points at Chenna. "She broke it."

"I'm not interested in who did what," Mistress Azami snaps. "The tub is ruined, and we will have to find a new one, as well as water. Blue, Zhen, Zhin, Aoki—clear this mess. Chenna, come with me and Lei-zhi to the storerooms." Then she spins on her heels, marching the two of us from the room.

Commander Razib looks surprised to see us again so soon.

Mistress Azami waves a hand at him. "Like I told you. Silly female squabbles. What did you expect cooping six girls up in one room? We need to fetch some supplies from the storeroom."

"We'll send for maids," he starts.

But Mistress Azami is already off, Chenna and me right behind. "A waste of time," she shoots over her shoulder. "Lei-zhi needs to be ready for the King in less than one hour. Anyway, a bit of manual labor will do the girl good. Gods know she's too spoiled for her own sake."

Commander Razib glares at me as he gestures to the guards to follow. "Yes," he says. "She is."

The storeroom isn't far. The guards take up station outside as Mistress Azami leads Chenna and me in. A Steel caste maid is gathering some materials from one of the shelves, and she bows when she sees Mistress Azami. Then she straightens, catching sight of me. Her feline eyes go wide.

"You *dare* look at the King's Moonchosen?" Mistress Azami rumbles at her, and the girl scurries off with her tail tucked between her legs.

I raise my brows. "Enjoying this a little too much, aren't you?" I say, low, so the guards can't overhear.

Mistress Azami gives me a steely look in response. Checking

the guards are still at their stations, she leads us to the back of the storeroom where a row of tubs line the wall. They remind me of the mixing barrels back in our herb shop, which reminds me of Baba and Tien—which in turn brings a fresh wave of the worry that is always there.

I hope Wren is keeping them safe.

I hope *Wren* is safe.

"Fill these buckets with water!" Mistress Azami shoves wooden buckets into our arms, bringing us to a fountain in the corner of the room where water is pumped up from heated wells beneath the palace. Under its noisy splashing, she whispers, "Nice distraction. I suppose it *was* you two who planned this?"

Chenna and I swap a pleased look.

"We thought we could use some time alone to talk," I say.

"Quite right. I hear Madam Himura's recovering well, so we might not have much more time together." Mistress Azami narrows her eyes at me, though her look is not unkind. "So. *Lei*. I was surprised to be called as your chaperone, given how I helped arrange your escape."

I hesitate. "And I appreciate you doing that, but...I couldn't go, Mistress Azami. Not like that. Not when it meant putting the girls in danger again."

"I understand perfectly."

"You're not angry with me?"

She gives me a surprisingly tender look, her usually tough features softening. "Lei, we arranged that for *you*. To spare you being here again with the King. But you chose differently. And I must say, what you chose was admirable." She cocks her head, a sharp smile tucking her lips. "Your trick with the bangles was clever. I only wish I'd thought of it."

I grin. "How did you know about that?"

"One of our allies visited Ruza yesterday." She raises her voice for the benefit of the guards. "Now these, too! And hurry up! Aiyah, you two are as slow as newborns!"

Water splashes over my hands as we allow the buckets to overflow. Chenna leans in. "Any news of the war?"

"Reports are coming in that the Hannos will shortly be on the move. The King has redistributed more soldiers to Marazi and the Black Port in anticipation of assaults there, and reinforcements are arriving here at the palace every day. The King expects an attack— and soon. He is fortifying the palace. He wants the Hannos to come to him."

"Why?" Chenna asks.

"He thinks he'll have the upper hand if he fights them on his own turf."

My throat tightens. "Will he?"

Mistress Azami answers with her typical frankness. "Most probably." She raises her voice again. "Now the tub! And handle it carefully, or I'll have your food rations cut in half for a week to repay for a new one!"

We move to the farthest tub so we're half hidden by a shelf of supplies.

"Our allies within the palace are working on weakening the King's forces," Mistress Azami tells us in an undertone. "You heard about the recent illness that hit Military Court? Or the 'accidental' death of General Nakhor during a drill? And we are doing what we can to spread discord and miscommunication throughout the court. A few of the recent executions of council members loyal to the King were thanks to our spies' hard work."

"Any chance you could work on getting Naja implicated in something?" I mutter sourly.

"Trust me, Lei. She'd be the first to go if it were up to me—"

"Hurry up in there!"

Commander Razib's call makes me jump. He's standing in the storeroom entranceway, the twisting lance of his gazelle horns framed in the light. For a second, I almost mistook him for the King.

How lucky demons are to be born with weapons built into their bodies. I always imagined if I had the choice I'd be a bird-form. Some fast, graceful demon who could soar through the skies so she'd never again be trapped. No one would ever be able to cage her, keep her from the ones she loves. Recently, though, the thought of having horns has started to look appealing. There's a reason Papers find bull and other horned demon forms so intimidating. Plus, I'm beginning to *feel* dangerous. It would be fitting to look it, too.

Under Mistress Azami's instructions, Chenna and I lift the tub. We lug it slowly toward the doorway.

Mistress Azami shifts in close behind me. "Look after the girls," she mutters into my ear. "When the time comes, they'll need to be ready to run."

"I could use some herbs," I say. "Blue and Aoki's injuries are still pretty bad."

"What do you need?"

"Milk thistle. Cinnabar. Lei gong teng, if you can get it."

"I'll see what I can do."

"We're given herbs for my baths," I tell her. "Maybe you can sneak them in with them?"

"Excellent idea."

We're almost at the door now, and I know we only have a few seconds left. "Is there anything else I can do?" I ask in a whisper.

She answers simply. "Stay quiet. Stay safe. And stay prepared."

When we return to the room, the others are still cleaning the stained mat. Zhen and Zhin jump up to help Chenna and me with the bathing tub, while Blue cuts us a glare before resuming her aggressive scrubbing.

"Lei-zhi is to be ready for an appointment with the King in exactly forty minutes," Mistress Azami announces. "She'd better be ready when I come for her. You have already wasted my time once today. None of you wish to find out what will happen if you do so a second time."

"Yes, Mistress," the girls murmur.

As she leaves, the dog-woman slips a folded scrap of paper into my hand. "A letter from a friend," she says.

I tuck it quickly into the fold of my robes. Warmth thrums through me—until I find Blue staring straight at me.

Once, I would have been afraid of her. But for some reason, her glare only fires me up. I stride toward her, and she grimaces, throwing her rag on the floor and starting to her feet. She has to push off her good knee with both hands. She wobbles, and I rush to steady her.

She bats me away. "Get your filthy paws off me, Nine."

Aoki is the only one of the girls paying us attention. Chenna, Zhin, and Zhen are busy filling the new tub with the buckets of water we brought. Lemongrass and ginger fragrance the air as Chenna sprinkles them into the water.

Blue bares her teeth at me. She's become even more of a feral creature since the Moon Ball, every flint-edged angle honed, the wild look in her eyes like that of a trapped cat: angry, scared, defiant. "Any excuse to touch a girl," she spits.

Instead of embarrassment, all I feel is pity. Just like a feral animal, Blue has learned to bite first.

"Take your clothes off," I say.

Blue's eyes widen. Aoki's face flashes up.

"You *sick*—"

"I've seen you naked a million times, Blue," I interrupt. "And while you are undeniably beautiful, I'm not interested. Sorry. But you stink, and your leg needs cleaning. *Proper* cleaning."

None of the girls have been allowed fresh water for bathing since they got here, left to use the tub after I've already dirtied it. I asked Madam Himura for their own bath supplies, but of course her response was a sneer and a jab to the ribs with her cane.

"The warmth will help with the pain," I tell Blue.

She juts her chin. "I'm not in pain."

"Yes, you are. Aoki? Could you help Blue into the tub? I'd do it myself, but..." I don't need to explain. Blue's glower is still boring into my skin. I reach for the cloth Aoki's been scrubbing the stained mat with. "Let me do that."

As I take her place, Aoki moves aside slowly, eyeing me almost timidly. "You need to be clean for the King," she says quietly.

I look away, my chest tight. "No, Aoki," I say. "*He's* the one who needs to get clean."

SEVENTEEN

LEI

A S THE CARRIAGE PUSHES THROUGH THE braying crowd of Ceremony Court, I thumb a spot in the fold of my black and gold hanfu where I hid a scrap of Lill's letter.

I'd read her message in secret last night, once the rest of the girls had fallen asleep. I hadn't realized how much I missed her. Like Aoki, my young Steel doe-form maid buoyed me through so much of my time as a Paper Girl with her sweet, optimistic presence. I'd cried happy tears, laughing at her jokes and vivid descriptions of life in the Night Houses, with the courtesans doting on her just as she deserves. Then I'd torn a single character from her letter before holding the paper to my lantern, the edges curling and blackening, Lill's scrawl disappearing into ash.

"Stop fussing," Madam Himura snaps. "You need to look presentable at dinner."

The warmth Lill's letter gave me has all but dried up now.

I twine my hands in my lap and press my cheek closer to the window—not that I want to look at the blur of demon faces passing by. Their noise is a wave, seeming to batter the palanquin even though our carriers hold us steady. Along with the crushed-cherry sunset, it only serves to remind me of what I just saw.

What I was *made* to watch.

"Didn't fancy volunteering this time, hmm?" Madam Himura asks, sly.

I grit my teeth, trying to block out the images. The King's wicked grin. Naja and five guards, raising their blades. Crimson bursts and the slump of six bodies falling in unison. The wild sound of the audience, eager for blood, or perhaps just for blood that isn't theirs, grateful each time the King punishes another because it means they have been spared.

Another execution. And this time, no Wren to comfort me. No secret fingers woven through mine. No hidden white offerings or furtive sky salute.

From my place at the King's side, I could practically smell the terror of the demons as they were forced to their knees before us. Even with their faces half covered by the blank, flesh-colored masks customary for court executions, their fear—and defiance—was evident. One of them, a boar-woman who ran a stall in City Court that made the best cendol in the palace, shouted out after the King called for the guards to ready their weapons. A desperate cry of *The gods see the truth!* before the plunge of a sword silenced her.

"I doubt they did it."

Madam Himura's tone is goading. Heat rises in me, but I hold it down.

"Not that it matters," she goes on, pressing, pushing, fingers in a wound. "If they incited enough suspicion for the Heavenly Master to have them executed, the palace is better off without them. And yet. Simple restaurant and shop owners from City Court. How would they have had the resources to pull off such an attack? No," she says. "Something like that would have been well coordinated. Part of a larger plan. It would have come from *within* the court. Demons with power. Connections." She clicks her beak. "I've been wondering about that smug Night House mistress for a while now."

"Oh?" I say. "Then perhaps I'd better tell the King. He should know he made a mistake with today's execution—and that *you* are the one to accuse him."

Madam Himura's eagle eyes flare. She looks as if she is considering reaching for my neck.

How easy it would be for either of us. I wonder if this is part of the King's twisted punishment. Every day, be near those you hate without being able to do a thing about it, and be close to those you love now they do not love *you* anymore.

The crowds of the Outer Courts disappear as we return to the heart of the palace, shadows deepening as the sun dips behind the palace walls.

Tonight's celebratory banquet—because of course, an execution is to be celebrated—is being held in a garden in Royal Court. A perfectly trimmed lawn stretches to high stone walls trailing with wisteria and roses, their red buds like gaping wounds. A servant welcomes me as I step out into the dusky spring eve. Under a canopy of magically suspended lanterns, demons swill about, their idle chatter abrasive after the scene we just left.

"Stand up straight," Madam Himura hisses at me. "Honestly, did you learn nothing from Mistress Eira and I?"

"I learned about cruelty," I say. "And betrayal. I learned how some people, *weak* people, will do anything for a bit of power or comfort, even if they have to trample over others to get it."

And for once, it's Madam Himura who looks as though she's been slapped.

While she gapes at me in offense, Commander Razib approaches. "Lei-zhi. Madam Himura. This way."

We cross the busy lawn to an emerald pagoda at the far side of the garden. Conversation drifts under the pipes and flowing urhu music. Most is the usual court chitchat that accompanies these events: plum-wine stock discussions between two financial advisers; an official's wife simpering to her counterpart, *Oh, you* must *visit the lotus ponds in Marazi, they're simply* stunning *this time of year!* But halfway across the lawn, my ears snag on hushed tones so clearly out of place.

"You heard what happened to the Hua-lings?"

"Terrible, just terrible. As with General Brahm's and Councilor Lee's families in the eastern Xienzo uprising. Poor Councilor Lee has been inconsolable ever since. He wasn't even at the execution today. Faked sickness, I'm assuming, though gods forbid word gets back to the King. So many good demons lost."

"And how many more until the King takes action?"

"Hush! You cannot talk like that, Yong. Not here…"

I spot the retreating backs of two low-level court officials. Madam Himura glares after them, no doubt making a mental note of their names.

"What eastern Xienzo uprising?" I ask her.

"Nothing that concerns you."

"It's my province. Of course it concerns me."

"Han is your province."

"Han is *nothing* to me."

In a whirl of feathers, Madam Himura drags me into the shadows of a nearby magnolia tree, bringing our faces so close my startled reflection is mirrored in her glassy yellow eyes.

"Listen to me, girl," she snarls, her rancid breath hitting me full force. "You think you are so powerful now you've gained a touch of status in the court? Well, enjoy your snappy remarks. At the end of the day, we both know how little it means. Once the war is over, this Moonchosen charade will be done with, and the King will cast you aside like the worthless keeda you are."

"*You* should know," I shoot back, "given how easily he cast *you* aside."

Madam Himura seems to double in size as her feathers stand on end. "The King still needed *me* enough to keep me in the court. What do you think happened to Mistress Eira, stupid girl? She was executed. What else?" For a second, her fearsome look falters. That tiredness I saw in her when we first met after my return reappears behind her composed exterior. Then her beaked face twists back into its ugly sneer. "Mistress Eira's position in the court was expendable—just as yours will be. So go ahead. Spout witty comebacks. Be proud of your kin's pathetic uprisings. For every handful of demons Papers manage to kill, we will tear down a thousand more of you." She rakes a taloned finger along my brow. "There will be no need for Doctor Uo this time. When the King is done with you, I'll personally inscribe your brand myself. You're more than rotten, girl—you *are* rot. You have brought poison into this palace. You have destroyed everything."

Something pained lies behind Madam Himura's tone; it's clear her fall from grace has hurt her far more than she lets on. But I have little sympathy to spare her. I'm reeling from the news about Mistress Eira. Her beautiful, serene face floats across my vision, twisting a clot of horror under my ribs. Because no matter how much she let me down, I still cared for her. Had hoped she'd be spared after the Moon Ball even though Madam Himura is right—*my* actions condemned them both.

"Honorable members of the court!" A magnified voice rings out

across the garden, the music trailing away. "Presenting our Heavenly Master, our gods' blessed ruler and commander of all beings
who walk the mortal realm, the Demon King!"

Clothes rustle as we all sink to our knees. As we wait for hoof-
fall, my mind still whirring from Madam Himura's revelation, I
note grimly that I've heard the King's official announcement so
many times I could recite it in my sleep—

I take a sharp breath.

Tonight's announcement was different.

Demon King. The royal announcers have only ever called him the
King before—because why clarify? Of course any King of Ikhara
would be a demon. I try to tell myself it doesn't mean anything
as the King's hooves sound, muffled by the grass. Yet, I know well
enough by now nothing in the court is done without intention.

When we lift our heads, the King stands on the pagoda, arms
wide. "Moonchosen," he calls. "Come join me."

I don't move.

Whispers slink through the crowd. There's an awkward cough as
the wait stretches on.

"*Moonchosen*," he repeats, harder now.

The title seems to be a condemnation. Chosen for what? Great-
ness, my parents told me. Power and purpose, according to Ketai.
Luck, for my customers back in our herb shop. For the King and
his court: the gods' blessing. A Paper Girl tied to her Demon King.

Madam Himura jabs her cane into my side with only a mild
attempt at discretion. "Go!"

I lurch to my feet. Demon eyes glint at me everywhere I turn. The
thrum of my heart pools into the soles of my feet as I pad through
the packed gathering. Only the guards remain standing, ready to
act upon a second's notice.

When I reach the pagoda, I finally lock eyes with the King.

His arms, draped in matching black and gold, are still flung wide, and as I get closer, I notice they're trembling. His smile seems stretched, weird and shaky at the edges, as though it's pinned to his face.

The King is *nervous*, I realize.

Why?

A dark premonition wings to life in my chest.

My shadow grows heavier as I step up to join him on the pagoda. The moment I'm within reach, he grabs for my hand. I instinctively flinch away, making him fumble before he captures my fingers.

He addresses the expectant crowd. "Members of the court. My fellow demons. After an ugly yet necessary afternoon, I am pleased to bring you something more...joyful."

The way he speaks the word makes it sound anything but.

"As your King," he says, "I've always tried my best to unite our three castes. As a court, we strive for unity. Patience. Peace. We work hard to ensure every demon and human is able to take his proper gods-given place in our great kingdom. Yet here we are, at war with those we once considered friends. Have our efforts been for nothing?"

The stillness deepens. My gaze skims the audience—latching on five figures kneeling directly in front of the pagoda.

The Paper Girls.

They stand out in a sea of demons. Each of their faces—even Blue's—is painted in shock, but it's Aoki's expression that breaks me. Tears stream down her face. Her mouth hangs open in a silent scream. She's grasping a fistful of her robes as if it's the only thing stopping her from flying to her feet and running from this place. Running from the King.

From *me*.

And I know then that my premonition is right.

Wondering why I sent them back to you, perhaps?

Yes, my King.

Don't worry. You will find out soon enough.

The King's maniacal grin pushes wider, his nails digging into my skin, and for a second, I feel pity so strong it blisters everything else away; pity for this sad, half crazed demon, every bit as trapped as I am, forced to wear a mask, day in, day out, until he's worn it so long it's welded to his skin. How can he even *breathe* if it's every bit as suffocating as the one he's forced upon me?

The King called me haunted. But he is the one who lives as a ghost, a shadow self inhabiting a dying world.

"The gods have spoken to me!" the King exclaims. "In this time of conflict, we must come together even stronger than before. In place of discord, we must cultivate harmony. And so it is thus I announce, just as the gods have blessed me with an heir, they also blessed me with the Moonchosen's return for a special purpose. In eight days, under the prosperous eye of the full moon, Lei-zhi will take her place at my side as my wife—as our Paper Queen!"

For one long beat, nothing happens. Everything is frozen: the garden, the audience, my soul, the air.

Then a few tentative cheers break through, before, in a sudden wave of noise, the crowd goes wild. The force of it drowns me. Like at the execution, the demons shout and roar and drum their feet so wildly it's impossible to tell whether they are excited or alarmed, joyous or mad with rage. Frenzied faces stare out at me, but my eyes are fixed on my friends.

Aoki is a wreck. She shakes her head slowly, hands shaking where she's clutching her chest, as if trying to hold together a breaking heart.

Back when we were Paper Girls, she told me that the King had said he was considering making her his Queen. Now here I am, exactly where she fantasized about being.

Aoki's dream.

My nightmare.

As the King holds our arms aloft in fake celebration, a single thought floats to the forefront of my mind: the character concealed within my robes. The single word scribbled in Lill's messy hand.

Love.

It's what I see on Aoki's crushed face.

It's what I hoped to share one day with the person I'd marry—not through force, but choice.

Not a husband, but a wife.

A girl with warm catlike eyes and dimples in her cheeks when she smiles, which is not often, but when it does happen it feels like magic. A girl who gave me hope when everything seemed lost. Who drew me up when I thought I might forever be on my hands and knees, crawling blindly through the dark. A girl who taught me a heart could be as powerful as a blade—even if, right now, it feels like the worst thing of all. Because while a blade may only be broken once, a heart can be broken eight thousand times over.

Still holding our hands high, the King hisses at me from the corner of his lips.

"Smile."

EIGHTEEN

WREN

LEAVING THE SOUTHERN SANCTUARY was harder than Wren anticipated. Five days of respite and care had replenished their group. Lady Dunya and her bird demons looked healthy again after long baths in the healing waters and the shamans' attention—just as they'd helped Wren's pain from her injury. Some of the darkness that had clung to Merrin since his return to the Jade Fort had sloughed off. He'd made jokes around the fire at night, and though Wren didn't join them, the others snorted with laughter, Ahma Goh loudest of all. Khuen had even made friends with one of the bird demons, a pretty hawk-girl called Samira who was a fellow archer. She seemed to have melted his apathy a little, encouraging him to integrate with the group. That's what they'd become in those five days—a group. And the sanctuary a home.

They left at twilight. No one spoke as they made the hike to the rocky outcrop from where they'd take flight. A few of the shamans came with them to weave enchantments of concealment. Wren had offered to help, but Ahma Goh insisted she save her energy. She didn't need to say what for.

Though Wren had done her best not to think too much of the upcoming battle or the dark plans her father might have for her Xia magic, trying instead to do as Ahma Goh said and use this rare opportunity to relax, she hadn't been able to push the war from her mind. Now the anticipation reared again with full force. In less than twenty-four hours, the Hannos would storm Marazi and the Black Port in a simultaneous attack. If things went well, the Hidden Palace would be next.

And with it, Lei.

Wren still dreamed of her every night. And she still woke each morning feeling as though she'd lost a limb. More than a limb; half of her heart.

Half of her *soul*.

Ahma Goh embraced Wren warmly when they arrived at their departure point. "Good luck, child," she said. "Remember what I told you."

"You told me a lot of things, Ahma Goh."

The old shaman laughed, but her face was serious. She grasped Wren's hands close. "I mean it, child. Life is a gift from the gods. Do not waste it on war and suffering."

"I'll do my best," Wren replied.

"Well," Ahma Goh said proudly, "as a daughter of both the Xia and the Hanno, *that* is a lot."

They shared one last smile before Wren led her group to the cliff edge. Lady Dunya had proposed to carry Wren herself, and Wren hadn't the heart to argue. When Wren made the signal, the swan-woman took off with a push of her legs and firm strokes of her feathered arms. There were more wingbeats as the rest of the birds followed.

Wren hunkered low against the wind. She scanned the skies and land for signs of danger. What she found instead was almost as bad.

On their way to the Cloud Palace, Wren, Merrin, and Khuen had flown over a handful of demon-destroyed settlements and places where the Sickness had clearly taken root: miles of dead farmland; riverside towns where once-fishable banks had turned to sludge. Now they were nearing the heart of the kingdom, the effects of the Sickness were even more prominent. They passed fields of rotten crops, burst riverbanks, forests dank with decay. Halfway through the flight, they saw a ruined village. Next to it was a strange mound, flickering with dying cinders.

Even at their height the smell of charred flesh was unmistakable.

Wren's stomach roiled, hate reawakening dark wings in her chest. The sanctuary had provided her respite from it, too, with its peace and laughter and conviviality. But now her bitterness returned. The way the King was going, never mind a war to decide Ikhara's fate.

They'd be lucky if there would be anything left to save.

When they reached the tented encampment outside Marazi, Wren's boots barely hit the ground before Commander Chang was storming toward her, voice booming over the clamor.

"Lady Wren! You're late!"

Wren swept back her wind-tangled hair, resisting a sigh. She drew herself to full height as he pushed his way through the throng, the bird demons stretching after the long flight. Hanno clan members welcomed them with cups of tea while a few shamans and doctors—presumably expecting the White Wing to be in worse shape after months of imprisonment—wove between them, looking both wondrous and a little lost.

"Who is that idiot?" Lady Dunya asked, smoothing down her pearly coat.

"The head of our army," Wren said.

The swan-woman shot her a disdainful look. "You trusted a *man* with that position?"

"Lady Wren!" Chang was still fighting toward her. "We were expecting you at least half an hour ago! This is—*oof!*"

Khuen had stepped in his way. "Oops," the boy drawled, sloping off with a disinterested yawn.

Chang strode forward, his cheeks red. He looked between the two of them. "I thought the famous White Wing army would be more organized than this," he huffed.

Lady Dunya's glare hardened. "I shall let you deal with . . . *this*," she told Wren, shooting one final imperious look at the Commander before sweeping away.

As Chang began to speak, Wren cut him off, already moving. "Where is my father?"

The war-tent brimmed with activity. Soldiers drank and polished weapons, blue-robed Hannos and warriors from their allied clans alike. In one corner, a kitchen had been set up. In another, a make-shift gambling den had popped up, cheers and groans sounding over the clatter of mahjong tiles. There were many cat demons, and Wren's mood lifted at the thought of seeing Lova and Nitta again.

The Commander hurried after her. "There's been a change of plans," he said. "Lord Hanno is to lead the attack on the Black Port. I have been sent here to oversee—"

Wren whirled. "My father isn't here?"

"If you'd let me *finish*, Lady Wren, I was about to explain that, after great deliberation, the council decided it would be better if Lord Hanno leads the Black Port attack while I conduct the take-over of Marazi. With your help, of course."

A hand clapped Wren's shoulder.

"What dear Chang here means is," a husky voice corrected, "your father has chosen *you* to lead us tomorrow. Chang is simply here to help. He's to listen to—and follow—every order you give. Isn't that right, Commander?"

The man blustered, growing redder by the second.

Wren turned to find Lova's grinning face. Nitta appeared on her other side. The leopard girl had one hand on the wheel of her chair and a half eaten cone of roti in the other, the wrapped bread almost overflowing with the fragrant curry ladled within.

Nitta caught some of the sauce with her tongue. "Nice trip?" she asked, jade eyes twinkling.

"It wasn't exactly the warmest of welcomes," Wren said.

"Hope you left a bad review in the guest book."

Despite herself, Wren's lips quirked. "You know, it wasn't exactly high on my list of priorities."

Nitta and Lova snickered. Commander Chang—chest still puffed like an overstuffed duck at a New Year's banquet—said loudly, "Lord Hanno *personally* entrusted me with the care of this battalion—"

"Wren's battalion," Lova corrected.

His teeth were gritted. "Yes. And having been Lord Hanno's chief army Commander for over twenty years—"

Nitta pulled a face. "Getting along a bit for a warrior, aren't you?"

"—I *imagine* your ladyship would *appreciate* my advice as to the coming battle. Lord Hanno has outlined a detailed plan of attack—"

"Then I think that should be good enough, Commander, don't you?" With a patronizing wave, Lova stole Wren away. "Come on. You can deal with Chang later. Tien demanded we bring you straight to her when you arrived. Says if you're to lead us into battle tomorrow you had better be properly nourished. And I don't know about you, but that woman scares me eight thousand times more than *Chang*."

"Wren!" Nitta exclaimed, grabbing her attention. "Look what I learned to do!"

Nitta was leaning so far back in her chair it looked as if she'd fall out any second. Then, with a swift jerk, she tipped to one side to balance on one wheel. She spun, head thrown back in laughter.

A group of nearby soldiers let out an appreciative whoop.

Nitta grinned. "See? Even better than legs."

Though Wren felt a guilty tug, she returned Nitta's smile. She couldn't believe how well Nitta had adapted to her situation. Or rather, she could, because it was Nitta. This was the demon who'd lost her brother yet had pushed on with their mission without complaint. The demon who always had a kind word for anyone who needed it, even if they had none to offer in return.

"It's amazing," Wren told her.

Lova rolled her eyes. "If you want to join the circus. You're a warrior, Nitta. I didn't make the chair for silly tricks."

Nitta ignored her. "Bo would be *so* jealous," she said, with the tiniest crack of grief.

Wren clasped her shoulder. "He would be so *proud*."

As Nitta beamed at her, Lova leaned in. "We've got a lot to get caught up on," she muttered.

Wren immediately braced for bad news. "What happened?"

"I'll tell you in a minute. Anyway, how did things go on your end? Seemed the prison break went well—though I saw Feathers made it back alive. Suppose you can't win them all."

As they neared the kitchen, Wren slowed, but Lova steered her on past the crowd milling about the bubbling pots.

"Lo, I thought you said—"

"Wait," she hissed. "He's still following. Ugh. I was hoping he'd have given up by now." She angled her head. "Nitta?"

"On it."

The leopard-girl dropped back. There was a blast of steam as one of the cooks lifted the lid of a pot of curry, and as they disappeared within the warm pillows of vapor there was a crash behind them and a yowl of pain.

"Oh, Commander," Nitta chirped, "I am *so* sorry! I'm so clumsy these days, you know, this big ol' thing."

Wren spotted Tien throwing a towel over her shoulder and storming toward the mess Nitta had created.

Lova and Wren slipped through the mob of hungry clan members. Then they were out, food-scented steam billowing behind them as Lova drew Wren away from the tent. The nighttime chill pricked goosebumps along her skin, along with the buzz of perimeter enchantments the Hanno shamans had set.

"Lo," Wren said, twisting from Lova's hold when they were a good way from the camp, "if my father trusts Chang, then so do I. We don't have to like the man, but whatever you've got to say, we shouldn't have to hide it from him."

"I'm not. I'm hiding *him* from *you*."

Their war-tent was pitched in an expanse of fields a few miles out of Marazi. Wren was distracted from Lova's odd statement as, eyes adjusting to the dim light, she began to make out other settlements nearby. The refugee camps. People who'd lost homes and work to the Sickness had flocked to Marazi for help, when in actuality they'd been all but ignored. It was terrible, but it offered the Hannos the perfect hiding place.

The shelters were spread out in haphazard bunches of tents, some lit with lanterns, most shadowed. A few sported flags with clan crests, though in the dark Wren couldn't make them out. They no doubt mostly belonged to Paper clans, though according to everything she'd heard, more demon clans were being displaced by the effects of the Sickness, fueling rifts between Steels and Moons over which side of the war to support.

The settlements were more tightly knit the closer they grew to the city.

Marazi. Han's capital.

Unlike the Hidden Palace, Marazi had no perimeter walls. Instead, it'd been built in the middle of the River Zebe on a great spur of earth that split the river in two, the water and the rocky bluffs acting as the capital's barricades. With only four bridges leading in—one at each compass point—and its high advantage, the city was well defended. Over time, Marazi's population had expanded, spilling past the river's borders, though the densely packed buildings along the banks across the waters were not as elegant as those within. They made up the New City, home to Marazi's poorer districts. The area within the river's borders was known as the Old City, where the capital's wealthier residents lived.

The glow of Marazi's lights were hazy, wreathed in mist rising from the river. Wren's heart hammered. Tomorrow, in just a few hours, their army would be there, right where those lights were— with her at the helm.

"It's poisoned," Lova said.

They were standing side by side, staring across the camps to the dim glitter of the distant capital.

"I know," Wren said, thinking of the ugly current that lay at the heart of everything the King and his demons did across Ikhara.

"No. I mean it's actually *poisoned*. The river. The water."

Wren turned. "What?"

"Your father had Chang and a small group of soldiers ride out early to poison the river," Lova explained heavily. "Marazi gets its water from the Zebe. It feeds through channels into reservoirs beneath the Old City. There are filters, but Ketai must have gotten his spies within the city to damage them. None of us were supposed to know, but when we arrived yesterday there were bodies in the river—too many to be coincidence. Papers from the camps. They must have been drinking from the river. Chang gave us strict orders not to do so ourselves. Now we know why."

Wren's throat was tight. "You're sure?"

Lova's mouth twisted. "I didn't even have to force it out of him. When I confronted him, he was practically boasting—*Wren!* Wait!"

Wren had begun to charge off without thought. Lova grabbed her. Wren threw her off with a burst of power that crackled the air between them, snapping awake the pain in her hips.

"There are innocent people in that city, Lo!" she shouted. "And the *camps*—"

"Wren," Lova said evenly, "this is *war*. I don't approve of Ketai going behind our backs to do it, and I certainly don't like Chang's attitude, but you have to admit, it was a good idea—"

Another surge of magic flew from Wren, a wave of glacial wind that made Lova throw a hand in front of her face, her marigold tunic and trousers flapping.

"A good idea." Wren pushed the words past gritted teeth. "To poison *an entire city*."

Lova cocked a hip, her brows raised. "What were you planning on having us do tomorrow during the attack? Talk to the soldiers? Ask the city's people to kindly let us take over their home?"

"We were only to attack when necessary—"

"And what is necessary, in a war? Killing one soldier? Two? A whole battalion? What about the innocents caught in the cross-fire? What about a shaman boy giving his life to save yours? The murder of a Clan Lady's daughter? A family of Papers burned alive? A young soldier tortured for information?"

Blood roared in Wren's ears. Each of Lova's words impaled her, drove through her like swords.

Why was it truth hurt more than lies? She supposed there was at least comfort in lies. Truth forced you to stare yourself in the mirror, bare in every sense of the word, and acknowledge the person looking back at you as your own doing.

Truth always caught you in the end.

And it was merciless.

Wren looked back over the mess of encampments jumbled across the fields—then on to the city in the distance, where silver mist lifting from its waters made it look as though it were already haunted.

She asked, "How long does it take for the water in the reservoirs to be distributed throughout the city?"

"It's a two-day turnover. They'll already have started to drink the poisoned water."

Wren faced Lova. "Is the attack tomorrow *necessary*, then?"

"The poison was only to weaken the King's forces," Lova replied tiredly. "There'll be plenty of demons who didn't drink the affected water, or who aren't too sick to fight. It'll still be a difficult battle. Just not quite so difficult as before."

Wren spun on her heels, making for their camp.

Lova fell in beside her. "You're not planning to murder Chang, are you?" she asked, her teasing tone not fully convincing. When Wren didn't reply, she added, "Or your father, the next time you see him?"

Wren stopped, her heart clenching. "Do you know if he poisoned the Black Port, too?"

"I asked Chang," Lova admitted. "But he claimed he didn't know and I believe him. Honestly, I doubt Ketai would have risked it. Marazi—it's the court's cultural heart. The Hidden Palace is its political one. They're both symbols of the King's power. But the Black Port is integral to Ikhara's livelihood. Every clan and caste depends on the city and its trade. Ketai will want to take it with as little force as necessary."

There was that word again. *Necessary.*

"Gather as many of your cats as possible," Wren ordered Lova. "I'll assemble shamans and medics. We're going to spread the word among the refugees they're not to drink any water they've collected from the river. We'll do what we can to help those who are already sick."

Lova shook her head. "That'll take hours, Wren. You need to rest—"

"Then it'll take hours. And I will not rest."

"Don't you think Nitta and I thought of all of this already?" Lova said with an impatient growl. "I'm not as coldhearted as you seem to imagine. But it's too dangerous. There are bound to be spies among the refugees. They could ambush us, or warn the guards at Marazi—"

"Then those are *necessary* risks. The court knows Marazi is one of our targets. Our attack won't come as much of a shock."

"Even so—"

Wren raised her voice. "I am in charge here, Lo, and these are my orders. Are you challenging them?"

The lion-girl's bronze eyes flashed. She looked slightly taken aback—but mostly impressed. She lowered her head, a smirk playing on her lips. "No, General Wren," she said. "I am not."

NINETEEN

WREN

WREN HAD HEARD ENOUGH SCREAMS in her lifetime to recognize what kind of distress triggered each one.

She was holding a wet towel to the forehead of a feverish Paper child, the boy's fathers whispering prayers at his side, when they began. High-pitched, quick, sharp; these screams flashed like fire. They came straight from the gut. They weren't the undulating wails of anguish that had chorused the long night and day Wren, Lova, Nitta, and the others spent tending to the sick and the dead in the refugee camps. These were screams of terror.

Wren handed the towel to the closest of the boy's fathers and strode from the tent.

The orange light from the sinking sun rolled across the fields like molten gold. In the distance, the striking silhouette of Marazi's Old City loomed. The faraway cries and yells seemed to be growing louder, a rising tide of panic.

Wren's horse was waiting for her, a black mare with a plaited chestnut mane named Eve. Wren swung herself onto her saddle. She kicked Eve into movement when Lova rode into view on the horse she'd taken as her own from the Jade Fort, the great black-and-white stallion called Panda.

"Marazi officials are blaming the poisoning on the refugees," Lova said, pulling Panda around to fall in beside her. They wove through the packed campsite. "Lord Anjiri has ordered the camps to be razed to the ground. I've sent Nitta back to warn our people. One of the shamans is rounding up the others who were helping."

"Have them evacuate the Papers to our camp," Wren said. "I need you to find Chang. Tell him to ready our soldiers. We can't wait until tonight—we attack now." Knowing what was coming, she turned to glare at Lova, drawing one her swords. "I can handle them until the rest of you join me. Go."

Though she looked reluctant, Lova did as she said.

Wren rode Eve in the opposite direction. Papers and the occasional demon face peeked out from the ramshackle shelters. Many were already fleeing, recognizing the signs of approaching danger all too well.

Wren pulled Eve through deft swerves to avoid crushing the running figures. She lifted her sword over her head so the light caught the metal. "Leave your things!" she bellowed. "The Demon King's men are coming, and they will not hesitate to kill you! Head south—our people will help you to our camp. Anyone strong enough to assist, carry the sick!"

Wren urged Eve through the increasingly frenetic campsite. Fire bloomed ahead, where tents closest to the city burned. Demons on horses and even war-bears rode through the crush, thrusting torches to set alight both fabric and skin.

Wren charged. Pain screamed from her injury with each buck, and she welcomed it, hunting for the familiar slip into her Xia state—

A throwing star was flying at her face before she could find it.

She moved just in time. The metal star whistled past her ear.

Wren ducked the second, then deflected the next with her sword. She couldn't see her attacker. Everything was fire-lit, distorted shadows making it hard to pick out individual forms.

Another star came hurtling at her. The metallic clash of it meeting her sword made her teeth shiver.

She was almost at the northernmost part of the campsite now. Smoke billowed into the sky. Eve leaped over bodies as Wren took in the scene: demon hordes sweeping through burning shelters; refugees fleeing on foot. She marked the amethyst-and-bronze-tipped flag of Marazi's most prominent clan, the Orchids. Lord Anjiri was its leader and the ward of the city—and thus the demon who'd ordered this attack.

The demon Wren would need to take down if she was to stop it.

Another throwing star came at her. She moved too slow. It sliced her cheek, spilling blood—but she'd finally spotted her attacker. Wren pulled Eve around and stormed right for him.

The ape soldier rode a black bear. The creature was wild, frothing at the mouth. As it held its position, the demon put away his stars and drew a pair of spiked wheel-like rings the size of Wren's face: feng huo lun. He brandished them with a grin, still not moving, though they were only moments from colliding—

Wren swerved at the last second.

The ape demon jumped.

He slashed out as he flew past. Wren parried his attack, then pulled Eve around to face him again—only to find his war-bear rearing up.

It struck out with inches-long claws. Eve whinnied and stumbled back, almost pitching Wren off. She clung on, gripping her legs tight.

The ape soldier leaped again.

Wren flipped her blade up as a shield. As he crashed into her, both of them tussling on Eve's back, she drew her second sword and brought it around in a flashing arc of silver.

It dug a line up the soldier's side from hip to ear. Blood gushed over Wren in a torrent. She shoved the demon off her, then spat out blood and spurred Eve into movement before they were caught by the riderless bear as it thrashed in a rage.

Flames beat on all sides. The haphazard manner in which the refugee settlement had grown slowed the Marazi's soldiers in their attack, funneling them down narrow pathways between burning tents. It worked in Wren's favor. She followed each channel and cut down soldier after soldier, adding to the corpses spread-eagled on the blood-slick grass. Time passed not in seconds but in bodies. War was a rhythm, and Wren had found hers.

Then: hoof-beats. Familiar cries.

A wave of cobalt-robed riders interspersed with Amala yellow and splashes of other clans' colors rolled in across the plains. Flying above, the pearlescent armor of the White Wing loyalists reflected the firelight.

Commander Chang hollered something above the tumult. It was the first time Wren had been glad to see him. He charged into view on a black stallion. He wore an iron face mask, its exaggerated face twisted in a grimace. Lova was right behind him, blood on her clothes and fur. As they drew close, she led her horse, Panda, directly in the path of a Marazi soldier crawling on the ground. Bones crunched.

Even with his mask, Wren could tell Chang was livid. He drew level with her. "What in the *gods*—"

A discordant riot of horn blows drowned him out.

Beyond the twinkling lantern light of Marazi's New City, the bridge that led to the Old City was teeming with soldiers. More swarmed down its broad boulevards. Other guards rushed to man what Wren knew from preparations with her father's war council were cannons, located at intervals along the riverside of the Old City. Part of their plan had been to have their spies within the city rig them so they'd backfire—

Boom!

A shudder tore through the earth as one of the pavilions where a cannon was being loaded exploded. There were distant shrieks as debris and bodies slammed down upon nearby soldiers or splashed heavily in the Zebe.

"Oooh," Lova cooed, as if watching a fireworks display.

A second blast rent the air.

This time, the cannon worked as it was supposed to. There was a hurtling flare of smoldering metal before it crashed nearby, bowling over both Marazi and Hanno soldiers.

Across the smoldering campsite, the battle raged on. Their White Wing allies, though few in number, were taking out batches of Marazi demons at once, clutching them in their talons before flinging their screaming figures through the air. Some paces away, Khuen and his White Wing friend Samira sent arrows through the necks of soldiers with astonishing speed.

Chang was blustering something about how Wren had ruined their plans and *now* look at the mess they were dealing with.

She held up a bloody hand. "Time for a new plan. Let the soldiers come here. The refugees are being evacuated, so we may as well use this as a battleground, and we'll be at an advantage since we can see them coming. Plus, it'll minimize casualties."

"What about Lord Anjiri?" Chang said. "We need to capture him in order to take the city—"

"I can get to him."

"*You*, on your *own*—"

"Yes, Commander." Wren lifted her neck. "*Me*. Ketai Hanno's daughter and the only living member of the legendary Xia warriors, trained from birth to assassinate demons. Or perhaps you'd prefer to volunteer your services in my place?"

His face purpled.

"Return to your soldiers," she ordered. When he didn't move, Wren barked, "*Now!*"

As he drew his horse around, Wren addressed Lova. "It's too far to the next bridge. I'll have to swim."

"They'll spot you," she said.

"I'll hide myself."

"No, Wren. No more magic. You need to save your energy. Let me help—I'll create a distraction."

"With what?" Wren retorted impatiently. "Your beauty?"

Lova arched a brow. "Who's the one joking at inappropriate times now? While that would *obviously* work, I've got something else in mind."

"Fine." Wren yanked Eve around, knowing what Lova meant. "Blow something up, then."

"Oh, honey. I thought you'd never ask."

They kicked their horses into motion, hurtling away from the campsite and into the eerily quiet streets of Marazi's New City.

Its citizens were hiding in their homes, nervous faces peeking from shutters and cracked doorways. Wren and Lova took a less direct route to avoid the fresh wave of soldiers arriving from the southern bridge. Bird demons—some of Qanna's White Wing, perhaps—flew with them.

They left the horses in a deserted street before slinking through the shadows to the Zebe.

Lova peered over the stone wall that bordered the river. "Looks pretty grim," she said. The water roared past, murky and flashing from the burning pavilions. "Sure you're feeling up to it?"

Wren ignored her, already climbing over the wall. She rolled the sleeves and hems of her bloodstained clothes. Tying her hair back, she calculated her crossing by eye.

"I'll meet you at the Orchid Hall," Lova said.

"I don't need help," Wren replied automatically.

"I know you don't," Lova snapped. "If you hadn't realized by now, Wren, it's not always about you. *I* need to know you're going to be all right." Then she disappeared into the shadows with a swish of her tail.

Facing the water, Wren took a deep inhale—then leaped into the inky waters of the Zebe.

The cold shocked her, a frozen hand around her lungs. In an instant, the current clutched her, dragging her downstream far quicker than she'd anticipated. She kicked out and forced through the icelike water. Each movement was arduous, pain flourishing from her injured hips, lungs screaming, thighs aching.

Light rippled on the river's surface before the muted rumble of an explosion reached her through the water.

Wren sped upward. She gasped as she burst out, switching her strokes to cut through the choppy waves. A magnificent three-tiered pavilion close to Marazi's southern bridge was on fire, flames spilling into the sky.

At least Lova was having fun.

It took five more minutes of hard swimming to reach the steep bank of Marazi's Old City. Wren splayed on her back to catch her breath. Water splashed her legs. She ached all over, pain radiating from her burning hips into every inch of her. Even her *hair* hurt.

Lying there was the first break she'd had in almost twenty-four hours; already those magical days of peace at the Southern Sanctuary seemed like lifetimes ago. Would she be able to return, one day? Simply lie somewhere, without pressure weighing down on her, without the constant shadow of danger, and just feel the world turning?

As if in answer, a sweet voice whispered in her ear.

Get up, my love.

"Lei," Wren breathed.

She couldn't stop. Not until Lei was safely back at her side.

Gathering her strength, Wren staggered to her feet. She wrung out her clothes as best she could before clambering up the muddy slope.

The city center was busy with activity. Guards shouted, soldiers running this way and that. Lova's fire leaped from building to building, already eating up much of the quarter directly across from the bridge, causing bedlam among its residents, which in turn obstructed the soldiers trying to pass.

Wren turned her attention to her own target.

At fifteen levels, the Orchid Hall was by far the tallest building in Marazi. Its curved eaves reached high over the city like a giant bird's outstretched wings.

Wren made her way toward it, slinking like a cat through oil-dark shadows. The clan's pavilion was set within elegant gardens, its lacquered indigo walls carved with floral patterns. The edges of each roof, door, and window frame were bordered in bronze to match the clan's colors.

The Orchid were fox demons. Hanging lanterns glinted off their guards' russet pelts as they stalked the balconies and grounds.

Wren crept closer. She waited until the guards patrolling the base of the building passed before launching herself up the closest pillar.

She climbed swiftly. She swung herself up and over the curved edge of the roof, then crept nimbly across the stone tiles, repeating the same process for each floor.

By the time she reached the top, Wren was panting. Her pain was strong, fiercer after the respite the sanctuary had given her, and up this high the air was cold, lifting goose bumps beneath her wet clothes. Guards marched by, unaware of the girl watching them from the shadows. Beyond the balcony, light glowed from behind rice-paper doors.

Lord Anjiri's throne room.

Wren snuck across the tiles, approaching the southern side of the room. A few of the sliding screens were open, offering an unobstructed view of the city, all the way to where the battle at the refugee camps still raged.

Harried voices floated out.

"—three hundred and counting—"

"—the Lunar Pavilion just went down—"

"—General Gombei is requesting backup at South Bridge—"

Wren could see into the room now, and took stock in one sweeping look. Five guards to each entrance; eight maids kneeling along the edge of the room; two more serving tea for the six advisers huddled over the table, poring over maps and military legers. The throne in the center of the room sat empty. Its Clan Lord stood instead past the open screens, half blocked from view by a beam. The old fox gazed out over his city. Wind rippled his wizened auburn fur.

Wren drew one of her swords. She was about to make her move when the air blurred.

She had just enough time to draw her second sword as a demon dived at her.

The shriek of clashing metal shot through the night.

Wren's boots slid on the tiles as the demon pushed her back, until she felt her heels digging into the edge of the roof. Wren threw all her weight forward, but the demon girl was strong.

And Wren's grip was slipping.

From behind their grinding swords, Qanna's black eyes glinted. Qanna—Lady Dunya's daughter and her usurper. The new leader of the White Wing, allied now with the Demon King. Sister of Eolah, who Wren had murdered accidentally in Qanna's stead.

The pretty young swan demon's face was wrought with rage and a deep, hateful satisfaction. "Lady Wren," she spat. "So good of you to come. I had a feeling you would."

"Qanna—" Wren began.

She didn't get a chance to continue. With one strong thrust of her heavy jian, Qanna shoved her.

Wren felt her feet lose purchase. Then she was tipping, falling into the opening arms of the smoke-churned sky.

TWENTY

WREN

SHE GRABBED A FISTFUL OF QANNA'S robes at the last second.

Qanna lurched forward, opening her feathered arms wide to combat the sudden extra weight. In doing so, her sword caught Wren across the arm, tearing through her tunic and dragging a slash of red along her skin. The pain was fast and sharp. From where she hung, Wren still had hold of both her own swords. One was in the same fist that clung to Qanna's robes. The other swayed in the air behind her as she dangled from the roof.

With a grunt, Wren swung it around, using the momentum to fling herself back onto the rooftop.

Qanna batted her away the instant Wren's feet gained purchase. But Wren stepped back anyway, dual blades poised not to strike but to defend. "I don't want to kill you, Qanna," she said, almost the exact same words she'd used on Commander Teoh at the Cloud Palace.

And she hadn't killed the Commander—though someone else had. The girl glowered. "Pity," she snarled. "I'm very keen to kill *you*."

She lunged, just as Orchid guards came running.

In the moment she had to react, Wren threw all her energy into accessing her Xia state. She forced through the mudlike resistance—goddamned Sickness—and then, *oh*, being submerged in that vast lake of magic and might, a sensation so right, so fierce, so *good*.

Then she was moving.

Wren became a spinning top in slow motion, calm and poised, vibrating with a deep awareness. She noticed everything. The panting breaths of the guards as they ran to attack, only to be mowed down by her swords. Qanna's wingbeats as she retreated to the air. Lord Anjiri's surprised shout as he ran to take cover within the throne room. And smoke, smoke everywhere, clouds of it turning the air ashen.

More of Marazi was on fire than before. Had the battle reached the city? Had Lova simply gotten carried away with her explosives?

The questions entered and left Wren's mind, swift and fleeting. Right now, her job was to get to Lord Anjiri.

And there were demons in her way.

Blood sprayed her as she took out the fox guards one by one. Static crawled across her skin. Beneath her own pain—louder now, a weighted thrum in her bones and muscles—the enchantments Wren called were painful themselves. But she dragged the magic out, bending it to her will.

This time, Wren was prepared when Qanna dived for her.

She'd cut down the last of the fox guards. Only the cowering maids and advisers were left, huddled in the throne room behind furniture or pressed against the walls, too scared to move in case it risked drawing her attention. Then there was Lord Anjiri, who *knew* he had Wren's attention. He was running full pelt for the stairs.

The skirr of wind from Qanna's wings hit Wren's neck. A moment later the girl was upon her, slashing out with razor-laced talons.

Wren parried. Thrust upward with a kick. Qanna dodged, then

came barreling toward her, trying to push her closer to the lip of the roof.

Wren rolled sideways, then leaped down to the veranda. Ignoring Qanna's screech of impatience and the howls of the terrified maids and advisers, she sprinted across the throne room—stowing one of her swords as she went—to where Lord Anjiri had just disappeared out of sight.

She launched herself over the edge of the staircase and landed on top of him with a crash.

The crisp *snap* of something breaking shot through the air. The old demon let out a wail.

Wren dragged the Clan Lord to his feet by the wizened hair at his neck. Blood gushed from his nose. By the way he whimpered, clutching at his ribs, he'd broken at least one of them, too.

"*Stop,*" Wren told the guards running toward them, bringing the blade to the Clan Lord's neck. Her Xia voice echoed with power.

They stopped.

Wren sensed their fear at the sight of her—a Paper Girl unlike any they'd seen before, white-eyed and blood-soaked, magic billowing off her in icy waves.

"*Where are the war-horns?*" she asked Lord Anjiri.

He answered haltingly. "In...throne room."

Keeping hold of him, one sword still at his throat, Wren backed up the stairs. Pain was rippling through her in brighter waves, and she felt her connection to the earth's qi flicker. She almost lost it, just as she'd lost her footing on the roof minutes ago. But like then she clung on, even as the effort made her vision swim.

"*Tell your guards to stay away. They are not to follow. Some should alert the rest of your men that I have you. The battle is over.*"

"Do...as she...says," the demon choked out.

Though half his soldiers looked as if they wanted to object, they held off. Some hurried away, presumably following Wren's directions, as more arrived, footsteps pounding from rooms and stairs below. While Wren hoisted Lord Anjiri out of sight, one of the guards shouted, "No! The Hanno girl has him. If we go, she'll kill him."

Back in the throne room, the maids and advisers were still huddled for cover. A few squealed when they saw Wren and their freshly bloodied Clan Lord reappear. Wren was braced—she'd expected Qanna to be there, barreling toward her the second she returned. But the swan-girl was nowhere to be seen.

"*The war-horns,*" Wren hissed in Lord Anjiri's ear. "*Now.*"

"In the . . . alcove. North side . . . room."

Wren dragged him to the opposite end of the room where a spiral staircase was tucked into the corner. It twisted upward out of sight.

Wren's sight pulsed, a wave of dizziness flowing over her. Her Xia state fell away. Clenching her jaw, she threw herself back into it.

It felt less like entering a lake and more like crashing head-first into a wall of ice. Wren hissed, but didn't relent.

She lugged Lord Anjiri up the steps. They arrived in a small room within the building's pitched roof. Ash-thick wind hit them. The space was open at the front with a view over the smoking rooftops of Marazi, the darkness broken with flickers of cinnamon flames. A series of bone-carved war-horns lined the balcony.

Wren shoved Lord Anjiri at them, sword to the nape of his neck. "*Call the battle off.*"

Cradling his ribs, he stumbled to the middle war-horn, pressed his mouth to it, and blew.

The sound resonated out across the city. Unlike earlier, this horn's call was light-pitched, almost melodic. It was a sound of peace. Of surrender.

"*Again,*" Wren said.

Halfway through the second blow there was a flash of white beyond the balcony.

In a flurry of feathers, Qanna smashed into the Clan Lord, sending him sprawling across the floor, before crashing into Wren.

The impact winded Wren—and threw her from her Xia state.

Knocked from her hand, her sword slid across the floorboards.

Wren reached for its twin. But before she could free it, Qanna dug her talons into Wren's shoulders and, with heavy strokes of her wings, flew them backward over the balcony and up into the flame-limned sky.

Wren's legs dangled. Pain screeched where Qanna's talons pierced her flesh. She clasped Qanna's ankles with both hands; if she released her, Wren would plunge to her death.

Qanna flew higher.

Wren struggled. She grasped for her magic, daos streaming from her mouth. Yet nothing worked. She was too tired. Too weak. As everyone had warned her since Jana, she'd used up too much energy and not rested enough to replenish it.

This is it, a small voice in her head said.

For a moment, Wren felt relief. How simple it would be to let go. It'd be like reaching for magic when it was easy: a slip, a fall, then that wide, eternal lake. Only this time its waters would be black, and she would not reemerge. She would sink like a stone. It would be quick and pain free.

And then horror snatched the idea away. Because this could not be it. It was not how this would end.

It was not how *hers and Lei's story* would end.

"Let *go!*" cried Qanna.

She was jerking, trying to toss Wren off. Her flying was erratic, unbalanced by Wren's weight.

Wren clung to Qanna's ankles with every scrap of energy she had left. Because falling through a burning sky to crash upon tiles or trees or stone was not how she would go. She had so many things still to do. A war to win. Friends to save. A new, better nation to build. A lover to kiss and hold and whisper velvet truths to in the middle of the night; to apologize to; to heal with; to just lie alongside, feeling the slow turn of a peaceful world.

A memory came to Wren then, as cleanly as the first scent of snow.

A night at the Hidden Palace, a few weeks out from the New Year. Lei in her arms, the pair of them twined in the darkness of her bedroom. Lei asked Wren where her name came from and Wren said she didn't know, which was true. Ketai had never told her.

"Well," Lei said, "can I tell you what it means to me?"

Love bloomed through Wren's chest so strongly then she could have cried. Instead, all she'd said was, "Tell me."

Lei. Whispering in the dark. "I didn't think it suited you at first. Remember that morning at the bathing courtyard, when Blue insulted my mother? You stopped me attacking her, and after you left, Lill told me your name. I remember thinking how strange it was a girl like you"—she giggled—"I called you Cat-girl in my head before that, because you were—*are*—so fierce. And wrens... they're these common birds. They fly across our skies every day, without ceremony. Hunted by bigger birds. But now I think it's perfect. Just like your namesakes, you've done your work day in, day out, all your life, without complaint. Without ever knowing what a wondrous thing that is. How wondrous *you* are."

Tears slipped from Wren's eyes then, though the shadows hid them. Lei started to say more, and Wren silenced her with her mouth, hoping she could feel everything she felt and everything she wanted to say within the liquid dance of their lips, the roll and slip and tender glide of their bodies as they moved together in the dark.

Wren would be that bird for Lei. She would cross the skies a million times over to get back to her. That's exactly what there was now: miles between them, and in those miles waited the King's men, with teeth and fire and a hunger for revenge. Yet Wren knew she'd fight as hard as she could to find her way back to Lei. Because that is what birds do.

No matter how far they fly from home, they never forget their way back.

Fresh vitality roared through her. With a cry, Wren kicked her legs forward, then threw them back, swinging herself in a backward arc, so her boots smashed into the small of Qanna's back.

Qanna dipped.

Before the girl could reassert herself, Wren swung herself up again, this time releasing her hands from Qanna's talons so she was twisting, gliding through the air. Then she threw her arms out and grabbed Qanna's robes, hooking her arms over the swan-girl's shoulders.

Qanna screamed in fury as Wren clung to her back. Her wings flapped hard, batting Wren where she was nestled between them.

Ember-flecked air streamed past Wren's cheeks. Qanna was soaring lower, back toward the Orchid Hall rooftop. She knew she couldn't fight Wren while the girl was on her back—and Wren wasn't sure she was strong enough to fight Qanna once they landed.

"Your mother and the rest of the White Wing fight with us!" Wren shouted over the wind, the burr of flames. "Join us, Qanna! I don't know what he promised you, but the King will only betray you—"

"And you won't? I know what you did, Wren Hanno! You're a monster, you're just as bad as him! You killed my *sister!*"

Wren's blood ran cold.

"The King told me," Qanna snarled. "Not that he had to. I already suspected. But once I got to the palace and met his other allies and heard their stories, everything fell into place. You and your traitorous clan have been killing and pinning the blame on the King to turn clans like ours in your favor! He might be abhorrent, but at least the King claims the blood he spills!"

Wren's fight faded. There was only the ugly black truth of Qanna's words. The truth she knew would catch up with her eventually, no matter how hard she tried to run.

Then something collided into them.

Wren was thrown from Qanna's back.

A blur of speeding air, flying limbs, *pain*—

Wren slammed into the Orchid Hall's slanted roof.

Tiles shattered beneath her. A yell tore from her throat as she tumbled across them.

She caught the lip of the roof with one hand as she dropped over its edge. The torn flesh of her shoulders screamed. Wren wasn't strong enough to hold on, but she'd done enough to stop the momentum that would have carried her off the side of the building. Instead, she fell to the veranda.

Her right ankle cracked as she landed on it. Ringing pierced her ears.

Through blurred vision, Wren saw a rush of honey-colored fur and the sweep of black robes. A pleasant, sudden thrum of magic flowed toward her. And then the thing she had been outrunning the past hour—these past weeks, months, perhaps even years—finally arrived.

A slip.

A fall.

The surprisingly warm embrace of a very dark lake.

TWENTY-ONE

LEI

THINGS THAT HAPPEN IN THE WEEK before you marry a
Demon King:

Your friends will love and hate you. They will pity you.
They'll not know what to say. Some of them will stay up with you
during the long nights, holding you as you stare into space, unable
to form words amid the turmoil of your raging, tearing heart.
Some of them—one of them—will ignore you completely. It is not
new, but it hurts more now all the same. Another will surprise you,
swapping their usual sneer for something tentative and foreign—not
quite a smile, not quite so friendly yet, but not unkind.

You'll be examined by doctors and shamans and fortune-tellers.
Demons who were once cruel will now pander to your every need—
not that you have any. Nothing they can offer you, anyway. You will
be fed well to fill out the gaunt lines of your face. You'll be fitted
for your wedding dress, a midnight cheongsam with gold threading,
exquisitely woven, that clings to your body like a shroud. An impossible number of demons will fuss and argue over how your hair and
face should be made up while you ignore them, retreated somewhere

deep within yourself. Their faces will blur into one another as they shuttle you from bathhouses to tea salons to massage parlors, where hands shape and mold your exterior while tinctures and infusions gild your insides.

You must be beautiful beyond belief.

You must look like the queen you are to become.

You will be forced to pray for the gods to shower prosperity on your upcoming nuptials. Three nights before the wedding, you will partake in a sacred ritual. As you bathe in the River of Infinity while the gods look down from their starry citadel in the skies, you'll look up at them and wonder when it is they decided to abandon you.

You will think often of your mother and father. The joyful wedding day they must have shared. The way they used to dance, and laugh, and hold each other close, aglow in that secret way of lovers. Sometimes, the memories will make you smile. Other times, they will make you want to *scream*.

News from gossiping maids and guards will reach you about how the announcement of the wedding is beginning to take effect across the kingdom: a drop in uprisings, even a clan or two switching their allegiance from the Hannos to the court, Papers quelled by the false idea they may gain some power now one of them is to become queen. You know this is what the King and his court hoped for by arranging the marriage. You'll wonder how far the news has traveled, though to you only one distance is important.

The distance between here and *her*.

All of this will make you unspeakably angry, yet you will—can—do nothing but swallow the rage down. Still, you are used to this, brewing anger in your core like a poison. You have learned how to harness it. How to sharpen it into a weapon.

You'll remind yourself of your plans, that your marriage to the

King will not last forever. You and so many others are working to bring him down; you only have to endure this so long. Occasionally, this will be enough. The rest of the time it'll offer you no comfort at all.

You will begin whispering your Birth-blessing word to yourself, clinging to the hope it suggests. And at night and in carriage rides, you will thumb the torn scrap of your friend's message so many times its ink has long since worn away, though the imprint of the word it contained is embedded in the grooves of your fingertips, embedded in your heart.

Love, love, love.

You will wonder at its meaning. At how a thing can be at once so beautiful and so soul-crushingly cruel.

And every moment of the week before you marry a Demon King, every single moment, you will think of her.

TWENTY-TWO

WREN

QUIETNESS. THAT WAS THE FIRST THING that struck her. Quiet, after coming from what felt like just seconds ago a roar of action and noise, screams and rushing flames and the multi-pitched singing of pain.

Wren smelled incense. Felt the softness of blankets on bare skin. The air flowed with warmth and low chanting: daos. If shamans were here, and it was calm, then the battle was over.

Relief cascaded through her. Then—worry.

She opened her eyes to find the grand space of Lord Anjiri's throne room. Sunlight spilled through the tattered screens, painting buttery patterns on the floor. A group of shamans knelt nearby.

"Welcome back, Lady Wren," one of them said. The others continued chanting, weaving their magic.

Wren's voice was a rasp. "How long…?"

"Two days. Don't worry. Your friends are safe."

"That makes it sound like others aren't."

"It was a battle," the shaman replied. "Casualties were unavoidable."

"How many?"

"I'm afraid I don't know the details, my Lady. The ten of us have been at your side since General Lova and I found you. But I'm sure once your father returns from his inspection, he'll be able to give you a full rundown—"

"My father is here?"

Wren sat up too quickly. Even with the enchantments, pain swelled to life in her shoulders and hips and ankle. She hissed, eyes watering. Head swimming, she threw aside the blankets and got to her feet. Though her right ankle was still tender where it'd been crushed from her fall, it was healed enough to put weight on, and she pushed out a breath to steady herself.

"Lady Wren," the shaman said patiently, "you must take it slowly. You've been out a long time."

"Even more reason to rush," Wren retorted. "I need to check on everyone. Make sure things are in order." She examined herself as she spoke, unabashed by her nakedness; she'd grown up with maids primping and polishing her. A web of bandages crisscrossed her body. She skimmed her fingers over pale pink scars and fading bruises. The shamans had clearly worked hard.

Wren called to a couple of Hanno maids working over a wooden basin. "Jumi, Hai-li—I need clothes. Anything practical will do."

"Yes, Lady Wren," they intoned, hastening at once to where supplies had been piled up against the walls. The Hannos must have moved from their war-camp and were using the Orchid Hall as their base.

So Marazi really was theirs.

The maids helped Wren into a cotton tunic, trousers, and soft leather boots. Ignoring their requests to do something with her hair, Wren absentmindedly swirled half of it back from her face and went to her weapons. They were laid out on a satin cushion. Like her, they'd been cleaned. Wren swung them onto her back.

"Lady Wren," the shaman tried again as she went to leave, "your father ordered us to keep you here. He's concerned for your health."

"You mean he wants me to be rested for the next battle. Thanks to you and your shamans, I'm healed and well rested. Please, you all should rest, too." As he began to protest, she added, "That is a command."

The shaman sighed. "Very well. At least let me offer you this."

He pushed out his hands. After a moment of pained concentration, a gust of warm air flew from his palms. It eddied around Wren in a golden ripple, lapping at her bare skin. Immediately, she felt energy flood her body. Her pain dulled to a low hum. She smiled, about to thank him when the shaman gasped, crumpling suddenly to the floor.

Wren jolted forward, but he held up a hand.

"Please," he croaked. "All is well."

There was a guilty clot in her chest. "Thank you for your efforts."

"It is our duty to serve you, Lady Wren. You do not need to thank us."

Wren headed down the staircase, discomforted by the shaman's words. They brought to mind what Ahma Goh had told her at the Southern Sanctuary.

That was why your shaman friend's death offered you such intense power. You didn't take his life—he gave it to you.

The more she understood about her Xia magic, the more Wren suspected her father's intentions. Had the other shamans guessed them, too? They'd have heard what had happened to Hiro by now, and, like Wren, would surely be putting the pieces together.

And here were ten shamans who'd spent two days keeping alive the girl they might soon be forced to give their own lives for.

*   *   *

Lova and Nitta were uncharacteristically quiet as they rode along-side Wren through the ruined streets of Marazi, surveying the changes the battle had wrought upon the city.

While most of Marazi's soldiers had surrendered when Wren had forced General Anjiri to call off the battle, some refused to back down, leading to a protracted, messy conclusion. It hadn't been until sunrise the next day that the Hannos had secured the city. Lord Anjiri was being held in the prisons of the Orchid Hall, along with his closest advisers and demon families known to be affiliated with the King. Many had fled before they could be captured.

"This is the worst of the fire damage in the Old City," Lova was saying now, indicating the district they were passing through, which was barely more than a rubble-strewn wasteland.

"Merrin supervised the rescue," Nitta added. She was sitting in front of Lova on Panda's back. "He worked so hard, and with barely any help, what with—"

She cut off abruptly.

Wren glanced sideways to see Lova draw back from where she'd whispered something into Nitta's ear.

"I—I mean," Nitta continued quickly, "what with the aftermath of the battle and everything. It took that whole first day to get the fire under control. We'd have lost far more of the city if it hadn't been for him."

They crossed the bridge that led from the Old to the New City before heading toward the maze of buildings that made up the New City's southern district. Lova led them off the main road. "This way," she said.

Wren pulled Eve to a stop, noticing a strain in Lova's voice. "Why?"

Nitta laid a hand on Panda's neck; the horse was snickering, sniffing at the air.

"Why, Lo?" Wren demanded.

The lion-girl pulled Panda around. "Because we used the square over there to put the bodies," she answered flatly.

Wren stared. "Then I need to go."

"Wren!" Lova growled, as Wren kicked Eve toward the square. She rode after her. "It won't do you any good to see that—"

"Stop telling me what is or isn't good for me!"

Wren swirled. She felt lit up all of a sudden, as if someone had taken a torch to her blood.

Nitta cringed. "Wren, please..."

Wren drew herself tall. "I've had enough of everyone tiptoeing around me. Ever since we got back from the deserts, all I've heard is 'Lady Wren, don't,' or 'Lady Wren, be careful,' or 'Lady Wren, you need to rest.' *Look after yourself*, Lady Wren.' But leading a clan is not about looking after yourself. My first and foremost duty is to look after others. My clan. My family. My allies. My friends." She shot Lova a penetrating look. "You should know that, Lo, after more than four years as the Amala's General. And you should *especially* know why it's so important to me."

Apart from Lei, the only other person who knew what was within Wren's Birth-blessing pendant was Lova.

"I'll go where my people need me," Wren said. "If I can help others, if I can save others from the King, then that is what I am going to do. I need to help them, I *need* to, Lo, I can't fail again—"

She broke off. She turned from Lova and Nitta, hating the pity in their eyes. Without a word, she pressed Eve on toward the square. Hoof-clops rose behind her as her friends followed.

Part of the square came into view as they reached the house on the corner, its roof splintered by debris. Wren braced herself for the smell, but the air was fresh. When they turned the corner, she saw why.

Dozens of shamans lined the square. They knelt in prayer formation, a peaceful chant lapping magic in warm waves across the square—and the dead that inhabited it.

There were rows of them, laid out neatly from one end to the other. Most were covered. A few looked as if they'd simply fallen where they were killed, clothes and armor slashed open, skin dark with blood. Many were hidden behind the bent backs of weeping family members. Even now, more bodies were being carried in from all directions. Wren spotted Khuen and Samira carrying in a body together. It trailed long, silver-feathered arms: a White Wing.

The whole clearing glimmered from the shamans' dao. Their magic must be what was preserving the bodies, offering mourning families time to prepare appropriate funerals. For most, it would be pyres, given the majority of central and northern Ikharans believed in releasing spirits to the sky, while southerners buried their dead.

"They've been working in shifts," Nitta said. "They've been tiring quickly. The Sickness. You know."

Wren's throat was thick. "It's beautiful," she managed.

"Your father has ordered them to stop at sunset."

Wren tensed. "What?"

"He isn't wrong, Wren," Lova said carefully. "They need rest for what's to come, and we have plenty of injured soldiers who need their help."

"He wants us to move out first thing tomorrow," Nitta explained. She was smoothing down Panda's mane absentmindedly, her eyes wet. The scene must have been bringing back memories of her brother. They'd buried Bo on an island in the Mersing Archipelago after he'd been killed in a confrontation with royal soldiers. Wren knew it wasn't the proper burial Nitta would have liked to give him.

She reached for the leopard-girl's hand.

Nitta flashed her a tentative smile. "It's all right," she murmured. "I'm all right."

"You don't have to be. I'm sorry, Nitta."

"Is it terrible that sometimes I'm glad he's not here to see any of this?"

Wren looked away. "I don't think that's terrible at all."

Close by, a lone Paper man kneeled over a covered body. Who had he lost because of her? Wren wondered. Whose happiness had she crushed this time?

"We should leave some shamans here," she decided. "We can't storm a city then abandon its people." *We aren't the Demon King,* she added in her head. "It's our duty to care for them."

"Tell your father that," Lova said coolly.

Wren followed her gaze and saw Merrin soaring across the square, Ketai riding on his back.

Merrin banked, descending in their direction. Wren's father sat tall, looking every bit the regal Clan Lord, yet there was a rigidness to his posture that struck Wren. As they drew closer, she saw that same tension etching his face.

He was angry—with her.

The instant Merrin landed, Ketai jumped off and stormed toward them. His hair was ruffled from flying, choppy strands falling into his dark eyes, which glinted from behind knitted brows. "Come with me," he ordered Wren, striding past without waiting for a reply.

"Hello to you, too," Lova muttered.

Wren tugged Eve's reins. "Don't wait," she told them.

Lova scowled after Ketai, who was headed to the riverfront where the water would ensure they wouldn't be overheard. "No way," she said, kicking Panda into movement. "I'm not leaving you alone with *that*."

As they left, Wren stopped, remembering Merrin. He was hanging back, looking nervous to approach her. She thought of the times laughing with him during their journey, their group passing around bottles and sharing fire-cooked meals, Lei at her side and her friends nearby: Caen, Bo, Nitta, Hiro. They'd been happy. Whole.

Wren blamed Merrin for breaking them. But that wasn't fair. She'd played her part, too.

Perhaps an even bigger one.

"Thank you," she said stiffly. "For your help with the fires. Lova and Nitta told me what you did."

"It was the least I could do." Merrin hesitated. "Wren..."

Something softened in her as she realized for the first time since his return she felt ready to talk to him. But as he began to speak, raised voices came from where her father, Lova, and Nitta were arguing by the riverfront.

Wren flicked Eve's reins, hurrying to join them.

"It wasn't her fault!" Nitta was shouting. She was on Panda's back; Lova had dismounted. "If you dare make her feel as though it is—"

"As the Clan Lord in charge here," Ketai said, "I will do whatever I please. With or without your permission, Nitta."

Lova rounded on him, her blond fur bristling. "Careful, Ketai," she snarled. "You're not the only Clan Lord around. Given what's happened, you might want to be a bit more careful when it comes to keeping your allies happy."

Ketai stood tall, rage flowing off him in waves. As Wren slid from

Eve's back, he turned to face her. "The White Wing abandoned us," he said.

Wren was about to say they already knew that—hadn't that been why she'd gone to the Cloud Palace? To free Lady Dunya and the clan members still loyal to her? Then comprehension struck.

The lack of bird demons in the city today. The awkward exchange between Nitta and Lova earlier when Nitta said how hard Merrin had worked to put out the fires—because, she realized now, he'd had to do it from the sky alone. And of course, that awful exchange between her and Qanna the night of the battle. Words Wren wished she could forget.

You're a monster, you're just as bad as him! You killed my sister!

Something—some*one*—had slammed into them after Qanna had thrown that damning sentence at her, had explained how she'd worked it out.

He might be abhorrent, but at least the King claims the blood he spills!

"Lady Dunya," Wren breathed.

That's who had collided with them. She'd probably come to *help* Wren.

Ketai's expression confirmed it. "That," he said slowly, each word a cold, brutal slap, "was a secret that should *never* have gotten out. How did it happen, Wren? How did you *let* this happen?"

"They've gone?" she said. "All of them?"

"One remained. Some Steel girl. Khuen convinced her, apparently. But yes. The others left."

"To go where?"

"We don't know."

Wren struggled for breath. If Lady Dunya heard what Qanna had said, then...

"They must have gone with Qanna," she choked out. "To the Hidden Palace."

"Qanna is dead," Lova said. "I killed her," she went on matter-of-factly as Wren turned her wide eyes on her. "On the rooftop. I arrived with that shaman just as you fell. Qanna was arguing with her mother, asking her how it felt to be working for a traitor, the Paper that murdered her own daughter. They were flying low enough for me to reach. I managed to catch Qanna and drag her down. I only wanted to stop her from saying anything more to her mother, but she fought me. She was strong—impressively so. She'd have killed me if I hadn't done so first."

"What did Lady Dunya do?" Wren asked.

Lova jerked her head in Merrin's direction. "Ask him. He fought her."

Merrin's owl eyes were full of sorrow. "I had to," he said, sounding pained. "She'd have attacked all of us if not. I saw it on her face. She knew Qanna spoke the truth, even if she didn't want to believe it." His feathered arms hung limp at his sides. "Lady Dunya was always fair. She saw the best in people. We let her down."

"You killed her?" Wren whispered.

Merrin shook his head. "She was injured. I managed to hold her off long enough to force her to retreat. The fight was mostly over by then. Everyone was busy tending to the wounded. I think the other White Wing assumed Lady Dunya was moving them somewhere as part of our plans, but I suppose she's told them the truth about Eolah. It would explain why they haven't returned."

"That leaves us with two bird demons," Ketai declared. "*Two*, when we are mere days away from facing the most difficult battle of our lives. Where the use of bird demons was integral to our plans. Bird demons who also happen to carry invaluable information as to said plans—with a compelling reason to betray that information to our enemies."

He spoke with barely restrained fury.

"Maybe..." Nitta began, "maybe Merrin and the hawk-girl can

find them, persuade them to come back." But she didn't sound convinced, and none of them responded.

They all knew the truth. Lady Dunya and the White Wing loyalists wouldn't be returning. They'd be lucky if they hadn't gone straight to the Hidden Palace with the Hannos' strategy for the upcoming siege.

"Go back to the Orchid Hall," her father shot at Wren, already marching away. "Let the shamans finish their healing. We leave first thing tomorrow. Try not to ruin anything more until then."

"How dare you talk to her like that!" Lova growled. "Wren has given her life to you, sacrificed everything important to her, and this is how you treat her?"

Ketai didn't falter. "Wren understands her duty."

Her duty.

Xia. Hanno. She'd inherited the responsibilities of two clans, and for the first in her life Wren felt truly ashamed of it. Both clans were tainted in blood and death.

While Lova continued to insult Ketai—and he continued to ignore her—something fluttered past Wren's face. It was a sheet of paper. She was about to pick it up when another fell.

In moments, the sky was full of them: colorful sheets of crimson, black, and gold drifting down from where, high overhead, a trio of bird demons flew, releasing the pamphlets as they went.

There were shouts. Nearby soldiers sprang into action. Merrin leaped into the air, shooting so fast toward the demons he was a gray-white blur. Cries rose up as residents ran for shelter, mourning families scattering from the square.

Ketai snatched a poster from the air and scanned it in one grim look. "Do not panic!" he called. "This is merely more of the court's propaganda. It is no attack!"

Wren, who'd grabbed one of the sheets for herself, thought how wrong her father was—because what was splashed across the paper in her trembling hand felt *exactly* like an attack.

It felt like being stabbed in the heart.

Her knees shook, but she didn't fall. As if from underwater, she heard her father shouting instructions and reassurances. She heard Nitta's gasp as the leopard-girl finally got hold of one of the posters for herself. She sensed movement nearby, then a hand on her shoulder.

"Honey," Lova started—

Which was all it took for Wren to explode.

Magic burst from her in such a fearsome blast Lova was knocked off her feet. Nitta ducked low against Panda's neck. Even Ketai's voice cut off as the icy gust slammed into him.

He swirled, robes whipping in the furious flurry of Wren's power. Nearby Papers and demons gaped in awe. The falling pamphlets whirled around her, wreathing her in scarlet and glinting gold.

"Wren!" her father roared. "Control yourself, for gods' sake!"

"*That*," Wren said, her Xia-state voice echoing, "*is all I've been doing. And I have had enough.*"

Every inch of her was agony. A wild, animal pain that threatened to rip her apart. But her magic didn't waver. It roared, charged by each dark beat of her heart, the flashes of red, black, and gold as the court's posters continued to rain down.

Ever since she'd lost Lei, Wren wondered at the next time she'd see her. Not in a dream, but touchable, present. She'd imagined a million scenarios, but not this.

Never this.

Lei's face stared at her from every poster. The artist had detailed the slow arch of her eyebrows perfectly; her slender lips; the soft

curve of her cheeks and jaw. Yet it was her eyes that had been captured best.

Golden. Bright. Bold. *Burning.*

The artist had re-created the King's appearance just as accurately. His face loomed from behind Lei, arctic stare piercing Wren
straight to the core.

Lova approached her again, more cautiously this time. "I doubt
it's even true," she said. "The King is trying to get to you. To us.
The court knows this will make some Papers reconsider their griev-
ances against them. They're desperate, they're trying anything…"

Wren swung onto Eve's back and pulled her reins, making her
neigh and kick up. *"I won't risk it,"* she said. *"I am done waiting. Lei's been
in the palace, enduring gods know what—and now* this. *I won't let her down any
longer. She needs me."*

Her father blocked her path. "It won't make any difference!" he
roared. "We attack the Hidden Palace in less than a week. We cannot let anything else disrupt our goal. We must focus on what is
most important!"

Wren gave him a humorless smile. *"Thank you, Father. You are exactly
right. I'm glad I have your blessing."*

"I am talking about the war," Ketai said through gritted teeth.

"And I am talking about saving the girl I love."

It came out before she realized what she was saying.

Despite everything, Wren still felt a childlike stab of fear at her
admission. Perhaps her father had suspected, at least wondered…
but still. Her words were a confirmation she couldn't take back.

A strange expression crossed Ketai's face. Behind the fury and
indignation, there was something else. Something dark and excited.
Something almost *hungry.*

Then it was gone.

"I, too, have lost those I love, my daughter," he said, softer now.

"I'm sorry I didn't recognize the true nature of your relationship, and I am sorry this is happening to Lei. But to go to the palace now is futile. The wedding may have already happened."

Wren's heart beat so fiercely she was amazed it hadn't punched clean through her chest. *"If you had let me go earlier,"* she seethed, *"I'd have stood a chance. I could have saved her."*

Ketai lifted his chin. "You have responsibilities here, Wren. There will be consequences if you abandon them."

"There have been worse ones because I abandoned her."

And, with a kick of Eve's haunches, Wren charged.

Her father threw himself aside. He shouted after her but his voice was drowned out as Eve's hoof-beats churned across the ash-strewn lawn before hitting the cobbles of Marazi's damaged streets. Wren's magic pulsed around her, stirring up a whirlwind of posters and ash-black air as she rode.

One of the pamphlets was crushed in Wren's right hand. If only its contents were so easily destroyed.

LOYAL SUBJECTS, FELLOW DEMONS AND HUMANS, THE HEAVENLY MASTER IS PROUD TO ANNOUNCE HIS MARRIAGE TO LEI-ZHI, THE MOONCHOSEN. MAY THEIR GODS-BLESSED UNION BE A REFLECTION OF THE UNITY THE HEAVENLY MASTER AND HIS COURT WISH FOR ALL OF IKHARA, AND A REMINDER OF EVERYTHING OUR GREAT KINGDOM CAN ACHIEVE IF PAPERS, STEELS, AND MOONS WORK TOGETHER IN LOYALTY, FAITH, AND DEVOTION.

The last line sounded like something her father would say.

As Wren turned onto the main road that led out of the city, Wren's dao finally flickered out of life. The pain did not, but Wren didn't care. It was nothing to how much her heart was searing, how badly she wished there existed enchantments powerful enough to get her to Lei in mere seconds, because every moment she wasn't with her was another the girl she loved had to spend married to—

Her brain cut off the thought.

Hoof-beats rose behind her.

"Gods*damnit*, Father!" she bellowed, going to pull one of her swords.

"I very much hope we're not related in such a way," came Lova's response. "Otherwise, some of the things we've done in the past are rather questionable."

Lova and Nitta had caught up with her. Panda was larger than Eve, and even carrying two demons he could move as fast as her. Lova's honeyed fur flowed in the wind. She was grinning, while Nitta flashed an anxious smile.

"You won't change my mind," Wren shouted over the hooves.

"We know," Lova replied.

"We're coming with you," Nitta said. She stopped her as Wren began to protest. "You can't change our minds, just as much as we've never been able to change yours. We care about Lei, too, Wren."

And though Wren wanted to argue, she couldn't help the warm rush at the thought of her two friends by her side.

All her life she'd felt as though she were meant to be alone. Even when she'd had Merrin, Caen, and Kenzo to count on, then when she'd fallen for Lova, then fallen a hundred times harder for Lei, she still felt separate somehow. As though this was her burden, her sacrifice. Ultimately, she knew—surely they *all* knew—how it would end. The fewer people Wren cared about, and who cared for her, the less it would hurt when she was gone.

But Lei had taught her there was power in being vulnerable. Wren wasn't alone. She hadn't been for a long time.

She squeezed Eve's reins tighter. She turned to thank Lova and Nitta—

Only to find Nitta drawing a bow and Lova's amber eyes full of fury.

For one horrible moment, Wren thought she'd gotten it all wrong. Then Nitta arched her back, aiming high, and Wren saw Lova's eyes were on the sky.

"Shoot!" Lova snarled.

The leopard-girl held steady. "I want to hear what he has to say!"

"Feathers has had enough chances. We know where his allegiances lie."

"We can be loyal to more than one clan or cause!" Nitta fired back. "Or do I have to remind you who taught me that?"

"What are you both talking about?" Wren cried.

Neither one of them answered, and a second later winged silhouettes cast them in shadow as Merrin and Samira scooped overhead. Khuen clung to Merrin's back, his face a mask of sheer terror.

"Wren!" Merrin called, diving to fly alongside her.

"I'm not going back to my father, Merrin!" she yelled, preparing to draw one of her swords. She'd cut down anyone who got in her way. She should have done so a long time ago.

Merrin didn't back off. "We're not here to ask you to go back."

"Couldn't we be?!" Khuen groaned hysterically.

"Wren," Merrin said, "we want to help."

"Your version of help is pretty damn warped, Bird!" Lova barked. She swung Panda in closer at Wren's side. "Let me get rid of him once and for all. I have a new explosive in my pocket I've been looking for a good reason to debut."

"Lova!" Nitta cried. "How many more times does Merrin need to prove his loyalty to us?"

"Martyrdom might convince me."

Wren held up a hand. Close up, Merrin's eyes were sincere, his feathered face a picture of regret and hope and sorrow and anger and guilt, all jumbled in a complicated mix—and in it, Wren recognized herself.

"You can come," she told him.

Khuen practically wilted. But Merrin's eyes were bright. He gave her a grim nod.

They were both guilty for Lei being back in the palace.

It was fitting they'd free her together.

TWENTY-THREE

LEI

THE EVE BEFORE THE WEDDING, the girls are getting me ready for a private ceremony with the King to exchange gifts, a tradition common among demons. The only gift *I* want to give the King is a knife to the heart, but a range of less dangerous items have been selected for me by Madam Himura.

By now, the girls and I are used to the routine, and we play our parts with faded resignation. Still, the mood is particularly sullen, despite Zhen and Zhin's efforts to lighten it. Even their story about how they and their brother once let a monkey loose into their mansion and it ended up going to the toilet in their mother's dressing room doesn't raise a laugh. All week, the air has been heavy. Tonight it's leaden, as thick and sour as lassi left out too long in the heat.

Zhen perfects the cherry-dark paint on my lips. Her sister smudges a stain from my cheek. Blue and Aoki bicker while fixing an unspooled thread of embroidery in my hanfu. Chenna threads the last of the flowers into my hair: orchids for abundance, peonies for peace. A single anemone for anticipation. Her fingers are cool and gentle. She rests them against my neck in silent encouragement.

Once, I dressed for an evening with the King and imagined each layer of my clothing and paints as armor, transforming me into what the King called hours later a "beautiful lie." Right now, I hardly feel strong, and couldn't care less if I look beautiful. But I do feel like a lie. The flowers in my hair were chosen for a blushing bride. I am not her. Instead of an abundance of joy, what I wish the orchids to bring to my marriage is an abundance of *blood*—the King's, at my hand. Instead of peace between us, I hunger for war. And the only thing I'm eagerly anticipating is my soon-to-be husband's death.

Chenna sweeps a critical eye over me; even a stray wisp of hair can earn the girls a backhand from Madam Himura.

I give her a sardonic curtsey. "How am I? The perfect Moonchosen?"

My voice drips in sarcasm, but her reply is serious. "Yes. The perfect Moonchosen."

She doesn't say it the way the King and the court do. She doesn't mean chosen for *him*—she means it like the rebels do. Chosen to fight. Chosen to change the course of Ikhara's future. Her words bring me a glow of pride. Chenna's faith is important. She doesn't invoke the gods without truly meaning it.

"*Perfect* is hardly a word I'd use to describe Nine," Blue says, but her jibe has little bite to it.

As the twins jump in to reassure me how stunning I look, a smile touches my face—dissolving the instant I catch the look on Aoki's face.

"Aoki," I croak, wanting to explain I'd only been smiling at the girls' friendship, not their words. But before I can say anything more, the clack of talons comes from the hallway.

Madam Himura sweeps into the room with her usual impatience.

She stomps over to inspect me. "Sufficient," she says. "The rest of you, however…" She clicks her tongue. "Girls!" She jabs the floor with her cane, ushering in a flock of Steel caste maids. "Get to work!"

Instinctively, I move to shield the girls from the approaching demons. Madam Himura shoos me aside. "Not everything is a battle, Lei-zhi," she snaps.

I scowl at her. "Isn't it, here?"

As maids begin picking at Aoki's dirty hair, and Blue shoves away those trying to touch her, Chenna's voice rings out.

"Madam Himura? What's this about?"

The eagle-woman casts her yellow eyes over us, looking half bitter, half exhausted. Something in her manner strikes me as off; she's a little too stiff, even for her. "The King has requested all of you be present tonight," she announces.

The twins' eyes widen. Aoki gasps. Chenna goes to speak, but Madam Himura gestures for silence. Without any more explanation, she goes over to the nearest pair of maids, who are trying to peel Blue's filthy robes off her without success.

"The—the King has called for us again?" Aoki asks eagerly.

How well did the last time turn out for you? I want to say.

Madam Himura ignores her. She directs the maids with a touch more ferocity than usual, and they swarm over the girls, working fast. I watch helplessly, foreboding coursing through my veins. What could the King possibly want with the girls? He kept them around after the Moon Ball to punish me. To make them serve me, all the while heaping every luxury upon me, pushing their faces in the unfairness of it all, turning me from peer to usurper, tying my rise to their suffering. He tried to take the one thing from me he knew I valued in this place: their companionship.

Are we in for more of his mind games tonight?

When Madam Himura goes to discuss something with Commander Razib in the hallway, Zhin checks she's out of earshot before addressing us in a hopeful whisper. "Maybe now Lei is to become the Queen, we're to be upgraded, too!"

Blue snorts. "You think the court would let Papers look after the Queen?"

"She's a *Paper* Queen…"

Chenna shakes her head. "It's not how the palace does things, Zhin."

I meet Chenna's eyes past the crowd of maids. She's already half made-up, looking striking with her long hair plaited into the braids of her province, shimmer dusting her brown cheeks. From the look she gives me, I know we're thinking the same thing. Could this have anything to do with the rebellion?

"Maybe—maybe it's to thank us," Aoki suggests. "It *is* a gift-giving ceremony, after all."

Blue laughs harshly. "Oh yes, because that's just like the King. *Such* a generous demon, that one."

Some of the maids stop in their work, looking scandalized. Others look afraid, as if worried to even be associated with such sentiments.

Blue rolls her eyes. "What? We're already prisoners. It's not as if they can do much more to punish us—unless they mean to kill us." She regards us wryly. "Honestly, it would be a relief to be spared from spending more time in such close quarters with you lot."

Though she's teasing—it hits me dully: Blue, *teasing*—none of us laugh. When I glance back at Chenna, her wary expression has deepened. I want to talk to her, discuss how we might prepare for whatever's about to come, but with the maids and the other girls around, it's impossible. Then Madam Himura is back, deeming the girls presentable, and before I know it we are shepherded from the room, my guards marching us single-file down lantern-lit corridors.

We're still in the Moon Annexe, our shadows silky on the polished white marble, when Commander Razib halts outside an archway. A silver veil hangs over it, unnaturally still.

"The Moonchosen and the Paper Girls," he announces.

The veil furls aside, bidding us in.

Magic grazes my skin as I pass through. I've seen enough beautiful locations in the palace that I'm rarely taken aback by a new setting, but what waits beyond is so gorgeous and unexpected I can't help but falter.

At first, I think we must have stepped through some portal that has transported us to the gardens of the Floating Hall—the place where, on New Year's Eve, I tried to kill the King. Then I realize the room has only been enchanted to look that way. The floor is not a real lily pond, but a mimicry of one, ripples spreading underfoot. Garlands of caught fireflies and leaves drip from the walls and colonnades. The night sky has been re-created overhead, complete with scudding clouds and the passing skim of birds. Even the air is fragranced. It's balmy and sweet, just as it was the night of the Moon Ball.

A beautiful lie. That's what the King called me then. Now here we are, in a beautiful—not to mention elaborate, and *specific*—lie of his own creation.

There are sounds of awe as the other girls enter, filing out on either side of me.

"Oh, it's stunning!" Zhen gasps.

"How lovely!" Zhin coos.

Then a whisper from the girl beside me: *"Father."*

I catch the stunned look on Blue's face before following her stare to the far side of the room where a raised podium lines the wall. The King sits in the center on his golden throne, backed by guards. Beside him kneels Naja, along with a few high-ranking court members—Mistress Azami among them. At the end of the podium is a short, graying Paper man I take to be Blue's father, given he's the only human in the room besides us.

The King beckons us with a lazy wave. "Come."

The clunk of the guards' steps is loud in comparison to the soft brush of our satin slippers, our long skirts trailing the waterlike floor as we approach the podium. It's then I notice the shamans. They line each side of the room, half hidden by the columns. Their presence strikes me as odd; usually shamans weave their decorative magic before an event. Could the Sickness have worsened, making it harder for their enchantments to last? Or is there another reason they're here?

Blue's father. The shamans. The way the room has been made to imitate the gardens where I tried to kill the King.

My unease spikes. Nothing the court does is accidental.

"Welcome, girls," the King drawls as we bow before the podium. His tone sharpens. "Lei-zhi. Join us."

I mount the steps, every eye on me. I have to pass Mistress Azami to reach the King, and when I do she shoots me the briefest of cautionary looks. In front of the others, we can't communicate any more without giving ourselves away, and my mind whirrs to decode her silent warning as I reach the King's throne.

He points at his feet. "Kneel. Face your…*friends*."

The girls look so vulnerable from here, as if the fake flooded floor could swallow them any moment. Blue's eyes are still trained on her father. Aoki gazes over my head at the King, her face hopeful, vying for his attention.

The King stands over me, casting me in his shadow. "It is tradition," he begins, "among demon clans to partake in a gift-giving ceremony the night before a wedding. The future husband and future wife offer each other five gifts, each representative of one of the core elements. Wood, fire, metal, water, earth. These are the elements that are the foundation of our world, and so, too, do they form the foundation of a successful marriage."

Relief cascades through me. Presents. Gifts. That's really all this is.

"As is customary for the groom," the King explains, moving along the podium to the steps at its end, "I shall offer my gifts to Lei-zhi first."

Each hoof-beat is a heavy, threatening thud. He makes his way toward the girls, and my eyes scan the room, confused, waiting for a servant to appear with the King's presents.

None come.

The King stops beside Zhen.

She looks up at him, brow creasing. "Heavenly Master...?"

He leans down, tucking his hand under her chin. "Lovely Zhen," he murmurs. "Noble. Imaginative. Features as perfect as a wooden carving itself." He moves to her sister. "Graceful Zhin. Energetic. Intense. Like the dancing flames of fire."

When the King reaches next for Blue, she jerks away, and from the end of the podium I hear a man hiss, "*Still* this. The stupid girl."

Blue's father.

I feel a dash of pity for Blue before pride replaces it. She's leveled her coldest glare on the King, derision etching her features, though I can see she's trembling even from here. The King seizes her cheeks, yanking her so hard she's half lifted from her knees.

"*Blue.*" He speaks her name as though it taints his tongue. "What else for a girl like you—so rigid, so willful—apart from metal?"

He casts her down. The slap of her hands against the floor as she catches herself is harsh in the silence.

The King moves on. "Chenna."

My friend remains composed, even as he grazes his furred fingers down her cheek and over the dark blush of her lips. "Wise, mindful Chenna. A calm ocean surface masking turbulent depths."

I want to scream out, run forward, and shove the King away. But dread locks me in place.

The look on Aoki's face when the King finally reaches her. If I had any breath left, this would be what steals the last of it.

"My King," she murmurs, in the bared, reverential tone of lovers. *"Please..."*

The King holds her gentler than the others. Tears stream down her cheeks as he brings his face lower, close enough they could kiss, slipping his fingers through her hair then along her jawline, to trail a tender line down to her throat. "Sweet Aoki."

She lets out a whimper, a whipped-puppy noise. At first, I don't understand what's wrong, because their pose is so intimate and the King doesn't seem to have moved. Then I see her eyes bulge. Her tears come harder, cheeks flushing violet, and I realize with a sickening lurch the King's hand has tightened around her neck.

"Sweet Aoki," he repeats. "Honest. Loyal. You have upheld your earth roots this long, at least."

I am on my feet in a second. Before I can jump from the podium, guards restrain me. I scream and thrash as they force me back to my knees, and then something else grips me, trapping me in place.

Magic.

A pair of the shamans have prowled forward, arms thrust out. My yells die in my throat.

The King rears back from Aoki so abruptly she drops to the

floor. Chenna grabs her, drawing her sobbing form close. She looks up at the King with unleashed fierceness as he turns his horned head to me.

"Well, Lei-zhi. How do you like your presents?"

A wild rage burns me. But I'm locked by magic. I can watch uselessly as the King returns to my side. He flicks a hand—so horribly careless a movement to what it pertains—and five of the guards that had been flanking the podium fan out, each one positioning themselves behind one of the girls.

The metallic *shing* of five blades being drawn echoes out. And suddenly, everything makes sense.

The way the room has been made up to remind me of the night I tried to triumph over the King—and failed. The presence of Blue's father. The shamans, here not for their decorative skills but as weapons. And the Paper Girls.

My Paper Girls. My friends.

My family.

Wondering why I sent them back to you, perhaps? Don't worry. You will find out soon enough.

It wasn't about them seeing me become the King's Queen—it was about this.

Five gifts.

Five *sacrifices*.

The girls are panicking now, Zhen demanding answers, her sister clinging to her, eyes wide and wet with disbelief. Chenna is still comforting a sobbing Aoki even as her own face betrays her fear.

Blue scrabbles forward. The guard standing over her grabs her by the collar and jerks her back, bringing his blade to her throat. She lets out a shriek that penetrates right to my bones. "Father! Tell them to stop! Make them stop! Baba! *Baba!*"

I hear a faint *tssk* from where he's watching. Irritation.

"Please!" she cries. "Baba, please! *Please*—"

"I'm not here to *help* you, stupid girl! I am here to watch as you finally make yourself of some use!"

His words shock us all into stillness.

Blue makes a tiny, stunted sound.

Chenna's face is murderous.

The King laughs. "Well said, Adviser Lao—"

There's a whirr of silver; two strangled shouts of surprise.

The shamans who trapped me reel back, throwing knives buried in the center of their foreheads. I sense their magic wink out.

I whirl around, seeing Mistress Azami on her feet, face blazing as she draws a fresh pair of knives from her robes, and the whole room breaks into chaos.

TWENTY-FOUR

LEI

ET THE GIRLS AND GO!" Mistress Azami bellows at me.

She has just enough time to hurl her knives at the guards lurching in her direction before Naja is upon her, a spitting blur of white fury.

I stumble into movement, ducking the arms of a guard to leap from the platform. Everyone is shouting and yelling, running either for cover or to join the fray. Somewhere behind me, a man is screeching incessantly; I'd bet anything it's Blue's father. Shamans who'd been waiting behind the colonnades fly forward, hands thrown out. Enchantments soar over my head. The air froths with their electric power, and something else—a swarm of tiny flashing bodies. Fireflies. The shamans must have freed them from their decorative stations, and now they're loose, whipping everything into even more of a frenzied mess.

So some of the shamans are on our side. Mistress Azami must have organized it.

I hardly have time for relief.

"KILL THEM!" the King roars.

I see *them* through the roiling firefly clouds. Chenna, Aoki, Blue, Zhen, and Zhin. They're grappling with demon guards who only moments ago had been about to open their throats. Some of the shamans lob daos at the guards, blasts of wind that toss them back or send squalls of fireflies and razor-edged leaves torn from the garlands at their heads. But other shamans—the ones not allied with us—weaponize *their* magic, too. I'm helping Zhen to her feet when a pained squeal rents the air.

Blue rises high, eyes rolling back. Her body contorts in agony.

Chenna grabs her leg and tries to drag her down, but the shaman's magic is strong. In seconds, Chenna's feet leave the floor, too. She kicks desperately—

There's a whirr of movement.

Chenna and Blue collapse to the ground. Zhen and I run to them, hauling them up. Nearby, a shaman is spluttering. A sword—stolen from one of the guards—protrudes from his chest. He drops to his knees, face going slack.

Behind him stands Zhin. She's trembling, her eyes wide. Her hands are slick with blood. She drops the sword and steps back, slipping in the pool of red at her feet.

Zhen goes to her. Comforting words tumble from her lips, but there's nothing comforting to be found in any of this, the before-peaceful room now a pandemonium of clashing magic and battling figures.

"We need to go," I tell Chenna. *"Now."*

"Can you walk?" she asks Blue. She fell on her injured leg; it must be hurting even more than usual.

If it is, she gives barely any sign of it. Instead, her eyes are locked ahead through the flashing clouds of magic to the back of the room. "He came to watch me die," she whispers.

"Blue, can you walk?" Chenna repeats, louder.

Blue's attention snaps to her. "Can I *walk*?" Some of her usual spite has fought its way back. All of a sudden, she's pitching forward, crawling to the shaman Zhin killed, reaching for the hilt of the sword sticking from his back. "I can do more than walk!" she hisses, hysterical. "What father...? What—what *monster*...? I'll kill him! I'll *kill the bastard*—"

As Chenna hurries to control her, I leave them, looking for Aoki.

Out of all the girls, she's the only one who has remained still. Kneeling in the same position she was in earlier, she gazes blankly, tear-streaked and shaking. Her mouth moves, and while I can't hear anything above the din I make out the words on her lips.

My King. My King.

"Aoki!" I seize her by the shoulders. I drag her up, but she resists, wriggling from me like a fussing child. "*Aoki!*" I snap. I clasp her wrists. She tries to pull away, rocking to where the King is hidden behind the swirling vortex of leaves and fireflies and blood. "Leave him! We have to go—"

And then Aoki jerks—not out of my grip, but pulled in the opposite direction by another's.

Commander Razib.

The towering gazelle demon looms from the shadows. He is splattered in blood, his vicious-looking parang sheathed in red. He clutches Aoki with one hand. With the other, he lifts his scythe high—

A girl barrels into him, trailing a streak of braided brown hair.

Chenna.

She's only half his size, but she's strong, and he's not expecting her. Knocked off balance, his weapon sweeps through empty air instead of Aoki's neck.

I dive forward, grasping its wooden handle. The Commander roars, batting Chenna off—I hear her slam into the marble with a cry—but I'm weighing down his arm, and before he can reassert himself I fling my knee up, catching him in the groin.

He drops the parang with a strangled grunt. I snatch it up and slash out.

The hook tears through the front of his robes, releasing a hot spray of blood as it lodges in his gut. Red oozes in great pulses around the blade.

Commander Razib pitches, staggering to remain standing. I let go of the parang's handle and grab Aoki. In her daze, she doesn't try to fight me anymore, and I drag her with me to check on Chenna, who's already getting to her feet.

Though she looks slightly stunned, she gives me her trademark smile: small, grim, determined. "I'm fine," she says.

Just as, from behind her, a pair of talons grasp her head—

And twist.

The *crack* shoots through the room.

There is no blood. No gore. Only an abrupt dimming of light in those astute, tawny eyes, and the off-kilter tilt of Chenna's lovely head on her broken neck.

Blood pumps in my ears as I lift my gaze to meet Madam Himura's piercing yellow eyes. She's incensed, her feathers sticking on end. She drops Chenna unceremoniously—and comes for me.

My fingers are torn from Aoki's as the eagle-woman kocks me off my feet. I slam into the marble. Madam Himura pins me down. One knee presses my chest, right below my sternum. I gasp emptily as she leers over me.

"I have her!" she screeches. "I have the Moonchosen!"

Her triumphant cry pitches into a shriek as she's dragged off me.

Hands—small Paper hands—clutch at her feathers, the ruff at her neck, her winged arms.

I push myself up, winded, to see the remaining girls—the twins, Blue, even Aoki—wrestling Madam Himura to the floor. Behind them, one of Chenna's arms is visible, flung where she fell. Her hand is turned up, long, slim fingers open, as if expecting something to drop into her palm. Not that she could catch it. Not now.

Chenna. Dead.

The thought paralyzes me.

Nearby, Commander Razib, still leaking blood, fights with Mistress Azami. The magic-powered whirlwind buzzes furiously around us, a kaleidoscope of sparks and ruby droplets. Beyond, there's the dim shadow of battling figures. Shamans and guards, both allies and enemy. Fighting to get to us—and fighting to get us *out*.

The girls are still struggling to hold Madam Himura.

"The sword!" Blue yells.

It's still stuck in the shaman's back. I yank it free and stand over Madam Himura. She strains, spittle flying from her beaked mouth. The girls restrain her, Zhen practically lying on her in her effort to keep her down. They are strong.

We are strong.

Strong*er*, together.

"L-Lei," Madam Himura chokes.

She looks stricken, truly scared for the first time, just like Chenna earlier. Two women, usually so composed, threatening to come undone in their final moments. Yet while Chenna remained collected, self-possessed even at the very end, Madam Himura is unraveling.

A final word scrapes from her. *"Please…"*

"Look away," I tell the girls, though only Aoki does, burying her head in Blue's shoulder.

I score the blade in one sure movement across Madam Himura's throat.

Zhin yelps, turning as blood splatters her cheek. But her sister stares, along with Blue and me, the three of us watching as blood spills down Madam Himura's feathers and she makes her last sounds, gargled and muffled, until her eyes roll back. Eyes that spent so long judging and disparaging us. Eyes we feared, felt we'd never be free from their inscrutable glower. The first demon eyes at the palace that ever evaluated us and found us lacking.

A whir of movement to my left snatches my attention.

Commander Razib and Mistress Azami's duel has come to a close.

The girls gasp, but I only watch in horrified silence as the dog-woman—Mistress of the Night Houses, ally to the Hannos, protector of Kenzo and Lill, *my friend*—is lifted off her feet, Commander Razib's half moon blade buried so deep in her torso its hooked tip sticks from her back. She grips the blood-slick handle where it's embedded between her breasts with both hands, her face ashen. A crimson line trails from one corner of her mouth.

She doesn't cry out or whimper—she won't give the Commander the satisfaction. Instead, with what must be a supernova-level of effort, she looks to me. "Go to Kenzo," she breathes.

Then her head slumps.

The Commander slams her down, placing a hoof on her chest to rip his parang free with a wet, sickening tear.

I reach for the hand of the girl nearest to me, not even knowing who it is, and shout, *"Run!"*

The whorl of fireflies follows, tightening so Commander Razib is immediately engulfed as he gives chase. I lead the girls in what I hope is the right direction, barely able to see past the buzzing cloud, as the Commander's growls of frustration die behind us.

Another shout rings out: the King.

"CAPTURE THE MOONCHOSEN! KILL THE OTHERS!"

I sprint fast, dragging whoever it is along with me, praying the others are keeping up. The crash of swordfight sends shockwaves through the air. There are thuds as bodies are flung against the columns and floor.

We reach the doorway and skid out into the hallway.

The fireflies scatter, too distant from the reach of their shamans' binds. My ears pop. The sounds from the room are muffled here, barely more than a rumbling murmur. The King must have wanted the shamans to keep out the sounds of the girls' executions, and now his plan has backfired, keeping the noise of what's actually happening from drawing the attention of the rest of the palace.

I lead the girls westward. By now I know the King's fortress by heart: another failure of his arrogance, not believing I'd be able to escape from him a second time and use my new knowledge of the palace to do so. I take us down passageways and staircases, heading for a servants' entrance I know is minimally guarded.

We pass a few maids, who fling themselves out of our way with surprised squawks. When we cross three guards, I dispose of them with the sword I used to kill Madam Himura, her blood still coating it red. The demons are strong, but somehow I am stronger. My blood is wrath and vengeance. Recklessness and desperation.

"Arm yourselves," I say, panting over the guards' bodies.

After a moment's hesitation, Zhen and Blue take weapons from two of them. Aoki is still blinking dazedly. Zhin backs away with a whimper.

"Zhin!" her sister hisses, shaking her by the shoulders. "You want to live, don't you? You want to see Mama and Baba and Allum again?"

Zhin whimpers louder. Madam Himura's blood stains her cheeks; more red coats her hands from the shaman she cut down earlier. "We're killing..." she whispers. "*I* killed..." Realizing she won't be able to do so herself, Zhen stoops, prizes the pata from the clenched hand of the last guard, and pushes it on her sister.

At the sound of running footsteps, Zhin starts, fingers closing around the sword. I grab Aoki and the five of us disappear around the corner just in time. There's shouting as guards stumble upon the bodies of their comrades.

"The whole palace will be looking for us now," Blue hisses at me. "How in the gods are we meant to escape?"

"We just need to make it to the Night Houses," I say. "That's where Kenzo is hiding. He'll know what to do."

"Kenzo." Disbelief etches her words. "*General* Kenzo Ryu? Isn't he imprisoned at Lunar Lake for treason?"

"Our allies got him out. Mistress Azami's been hiding him—"

I break off at the clashing of an alarm.

All of a sudden, the hallways are alive with noise as guards respond to the warning bells. I drag the girls into a small courtyard with a water fountain to let them pass. Once the way is clear, we dart back out.

It takes us fifteen terrifying minutes to make it to the servants' entrance, hiding in rooms and side corridors each time we hear approaching demons. I keep tight hold of Aoki; I don't trust the way she's still mouthing those two words, *My King.* It feels as if any moment her whispering could turn to a scream that will give us all away. When we finally reach the narrow door, I inch it open.

Cool air hits my face. Outside, it is dark, the sky a lid of clouds. This part of Royal Court is deserted, but the night air is full of clanging bells and running demons. I'm about to usher the girls out when a scaled hand grasps the doorframe.

"Lei. You took your time."

Kiroku, Naja's maid—and our ally.

The other girls tense, not knowing who the reptile demon is. Blue even thrusts up her knife, barging toward the doorway, Zhen right behind her. I hold them back, explaining quickly, "She's a friend. How did you know we'd be here?" I ask Kiroku.

"Mistress Azami had a feeling you'd come this way given your knowledge of the building. But we posted spies at every possible exit in case." Her reptilian eyes narrow. "There are only five of you. Where's the other girl?"

Chenna's name sticks in my throat. "We're it."

Kiroku doesn't press me. She holds out a bundle of black cloaks. "You're going to pretend to be shamans. I'm accompanying you to the main gate on Naja's orders."

We drag the robes over our heads. I have to put Aoki's on for her. "I know this is hard," I whisper, tucking her auburn hair behind her ear, "but I need you to stay close. Can you do that?"

When she doesn't answer, Blue steps in and takes her arm. "I've got her."

I nod gratefully.

"Make sure the hoods don't slip," Kiroku reminds us, before leading us out, as if we need reminding of the deadly cost if our disguises should fail.

TWENTY-FIVE

LEI

PANIC THRUMS UNDER MY SKIN AS we make our way south through the palace using the servant passageways between the walls of the courts. When we cross guards or maids, I tense, bracing to be called out or at the very least challenged. But Kiroku plays her role with ease, sniping when one of us starts lagging, all the while prowling down the center of the walled path with little regard for anyone else, forcing them to scatter as if we are the ones in power here.

As royal shamans, that's exactly what we are. It's the perfect disguise.

My heart squeezes at the thought of Mistress Azami planning this. She clearly knew what the King had in store for us tonight—and that I wouldn't be able to live with myself if I lost the girls. She died for them. For *me*. Because if I'd escaped the palace as she'd arranged weeks ago, I wouldn't be here now, and the girls might not have been ordered to be executed, and Mistress Azami might not have had to reveal herself as a traitor to the court. Like so many others, her death is on my hands.

Wren told me once how no one prepares you for what taking a life costs. She was talking about murder, but there are more ways to be responsible for someone's death than plunging the blade with your own hand. I wonder if there's a way to ever get those pieces back, or if you keep existing without them, a house with so many cracks the wind whistles through you at night, lets in the cold so your bones are always chilled, your heart never quite as warm as it once was.

After forty minutes, Kiroku leads us out through an archway into the southernmost part of Women's Court. "It'll be quieter here," she says. "We can move quicker."

"Mistress Azami told us in front of Commander Razib to go to Kenzo," I say. "Are you sure they don't know…"

"I doubt it. Our spies have been feeding rumors of him hiding somewhere in the Demon Ridge Mountains. They won't think to look for you here—at least, not just yet. The whole palace will be searched eventually."

We dash along the midnight grounds, sticking to the pathways between the raised platforms with their covered walkways and interlocking houses. At the sight of the gates of the Night Houses, the lizard-girl holds up a hand.

A shaman peels out from under the boughs of a nearby saga tree; a real shaman, unlike us, tattoos knitting his dark skin.

"Ruza!" I exclaim. It's the young boy who helped me in Temple Court.

"The small bird flies," he recites, ignoring my greeting.

"On the wings of the golden-eyed girl," Kiroku finishes.

Ruza nods. His pale eyes sweep over us. He looks even more tired than when I last saw him, and though he's free of the collar at his throat, the skin there is blood-crusted and bruised. Still, the first thing he asks is, "Any wounds need looking at?"

I reach for Blue. "My friend fell on her leg—"

She swats me away. "My leg is perfectly *fine*. Why don't you ask him to fix that horrible face of yours, Nine? It'd do us all a favor."

Zhen lets out a wry bark. It dissipates some of the tension.

"We shouldn't be long," Ruza says, eyeing the guards lining the Night House grounds. "Word is traveling fast of Lei and the girls' flight. We can't risk losing their escape route."

He gathers us close, then shuts his eyes and holds out his hands. Golden characters spin from them, swirling around us with a warm hum.

The young shaman sags when he finishes, looking winded. "A protective charm," he says. "It'll keep us hidden. Come on. Stay close."

None of the guards turn our way as we pass through the gates. Immediately, the musk-sweet fragrance of jasmine and frangipani hits my nose. I've only been to the Night Houses in daytime, and the grounds are even more beautiful at night, lanterns illuminating the winding pathway through the gardens. Fireflies—unentrapped by magic—flit through the balmy air. There are couples in the pavilions half hidden within the trees, and sounds of pleasure drift out, while music and laughter float on the breeze from the cluster of buildings in the distance.

Once, these sensual sounds both embarrassed and stirred me. Tonight, all I think is how wrong it is, people having fun when hardly any time at all ago I was in a nightmare room watching two of my friends die.

The bodies of my two friends are still *in* that room, along with how many others of our allies.

Chenna. Mistress Azami.

Chenna.

When we reach the main clearing, we skirt the buildings and their bubbling chatter and noise. Though it pains me that Lill is so close by, I know it'd be too dangerous for me to try and see her. Ruza brings us to a small pavilion set back from the rest. Peacock-green sashes cover the entranceway. Instead of the banners adorning the other buildings, which are marked with the character *ye*, denoting them as the home of the palace courtesans, this structure's calligraphy marks it as a tea house.

"We'll keep watch," Ruza says, lifting his protective magic with a relieved exhale before he and Kiroku usher us inside.

I barely make it through the entrance before I stop, reeling.

"Hello, Lei," says Kenzo gruffly, one corner of his muzzled mouth lifting.

I throw myself at him, the wolf demon's strong furred arms closing around me as I bury my face in his neck. The reassuring scent of him envelops me—woodsmoke and jade-green fields—and for a moment I'm so buoyed by relief I could laugh. Then I notice how different his body feels. The poke of jutting bones against my flesh; a mangy patch of fur above the collar of his robes where my cheek is pressed. Even the way Kenzo is holding himself is stiff and careful.

I draw back, taking him in with glassy eyes. "Oh, Kenzo…"

He shakes his head. Despite his diminished form, his burnished bronze eyes haven't changed, and he gives me a fierce look. "No sympathy. Please. I am alive, and we are almost free. That's what's important."

"Excuse me." Zhen's voice breaks our focus. "I don't mean to be rude, but I'm aware we're a little pressed for time…"

Blue snorts at the understatement.

Kenzo sweeps a look over the girls. I can tell he notes Chenna's absence—while he didn't know her personally, he spent enough time as the King's personal guard to know who she was. Though his brow furrows, he doesn't remark upon it, for which I'm grateful.

I can't bear to say the words out loud yet.

"So?" I ask. "What's the plan? I'm guessing we'll be getting out the way I was meant to leave by last time?"

That earns me curious glances from the girls.

Kenzo nods. "Our allied shamans have been keeping hold of a part of the perimeter wall nearby," he explains for their benefit. "Ruza broke free to help bring us safely there."

Zhin looks panicked. "Then what? We can't just walk out, they'll find us, we won't get away, we *can't*. Oh, gods, we're going to die like Chenna—"

Zhen shushes her sister.

"We've planned a diversion," Kenzo says. "It should keep the King's soldiers distracted while we hide in the forest to let them pass. Kiroku is going to head back to the King now to tip the court off. They should take the bait."

Blue scoffs. "They should? What if they don't?"

"Do you have a better idea?" I snap.

"Give us more magic."

"You don't understand the cost of it, Blue," I say.

She glares at me. "Perhaps I would," she replies coolly, "if you'd bothered to let us in on any of this before we were being *dragged to our deaths*—"

A loud bang from outside makes all of us freeze.

There's the pad of running footsteps. Laughter. Another door slamming.

Kiroku thrusts her head through the curtains. "We should get going," she says. "News is guards have begun to search all the courts."

Kenzo hands me a pack of supplies, shouldering one himself. As we file out of the tea house, Kiroku stops me in the doorway. "I almost forgot." She presses something into my hands. "I believe this is yours."

The weight is instantly familiar—my dagger.

"I stole it from Naja's chambers," she says.

"Thank you," I say, and as we step back out into the dark night, I stow it within my robes, already feeling bolder. My knife has gotten me out of difficult situations before. Let's hope it can help me with one more.

"Oh, my gods," Zhen says when we enter Temple Court.

Knowing what to expect, I'd fortified myself for the sight of the imprisoned shamans. Now I wish I'd thought to warn the others. But how to prepare anyone for something like this? How to explain the sight of hundreds of shackled persons packed so tightly they have no room to move? The chains and collars at their necks, worse than anything a farmer would subject his cattle to? The reek of bodily fluids and dirt? The cowed posture of the shamans, their starved, hollow cheeks?

Blue's face twists with revulsion as we cross the crowded floor. "What *is* this?" she hisses. "*This* is the home of the royal shamans?"

"*This* is the cost of magic," I say, gaining no satisfaction from it.

The rhythmic chanting and the crackle of the shamans' daos thrums in our ears. It's like moving through a monsoon storm, the air a physical thing with body and bite. Its golden sheen would be beautiful were the source of its creation not so terrible.

"Where's the passage?" Zhin asks, panicked, when we stop by the far wall, its enchanted stone no different looking than the rest of Temple Court. "There isn't one! We're going to be trapped here, aren't we!"

Zhen rubs her shoulders, trying to calm her. Ruza, who's closest to the wall, reaches to touch it.

His hand passes straight through.

The twins gasp. Blue swears. My own stomach lurches. Even after all the incredible feats of magic I've seen, this is something else. These are the palace walls. The great protectors of the Hidden Palace that have stood for almost two hundred years—breached now by a young shaman's hand.

Ruza withdraws his arm, and the twins gasp again, as if not quite believing it would reappear. "It doesn't hurt."

Kenzo lines us up in front of the concealed opening. "We'll leave one by one," he says. "As soon as you're out, take cover in the trees. Don't go any farther. Wait for me."

"Are you coming with us?" I ask Ruza.

He shakes my head. "I need to retake my place. Otherwise they'll know something's off."

"You can't be serious," Blue says, disgusted. She scans the rows of enslaved shamans. "You—you can't—"

"I have to, and I will." Ruza looks each of us in the eye, that determined smile on his lips. "Take care, Paper Girls. I hope to see you all again soon."

He holds my gaze a little longer. Then he steps back, and Kenzo ushers me toward the wall that has held me prisoner for so long.

I hold my breath as I step through.

There is no pain—but there *is* a riot of sensation. Tingling and strumming and pulsing in my ears and an electric crawl that makes my tongue curl in my mouth. I stumble on, blinded by the enchantments, like a million light spots from staring at the sun.

Then, as abruptly as it started, it's all gone.

I'm out.

Outside the palace.

I have no time to revel in it. Disorientated by the sudden darkness, I lurch to a nearby bamboo tree and press against it. The strange hum of Temple Court has been replaced by thin night sounds: animals scurrying in the forest; the distant pound and shout of guards; wind rustling leaves. Then there's a sharp inhale as Blue appears, materializing like a ghost from the solid-looking wall.

She darts to join me. She looks around, chest heaving, scattered firelight from the braziers atop the high balustrade reflecting in her ink-dark eyes and flashing off her azure hair.

"Gods," she says.

"I know," I whisper.

Zhin is next, quickly followed by Zhen, who has to drag her sister with her to the cover of the trees, a hand over her mouth. Then Aoki, and finally Kenzo.

I watch the wall, as if Chenna might slip from it, too, her serious eyes blazing and her mouth a tight, resolute line.

But of course she doesn't come.

Beside me, Kenzo peers into the forest. The eerie white stalks of the bamboo trees give off a faint pearl-green glow, and I remember the forest is also covered by the shamans' enchantments. Before I can ask Kenzo whether that'll affect us, an earsplitting caw rings out.

Kenzo lifts his finger to his lips.

A large shadow arcs overhead.

Zhin whines. Her sister clutches her tighter. Nearby, Blue is holding Aoki, who is still quiet, though tears flow down her round cheeks as she mouths that same silent prayer: *My King. My King.*

We wait an agonizing minute for the flying figure to move on. I don't know whether it's one of the Tsume, the King's elite bird demon guard, or one of Qanna's White Wing. Either way, the demon is looking for us. When they sweep back over the palace with a beat of strong wings, Kenzo motions us forward.

We've barely taken a step when there's another caw.

This time, Zhen isn't covering her sister's mouth.

Zhin's alarmed cry isn't so loud—but like the snap of a twig in a midnight wood, it carries through the hush.

The bird demon screeches and dives straight for us.

We break into motion, stumbling deeper into the forest. Zhin's sobs of terror accompany our beating feet and frantic panting. Another cry joins the shriek of the first bird demon. Something whips the canopy overhead. There's the crack of branches, a scatter of leaves tearing free, and then a winged figure slams down through the forest ceiling.

A girl's high-pitched scream rents the air.

It all happens too fast to make sense of. We've scattered in our panic, and I can't tell who the scream belongs to until the bird demon—an enormous crow-woman fitted with the Tsume's golden armor—flaps upward, a girl dangling from her razor-fitted talons.

"Aoki!" I cry.

I propel myself at her, but I'm too late, she's lifting out of my reach—

There's a whir of gray fur.

The crow-woman screeches. Cants to one side.

Her wing catches the trees, and she dips, tumbling to the forest ground. Kenzo clings on. He's lucky the demon hasn't crushed him, falling instead on her other side. He clambers up to her feathered neck. With a rumbling growl, he drags a blade across her throat.

As the demon's body goes slack, her talons release, and Aoki rolls free.

I fall over her, pushing her coppery hair from her face. "Aoki!" I shout, all sense of stealth forgotten in my panic. "Aoki, speak to me! Are you hurt? Aoki!"

She groans. Her face is gray. A bubble of blood balloons at the corner of her mouth. My lap feels wet, and I look down to see more blood—glossy torrents of it—gushing from her stomach. While my own hanfu is the usual black with gold trim, Aoki's is light green, but it's already turning dark.

There's so much blood I can't make out her wound at first. When I do, the earth drops out from under me.

From nearby comes the clash of talons and metal. Kenzo is fighting the second bird demon. Their whirring movements whip the hair about my cheeks, but I barely notice, crouched over Aoki's limp body, my tears dripping onto her upturned face. I drag off the pack of supplies Kenzo gave me and empty it desperately, snatching the first roll of fabric I find and stuffing it against her shredded flesh.

It's soaked through in an instant.

Sobbing, I press the jagged line in her belly where she was caught by one of the crow's blade-tipped talons, but blood keeps pulsing past my fingers, vanishing them like Ruza's hand in the wall. Then Kenzo is here, gathering Aoki into his arms, and the other girls are back, muffling their cries at the sight of her, and Blue locks onto my hand with viselike fingers, and we are moving again, dashing through the dark forest, the carrying calls of more bird demons chasing us as we run and run, Aoki's blood leaving a trail in the soil.

Her ghost-pale face hangs past Kenzo's shoulder, her lips finally unmoving.

TWENTY-SIX

LEI

"I NEED ANOTHER BIT OF FABRIC, this one's drenched—"

"Here—"

"Keep pressing. Kenzo, could you…?"

"Lei, take care with that part—"

"I'm trying—"

"Oh, gods, there's blood *everywhere*—"

"Zhin! Keep your voice down! We can't have them find us again!"

"Oh, thank you, Zhen, that *really* helps calm me!"

"Well, it seems nothing will!"

"How come *you're* not all panicking? Don't you realize we just broke out of the palace while killing Madam Himura and a bunch of guards and shamans—*I killed a shaman*—and Chenna's dead, and Aoki's almost—"

"Don't say it. Don't you *dare* say it."

My snarl shuts Zhin up. I return my full attention to where I'm bandaging Aoki. Her flesh is soft and slick. My fingers slip as I tie the knot. Kenzo holds her wound together so we can make the dressing as tight as possible, while Zhen wipes away blood and Blue tears spare scraps of our clothes into bandages with her teeth, making it look as though she's been feasting on raw meat.

Zhin wasn't exaggerating. There's blood *everywhere*.

Aoki's head is cradled in Zhin's lap, Zhin smoothing her hair with shaky fingers. In the dim light of the forest, Aoki is startlingly pale. Her eyes are shut, her expression calm. Only her complexion and the trickle of blood running from one corner of her mouth make it clear this is no typical sleep.

I slip my fingers to her wrist. Her pulse flutters weakly.

"You're going to be fine," I say. "You hear me, Aoki? You're not going anywhere."

"Lei," Kenzo says gruffly. "When she wakes, she'll need something for the pain. There are herbs in your bag. Mistress Azami packed them in case something like this happened. She said you'd know what to do."

I go cold. "I emptied the bag when Aoki was injured," I breathe. "I...I don't have it."

There's a painful silence. We all study Aoki's ashen face.

I get up. "There must be some herbs around here."

"You can't leave!" Zhin hisses. "There'll be hundreds of soldiers searching for us by now!"

"The diversion will keep them occupied," Kenzo says.

"We haven't heard anything for ages," I point out.

Zhen wraps an arm around her sister's shoulders. "Still, it's probably best to stick together."

"I'll go with her," Blue snaps. "We're not helping Aoki sitting around squabbling like aunties over a mahjong bet." She wipes her red-stained hands on the thin underlayer of her hanfu, leaving smudged prints; like me, she stripped off the outer layer of her robes to use as dressings for Aoki's injury. The nighttime chill pricks goosebumps across her skin.

I nod at her, then turn to the others. "We won't go far."

"If anything happens," Kenzo reassures me, "I'm here. Just stay close, and be careful." He speaks calmly, but when our eyes meet there's an urgency he can't hide.

None of us can be sure of how long the diversion will work. Kenzo explained it to us earlier, once we'd found a safe place to hide from the King's bird demons. A group of guards allied to us will leave the palace via the southeastern ramparts and take off on horseback, leaving the coast clear for us to move to the northwest part of the forest, from which we'll head to the secret war-camp the Hannos have set up a few miles out in preparation for the siege on the palace. Still, it could be days or mere hours until the court knows we fooled them. Then what?

I brush a kiss to Aoki's brow before leading Blue away from the small clearing. The clouds have begun to clear, and snatches of starlight wink down through the canopy. It fills the forest with flickering shadows, making me even more on edge as we wind through the trees. My eyes strain to pick out useful herbs from the sparse foliage on the ground. I'd rely on my nose were it not for the stench of blood. My clothes and skin are caked in it, scraps of my hair stuck to my cheeks with Aoki's gore.

Blue tracks alongside me. "What are we looking for?"

"Mostly the same herbs I've been giving you," I say, inspecting the roots of a tree. "Ginseng. Milk thistle. Anything to dull pain and protect from infection. If a wound like that turns septic..."

Blue either doesn't sense my concern or chooses to ignore it. She snorts. "Very helpful, Nine, given I don't know what in the gods any of those look like when they're not in a mush and stinking up my leg. Not all of us work in some peasant herb shop."

"Then why offer to help if you think this is beneath you?" I reply impatiently.

"*Someone* had to make sure you didn't get the rest of us in even more trouble than you already have," she shoots back with a scowl. But there's a softer note that suggests I'm not the only one of us concerned about Aoki's well-being.

"Our best bet here is yan hu suo," I say. "They grow well in bamboo groves. Look for small bell-shaped flowers, blue or yellow, and thick vegetation. It's their tubers we're after."

Blue grunts in acknowledgment. As she moves to search some bushes close by, I notice her limp is more pronounced than usual. After all this running, and her fall on it earlier, it's a wonder she's moving as well as she is.

"How's your leg?" I ask.

"Fine," she replies brusquely, and I don't press her. Still, when I come across a bunch of wild poppies ten minutes later—a good enough substitute for yan hu suo—I pick a few extra.

We're hunting for more herbs when Blue says, "What was that about, an escape route you should have taken before?"

I stiffen. "The rebels within the palace. They had a plan to get me out."

"And you didn't take it?"

"It wasn't the right time."

She makes a scathing sound. "Unbelievable."

I glower. "What?"

"You had a way out, and you didn't take it. How dense *are* you, Nine?"

"You'd have been punished if I had," I say heatedly. "The King probably would have killed you."

"So what? What has living ever done for me? Gods, my life is just so *fantastic*, who wouldn't want to be me?"

The hostility in her voice stings me. "Blue..."

But she turns her back on me, making it clear the conversation is over.

When we head back, having gathered enough herbs, I say gently, "I'm sorry about your father."

She doesn't reply—and I don't expect her to. Yet as we approach the clearing, Blue's words come sudden and fast. "I shouldn't be surprised by now. It's ridiculous. Clinging on to nothing, all this time. I mean, *gods*, after *everything*..." She makes an angry, animal sound at the back of her throat before releasing a shuddering breath, her voice withering to a whisper. "Why am I still surprised?"

"Because," I say, "when you love someone, you can't help but hope for the best."

"Even when all they show you is their worst?"

"Because they have shown you *more* than their worst. Because you know they can be better. Because you've seen it. You've *loved* them for it."

Blue's dark, suspicious eyes flick my way. "What happened between you and lover-girl? You've not even spoken her name. Not that I care, of course," she hastens to add. "I'm just surprised you didn't spend every waking moment gushing about her."

This time, it's my turn to ignore her.

Once we're back with the others, I tend to Aoki, creating a poultice for her wounds and crushing some poppy seeds on her tongue for her pain. Afterward, I touch up the minor scrapes Kenzo and the girls picked up in our escape. The hours pass with no signs of trouble, and as the tension drains, the twins fall asleep. It feels almost safe now amid the softly rustling bamboo and the dancing light of the stars painting lullabies across the earth. After the night's events, exhaustion must be hitting the girls hard.

Earlier this evening, they were told they were going to die.

Then one of them *did*. And another isn't far behind.

His watchful eyes on the trees, Kenzo cradles Aoki to him to keep her warm. She still hasn't stirred. I check her pulse often, scared she might slip away without us knowing. Half of me wishes she'll remain unconscious so she's spared the pain that'll undoubtedly storm her the second she wakes, while the other part of me wishes she'd open her eyes, just so I know she's still in there. That she still has energy to fight.

"Rest," Kenzo murmurs to me.

The dark is ebbing, sunrise fast approaching. Zhen and Zhin snore lightly. At the edge of the group, Blue is curled tight, facing away from us so I can't tell if she's sleeping, though after what she learned about her father earlier, I doubt it.

"I'm not tired," I tell Kenzo.

"Of course you are. Lei, we'll have to move soon. You might not get another chance to rest."

"I don't need rest," I snap. I blow out a breath. "Every time I shut my eyes I see Chenna and Mistress Azami. The look on their faces as they died. How they died to save *us*. Sleeping won't bring me peace."

"And torturing yourself with thoughts of them will?"

"It will give me strength." I meet his astute wolf eyes. "With what's to come, I need that far more than peace."

He tips his head, assessing me fondly. "How far you've come from the girl I once trained with in the forest. That girl barely knew how to wield a knife. Now look at you. You cut down demons with the confidence of a seasoned warrior. You saved the lives of four of your friends. Wren would be so proud."

Despite their warm delivery, the words bury into me like daggers.

I bite back the sour reply I want to hurl at him—that maybe Wren *is* proud of me becoming a ruthless killer, just like her.

Yet I can't help but recall the look on her face when she shared her Birth-blessing word with me. How broken she looked when she admitted what really happened to Aoki's family. How, when we talked about the night of the Moon Ball and why she came back for me, Wren said she couldn't let me go through it alone.

I know how it feels. They don't tell you about that—how taking a life takes something from you, too.

Will she still look at me the same way, even now? After all the things that have been taken from me? That I've taken from *myself*?

"I doubt you've been out of her thoughts this whole time," Kenzo says. "Maybe you forget, Lei, but I was there when Wren announced her love for you. I've never heard her speak like that before. It's the only time I've ever seen her not in control. You were the only thing in the world that existed right then. The only thing she cared about."

A few tears slip from my grasp. Kenzo reaches for my hand. His wolfish paw is large and heavy. It covers mine, and like the first time he touched me, instead of making me feel threatened, I feel safe. Protected.

How Wren's love used to make me feel.

How it still does.

Because even if I *am* scared, and disappointed, and angry, and confused, it always comes back to that: our love. Like I told Blue, I might have seen Wren at her worst, but I've seen her at her best, too. I know her, and she knows me. I called her heartless in my rage and despair once, but it wasn't fair. Not once has that been true. Wren has always had a heart.

She's just been taught to ignore it.

Kenzo smiles, and I return it through tear-blurred eyes—

At the same time an arrow whirrs past.

It embeds itself into the tree trunk inches above Kenzo's head.

I'm on my feet in an instant, knife drawn. Blue jumps up, too. Grabbing the club she took from one of the guards back at the palace, she dashes to my side. The twins stir. With Aoki lying across his lap, Kenzo doesn't get up, but he reaches for the staff propped behind him without shifting her, lupine eyes glinting as he stares into the darkness where the arrow came from.

"Wait here," I tell him and Blue, already moving forward.

"Lei," Kenzo warns.

"There might be others. Stay here and protect the girls."

I creep away before either he or Blue can argue. I hear Zhen mumble, "What's happening? Where's Lei?"

In the predawn light, the maze of bamboo plays tricks on my eyes, casting shifting shadows that mimic figures slipping in and out of view. I whip around at each snap of a branch, only to find more shadows.

Then a scream rises from behind me.

In an instant I'm hurtling back the way I came. More screams join it, and it strikes me that they sound wrong. They're high, almost giddy. As I get closer I make out voices and...is that *laughter*?

When I reach the clearing, I understand why the screams sound wrong. They aren't the type of screams I've become accustomed to, sounds of pain and terror.

They are screams of *happiness*.

I stumble to a halt, my panting loud in the sudden hush as every face in the clearing turns my way. Time slows, the world stilling on its axis, tuning its attention to this small space and the few people within it. Even the gods must be holding their breaths to watch.

For me, the world shrinks even further—until it is just her. All her. Only her.

Wren holds my astonished stare.

Nothing else exists apart from her eyes, that face, and my wildly beating heart, and my soul, shining so brightly that I wonder how I'm still standing—if I even *am* still standing—because all I am is breath and heartbeat and furious love burning so brightly it has scorched away everything else.

Wren opens her mouth. Nothing comes out.

Dimly, as if from far away, I hear Blue mutter disgustedly, "Look at them. It makes me sick."

And as if some strange enchantment has broken, I launch myself forward, just as Wren does, and we crash into each other, me leaping into her, her muscled arms strapping around my back to hold me, so safe, so strong, so *Wren*, both of us laughing and crying and clinging to one another, chest to chest, soul to soul, locked together as if we might never let go.

TWENTY-SEVEN

WREN

*I*T'S HER.

It's really her.

The words had been singing in Wren's mind from the instant she'd caught sight of Lei in the forest, her sweet face blank with shock at first, yet every bit as beautiful as Wren remembered. Then something had given behind those golden eyes and a fierce kind of joy had burst across her features, until she was blazing. Radiant. Lei had jolted into Wren's arms, and Wren finally got to hold the girl she'd been dreaming of for months, the girl she had thought of every waking moment, whose absence she felt with each heartbeat.

Lei's hand was in hers. She was here, *it was really her.*

Everything about her was a marvel. Wren looked and looked, drinking her in. And Lei looked back, as if *Wren* was a marvel, too.

After the initial euphoria of their reunion, some of Wren's anxiety at how Lei would receive her after the way they'd left things returned, but so far Lei was only shining eyes and glowing joy and wondrous disbelief—they were holding hands, *she was holding Lei's hand*—and though Wren knew it couldn't last, she basked in it. If only there was a way magic could affect time. She could live inside this moment forever.

"You didn't need to shoot at us," Blue grumbled.

Nitta shrugged. "Didn't want you attacking us by accident thinking we were soldiers sneaking up on you."

"Did you not think we'd have attacked you *because* you shot an arrow at our heads?" Blue returned waspishly.

Lova waved a hand. "Trivialities."

They were making their way through the forest together, heading for the northwest border, where Merrin, Khuen, and Samira waited with the horses. Lei and Kenzo had explained about the diversion, but none of them wanted to take any chances, so they'd got moving right after their reunion, making introductions for those who hadn't met. Wren had been relieved to see Kenzo with the girls, but it was tainted by the obvious cruelty he'd suffered during his imprisonment—and the half dead girl he carried in his arms.

Now, Kenzo walked carefully so as not to let the tiniest spur of torn bark or vegetation snag Aoki. Aoki's small body was limp, her skin pallid. Wren caught the concern on Lei's face, and she knew their blissful bubble had finally burst.

"I'll take a look at her as soon as we're at the camp," she said, squeezing Lei's hand. "I'll do everything I can for her. And we have amazing doctors. She'll be all right."

Lei nodded. Her expression darkened. "Wren, you should know...Mistress Azami was killed."

Though they kept walking, the loamy forest floor unchanged, it suddenly felt as if it were mud-thick, weighing down her steps.

"How?" she asked.

"She gave herself away to help us escape."

Of course. Mistress Azami, the proud, flint-eyed dog demon who'd been the first of their allies within the palace to make herself known to her. She'd told Wren she would do everything in her power to help her—and here was her final gift, delivering Lei safely to her at the cost of her own life.

It was Lei's turn to squeeze Wren's fingers. "I'm so sorry. She was an amazing woman. She did so much for all of us, put herself at risk every day. We wouldn't be here if it weren't for her."

There was a crack in her voice, and Wren knew it had to do with more than Mistress Azami. She asked quietly, "Chenna...?"

Lei shook her head.

Wren forced down her dismay, holding back the heat that rushed her eyes. She'd suspected as much, but some tiny part of her hoped Chenna had only gotten held back during the escape and their allies would hide her until they came to liberate the palace.

"I'm so sorry," Wren said. "Chenna was wonderful—"

"I don't want to talk about it," Lei interjected, and Wren nodded, understanding.

There were so many things she couldn't bear the thought of discussing yet, either.

Though Wren remained alert for soldiers, they reached the edge of the forest without incident. The sun was rising, a dome of gold on the horizon across the arid plains that stretched beyond the ivory-green rows of bamboo.

Wren felt Lei tense at the sound of hooves. "Our horses," she said, and then the large forms of Eve and Panda emerged from the trees to their left, led by Khuen, Samira, and Merrin.

Wren introduced everyone. She could tell Blue, Zhen, and Zhin were uncomfortable in the presence of so many demons, and they looked dazed still, smeared in blood, their pretty robes torn. Wren hated to think what they'd been through to get that way.

"Any guards?" Lova asked the others.

"Not on the ground," Khuen replied.

"A few of the Tsume are circling," Samira said. Like most bird demons, her voice was scratchy, but it had a pretty, musical timbre to it. "Want us to take care of them?"

Wren shook her head. "It'll only draw more attention. I'll hide us."

Lova's eyes searched her. "Are you sure that's a good idea?" When Wren shot her a sharp look, she lifted her hands. "Just saying. The last time you used magic you almost mowed us down. I'd prefer to stay un-mowed, thank you."

"What is she talking about?" Lei asked.

"I'm fine," Wren said, cupping her shoulder.

"So we're sticking to Ketai's plan?" Nitta, too, was giving Wren a penetrating look. "You still want to join them before the attack?"

"We'll need somewhere safe to stay, and to leave Aoki and the other girls."

"Wh-what do you mean, leave?" Zhin asked, her thin voice tremulous. "What attack?"

"Come on, Zhin," Blue said. "You can't be so dense."

As her sister opened her mouth to argue, Lova spoke over her. "We'll explain once we reach the camp. I'd rather not hang about here too long. This place gives me the creeps."

"Hang on," Kenzo said. "You never told us why you're here. It wasn't part of the plan, and if my timings are correct, you're a day early. Why aren't you with the others?"

"We'll explain later," Wren said, giving him a pointed glance.

"Going to be a lot of that, is there?" Blue remarked archly.

"Catch on quick, don't you, little one," Lova returned.

Blue's voice rose. "Excuse me—"

Lova moved fast, a hand clapping over Blue's mouth at the sound of wingbeats. Moments later, a shadow flew overhead. The bird demon turned in a slow, watchful arc, before moving away.

They waited until they were certain it was gone before organizing the group into those who'd ride the horses to the camp and those to be flown by Merrin and Samira. The busyness diffused the tension, though as Wren helped Blue mount Eve, the girl was still glowering daggers at Lova where she was swinging onto Panda's back. Once everyone was set, all that was left was Wren's magic.

It was the hardest she'd ever had to work to cast. But she focused on the sensation of Lei's arms around her waist and dragged it out, even as the effort made her vision swim and her head pound. She couldn't let up now, no matter how exhausted she felt, how depleted she was from the battle at Marazi and the long ride she'd made to get here. Wren had a responsibility to give every ounce of her energy into being what Lei and the others needed her to be.

A warrior.

A leader.

A Xia.

A Hanno.

If there was one thing Wren did well, it was honor her duties. And now Lei was back by her side, an honor all of her own.

Wren's resolve carried her through the effort of holding on to the enchantment as they crossed the plains. It underpinned her focus when they reached the war-camp where some Hanno clan members and shamans were waiting, having come ahead of the others to prepare for their arrival. It helped her grind out yet more magic so she could work healing daos into Aoki's fragile body under Lei and the Paper Girls' anxious gazes.

Lei was here, and Wren would never let her down ever again.

It was past nightfall, almost a full day after they'd arrived, by the time the camp had properly taken shape. The site hummed with an anticipatory atmosphere as orders were followed, dinner was cooked and dished out in banana-leaf bundles, and guards rotated lookout duty.

Having finally finished with her duties, Wren found Lei sitting with Nitta by a stack of boxes on the edge of the camp. They were looking out across the barren plains to the Hidden Palace. Even at this distance it was imposing, a black blot on the horizon nestled in a vast ring of green.

The night was clear, moonlight spilling down—the same light that gleamed off the horrid walls of the palace painted Lei's skin so beautifully. Wren had to stop herself from grabbing her right there and kissing all the places the silver touched. Lei had washed and changed from her ruined clothes. She was dressed in a simple cotton baju set in Hanno blue.

"Dessert?" Wren offered, coming to sit by her.

Lei raised her eyebrows. "You have to ask?"

"That is one word," Nitta said, reaching to grab one of the leaf-wrapped bundles Wren had brought, "that need *never* be followed by a question mark. Goes for anything edible, really. And naps." She smiled with glee when she found little jewel-colored diamond-shaped sweets within the leaf. "Kuih! I haven't had these in ages. Isn't this your province's specialty?" She directed the last part at Lei through a mouthful of the sweets.

"They are." Lei smiled, but it didn't quite reach her eyes.

Wren was still holding some out to her. "I asked for them to be prepared especially. Just in case."

Just in case you were still alive.

Just in case you were here to try them.

Just in case I wasn't too late.

The silence rang with the awful possibilities. Luckily Nitta was chomping away, her happy eating sounds softening the atmosphere. Wren was about to put down the banana-leaf parcels when Lei touched her wrist.

"Thank you," she said.

"I love you," Wren replied.

It came out as easily as breathing. Without thought, or even intention.

Something swirled in Lei's eyes. The light of the lanterns that hung from the posts holding up the stretched tarp of the camp turned them even more golden and molten—as well as her tears.

Nitta smacked her lips. "Well," she announced, spinning into motion with a push of her hands, "time for my post-dessert nap."

"It's nighttime," Wren said.

Nitta beamed. "Naps that become full-on sleeps are the best kind. Better squeeze one in if it's to be one of my last, hey?"

Though her tone was teasing, the air turned heavy when she left.

"Her back is broken," Lei said dully.

Wren felt a guilty stab. "The battle at Jana," she said, though Lei knew that already.

She could feel anger pulsing off Lei, full, dark waves of it. She'd been poised for it, but it still felt too soon. She wanted to live in her joy a little longer. They were together again. It was all she'd been waiting for.

Almost all.

In the distance, the palace loomed.

"She seems good, though," Lei went on. "Better than good, even. She's been telling me about the upgrades she's bugging Lova to make to Battlechair, and how Tien has been terrorizing your cooks and pretty much anyone else who dares cross her path when she's in a mood. Even your father." Her smile faltered. "I always admired that about Nitta. Terrible things happen, and she can keep smiling, even if it's agony."

Wren was quiet. "Isn't that something we all learn, through grief and suffering?"

Their fingers found each other at their sides, and wound together, tight.

"I wish I was better at it," Lei whispered.

A current of pain shot through Wren that had nothing to do with her injuries or exhaustion. "I wish it wasn't something you ever had to learn in the first place. Lei, I can't tell you how sorry I am you had to go back there——"

"No," Lei cut in. "I—I can't. Not yet."

"Of course. Only if and when you're ready."

Something hard pressed into Wren's forearm where she was holding Lei's hand: a golden band. It circled Lei's wrist, sleek and smooth. The trace of magic buzzed from its metal.

Wren had noticed it back in the Bamboo Forest. She'd not failed to spot a similar one around Aoki's wrist, though Aoki's had been bound far tighter—so much so it had crushed bone. When Wren healed Aoki earlier she'd tried to sense if there was anything to save, but the damaged tissue was too far gone. What had happened in those months back in the palace?

Wren was almost glad Lei wasn't ready yet to tell her about her time there. If she knew the details of what the King and his court had done, she didn't think she could stop herself from charging over there right now and hunting down every demon who'd dared harm a hair on Lei's head.

"None of it's important now, anyway," Lei went on tiredly. "Not to the war. And we got out just before...before the worst could happen." Her eyes slid sideways, and though they were as lovely and emotive as they'd always been, they were harder. As though some of their softness had been replaced by weathered stone. "But you and Ketai, and all the rest of it...Nitta's filled me in on some things, but I know there's more."

She paused, and Wren knew what was coming.

"Tell me everything," Lei said. "Everything that happened since Jana."

And so, Wren did.

It took a long time. She didn't leave a single important point out. Lei listened intently. Though her hand was rigid in Wren's, sometimes flinching in silent anger or shock, she didn't interrupt. She simply held space for Wren to speak.

Her restraint surprised Wren. Once, Lei would have pressed her for further details. Demanded why Wren had given in to her father so easily when he refused to allow her to rescue her from the palace, or burst with indignation at what Wren suspected Ketai had planned for the Hanno shamans. Then again, Lei used to *have* to push her for more. Tonight, however, her words kept private from the rest of the camp as clan members bustled in the background, Wren spoke freely.

You're making this so hard for me. Do you know that?

That's how it had felt once, when she'd first opened up to Lei. Now, what Wren felt more than anything as she talked was relief.

An hour slipped by. Wren's fingers grew numb where they were scooped with Lei's, her body sinking with exhaustion. But neither of them moved.

"Ketai will be pleased to know we escaped without your intervention, then," Lei said when Wren's story came to a close. "That your plans for the siege haven't been compromised."

Wren hesitated. "Unless Lady Dunya brought him the information when they abandoned us at Marazi. Gods know I wouldn't blame her for it."

"I don't think she did. It would've been pretty hard to miss their arrival, and I'm sure the King would have gloated to me about it." Lei's tone was rueful. "When your father arrives tomorrow, I'll be his Moonchosen again, won't I?"

A dark beat knotted Wren's stomach. "Lei," she began, "whatever he asks of you—"

She was cut off by running steps.

The two of them were on their feet before Blue ran into view. The bags under her eyes were deep, her hair mussed on one side as if she'd slept awkwardly. But her typically stony eyes glinted with something Wren hadn't seen in them before. It was almost warmth.

"Nine," she said. "Aoki's awake."

Lei jolted forward, only to stop, turning stiffly back to Wren.

Blue's eyes flicked suspiciously between them. "What's wrong?"

"Go ahead," Lei told her. "I'll be right there."

Blue folded her arms. She was thinner than the last time Wren had seen her but just as tough, every harsh edge and line more pronounced, as though she'd been honing herself like a weapon. "I am not your captive maid anymore, *Queen* Nine," she shot, and Wren's mind spun on the words. Captive? Maid? "Anyway, it was you who asked me to get you when Aoki woke."

Lei sighed. "We just need a moment, Blue. Please."

Blue threw them an affronted look. "Fine." Before she left, she jutted her chin in Wren's direction. "That ridiculous lion demon is looking for you." Then she spun on her heels, stomping back in the direction she came from.

"Aoki doesn't know about her family," Lei said as soon as Blue was out of earshot. "And now isn't the time to tell her. She needs all her energy."

Guilt twisted beneath Wren's ribs. "Lei, I am so sorry—"

"But she'll have to know eventually," Lei continued, "and I think you should be the one to tell her." Her lips quirked, wetness shimmering in her eyes. "Something to look forward to, after all this is over?"

Her mouth twisted. Wren wanted nothing more than to bundle her in her arms and tell her how, if they were lucky enough to survive what was coming, she would prove to Lei for the rest of their lives just how sorry she was.

"I was wrong earlier," Lei added. "When I said I didn't have any important news for you from the palace. I can't believe I almost forgot. I...I met the Demon Queen."

Whatever Wren might have expected, it wasn't that.

"The King took me to see her," Lei said. The lightness had gone from her eyes; they looked as solid and heavy as the gold at her wrist. "She's carrying his child, Wren. His heir."

Blood rushed in Wren's ears.

The King. An heir.

It was too awful to believe.

That at least had been one comfort, one thing her father and their allies had felt safe in—that the so-called Empty King of Ikhara was infertile. They didn't need to worry about his line continuing. They just had to kill him, dismantle his court, and they'd be free of his corrosive influence. But if another Demon King lived on...

"We have to find her," Wren said. "We have to—"

She stopped, the words too horrible to speak.

Lei's stare was caustic. "We have to *save* her. I promised myself that I'd free her, Wren. Whatever happens tomorrow, we're getting her out. I count on your support."

She strode away before Wren could offer it. Maybe she wanted to leave before she could read any more into the shock on Wren's face, and figure out what Wren had actually meant when she said they had to find the Demon Queen.

Or maybe she was walking away because she already knew.

"Trouble in paradise?"

Lova slunk from the shadows. Wren wondered if she'd overheard what Lei had revealed about the Demon Queen, but if she had, Lova didn't let on, and it wasn't like her to withhold her opinions.

"What did you want to show me?" Wren asked.

Lova led her to the northeast corner of the encampment. Apart from the guards patrolling the perimeter beyond, only a few clan members were still up. They bowed as Wren passed.

"Lady Hanno," one young Paper maid demurred, before moving on, and the name shot through Wren like a firebrand.

"Perhaps you'd prefer Lady Xia," Lova said.

"I'd prefer no *Lady* at all," Wren snapped.

"I'm with you there, honey. *Lady* suggests such a dull life, doesn't it? Even *General* has been getting on my nerves lately. I think it's time for an upgrade."

"Depending on how things go in a couple of days," Wren responded coolly, "*Queen* might be available."

Lova stopped. "Lei saved herself from getting married to that bastard. Why aren't you happier? I know you understand restraint more than most of us, but you're back with her, Wren. She's safe—at least for now. Don't waste the time you have. If it comes to an end, you'll regret you didn't make more of it."

There was remorse in her voice.

"Is that what you wanted to talk to me about?" Wren retorted, annoyance rising in her. "Me and you? How good we could be together, a Paper and Moon leading Ikhara? Because it sounds like someone else's recent plan, Lo, and I wasn't a fan of that, either."

Hurt dashed across Lova's features. "What I'm saying is to not let pride or some stupid fear get in the way of something true. Something good." She started on again, brushing roughly past Wren. "If you don't want my advice, fine. But as allies in a war, I am obligated to show you this."

She marched out from under the lit canopy of the camp. They went a short way before Lova pointed to the east.

"There."

At first, Wren couldn't make out anything, her human eyes not nearly as sharp as Lova's demon ones. Then she saw it.

Something was moving on the horizon. A low mass, lit by flickering pinpricks of light.

"But our army is coming from the west," Wren said.

"So that's not our army."

Coldness slunk down Wren's veins. She thought of Lei tending a gravely injured Aoki. Of the Paper Girls asleep in their hammocks. Of Kenzo and Nitta and everyone else back at the camp under her protection.

"Reinforcements," she whispered.

"But for the King, or for us?"

Wren scanned the horizon again. It was impossible to make out anything more of the slowly approaching mass, but it was clear they were headed right for them. If the group was coming to bolster the King's defenses, they risked being taken out—their daos weren't strong enough to protect them from such a large attack.

"We'll take the horses," Wren told Lova. "Just the two of us. And bring some of your explosives."

Lova gave her a sharp-toothed grin. "You always know the way to my heart, honey."

Wren recalled the barely veiled disappointment in Lei's eyes earlier.

If only she knew how to hold on to the one heart she truly wanted.

TWENTY-EIGHT

LEI

AOKI'S LASHES FLUTTER. SHE LETS OUT the occasional soft groan, or turns her neck, wincing. But she hardly seems aware of my presence as I check over the bandages the Hannos' medics wrapped her with—far better than our frayed scraps of hanfu—before I settle beside Blue.

"He's keeping her sedated for the pain," she tells me, inclining her head toward the shaman kneeling on Aoki's other side.

His chanting drifts over us, fluttering the curtain separating the sick bay from the rest of the camp. It's quiet. Only the distant sounds of guards patrolling the perimeter and the murmuring and clatters of a few restless clan members break the peace, along with a sudden flurry of hooves from the direction of the stables. Guards off to do some checks I suppose, or perhaps messengers. Once they fade away, everything settles back into a strange kind of serenity.

It won't last long. In a few hours, the place will be a hive of activity.

At least, I imagine so. I haven't prepared for a battle like this before. Perhaps this is how it will go on. The calm before the storm.

Aoki murmurs. Her eyes half open, and I hold my breath until she drifts away again.

"Sleep," I tell Blue. "I'll stay with her. You must be exhausted."

"I'm fine," she says, her words at odds with the shadows bruising her eyes. "*You* should be the one resting. It's not like I'll be going back there to kill the King. That *is* your plan, isn't it?" She makes a scornful noise when I don't answer. "I don't care, Nine. There's no need to pretend anymore—not for any of us. Go kill the gods-damned King, if that's what you want. Just make sure you do it right this time so we can all move on."

"Move on," I breathe. "It seems too much to hope."

"All *I'm* hoping for," Blue responds tartly, "is to finally live without *your* stupid actions dictating *my* life."

We glance at each other—and burst into laughter. It comes from nowhere, a sudden rush, as though it'd been bottled all this time. Tears rush my eyes. Blue's laughter is bold and true and wholly surprising. It's the first time I've ever heard it like this before, not a bark or derisive snort, and it's a wonderful sound.

"Wh-what's...f-funny?"

Aoki's croak makes both of us jump up.

"Aoki!" I brush the sweat-stuck hair from her brow. Blue lifts a cup of water to her mouth. "Don't worry," I say, stroking her face. "You're safe. You're safe, now."

After some sips, Aoki's head slumps. "The...the King." Her eyes open wider. She tries to sit up, then winces. Her hands skim across the reams of bandages covering the lower half of her torso. "Where is he? We were—I was just with him..."

Blue and I exchange a pointed look.

"Aoki," I say carefully, "we're not in the palace anymore. We escaped. Don't you remember? There was going to be...the King had planned..."

I fumble for words. *The demon you love ordered your execution* doesn't exactly roll off the tongue.

Aoki's forehead furrows. "He wanted to see me..."

In a flash, Blue leans over Aoki, their noses almost touching. "The King wanted to kill you, Aoki," she growls with revulsion. "He was going to kill all of us, except precious Nine. We only just managed to escape—apart from Chenna. Madam Himura broke her neck right in front of our eyes."

"Blue!" I cry.

She spins to face me, her dark azure hair catching the lantern light as it swings across her face. "She isn't a child, Nine. Stop treating her like one. Aoki can handle the truth. She *needs* to." She turns back to Aoki, who is looking between us with round eyes, her lips trembling. "There's going to be an attack on the palace the day after tomorrow," Blue says. "The Hannos and their allies are organizing it. Lei's been helping them this whole time. She would have murdered the King long before now if that stupid thing on your wrist hadn't held her back."

Tears streak Aoki's reddening cheeks. She gapes at us, then turns away, grimacing at the effort. "You should have let him k-kill me," she whispers.

I draw back, her words a slap.

She takes another juddering inhale. "It w-would be better than *this*."

Waves of contempt flow off Blue, as powerful as Wren's magic. "You care about that bastard, even now?"

"Blue," I warn.

She ignores me. "He didn't care if you were dead or alive, Aoki! You meant *nothing* to him. None of us did. Why do you think he even kept us around after the Moon Ball, instead of executing us like all the others with a connection to Nine? He used you for information about her, and then he saved us for *bait*. He knew we were the only thing stopping Nine from attacking him again. And when he no longer needed us, he arranged to have us murdered—"

"*Blue!*" I yell. "That's enough!"

As Aoki's sobs rack the air, Blue climbs to her feet. "For once, Nine," she says icily, "I agree with you."

She glares down at Aoki, a strange yet familiar expression contorting her face: a mixture of pity and resentment and deep disappointment. I recognize it as the exact look her father wore when his daughter arrived for her own execution.

"Enough of this," Blue orders Aoki. "The King doesn't care about you. He never has. The sooner you understand that, the better. Don't waste your tears on a man like him." Then she tosses the curtain aside and disappears.

"Ignore her," I say. "She's...going through some things. None of that was about you. You know that, right?" When Aoki doesn't answer, I go on tentatively, "Do you think you can sleep a bit more? You need to rest."

Aoki watches me, her eyes shining. Though her voice cracks, she pushes the words out. "Are you really going back there to try and kill him again?"

I nod, even though it hurts. "We're storming the palace the day after tomorrow. It should be the end of the war. One way or another."

Aoki takes a small breath. "The end," she murmurs.

The end of us being Paper Girls.

The end of her relationship with the King.

The end of Ikhara as we know it.

Whatever happens tomorrow, it will be an end—though that means there will also be a beginning. A future, no matter how changed.

"Not *the* end, Aoki," I amend, reaching for something soothing to give her. "*An* end. There's so, so much more for you to come. I know you think the King is your whole world, but he's not. You have an entire future without him, waiting for you to take it."

Her reply is scathing. "Is that what you'd say if this was about Wren? You're not the only one who's ever been in love, Lei. No matter how much you act like it."

There was a moment once when I thought I'd lost Aoki forever—when I first understood she truly loved the King, or at least believed she did. And really, what is the difference? Like faith, or hope, love isn't a substance we can take in our hands and hold out to someone and say, *Look, I told you it was real.* It exists purely within our own hearts. If anything, that makes it all the more powerful. If we *could* measure it, set it out on a platter for weighing, it would make so many things easier.

If only I could offer Aoki my love. It would barely fit in my arms; its brightness would be blinding. And she would see that in comparison the King's was never anything more than a hard, empty husk.

I was wrong when I thought I'd lost Aoki that time—even all the moments since I've been back in the palace, sure of her hatred of me. This, here, is the final break in our tether. Her words a slice of a knife, sure and devastating.

"Leave me alone!" she cries, and I do as she says, stumbling away before she hears the sob that escapes my throat.

The second I find a quiet corner, I fall to my knees and weep.

I don't know how long I cry. I must be well hidden, because no one disturbs me. My sobs have faded to a silent stream, my neck and the collar of my top soaked. It's only at the growing sound of hoof-fall that I uncurl from my crouch.

Hooves, approaching fast. Far more than I heard leaving earlier.

The sound stokes a drum of dread. In an instant, I'm ten years old again, screaming for Mama as her hands slip from mine in a throng of panicked villagers.

"You aren't a child," I tell myself, loosening the knife at my waist. "You have fought the King and his demons. You will not cower anymore."

All around come frantic footsteps and shouts as the camp bursts into action. I join the fray, passing Kenzo, who doubles back when he sees me. He towers over the mostly Paper crowd, gray fur glinting in the lantern light and the flash of weapons being readied.

"Lei!" he shouts. "Have you seen Wren?"

"No...?"

"I'd hoped you were together."

My heart flutters. "You haven't seen her? She's not here?"

He shakes his head. "Neither is Lova."

For one absurd moment, I imagine the two of them have gone off to create a life for themselves. It makes no sense, and I know it's only a cruel burst of jealousy on my part, but the image burns in my mind. Wren and Lova, the beautiful young clan leaders, spurring their horses on, faces thrown back in laughter.

That's when I remember. Hoof-fall. Wren and Lova *did* leave earlier—but not to abandon us. Wren would never do that. She came all this way for me because she loves me.

And what did I show her in return? Anger and contempt. I didn't even get around to apologizing for what I said to her that awful night on the Amala's ground-ship. Didn't tell her how I've regretted those words every day, wished and prayed and begged the gods I could somehow take them back. How, even though they came from a place of honesty, what I said wasn't fair and could never take away from how much I love *her*, too, and that if there'd been any way, I'd have crossed the whole of Ikhara just to tell her how fiercely I regret those words ever left my lips.

Now I might have missed my chance.

"They took the horses earlier," I say.

His bronze eyes flash. "Where? Why?"

"I don't know—"

He spins, cutting through the throng. I hurry after him. Clan members rush past, some pausing to ask Kenzo things or relay information, and my pulse skips as I catch snippets of their conversations: *a hundredfold*; *horse- and bear-back*; *Papers*; *demons*. But it's only when we reach the edge of the camp that the horror truly kicks in.

Before us, rocky terrain spreads to the horizon. The rough earth is silvered in starlight that glints off a mass directly ahead, speeding toward us across the plains.

It is unmistakably an army.

There are soldiers of all types—demons, but what appear to be Papers, too, recognizable amid their larger neighbors. Most are riding. Some sit or stand in the backs of open-topped carriages. Flags snap from poles attached to their mounts. With the lantern light at my back, it's difficult to make out what's stamped across them, but I identify enough different colors and designs to realize these aren't royal soldiers. They're a collection of warriors from clans from across Ikhara.

"The Demon King's allies," I breathe. I'm speaking more to myself than to Kenzo, though he listens at my side, staring ahead. "Wren must have seen them. Went to face them with Lova before they could reach us."

A scream builds inside my throat—how *dare* she? How dare she, yet *again*, take everything on her shoulders, deciding what I can or can't be a part of? A murderous desire to find the shaman responsible for her Birth-blessing pendant and the venomous word it contains sears me. *Sacrifice.* Wren has built herself around the concept. And if she did go to intercept the King's reinforcements, and they're now charging straight for us, that means—

A boom of laughter startles me.

Kenzo's head is tossed back, incisors bared as gales of thunderous laughter rock through him.

"What in the *gods*," I snarl.

Still grinning, he opens an arm. "Reinforcements."

"I know that—"

"Not the King's. *Ours.*"

The army draws closer, and I notice now what I failed to in my initial panic—the two figures riding at the head of the pack. Lova, towering on the back of her enormous black-and-white horse.

And Wren.

My Wren, sitting tall and regal, loose hair whipping her cheeks as she charges her horse on. Her face is set in a resolute look visible even at this distance. A look that tells the world *I have found what I was searching for—and I will have it.* The look she wore the night of a dance recital back in our early days as Paper Girls, when our eyes met across a sugar-dusted stage, and before I even understood what it meant I sensed how my life was about to change forever.

Kenzo grins. "The Black Jackals. The Hish. The Paper Warriors of West City. The Ice Plains Alliance. And is that…" He lets out an impressed whistle. "The desert bears of the Red Sand Valley. They're some of Ikhara's fiercest warriors. Ketai's been trying to win them to our cause for over a decade."

"There are hundreds of them," I say, awestruck. "Kenzo…we might stand a chance."

He crooks his neck at me. Though his smile fades, there is a sharp, hungry look in his features that reminds me of the time I was once just a terrified girl being taught by a wolf demon in the middle of a midnight forest how to kill a King.

Do not forget the last part. Right here, Lei. This is where you aim tomorrow. Push the blade deep, and do not stop.

"A chance is all it takes," Kenzo says, echoing other words he shared with me that night. "And I'd say this time, ours isn't bad. We've taken Marazi and the Black Port. We have recruited important allies— allies the King would have liked for himself. And, of course, we have *you*, Lei. The King lost his Moonchosen the night before he was to marry her, and the deepness of the roots of our rebellion's influence within the court has been revealed. Whatever he might be pretending, I imagine the King is the most vulnerable he's ever felt."

The dusty plains Wren, Lova, and our allies are crossing now make me think of the first time I was brought to the palace, almost one year ago. I was in a carriage with General Yu, and I'd looked at the stars and thought of the sky god Zhokka, Harbinger of Night, feeling as though I was about to be swallowed whole, just as Zhokka had attempted to eat all the light in the sky.

As the story goes, Zhokka was punished for his greed by the Moon Goddess Ahla, who blinded him when she attacked him in her crescent form. Ever since, I've thought of the King as Zhokka, consuming the world with his toxic heart, and Wren as Ahla: the only one with the power to bring light back to my sky.

The first time I came to the palace, I was terrified. I had no idea what awaited me. The second, I was a wild thing, fraught and lost. The next time I return, I'll be those things and more. I will be braver, and stronger, and I will have Wren at my side.

It won't only be her who'll be Ahla. *I* will be Ahla, too. A lancing blade in pursuit of my prey.

We know how the story goes by now. Zhokka falls to Ahla, and light is restored.

The King always said we must play our parts in this world. This is mine.

And for the first time, I feel truly ready to wield it.

TWENTY-NINE

WREN

IT WAS THE FOLLOWING AFTERNOON BY the time Wren was able to pause. Ever since she and Lova brought their new allies to the camp, it had been a whirlwind of delivering orders and overseeing their execution. Wren had only seen Lei twice in passing the whole morning. She wished Lei would rest, but Kenzo had drafted her and Blue to create a ledger of every Paper, Steel, and Moon in the now-overflowing site, and Lei seemed to appreciate having something to do. Wren knew her. She wouldn't sit around while others were hard at work.

Nitta was the one to alert Wren to her father's arrival. Lunch had been served a few hours ago, but Wren had been too busy to take it. Now, she sat on a crate in as quiet a spot as was possible amid the frenetic camp, lifting glass noodles tiredly to her mouth. She'd just finished the bowl when Nitta rolled into her vision.

"They're here," she said simply. "Want me to cover for you?" Nitta asked as they made their way to the main hub of the camp. "I could say you've got pre-battle nerves and haven't left the toilet all morning? I doubt even Ketai would want to confront you while you're, you know…"

"I wouldn't put it past him," Wren replied, making Nitta snort.

"Or I could tell him you're having a *very* amorous reunion with Lei."

If only that were the case.

Sensing her mood, Nitta said kindly, "You looked amorous enough to me back in the forest. In fact, in many provinces a public display like that would get you arrested."

Wren's smile disappeared the moment she heard her father.

He was at the center of a large group, Hanno clan members and warriors from their newly arrived allies gathering to greet the Clan Lord. Wren hung back, freshly anxious at the thought of facing her father after their confrontation in Marazi. Then another voice boomed from her right.

"Lady Wren!" Commander Chang pushed toward her. "What a surprise to see you. I worried we may arrive to news you'd been taken captive at the Hidden Palace."

"Sweet Samsi," Nitta groaned. "Do you *ever* shut up?"

Chang's cheeks reddened. "I suppose I should expect little manners coming from a common Cat like you. Not even wanted by your own clan—and one held in such low regard as the Amala—"

In a flash, Wren had a blade pressed to the underside of the Commander's chin and Nitta moved right up to him so the wheel of her chair pinned one of his booted feet in place.

Chang whimpered, attempting to free his foot while wary of Wren's sword.

"Careful, Lady Wren," he spluttered, and despite his precarious situation there was a knowing curl of confidence in his tone. "Fraternizing with outcasts seems to have rubbed off on you, and we both know your father values loyalty above all else. Indeed, he *demands* it."

"*You* want to be careful, Commander," Wren said smoothly. "Tomorrow, we fight alongside each other. We both know which of us is the stronger warrior. Should it come to a moment where you need my help, you might regret having accused me of disloyalty. I may decide to agree with you." She jerked her head. "Come on, Nitta."

As she strode away, she heard Chang's relieved welp as Nitta rolled off his foot.

The gathering around Ketai jostled, clamoring for his attention, yet when he spotted Wren her father stilled. He held up a hand. "Dear friends, I'm afraid I must ask you for a little more patience. My daughter is here, and there are things I must discuss with her. When I get back, I will answer every one of your questions."

"But, Lord Hanno—"

"My Lord—"

"Just one minute—"

Ignoring their pleas, Ketai walked over and slung an arm around Wren's shoulders. He led her to his private tent, set up close to the camp. Wren steeled herself for the berating that was surely to come. Yet when they stepped through the navy curtain, she was surprised to find others already in the tent.

At first, she thought something was terribly wrong. The figures were huddled together, sobbing and talking in stuttering sentences. Then she heard the joy in their voices. Saw that their tears were ones of happiness, not sorrow.

Her heart leaped.

Lei, Lei's father, and Tien. Reunited at last.

It felt as though she were intruding on something deeply intimate. Perhaps her father felt similarly, because neither of them spoke, waiting patiently for Lei and her family to realize they had an audience. When they did, Lei sat back where she was kneeling on the rug and beamed up at Wren, while both Jinn and Tien got to their feet.

Tien bundled Wren into so tight a hug it took her breath away. "Thank you, sweet child," she said. *"Thank you."*

Past her shoulder, Jinn gave her such a genuine, loving smile that it crushed something in Wren's chest. "Eight thousand times, thank you," he croaked, hoarse from crying. "How can we ever repay you for what you have done?"

The words should have warmed Wren. Instead, they chilled her. Lei's father might be grateful for whatever role she'd played in getting Lei out of the palace—which was essentially nothing, since Lei had freed herself—but what would other families say if they ever discovered what Wren had done to *their* families? What would Aoki say once she knew the truth about her own? All the other raids the Hannos framed on the King?

Wren extricated herself from Tien. "Thank you for your kind words, Jinn, Tien-ayi. You are too generous. I did nothing—Lei saved herself and Kenzo and the girls without my help."

"But I did have help," Lei corrected, her smile wavering a little. "We only escaped because of the shamans, and Mistress Azami, and Chenna, and the rest of our allies in the palace."

"Still," Jinn said. "Wren, we owe you and your father so much. We hardly dared to dream this moment would come, and you have been a part of making it so. Please, accept our gratitude."

Wren inclined her head, though she still felt uncomfortable.

Ketai came forward. "Jinn, Tien—will you please give Lei, Wren, and me a moment? Once we're done you may spend as much time together as you like. Tonight is cause for celebration on many fronts. Our chefs are preparing a fine banquet—in part, to honor your wonderful daughter, Jinn, and the bravery she continues to show. Tien, perhaps you'd like to keep an eye on the kitchen? I know my chefs haven't been quite up to your perfecting standards."

The lynx-woman laughed. "As we say in Xienzo, *No dish is better than one born from love*. Nothing will ever beat home cooking, Lord Hanno. No matter how many fancy chefs you employ."

Wren's father smiled graciously. "Perhaps one day I can tempt you to join their ranks."

"Too much work," Tien said, with a dismissive wave of her hand.

"That's what you always said about me and Baba," Lei pointed out.

"Why are you using past tense, little nuisance?" Tien retorted, and she, Jinn, and Lei laughed, a beautiful sound that Wren could have listened to forever.

Lei was happy. She was with her family, who loved her. She deserved every moment of her life to be like this.

Before they left, Lei sprung to her feet. "Baba, Tien," she said, clutching their wrists, her face serious now. "Promise me you'll think about what I said. I couldn't bear to lose either of you. Especially now."

Tien lifted herself high, though she was hardly taller than Lei herself. "You're forgetting my prowess with a gutting knife," she said, only half jokingly.

Lei's father's eyes were wet. "My dear, we should be fighting alongside you. It's only right."

Lei stared them down. "I had plenty of training with Shifu Caen and in all the fights I've been in since. Neither of you have battle experience. Please. I need you both."

"Let's talk later," Tien conceded.

Jinn pressed a kiss to his daughter's forehead. "Later then, my brave girl," he said.

The atmosphere changed as soon as the pair left the tent. Ketai was still smiling, but it had taken on a barbed edge. Wren instinctively moved closer to Lei, muscles tensed.

"Don't worry," Ketai said. Lantern light flickered in his granite-flecked eyes. "I'm not going to rebuke you for defying my orders. It would be a waste of our energies, and conflict is not what we need right now. Anyhow, everything turned out for the best in the end."

Wren didn't like the sound of that. She'd come to understand what was the best for her father was not necessarily welcome in her world.

Not anymore.

"What did you want to discuss?" Wren asked, twining her fingers through Lei's.

Ketai's smile disappeared, something strange twisting in its place. He looked almost feverish, touched with a desperate kind of expression Wren was more accustomed to seeing on the face of the King.

"I have been trying," he began, "to understand something for a while now, and I think the two of you hold the key to its answer."

Lei swapped a wary look with Wren. "Us?"

"If I am correct," Ketai said, "it's vital we figure this out tonight, as it may be the very thing that sways the battle tomorrow. Wren—you stayed at the Southern Sanctuary on your way to Marazi. Tell me, did the shamans there discuss the Xia with you? Did they share anything that might reveal more about your magic?"

It was as if a stone had been dropped into Wren's stomach.

"You knew," she said. "It was part of your plan for us to camp close to the sanctuary. You *wanted* them to find us."

"I'll admit, I wasn't certain they'd reveal themselves to you, but yes, I very much hoped they would. To provide you safety and comfort, of course—"

"But more to understand the workings of my magic," Wren finished.

Ketai came closer. Though Wren was the same height as him, she felt small in his presence. She forced herself to straighten, to project confidence—as he himself had taught her. He noticed, and pride shone on his face.

"What did you learn at the sanctuary? Please, daughter. It could give us the advantage tomorrow. After everything the two of you have been through, and our friends—Mistress Azami, Zelle, all our fallen allies who died to protect *us*—anything you may have heard or seen at the Southern Sanctuary could save others from the same fate. Isn't that what we're here for? To stop the King and his court from destroying more than they already have?"

Wren almost flinched. What did her father think? That all she'd given up, everything she'd risked—including the most important thing of all, *Lei's love*—meant nothing to her?

"Please, Wren." He braced her shoulders. "Even the smallest detail could be meaningful. Help us win tomorrow, so we can finally be free."

Free.

The word unlocked something in her.

It all came pouring out. Wren recounted the days she'd spent with Ahma Goh and the mountain shamans, Ketai interjecting now and then with questions, but for the most part letting her speak, just as Lei had earlier, listening intently.

When she finished, Lei was smiling up at Wren. "I still can't believe you found your Xia family's home. I'm so *happy* for you, Wren," she said, and Wren's whole chest glowed.

It was only the two of them in the tent then.

"I'd like to take you there," she told Lei.

"Then take me there. Please."

Almost the exact words that had followed her question one velvet night in Wren's room in Paper House so many months ago.

Can you imagine a world where we're free to be with each other?

Actually, I can.

Then take me there, Wren. Please.

Lei's smile was soft and knowing, and Wren knew she, too, was recalling the conversation. Wren felt the promise of that future held within their clasped hands. It seemed closer than ever before.

Then her father spoke. His face was alight with vivid focus. "So it is as I thought." He moved away, pacing the rug-covered floor. "The key to true Xia power. It's easier than I even dared to hope." He swung around. "We have everything we need to defeat the King, right here in this tent!"

Wren shifted closer to Lei. "We have more insight into the Xia now," she said carefully, "but we understood all this already, the dark sacrifice that powers their magic. That was why—"

She stopped. She hadn't yet confronted him about her suspicions as to his plans for the Hanno shamans. It had been awful enough with Hiro, but this . . . this would be a *mass execution.*

"That is unnecessary, now," Ketai replied, and relief charged through Wren.

Until his next words.

"We have something even more powerful. Or, I should say, some*one.*"

Ketai's zealous eyes were fixed on Lei.

Wren's heart roared in her ears so loudly she almost didn't hear his words. But she did. She heard, and she wished she hadn't. She wished she'd never entered the tent at all, never gave her father the confirmation he'd needed to come to this conclusion, worse than anything she could have imagined.

Worse than anything she could have imagined of *him*.

"Lei, my dear Lei," he explained fervently. "Don't you see? *You* are the key. The Xia didn't just sacrifice anyone for their magic, like the King has been doing with his Shadow Sect—siphoning our land of its qi in the process. That was the issue all along. We thought the Xia's power came from death, which it does, but only death given *willingly*. True sacrifice. For what is a more powerful sacrifice than to die for someone you love? Everyone thought the Xia traveled in pairs at a minimum because it was safe, but it was for *this*. If they needed to, one could sacrifice themselves for the other. Ultimate power, always at their fingertips." He was aglow with awe. "Such an elegant, intelligent, *simple* system. I should have guessed sooner." He gave a rough laugh, teeth flashing as he smiled. "But now we know—and just in time."

Lei stood frozen at Wren's side. She whispered, "You...you want me to sacrifice myself tomorrow. To kill myself, for Wren."

"*Yes*," Ketai confirmed eagerly.

At the exact time Wren said, "*No*."

And then she flew for her father. She slammed him down and pinned him to the floor, magic and wrath blazing from her like never before as she crushed his throat beneath her fist.

THIRTY

LEI

KETAI AND WREN'S THRASHING BRINGS GUARDS rushing into the tent. In seconds, Paper and demon hands grasp Wren, attempting to drag her off her father. Glacial waves of magic billow from her. She's so strong it takes more than ten of them to get her off of him—only for her to dive straight at him again. They just manage to hold her back. Nitta and Lova are among the pack. I hear Lova shout, "At least kill him *quietly!*" and a crazed laugh bubbles out of me before it chokes off in a gasp.

Wren's chest heaves. Her eyes are as white as fresh snow, as white as death. Her power shakes the tent walls.

"*How dare you,*" she snarls at her father, before collapsing to her hands and knees.

The air stills as she drops from her Xia state.

"Wren!" I elbow Lova out of the way.

She's panting for breath. Tremors rack her body. She retches, and I pull her hair from her face, though nothing comes up. I wrap myself around her and look over my shoulder.

Ketai is on the floor. Some clan members fuss around him, but he waves them away, propping himself up on one elbow. He coughs, rubbing his neck where the imprints of his daughter's fingertips are visible. His dark eyes meet mine.

There is no shame or regret. Not even compassion. Only pure, cold determination.

"What in the name of the Heavenly Kingdom!" one of the clan members—a burly, mustached Paper—bellows. "It is just as I was telling you, my Lord. The girl is *not* to be trusted!"

Everyone ignores him.

"Do...you...see?" Ketai's voice is a whispering scrape, his windpipe bruised, but I hear each word as if he's speaking right into my ear. "Her magic...is weakening. What do you think will happen... tomorrow?"

"Stop," Wren spits weakly. She tries to stand but only manages to plant one foot before she sags.

I clutch her close. Yet my eyes are pinned by Ketai's penetrating stare. His words ring in my ears, sink deep into my skin like a brand.

Her magic is weakening.

What do you think will happen tomorrow?

Do you see?

And the awful part is, I *do* see.

The assortment of guards and clan members look between us all, bemused. Mustering his grace, Ketai stands. He swipes a hand through his fallen mop of gray-black hair.

"Out," he commands. "All of you."

"Like hell," Lova growls.

Nitta smolders. "What she said."

"The insolence!" blusters the large man. "The audacity! The—"

"*OUT!*"

Ketai's roar stuns the tent into silence. The mustached man looks as though he's been slapped. As the other clan members hurry from the tent, the man shoots Wren and me a disgusted look before he stomps out.

Lova and Nitta don't move.

"Do as he says," I tell them. "This is a discussion we need to have alone."

Nitta's jade eyes swim with worry. "But—"

"It's fine, Nitta. Please."

Lova turns her furious glare on Ketai. "We'll be right outside," she snarls. "The slightest sign there's a problem, and we'll be back to finish what she started." Then she prowls from the tent with Nitta.

"You're all right," I whisper, pressing my forehead to Wren's. "You're all right. You're exhausted, my love. You've been going non-stop since Jana. We'll get a shaman and a medic to see to you, and then you're going to rest."

"You are not sacrificing yourself," she forces out, still trembling violently. "You're not doing that, Lei. Not for me, not for anyone."

"I know. Don't worry." I look at Ketai. "She needs a calm place to rest. A sleeping mat, food…"

"Stay here," he says. "I'll send for everything she needs."

Wren lifts her head, sweat beading her forehead. She speaks shakily but her tone is final. "You will not have her, too, Ketai."

Though he hides it well, I don't miss the surprise that flashes through him at her use of his name. After a beat, he says, "If that is your decision."

He sweeps from the tent in a streak of cobalt robes.

"Lei," Wren starts once we're alone, "I am so sorry. I had no idea—"

"Shh." I lower her down as her eyes flutter, shocks spasming through her body. Rage charges through me, white-hot. How much magic has she spent to get to this state? How much vitality—how much of *herself*—has she worn away to do her father's bidding, to be the perfect Xia warrior everyone expects of her?

I draw some nearby furs over her and lay her head in my lap. I brush my fingertips along the curves and dips of the face I know so well I could paint it with my eyes closed, every tiny freckle, every scar, every flawless detail. "Rest," I say. "I'm here. I'm with you, Wren. I'm not going anywhere."

Her lashes flutter. Her eyes are unfocused. "Promise?" she whispers, in the simple, trusting way a child would ask an adult.

Like so many adults, I answer with a lie.

"I promise."

I find Ketai by the stables. He's with a few of the Hannos and some of the other clan leaders. When he sees me, he says something to the group and leaves them, striding over to me. It's just past sunset. The darkening sky is the color of bruised plums. The brightest stars are beginning to emerge.

The group Ketai was with watch him go. Whispers trail him. News of his and Wren's fight must have traveled through the camp, and I wonder if any have guessed the terrible reason behind it. But how could they? Even after Hiro and Aoki's family, and Wren's suspicions about her father's schemes for his shamans, *I* still didn't expect it. Even Wren was blindsided.

We all have limits. Tonight, the three of us discovered ours.

"We're planning how best to allocate our mounted units tomorrow," Ketai tells me with forced casualness. "With last night's arrivals, we've far more numbers than anticipated. It's an enormous boost."

I turn away, gazing out over the dusty plains to where the Hidden

Palace rises from behind the dark-green armor of the surrounding forest. The fading light catches on the palace's dark, glittering walls. They remind me of Ketai's eyes.

"Wren's resting well," I say. "I thought you should know. A shaman is still with her to help her sleep. I told him to get some rest himself, but he seems to think he doesn't need much. I suppose," I continue when Ketai says nothing, "that's because you're going to have them kill themselves to give their power to Wren."

He responds calmly, with no trace of remorse. "Just as the King will have his shamans in the Shadow Sect do. It will help—but it will be only a fraction of the strength *your* sacrifice would offer her."

A cold laugh bursts from me. "You really are shameless."

"Shame has no place in war."

"And what of in life?"

"War is different."

"Is it?" I ask. "War is a part of life. It doesn't happen in a vacuum. One day soon, if you're lucky, you'll have gotten through all this—and then what? Will you keep punishing, keep killing, keep maintaining you're only doing what needs to be done? How will *you* rule, Ketai? How will you keep order when demon clans rebel against *your* court? When it is *their* turn to seek revenge?"

He makes an impatient noise. "I don't expect you to understand, nor do I need your approval. Your naivete is charming, Lei, yet unrealistic. I'd have hoped being with Wren would have taught you more by now."

I laugh again, an ugly sound. "She's more than you think, Ketai. She's so much more than you made her. Didn't you hear her? *You will not have her, too.* She wasn't talking about the Papers or demons you've killed. She was talking about *herself.*"

Ketai doesn't answer, and this time I know my words have cut him. Still, when he responds, there is an indifference in his tone that makes me shiver. "Well, Moonchosen. We both know why you came to find me. Let's not waste more time. Say it."

I look back across the plains to the palace.

I imagine turning away from all this. Taking Wren and Baba and Tien and the Paper Girls and getting out of here. We could go to the sanctuary Wren described in the mountains, or perhaps back to my home in Xienzo. Find a quiet corner of the world and make a life for ourselves. A life chosen by us, and not forced by the greedy hands of men like Ketai and the King. We could make our own kind of freedom.

When the world denies you choices, you make your own.

Yet I know these thoughts are pointless. Because if the King defeats the Hannos tomorrow, Ikhara will never be free for Papers. Everything will continue as before, always living with the fear that one day we'll hear horn blows and hoof-fall, and know our worlds are about to shatter. And even if the Hannos and their allies *do* win the war, I know Wren would regret it every day that she hadn't been there to do it with them.

I would regret it.

Because this has never really been about helping Ketai Hanno take the throne. It is about my mother, and Zelle, and the Demon Queen, and every Paper Girl who was ever imprisoned in the palace. It is about Bo and Hiro and Chenna and Caen, and all the Papers across Ikhara who live every day with a fear they should never have had to know in the first place. It's about shamans like Ruza who are risking their lives to help me keep mine. The Paper woman who looked at me the night of the Unveiling Ceremony and called me dzarja, a traitor to my own kind. And, perhaps above all, it is about the night the Demon King took something from me I'll never be able to get back. All the times he took and *took* from me, tiny parts and huge chunks, inflicting wounds that will never heal, no matter how much time passes.

And it is about Wren, and love, and hope.

I take a breath, steadying myself. Then I turn to Ketai.

"I'll do it."

The words sound as though they're coming from a foreign body. Surely I can't be agreeing to this. But I knew the moment the pieces came together in Ketai's tent that if this is what it takes, I will do it.

The first thing I picture once the words are out is Wren, Baba, and Tien crying over my body. The second is two characters, side by side, close as lovers.

Sacrifice.

Flight.

Wren's fate was never about her—it was about who she loved. It was this. It *is* losing me. And this time, it's my turn to give *her* wings.

"I'll do it," I repeat, "but not for you. For Wren. She's drained herself so much I don't know if she can get through the battle without it."

"You love her that much," Ketai says.

I shake my head. "More."

He begins to speak.

I hold up a hand. The tears are arriving, and I won't give him the satisfaction of seeing them. "I've seen how it's done. I'll know when the time comes." I take a shaky breath. "Wren will hate you for this for the rest of your life," I say as I move to leave. "I hope you know that. But she *will* have a life. And that's what matters to me."

Before he can say anything, I spin on my heels. Tears stream hot and fast now as I run back the way I came, desperate to return to Wren. To not waste one second more without her.

If I'm only to live a few more hours, I want to spend them by her side, in her light, in her love, her beautiful glow. I want to soak it all up. I'll remind myself exactly how it feels so that when the time comes for me to go, I won't be alone. I will have the memories of every moment we have spent together.

Even if I wish for so, so many more.

THIRTY-ONE

WREN

IT WAS JUST HOW SHE'D DREAMED it so many nights before. Lei waking her by slipping under the sheets, tucking a leg between her thighs and cupping her face in one hand, turning her cheek gently so they were face-to-face, those bright eyes blazing more fiercely than she'd ever seen.

"My love," Wren started, hoarse.

Lei shook her head. "Not now. None of it matters. Nothing before this moment, and nothing after. Can we do that? Can we just...be?"

Her eyes were shimmering with a rainbow of emotions, but above all else was resolve. Wren could drown in that molten gold, and gladly.

She knew she should apologize. They had so much to talk through. But tomorrow's battle was creeping ever closer, and their issues wouldn't be solved with one conversation. It was going to take months, probably years of patience and understanding and reopening old wounds until they found the formula to heal them.

Wren didn't mind. She was ready for it—anything that meant they might stand a chance.

"Let's just be," she agreed.

Their lives were about to begin, after all. Their futures were waiting just around the corner. They could have one moment suspended in time. One moment to ignore reality a little longer.

Lei smiled, and Wren's heart ached.

"How do you feel?" Lei asked, bringing her lips closer. "Do you think you have the strength to kiss me?"

Wren brushed back the hair that'd fallen across Lei's face. She smelled so good, like wild meadow flowers in the rain, like love, like hope. She smelled like home.

She *was* home.

"Always," Wren replied, and lifted her mouth to meet Lei's.

As the first boom of a war-horn rent the air.

THIRTY-TWO

LEI

THE CALL BLASTS LOUD AND CLEAR, shooting despair down my veins.

Not now. Not *yet*.

We were supposed to have one final night.

I was supposed to have more time.

Wren is already dragging me to my feet. She flings aside the flap and looks out. Bodies rush past, the entire site having burst into commotion at the alarm.

"Wren! Lei!" Kenzo sprints toward the tent, lobbing a large bundle to Wren as he nears: clothes, armor, the long lacquered scabbards of her swords. "Get dressed and meet us at the stables."

The wolf demon is already dressed for war, blue hanfu overlaid with a leather chest piece and metal-knuckled gloves. His bamboo staff is strapped to his back. Even in his diminished condition, he looks imposing, every bit the experienced warrior.

"What's going on?" Wren asks. "We're hours early."

Kenzo's expression is grim. "The Bamboo Forest is on fire."

"The entire forest?"

"They must have set it themselves."

My head spins. "But why? It was one of their defenses."

"They know we're coming," Kenzo says. "Instead of waiting, they've played their hand first. It is a bold one, I must admit, and not one we predicted. Not only does it give the palace guards a better view of our approach, they are sending us a message."

"Which is?"

"That they are not afraid."

He and Wren swap a hard look, then she brushes past me, slipping off her sleeping robe to draw on her various layers of gear. Kenzo spins on his heels, disappearing into the throng.

"Wait!" I shout, springing after him.

I elbow my way past rushing bodies. He stops midstride, turning at my call. We're crushed together by the throng, the rush and noise shielding my words from the wrong ears.

"There's something you need to know," I say. "But you have to promise not to tell Ketai." Kenzo begins to protest, and I cut him off. "I know you're loyal to him, but I need you, Kenzo. I need your help."

He hesitates a fraction longer. Then he nods. "What is it?"

"The Demon Queen is carrying the King's child."

His jaw ticks. "Why are you telling me this now?"

"We need you to get her out of there, Kenzo. I'm going to try, but if anything happens to Wren or me, I need you to do it. She's in a pavilion within the River of Infinity's southern curve—though the King might keep her with him during the battle for extra protection. I don't know. But I need you to promise me. After the battle, get her to safety." I clutch his arm. "Ketai *cannot* know about this. If he thinks there's any chance the King's reign could continue with the baby, he'll kill it, and the Queen, too. And she deserves to live,

Kenzo. Think of everything she's endured. Now, pregnant...it's her choice what she does with the baby. No man is taking it away from her without her consent, demon or not."

Kenzo gives me a long, searching look. Finally, he reaches down, curling a roughly padded paw around my shoulder. "I asked you once to help us when we needed it the most. Of course I'll do this for you, Lei." He draws me against his chest. Pressing his nose to the top of my head, he adds in a rough whisper, "But I pray I do not have to."

I squeeze him back.

"Wren's coming," he says, and slips away.

"Lei!" Wren calls over the clamor.

I snap on a neutral expression. "Sorry. I just wanted to see if Kenzo had an update on Aoki."

"She'll survive this, Lei," Wren assures me, taking my hands. "She'll be here when we get back. And the rest of the girls, and your father and Tien. Maybe it's a good thing we don't have time to face them before we leave. There's no need for good-byes when we'll see them again."

It takes all of my willpower to hold back tears at that.

I told Baba and Tien we'd speak more about them joining the battle. They'd promised me they'd think about remaining behind, and I could tell they understood how desperately I meant it. Now I won't have time to be certain, to give them one last embrace, and I won't be able to see Aoki or Blue or the twins to tell them how much they mean to me, how much their companionship over the past few months has kept me going, kept me alive—not in the physical sense, but in my *soul*.

Tears cloud my vision as Wren leads me back to the tent. "Let's get you changed. My father had clothes and armor made just for you."

Of course he did. After all, The Moonchosen must always look her part. First, as a symbol of revolution; then repentance; then a bride.

And now, the last of her guises.

A martyr.

The burning forest comes into view as we head out into the camp grounds. Even as we pushed through the swarm of bodies within the tent, the bite of smoke in the air was detectable. Now it hits us full force as we emerge into the night.

The rocky plains stretch before us. Past them, the Hidden Palace lives up to its name, veiled by swaths of flames. The whole horizon is alight.

Wren leads me to where her father is booming instructions from atop a crate.

"General Novari, to the west flank!"

"Lady Oh, your Commander is preparing your war-bears in stall twelve!"

"All remaining soldiers of mine who've been assigned to mounts, report to Commander Chang!"

Spotting our approach, Ketai presses the scroll in his hands to the adviser beside him to continue organizing the crowd, before jumping down and striding our way. Kenzo comes over from where he was helping a soldier steady her nervous horse. Nitta joins us, too, Battlechair gleaming in the firelight.

"Where's Lova?" Wren asks her, ignoring her father.

"Gathering the Amala. We'll be making up the bulk of the eastern flank during the first wave."

" 'We'?" I say. "Are you with the clan again?"

"I mean us cats. It's not like—"

"There's no time for this," Ketai interjects. "If we make it through the night, you can continue this conversation then."

His eyes skip over me as he says this, the words so careless on his tongue. I resist the urge to punch him in the face. He and I alone know I won't get a chance to finish this conversation.

I won't get a chance to finish anything.

"The forest being on fire changes things," he says. "We'd planned to travel through the forest, but it will be completely unnavigable like this. The court knew exactly what they were doing by setting it alight. They must have heard by now we lost our remaining White Wing allies, so our only route to the palace is by foot. They'll be expecting us to wait out the fire, forcing us to attack in daylight tomorrow, when they'll have a perfect view of our approach." His eyes flash. "We must not play into their hands again. We will attack now, while the fire still rages. *We* will be the ones to surprise *them*."

Two winged figures descend from the sky: Merrin and Samira. Merrin's coat is stained pewter from smoke. Samira doubles over, coughing, as Nitta goes over to rub her back.

"Everything is as we suspected," Merrin reports. "The soldiers are mostly gathering within the courts adjacent to the main walls in preparation of us attempting to scale them, with more in Ceremony Court in case we attack via the main gate."

"And the King?" Ketai prompts.

"Guards are mobilizing around his fortress. But they're concentrating on the perimeter walls."

"Good. That'll mean more will be caught in the blasts."

Blasts?

"But the shamans are in the walls," I say.

The group ignores me, talking fast, shooting information and queries back and forth as the sky roils ever darker.

"Are we still focusing on the main gate and the southern walls?"

"I don't see any reason to change plans. We always knew they'd anticipate a more front-loaded attack. Let's give them what they expect—then surprise them with what they don't."

"What about the Tsume? The White Wing? We never factored in this much smoke."

"It'll only make it harder for them. They fly in a pack. The bad visibility will cause problems."

"And Samira and I can keep them distracted."

My heart races as I try and keep up, try to make sense of the plans I wasn't a part of making, only ever truly expected to be useful to Ketai for one part of them. A part that requires neither preparation nor practice.

Knife, blood, magic.

The formula could hardly be simpler.

"Lord Hanno!" A blue-clad guard hurries over. "The army is ready. Everyone is in place."

It takes me a second to realize the buzz of the camp has died down. Although clan members are still rushing about, last-minute shouts for a doctor or a piece of equipment cutting through the air, the mass of arrivals Blue and I spent so much of yesterday inventorying has dwindled to less than a third. I swing around farther, looking to my right.

While we've been speaking, the collective army of the Hannos and their allies has assembled. The grounds facing the palace are *packed* with soldiers; thousands of Papers, Steels, and Moons from a myriad of clans, their colors muted in the flame-charred wind, flags emblazoned with crests flying from the masts of ground-ships and war-carriages and horseback. They are organized in precise blocks, facing ahead to where the Bamboo Forest burns, marking our target.

Ketai dismisses the guard. "Ready?" he asks us.

The others give their assent. Wren's father's knowing eyes bore into me as he waits for my response.

Am I ready to die?

Of course not. I want to run back to the camp and find Tien and Baba and hold them until all this is over. I want to go to the girls and keep them safe in a way I never could within the palace walls. I want to tell Wren that I lied to her, that these last few pitiful moments are all we're ever going to have, and it's not enough, it could never be enough, eight thousand lifetimes with her would not be enough. Then she slips her hand into mine, and suddenly what I am about to do seems not only reckless but impossible.

I can't, I can't, I can't.

I'm not ready.

"Lei?" Wren whispers. She moves closer. Her fragrance, that fresh ocean scent, once seemingly so exotic but now so wonderfully, bone-achingly familiar, is a reminder of everything I'm about to lose.

And everything I am about to save.

I steel myself, clutching the broken scraps of my soul.

"My love?" Wren speaks only for me. "You don't have to fight. You've done more than enough. Stay here with the girls and your family, if you want. I'll find him, Lei, and I will kill him for what he did to you. To *us*. I will kill him," she repeats fiercely.

"I know you will," I whisper back.

Then I return Ketai's stare.

Am I prepared to die?

No. But what is one more lie?

"I'm ready," I say, even as the words sear my throat.

Ketai nods, and the group splits, everyone heading to their various positions. No one spares time for good-byes or good wishes, perhaps believing like Wren it will bring bad luck—or perhaps knowing it'd be too difficult.

As Nitta joins the Amala, emerald eyes glinting as she flings us one last grin over her shoulder, Wren draws me into her arms.

"We'll be together the whole way," she says, soft lips to my brow.

I can't look at her. It would tear away my last shred of resolve. Instead, I watch the flames in the distance and think of the demon who waits within. I may not be ready to die, but I am ready for *him* to die, and this is how we make that happen.

Gripping Wren's hand, I walk forward before my determination weakens. "The whole way," I echo, knowing with numb, sinking agony that the way won't be far.

THIRTY-THREE

LEI

WREN'S HORSE, EVE, IS BROUGHT TO us by a Hanno clan member. Wren climbs up first, then swings me onto the saddle behind her. With a flick of her reins, we move past the lines of amassed soldiers to the head of the army. "Hold tight," she instructs. "We'll be riding fast. If anyone attacks, don't worry about fighting. Khuen will spot us. Just keep hold of me."

My heart hammers so hard I wonder if she can feel it through her back. I suppose not, since I'm jammed against the hard sheaths of her swords and she's wearing the same pitted leather armor as Kenzo and her father.

My own outfit is notedly different. Armor is heavy and takes getting used to fighting with, so Ketai designed something he felt I'd be able to move easily in. I'm dressed in the Hannos' signature navy, in a cotton baju set and supple leather boots, a belt at my waist to hold my knife. My hair is drawn back from my face with the same band Wren and the rest of the Hannos wear. Their insignia is stamped across the blue fabric, but while theirs is white as on their flag, mine has been stitched in shimmering gold thread to match my eyes, as well as to mark me as different.

Only Ketai and I know the reason for this, of course. But I *feel* marked, even without my new Moonchosen outfit. Though the soldiers we pass are probably more interested in Wren—their champion, their prized Xia warrior—it still seems as though they are watching me, each pair of eyes seeing through to the dark truth pulsing at the core of me.

Soon, I will be dead.

As I look back at the soldiers, it strikes me I'm not the only one riding to their death tonight.

Do some of these men and women feel marked, too? Do they also sense a swift blade and sudden rush of blackness awaiting them? Are their hearts also crazed with fear? A voice in their heads crying out this can't be it, there is so much more they wanted to do, so many years they hoped to have, so many more times they wanted to feel sunshine on their skin and the warmth of their lover's embrace. To close their eyes at the end of a long day, so certain there'll be a new one to wake to.

With a rough shake of my head, I blink my eyes clear.

No more tears.

No more pity.

I whisper the words that have always been there for me when I've needed courage. "Fire in. Fear *out.*"

We're nearing the front of the army now. A row of war-carriages is packed with both soldiers and cannons and other huge metal weapons I've never seen before, most likely Lova's creations. Then, making up the very first three rows in the central block, are shamans.

Even when they're not casting, they are impressive. Compared to the other warriors, many of them look out of place, too small, young, or old to be in an army, yet latent power ripples off them in a silent wave.

We take our place beside Wren's father at the head of the army.

Behind us, Khuen, the young Paper archer, rides a speckled gray horse, while to his other side, Kenzo—presumably charged with protecting Ketai—towers on the back of a colossal war-bear. The bear seems far calmer than the ones I heard panting and growling in the stables; it only rolls its thick shoulders side to side, its wet snout smelling the air.

Wren's father's mount is a beautiful white mare. His flowing cobalt cape is striking against her snow-white coat. An elegant jian juts past Ketai's shoulder. I wonder how much blood it has spilled. How much more it will spill tonight.

Ketai tips his chin at us before fixing his gaze upon the flame-wreathed forest, eyes narrowed against the smoke-dark wind. He lifts an arm. A hush ripples through the soldiers.

From overhead comes a rumble of thunder, almost as if Ketai called it himself. A summer storm must be couched behind the clouds.

Wren slides a hand over my linked fingers at her waist.

Half lifting myself to reach her, I press my cheek to hers, closing my eyes. "I love you," I whisper, urgent.

Wren's hand clasps mine tighter.

Her father roars.

"FOR THE FUTURE OF IKHARA!"

I jerk back as Eve leaps into movement, building into a charge in seconds. The deafening clamor of hooves fills my ears as, like one enormous creature, our army storms forward.

Wren's hair streams as she urges Eve on, keeping her level with her father's white mare. I can hardly breathe for the force of the wind, the stunning pace at which we ride.

There's the first flash of lighting, sapphire-white behind the ceiling of smoke, and in the afterglow I make out the winged silhouettes of Merrin and Samira.

"Bird demons!" Merrin shouts.

Ketai flings his arm high. "WATCH THE AIR!"

They drop from the clouds they've been using for cover with the next burst of lightning, a rush of speeding winged figures.

The White Wing have swollen the Tsume's ranks. There are two hundred, maybe even *three* hundred birds headed straight for us.

Wren draws a sword. It reflects the lightning—as a volley of flaming arrows rains down from the approaching birds.

"HEADS!" Ketai yells.

Wren flings an arm around, yanking me down. Air whirrs as she spins the sword over our heads, deflecting the arrows. Others aren't so lucky. There are shrieks of pain. Stumbling hooves as falling soldiers trip up those behind them.

I straighten as Wren lets go, my blood surging as I take in the sight of the bird demons, so close now I can see the colors of their plumage, the metal beak coverings and talon razors strapped to some—and the stone slabs others haul between them.

Merrin and Samira fly at their center, causing their tight formation to split.

Ketai punches his arm high. "ARROWS!"

From behind us, a hundred arrows hurtle into the air. There are yells. Grunts. Winged figures tumble from the sky.

A chunk of rock crashes down with one of them, right in our path. Eve leaps it. We land with a judder, only to swerve as two birds pitch another slab our way.

"SPLIT!" Ketai commands.

The world turns neon white, lightning illuminating the bird demons—just as they set upon us.

The plains resound with cries and screams, the shrill clash of metal as fighting erupts. Thuds punctuate everything as the heavy rocks slam down.

Wren draws in line with her father. Behind him, Kenzo is hunched over the neck of his bear. An arrow juts from his left shoulder. He cracks it in half and tosses the feathered end away as simply as if he were brushing off a fly.

"Father!" Wren shouts. "The wall, are we still—"

She cuts off as a feathered figure wheels toward us. Wren has her sword ready, but an arrow cuts the bird down before he reaches us: Khuen.

There's a sickening crunch as Eve's hooves trample the fallen demon.

We're nearing the Bamboo Forest now. A wall of towering flames rises like a tsunami of fire. The heat lashes out, sticks my thin clothes to me with sweat.

"SHAMANS!" Ketai shouts. "PREPARE YOURSELVES!"

Keeping my arms firmly around Wren's waist, I risk a glance over my shoulder. Behind us, the shamans—three rows deep—each mimic the same position, holding on to the reins of their horses with one hand, the other thrown forward, palm open. Their lips move, forming words I can't make out over the burr of the flames and the crush of hooves, gold characters already spinning from their lips. The magic travels down, circling their outstretched arms to the tips of their fingers.

I spin back around. We're meters from the inferno.

The heat is unbearable, searing the air and sucking the breath from my lungs. The flames writhe high, coiled with ribbons of smoke, the bitter taste filling my mouth.

I bury my face in Wren's back; brace for the burn—

"SHAMANS!" comes Ketai's bellow. "NOW!"

There's an astonishing blast of wind and light.

And the heat *explodes*.

My first thought is that we're in the forest, and we're being scorched alive. Even with my eyes clenched, face pressed to Wren's back, the light is so bright its sears my eyelids. Electric waves race over my skin. The howl and the heat and the buzz of magic builds into a formidable mix, until, just when I think I'm going to suffocate from the force of it, there's a sudden rush of air—

And it all falls away.

I lift my head and open my streaming eyes.

I once saw shamans put out a fire with a dao that transformed into water. This enchantment used air.

As Eve slaloms through the blackened husks of trees, the immense wall of air the shamans unleashed charges ahead in an all-consuming wave. Row upon row of blazing trees are snuffed out in an instant. The smoke is dispersed, too, pushed up to where it coils overhead in black clouds. And as the air in front of us clears, the walls of the palace come into view.

I'm cast back in time to the first moment I saw the palace. The way the curtain of ivory-green bamboo drew apart to reveal towering walls, golden characters swirling within the marbled stone. The might of the magical vibration coming off them. The demon guards flanking the perimeter and patrolling the parapet, each so terrifying I'd understood why the King felt invincible within these walls.

Almost a year since, and I've proved—*we've* proved, me and Wren and all the others—just how wrong he was to ever believe he was safe.

I look up at the walls and think of the King hiding behind them, and a satisfied smile twists my lips. Because I know this time, he does *not* feel invincible.

He knows we are coming for him.

And he knows exactly what we're capable of.

Ketai swings his horse close. The shamans' magic reaches the last of the flames, extinguishing them in a final billow of air before slamming into the walls of the palace themselves. The banners lining the parapet are ripped from their poles. They swirl through the ember-flecked wind, a cascade of red and obsidian.

The shouts of the royal soldiers are discernible now. There are demons everywhere: on top of the wall, before it, birds from the Tsume and the White Wing still swooping low over our charging ranks, their number cut in half but still too many.

Straight ahead, the main gates are blocked by a contingent of heavily armed soldiers. They're reassembling after the shamans' wind knocked many off their feet. To each side of the gate stand stone pecalang, the pair of guardian statues carved into the likeness of bulls. They are gigantic at over twenty feet tall. The braziers in their hooflike hands are still lit, unaffected by the enchanted air; like the walls, they must be protected by the royal shamans.

"Wren!" Ketai yells. "At some point they'll be forced to open the gates—make your move then!" He addresses me. "Stay close to her!"

It sounds so innocent, as if he's telling me for my own protection. But we both know what he means.

"Lei!" Wren draws her second sword. "Get your knife. When we reach the soldiers, we jump!"

I let go of her waist with one hand and fumble for my dagger. Its bronze blade flashes in the stormlight. For the briefest moment, my eyes are reflected in it, and I catch a glimpse of the thing that has brought me so much wonder and pain for what will be the last time.

A deep, almost calming sense of purpose flows through me.

No demon or god gave my eyes' golden tone to me—my *parents* did. My plain, Paper parents. And everything I am, everything I have been and done, is because of them. Before Wren, it was they who taught me about bravery, and fairness, and kindness, and love.

They would understand what I'm about to do.

They would be proud of their daughter.

Baba *will* be proud.

To our right, Ketai thrusts his fist high. We're almost upon the royal soldiers now, the palace walls close enough to make out the individual characters spinning under their stone skin.

"CANNONS!" he hollers, throwing his arm forward. "ATTACK!"

A series of colossal booms rip out.

Smoldering objects shoot over our heads, almost too fast to track. There's just enough time for a few warning cries before they crash into the wall, exploding in shocks of white.

"Lei!" Wren cries, as the air is suddenly alive with flame and screaming. Something that resembles an arm still clutching a spear flies past me. "Now!"

Together, we jump.

Air whips my skin. There's a rush of cold. I brace for an impact—

Which doesn't come.

My hair flaps about my cheeks, caught in a whirling ball of arctic air: Wren's magic. It lowers us gently to the ground. I'm on my hands and knees, dagger still in one fist. Wren is already fighting, twin swords swishing in a graceful dance. Her clothes flow around her in an underwater sway. As she spins, I catch the eerie white stare of her Xia state.

Battle has broken out. Wren's swords create a pocket around us, keeping soldiers at bay, but beyond, Hanno and royal forces fight in intense clashes.

I flinch as another round of projectiles fly overhead.

Figures are flung from the parapet as the wall is rocked, smoke unfurling with each strike. Yet though the wall is scarred, given the power of our cannon fire it should be far more damaged than it is.

I think of Temple Court, the rows of shamans chained within the walls, forced to cast endless daos of defense. They're what's keeping the wall standing—but if it falls, they will be killed. Shamans like Ruza. Shamans that helped me. Helped all of us.

I should warn them, try to help. But I can't leave Wren.

Knife, blood, magic.

I have a job to do.

I clamber to my feet. In the flickering firelight, my blade seems to wink at me, urging me on.

Wren keeps the demons at bay, but more soldiers arrive every second, rappelling over the palace walls or transported by bird demons.

That's when I hear it.

The palace gates. As Ketai predicted, the towering doors groan slowly open. For a second, I'm relieved. Not only can we get into the palace, but it means we won't have to destroy the walls and risk killing the shamans within.

When I see what waits beyond the gate, my body goes numb.

The vast square of Ceremony Court is packed with demons and shamans. They stand eerily still, stormlight and flames flashing off their armor. The soldiers are dressed in red, while the shamans wear midnight robes, the hems swirling at their feet like smoke. They're standing in pairs, creating a patchwork of the court's colors: crimson and black, like fire and smoke, blood and decay.

"THE SHADOW SECT!" roars Ketai from where he's fighting side by side with Kenzo a few feet away.

My heart flies into my throat. After all this time, all the rumors and slithers of gossip, I'm finally face-to-face with the King's secret weapon. The power that generations of his ancestors have been cultivating all this time based on information they stole from the Xia. The root of the Sickness. The mirror of Wren's power.

Pain. Death.

Sacrifice.

The doors of the gate come to a stop, fully open, and the Shadow Sect begin a slow march forward.

"Wren!" Ketai commands. "Now!"

But whether she's too occupied by the onslaught of demons, or too deep in her Xia state to hear him, she doesn't slow.

"WREN!" Ketai shouts again.

I watch, frozen in place, as the Shadow Sect shamans all take a single step forward.

"CANNONS!" Ketai bellows, giving up on Wren. "AIM FOR THE SHAMANS!"

There's the boom of gunpowder. The ground rumbles beneath us.

The shamans throw their hands forward.

A flare of magic strikes, so powerful it snatches the breath from my lungs. The air crackles. Time seems to slow, everything moving in a dreamlike flow as a series of cannonballs arc low over our heads, straight for the Shadow Sect—

And then pause.

For one incredulous moment, they hover in the air. Then the cannonballs are thrust back, flying fast the way they came.

I dive at Wren, flinging us down—before the impact launches us high then slams us into the ground. Pain judders me. My body groans in protest as I list to my knees, Wren and I crawling to each other.

The night is rent with screams and the crackle of fire. Whole swaths of dead trees and earth are wreathed in flames. Pits where the projectiles landed smolder, spewing palls of gray. Most of our carriages lie on their sides. Bodies litter the ground. One has fallen close, staring up with vacant eyes. I don't recognize her, but she's wearing Hanno blue. Wren closes the girl's eyes and makes the sky salute over her body. When she turns back to face the Shadow Sect, the focused expression I've come to know so well closes over her face.

Her hair lifts as she recites a dao. She gets to her feet, hands curling into fists. White crawls over her irises as she moves into her Xia state—only to drop to her knees.

I lurch to her side. "Wren!"

She rakes in ragged breaths. Lifting her head with a grimace, she starts to chant again, the warm brown of her eyes icing over before she slumps back down.

Around us, bodies wrestle in the firelight. Members of our army rush about, helping up friends and dragging the wounded away. The Shadow Sect hasn't moved from their position. Its shamans stand with their arms outstretched like eerie statues, their power forcing back anyone who gets too close.

I scan the vicinity. To our right, Ketai and Kenzo are locked in a fight with four demons. Nearby, Khuen sends volleys of arrows into the air, keeping the diving bird demons at bay. At our backs, our own shamans are occupied with countering the magic of the Shadow Sect, enchantments clashing in the charged air. For now, they seem evenly matched—but many of our shamans have been injured or killed, and the ones remaining look exhausted, pale-faced and racked with tremors like Wren.

They won't last much longer—and we haven't even made it into the palace yet. We need Wren's power, or every one of us is going to die here at the palace gates.

My knife is on the ground where it was knocked from my hand

in the blast. I snatch it up. Wren is still on all fours, sweat pouring off her as she struggles for breath, trying—and failing—to access her Xia state. I slip my arms around her and press a kiss to the top of her head. Then I draw back. Her eyes meet mine, then slide down to where I'm raising my dagger.

There's a flicker of confusion. But before it can fully take hold, her eyes snap to the left—and go wide.

The Shadow Sect shamans have lowered to their knees. Their black robes billow around them. Each soldier has taken the arm of the shaman to their left. As one, the shamans reach into their robes and draw a long, slim dagger. Firelight glints off the blades as, in perfect unison, one hundred shamans lift their knives to their throats—

And draw them firmly across.

I let out a strangled cry.

Knife, blood, magic.

The exact method I was moments from using myself.

The shamans slump, ruby torrents pouring from their opened necks. But just as the blood reaches the floor, it stops.

Horrified, I flash back to Hiro on the Czos' island. Like then, the shamans' blood begins to eddy, traveling in a loop to where the soldiers hold their limp hands. The liquid slinks higher, moving over the soldiers until each of them is armored in blood.

Shining red coats their skin and fur. It crawls up over their chins. Seeps into their mouths.

Some of the fighting dies as both armies take in the nightmarish sight. Along with the wasp-buzz of magic, a high-pitched ringing grows, and I clap my hands over my ears.

The blood from the emptying shamans spreads over the soldiers' faces in scarlet masks, glazing over their eyes, until they share

the same awful red stare. One of the soldiers—a hulking croco-
dile demon right across from us—opens his mouth in a grin. His
razored teeth drip blood.

As one, the Shadow soldiers let go of the dead shamans.

The second the bodies hit the ground, they charge.

THIRTY-FOUR

LEI

WREN AND I CLAMBER TO OUR feet as the wave of Shadow soldiers strikes.

Wren is back in her Xia state. It must be excruciating, but the threat of the blood-powered soldiers is powerful enough motivation. The air—already ringing, singing, *bursting* with magic—whips about us in a frenzy, lashing out in ice-cold flares and flame-hot blasts. Smoke is caught up in it, showering everything in spinning whorls of ash.

I fight instinctively. Wildly.

Action. Reaction. All fire, no fear.

I don't have time to be scared. I barely have time to think.

Before, Wren handled most of the demons, but now each one takes her full attention, so I'm left to face others on my own. I swerve and duck the towering demons' weapons, attacking with quick slashes to their ankles, groins, wrists—anything I can reach. I hack until they fall to their knees, then finish them with a cut to the throat or a thrust to the heart, the now-familiar sensation of my blade digging through sinew.

Ketai and Kenzo have closed in to provide Wren and me with more protection, each of them locked in combat with one of the blood-armored soldiers. Khuen's arrows stud the demons as we fight, though they barely seem to register the hits.

"Lei!" Ketai yells, face contorted with effort as he holds off an immense gorilla demon. "Do it! *Now!*"

Now, now, now!

The word throbs with the rapid trip of my heart. I know he's right. The Shadow Sect is too strong, and Wren is too tired to hold on to her Xia state much longer.

She's drifted some way off, fighting two Shadow demons at once. Even with her ferocious skill, she's lagging behind.

I lurch in her direction, climbing over the bodies of fallen soldiers.

"Knife, blood, magic," I pant. "Knife, blood, magic. Save her, so she can save them."

I'm almost there. Blood and cinders spin in the flurry of Wren's magic. Bracing myself against her power, I launch into a run, her name filling my lungs—

Someone slams into me.

I'm thrown to the ground. A wiry reptile demon with moss-colored scales and slatted eyes pins me.

"Sith," I snarl.

The tip of his qiang glints in the flamelight as he raises it, exactly like he did one year ago, with my sweet dog Bao on its end.

"It's been a while, girl," he sneers, a pink tongue darting over his lipless mouth. "Though I still recall exactly how you taste."

Revulsion twists through me. Even before the King, Sith was the first demon who touched me, who made me feel small and scared and ashamed.

I bare my teeth at him. "And I still remember how *you* cowered in front of General Yu. But you're right. It *has* been a while. It'll be nice to see your fear once more."

Sith lunges with a hiss.

I roll out of reach of his spear. When he dives again, I use a move Shifu Caen taught me, rolling under the lancing point of his qiang and exiting with a jump, knocking the spear and rendering him off balance. His arm flies up just enough for me to thrust my dagger into his armpit.

He lets out a yowl of pain. He stumbles back, trying to knock me away. I weather his blows and keep jerking the blade, blood gushing over my fingers.

Sith falls back with me straddling his chest—the opposite of the position we were once in.

"Look at me," I say, grabbing his collar. "It's only polite to look at a girl in the eyes when she kills you."

His reptilian eyes—wide with pain and shock—meet mine. I free my knife and, lowering my face right over his, thrust it into the underside of his chin.

Instantly, his eyes dim. I let go. His head drops back, body limp.

I get to my feet, buzzing with triumph, a dark, delicious satisfaction coursing down my veins, and it takes me a few beats more to notice the immense shadow I've been cast in. I look up to find what appears to be a giant bull demon looming over me.

A giant *stone* bull demon.

Magic has brought one of the pecalang that guard the main gate to life. It's carved from the same marble as the palace walls, ripples of magic swirling within its stone skin. It takes a clunky step closer and swings its enormous head. Then, with an earsplitting roar, it draws back a muscled arm—aiming right for me.

Then, with a rush of air that almost knocks me off my feet, the statue's arm passes over my head, smashing instead into a cluster of Shadow Sect soldiers nearby.

I whirl around to see a group of shamans—Hanno shamans—moving their arms, puppeteering the stone bull's movements as one unit.

The statue lurches across the grounds. Its huge feet and fists aim for royal soldiers as members of our army fling themselves out of the way.

All of a sudden, there's a blur of jet-black rock.

The second statue has come to life—and is charging for the first.

They collide with a colossal *crash*.

A clearing forms as the two pecalang wrestle. Lightning illuminates their grinding marbled muscles, the fiery glow of their eyes, their insides lit with magic. With each punch, chunks of rocks smash to the ground. There are shrieks as some fall on the legs of unlucky soldiers, while others are silenced before they have time to scream.

The Hanno shamans move in perfect synchrony, chanting furiously. But even I can tell their energy is fast draining; their skin is bone white, sweat pouring down their straining faces.

They need Wren.

I lurch over bodies, the earth wet with blood. The brawling statues block most of the firelight, smoke from the burning trees and war-carriages choking the air. In a flash of lightning, I spot Wren standing on a hunk of fallen stone close to the main gates, surrounded by a horde of Shadow soldiers. Her swords whirr, beating them back, but the soldiers are unrelenting and she is tiring, her movements becoming sloppy. Her eyes flicker, ice-white one moment then brown the next; she's falling in and out of her Xia state.

If she fails, if she loses her grip now amid all these soldiers...

The ground shudders as one of the warring statues finally topples, its head punched clean off by the other. The head of the remaining statue swivels, looking at Wren, and I know our shamans have lost.

As the stone bull heaves toward her, so do I.

I weave through the Shadow soldiers surrounding her. They're so focused they don't pay me any attention until I'm halfway up the slab of rock. By then, Wren has seen me, too. She cuts off the arm of a soldier as they grab my shoulder.

"Lei!" she cries, her voice normal, her eyes not Xia white but brown.

Lovely, rich, honey-warm brown.

Right now, she is just Wren.

My Wren.

I smile as she reaches for me. At least I got to see her as the girl I fell in love with one final time.

Our fingers clasp. But before she can pull me up, I cling on tight and draw my other hand around, lifting the edge of the dagger to my chin.

"I'm sorry," I say, so quiet it's whipped away by the roar of battle, but for a moment it feels as though she can hear me, as though my words find her, gentle as they are amid such carnage, slipping under her skin as lightly as a kiss.

One last kiss, I think. *That would have been nice.*

"I love you," I tell her. It's important this is the last thing she hears from me.

And then I jerk my arm, drawing the blade across my waiting throat.

THIRTY-FIVE

WREN

SHE SAW IT ALL HAPPEN IN slow motion. Lei, staring up at her with blazing eyes. Her mouth moving, words so clear Wren felt them even if she couldn't hear them: *I'm sorry. I love you.* The lifting knife. The glinting blade.

Surely Lei couldn't be doing this. Surely her father had never suggested it in the first place, because what kind of man would do that to his daughter, would ask that of a girl he'd already asked so much of? But here Wren was, watching it happen. It played out like a nightmare, but it was real. Wren knew what her father was capable of, and she knew what Lei was capable of, and she understood too late she had underestimated them both.

Wren grasped Lei's slipping fingers.

A sound tore from her lips.

Magic burrowed through her—and out.

It was like nothing she'd ever felt before. Wren had dived into that eternal lake too many times to count, yet now it was as though *she* were the lake. She could barely see. Her ears screamed. Her head pounded.

As if from afar, Wren felt herself lurch forward, heart crying out as she reached with straining fingers for that shining blade. But even in her Xia state things were underwater-heavy, the air almost impenetrable, and she knew with a terrible certainty she was moving too slow.

Then everything stopped.

One infinite second, in which all was suspended: life and breath, heartbeat and thought.

There was a soft glow, golden, like Lei's eyes. It built slowly to a warm shine, then a hot, yellow glaze. Then, with gathering speed, it grew brighter, until it was a dazzling white—

That was when the world split apart.

That's what it felt like. Like when Wren reached into her Xia state and power flooded her—a sudden blast of strength and magic, making each of her senses come alive. Except this time, it was happening not just within her but *all around*, a riot of noise and color and movement and change that swept into everything and everyone, churned the whole world upside down.

There was a blast. And like a blast, it created something: power, energy, force.

It also took something away.

Wren found herself on the ground. She was on her back. The smoke had cleared, leaving scraps of fabric and blackened leaves and burning embers fluttering down through a granite, predawn sky. Wren tried to move but found she couldn't. Her muscles throbbed. She couldn't hear anything apart from the shrill ringing in her ears. The air smelled bitter. And...there was something else. A strange wrongness that pulsed in her cells.

Her mind filtered back groggily. There'd been an explosion—a magical blast. *Her* magic? Before the explosion there had been light. Light that had begun as a gentle glow, the color of Lei's eyes—

Lei.

Everything came back to her in a rush.

Lei. The blade. Her waiting throat.

It couldn't be. It *couldn't.*

Muscles shrieking with the effort, Wren pushed herself up. She swayed, head spinning. Soldiers were splayed across the battleground. Many were dead, their eyes blank and staring. Many more were alive but reeling from the force of the blast, just as she was.

Heads lifted. Arms grasped at empty air. A few calls rang out, growing louder as the ringing in Wren's ears faded. The charged wind of the thunderstorm grazed her bare cheeks. Pain sang through Wren: her old injury, her aching muscles. And as the sensations of the world came back, the sense of loss grew more prominent.

Something was different. The world was changed.

How? *Why?*

Wren pushed the questions away. Finding Lei was more important. She forced past the pain and moved through the swaths of fallen warriors.

More of them were rousing now. Fights stuttered back into life as the blast-shocked demons and humans struggled to regain their rhythm. Wren skirted the messy scuffles. She kicked at hands that seized her ankles. One soldier jumped on her back, and she wrestled him off her—her swords had been lost in the explosion.

Another demon approached. Wren spun, knocking them away with a thrust of her elbow.

The demon rubbed his jaw. "Thank the gods you don't have your swords," he muttered, straightening.

"Kenzo!" Wren exclaimed. "I'm sorry, I thought—"

"I know." He glanced over her. "What happened? There was some sort of explosion, but no cannons were fired on either side. And something feels..."

"Off," Wren finished. "The royal shamans must have done something. Created some kind of magical blast."

"I thought it was you."

She shook her head. "Kenzo—I need to find Lei. My father asked her to sacrifice herself to unlock the full potential of my Xia power."

"So that's why you attacked him," he said.

"I won't apologize—"

"I should hope not. Ketai is lucky you didn't kill him." Kenzo sighed, running a hand through his fur. "Sometimes, I think he forgets love is the reason we fight. Revenge would be meaningless without it." He bent to tug a spear from the body of a soldier as lightning prowled overhead. "Go," he said. "I'll keep them busy."

Wren moved away, grabbing a sword from the hand of a dead demon in her path, as the sound of jarring weapons rose behind her. The battle was rebuilding in intensity. She swerved past wrestling figures, narrowly missed being taken out by a parang as it flew from the demon wielding it.

A glint of gold caught her eye.

Wren seized the bronze object that had caught her attention.

Lei's knife.

She spun around and spotted another flash of gold. Lightning illuminated navy robes with gilded hems. A pale face peeked out from a dark curtain of hair where a girl lay on her side. Her eyes were shut, her lips parted. One of her hands stretched on the ground as if reaching for Wren, fingertips red with blood.

Wren was by Lei's side in a flash.

"Love," she choked, drawing aside her hair. With trembling fingers, she lifted Lei's chin, not daring to breathe.

A thin line of red marked her throat, like the beginning of an awful smile.

A sob racked through Wren—cutting off when she noticed the

line was only an inch long. And, when she touched disbelieving fingers to the wound, she found it wasn't deep. It was light, a superficial cut.

Lei hadn't managed to open her throat. The blast must have thrown her arm off balance just when she'd drawn the blade.

"You're not dead," Wren gasped, collapsing over her.

"I'm...not?" Lei croaked.

Wren drew back, finding those bright eyes staring back at her.

Lei's lips crooked. "Because," she said weakly, "I've got to admit, this is a bit like what I imagined the Heavenly Realm to be like."

Wren laughed. Tears streamed down her face, warm and wet and wonderful, because Lei was alive, she was alive, *she was alive*.

"Like what?" Wren managed. "A battlefield?"

Lei gave the smallest shake of her head. "Like you."

With a half laugh, half cry, Wren pressed her face to Lei's, kissing her lips and eyelids and cheeks, every available bit of her skin until she could breathe again. She could have kept kissing her forever if the battle wasn't still going, a broken chunk of statue the only thing keeping the two of them partially blocked from view.

"Can you get up?" Wren asked.

Lei nodded. She took Wren's offered hand, and though she grimaced, she got to her feet without complaint. "My knife," she said, looking at Wren's belt. "You found it."

For the first time since Wren realized Lei was alive, she felt a beat of dread. She moved instinctively to cover it.

"I need to defend myself, Wren."

"Defend, yes. Hurt yourself? No."

Lei's eyes shone with a familiar ferocity, but her tone was sad as she said, "I don't need the knife for that." She spread her arms. "We're in a battlefield. I have my pick of weapons. I can just step out and scream, and someone will help me out."

Wren felt an angry burn in her throat. Where was her father? Was he still alive?

Did she want him to be?

Guilt flushed her. Of course she did—he was her father, and he'd done so many things for her since saving her life as a newborn. But she also knew that for as long as she lived, she would never forgive him for this.

Wren took Lei's hands. "Losing you wouldn't make me powerful, Lei. It would destroy me."

"Wren, you're tired, and we need you to win…"

Wren gave her a grim smile. "Someone once told me nothing is worth losing yourself. Maybe that girl should take her own advice. I lose you, I lose myself. We'll win, but not like this."

"How, then?"

"We'll figure it out. When the world denies you choices, you make your own, remember?"

Lei raised a brow. "Quoting yourself, now? Don't you think that's a little much?"

A laugh escaped Wren's lips—at the same time they heard the groan of grinding stone. Beyond the pile of fallen Shadow Sect shamans, the palace gates were shutting.

Without hesitation, they broke into a run.

The ground rumbled as the doors moved, slowly but steadily, crushing the bodies in their way or dragging them with them. Wren's hips cried and her vision swam, but she was zeroed in on the gates and drew strength from Lei's hand in hers. The pair of them clambered over dead warriors and leaped over bits of debris and chunks of broken rock.

Demons came for them. A bird demon dived from the sky, talons outstretched, but an arrow whistled past Wren's ear and a split second later there was a thud as the demon crashed to the ground.

Wren didn't have time to look to see who'd saved her. The gates were shutting. If they didn't make it through, she and the Hanno shamans were too weak to overpower the royal shamans' enchantments, and two bird demons alone weren't enough to transport them all over the walls.

This was their only chance to get inside the palace.

The gap between the gates was narrowing. Lei stumbled, but Wren's grip kept her on her feet, and they were almost there, *almost*—

They hurtled through, the doors scraping their shoulders. If they'd been any slower, they would have been crushed.

As the gates shut with a deep rumble, Wren drew her back against them so they could hide in the shadow the wall cast. She adopted a defensive stance, her stolen sword brandished, ready for danger.

But Ceremony Court was empty.

For the first time—at least when she'd seen it—the vast square was deserted, from the abandoned guard's pavilion to the usually bustling stables. Only the night-blooming jasmine was left. Their flamelike petals ruffled in the wind where the flowers crawled across the walls. Their perfume was so strong she could smell it even above the ash and blood and sweat of battle. It was a jarring sensation.

"Where—where is everyone?" Lei whispered. "Is it a trap?"

"Possibly," Wren answered.

"Maybe the guards have withdrawn to protect the Inner Courts?"

Wren waited, senses humming. There was a rumble of thunder. Lightning scrawled across the pale dawn sky; at some point during the battle, night had given way to a new day, though the sun hadn't yet risen. Behind them, the roar of fighting was loud.

"It appears so," she said. "Though I'd have thought they'd have left *some* guards to welcome us."

The emptiness unnerved her, especially with the battle raging on the other side of the walls. That strange sense of loss nagged at her again; the way even the weight of the air seemed to have changed since the blast. It was lighter, now. Thinner.

Something slammed into the gates, making Lei jerk away from them. There was a muffled cry. Another blow. The sound of bones breaking.

Suddenly, Lei gasped. "Wren," she breathed, hoarse.

She was staring behind them, at the doors. Wren whipped around, raising her sword. But nothing seemed wrong. Despite the noise, no soldiers had appeared. The gates were secure. They were hewn from the same stone as the palace walls, and looked as they always had—imposing solid slabs of onyx rock.

Wren went taut.

She saw now what had shocked Lei, and the understanding that came with it rendered her numb.

Because the palace walls were never *just* black. They only appeared so from a distance. Up close, you could see the amber shimmer of characters dancing beneath their dark surface, feel the buzz of the daos being woven into them without pause by the royal shamans, such powerful daos even Wren had been stunned by the magic she sensed when she'd first arrived at the palace. For almost two hundred years, they'd worked as the original Demon King had envisioned: a living shield of magic, impenetrable, unconquerable.

A shield that had now, finally, failed.

"The protective magic," Lei whispered, reaching for the wall. "It's gone."

THIRTY-SIX

LEI

WHEN MY FINGERS TOUCH THE STONE, I know it's true. There is no power within them.

That's why their golden glow has disappeared. Why we can hear the sounds of battle so clearly, when the magic of the shamans usually blocks out the rest of the world.

Behind my astonishment, a tentative elation builds. The palace's protection has broken—leaving it wide open for us.

A grin spreads across my lips. I turn to Wren, expecting to see the same growing sense of victory on her face, too.

Instead, tears stream down her cheeks.

"Wren!" I cry, grabbing her. "What's wrong?"

"There is no more magic," she says.

"I know. Wren, this is *amazing* news—"

"No more magic," she says, "*at all.*"

It takes a while for the meaning of her words to sink in. When they do, it drives the breath from me.

"That's what the explosion must have been." Wren gazes at the gates through wet, disbelieving eyes. "So much magic was being used in such a short period and all in the same place. The Shadow shamans killed themselves. Our shamans were using magic to attack the wall. To protect and heal our injured. I was using magic to fight. And then you... you were about to sacrifice yourself for me."

I shift guiltily, but her tone isn't accusatory. It's disbelief. Incredulity. The worse kind, when you know you're right, but you're desperate not to be.

"Qi draining," Wren whispers. "Too much taken from the earth without enough given back. That's what's caused the Sickness—the King torturing the shamans within the wall to perform the protective enchantments. Building the Shadow Sect. Forcing power without any thought of the consequences. The balance of energy has been tipping for years, and tonight it became too much. Now it's all gone. Magic. My power."

Before I can say anything, a shadow passes overhead.

Wren and I whip our blades ready. But the winged figure is familiar, despite the blood splashing his gray-tipped feathers and blue hanfu.

"Merrin!" I call as he evades arrows from the archers on the parapet.

Samira dives to distract them so Merrin can come closer.

"The shamans' protection is gone!" I say, raising my voice just enough for him to hear but not to draw the soldiers' attention. "The palace walls are unprotected!"

"Find Lova!" Wren tells him. "Get her to direct the cannons at the gate—it's the weakest point."

Merrin nods, lifting back high. He joins Samira in attacking the guards atop the parapet to keep their focus from us as Wren and I dash across the court, moving a safe distance from the gates.

"Wren," I say as we wait. I chose my words carefully. "Your magic—*all* magic... it's got to come back, right?"

She's scanning the court for danger, but I see her jaw clench at my question. "Magic is a fundamental part of the world. It lives in the earth, flows as qi through everything. It won't have gone forever. It just needs time to regenerate."

"How long will that take?"

"I don't know—"

Boom!

The ground shudders as the first cannonball hits its mark. The gates jolt. Dust billows, human-sized pieces of debris falling loose. On the ramparts, the royal soldiers reload their own cannons, ordering archers to send out more arrows.

The doors tremor as a second cannonball crashes into them. A few guards are flung from the parapets by the blast. I wince as they hit the floor, bones splintering upon impact.

The next two explosions ring out in quick succession—and then the great gate of the Hidden Palace finally gives, collapsing in a heap of broken stone and blooming dust.

There's a triumphant roar.

Backlit by the rising sun, a wave of soldiers emerge through the smoke: Papers in Hanno blue; the yellow robes of the Amala; demons sporting a myriad of clan colors and crests, some still on bear- and horseback.

The guards on the ramparts immediately turn their attention inward. Arrows rain down. Scarlet sprays the air as demons and Papers drop, disappearing under the boots of the soldiers coming up behind them.

Our own archers return fire, toppling more guards.

As the remainder of the royal soldiers rappel down the wall to meet our army head-on, Wren and I charge into the fray. Ceremony Court, deserted not even a minute ago, swells with clashing figures.

I spot Nitta, her face blood-splattered and furrowed in concentration as she shifts her chair with deft movements, aiming the blades jutting from its wheels at soldiers' legs. Beside her, Lova cuts down the maimed demons with her cutlass.

Wren and I fight side by side, slipping into an instinctive rhythm. I'm exhausted, each move making my muscles protest, yet the fight feels different now. Having pierced the palace's defenses, we finally have the advantage. Knowing that invigorates me—invigorates *all* of us, judging by the undercurrent of victory humming through our warriors.

Without their boosted power, stolen like Wren's by the blast, the soldiers of the Shadow Sect have lost their intimidating blood coats and savage strength. And though they're still highly skilled fighters, I face them without the same fear as before.

Even demons are no match for Paper Girls with fire in their hearts.

It doesn't take long for what's left of the King's perimeter army to fall.

When the last of them have been brought down, cheers burst out. A few young warriors climb onto the bodies of fallen guards, pumping their fists. Others drum their feet, embrace one another fiercely.

Wren grabs my hand. "Let's check on the others."

We weave through the throng. Our soldiers are spreading out, taking advantage of the pause in fighting to regroup. While some celebrate, the mood is for the most part somber. We pass medics tending to the wounded. Friends crying over the bodies of the fallen. Dazed Papers and demons sitting in silence.

There are a few last rumbles and flickers from the clouds overhead, but it seems the storm has spent itself at last. The rising sun spills through the gap in the broken gate beneath a haze of dust. I accidentally look straight at it, and am blinking my vision clear when I spot a flash of dark azure.

At first, I think it's a trick of the light. Then the girl turns to accept a flask someone is handing to her.

Porcelain skin. Gaunt cheekbones. Haunted eyes.

"Blue!" I burst, running straight for her.

She's slumped against a chunk of blasted gate, legs stretched before her. Her usually glossy hair is matted to her skin with sweat. There are patches on her navy robes, blood I hope doesn't belong to her.

"Nine," she says. Her eyes shift. "Lady Hanno."

It's the second time I've been grateful to hear that sardonic voice. I drop to my knees and throw my arms around her. We're both trembling. I clutch her tight, and after a few beats her hesitant arms wrap around me, before she's hugging me back with the same ferocity she usually reserves for terrorizing me with.

I look over her, hunting for signs she's hurt. "What in the gods are you doing here?" I demand. She doesn't seem injured, though from the way she's rubbing it I can tell her leg is bothering her. "How did you even get here? I didn't see you among the soldiers."

"One of the carriages," she says. She adds, quiet, "I have my reasons to hate this place, too, Lei."

I clutch her shoulders. "I can't believe you're here."

"Neither can I. I didn't—" A shudder travels through her. "I didn't think I'd make it. Not after... *that*. I thought after we escaped, I knew what I was doing. That I could handle this. I—I had no idea. I hid in the carriage for as long as I could. Even though I heard others dying outside. Some of them were calling for help. I didn't help them. Is that terrible?" She gives a barking laugh. "Of course it's terrible."

"Blue," I say, my heart aching at her venom, directed for once at herself. "You've been so brave just to come at all. You have no reason to be ashamed. Not one."

She avoids my eyes. "I have plenty."

"Ah," comes a loud, feline voice. "I see you've discovered our little stowaway. I've got to hand it to you Paper Girls, you are full of surprises."

"Lo!" Wren cries.

The two of them embrace. Then another cat demon joins us, and it's my turn to cry out.

"Nitta!"

She laughs in her bright, husky way as I launch myself at her, burying my face in her fur. "Hello, Princess," she mutters. "It's good to see you."

I pull back, surveying her with the same urgency I used on Blue. "Are you hurt?"

"By those weaklings?" She makes a dismissive noise. "As if. But I've got some mean blisters from my chair. Look at the size of them! I'll be asking my designer for some modifications as soon as we're back home," she says, nodding in Lova's direction.

Home.

The word glimmers in the air, palpable.

Bloodstained, wounded, the atmosphere still tense, and back in the one place I'd give anything to never have to set foot in again, the thought of home seems so distant.

"It's almost over," Nitta whispers, as if reading my thoughts. She gives me a crooked smile. "Just got to hang in a little longer."

"Oh, that's Nine's specialty," Blue says. "It's getting *rid* of her that's the hard part."

I laugh and throw my arms back around her. Though she groans, she doesn't push me off.

"Point proven," she grumbles.

"Is it true?" Lova inquires in a low tone. "The shamans are saying magic has somehow disappeared."

"It's true," Wren confirms.

"Oh, honey. I'm so sorry."

"Do you know if they've spoken to my father about it?"

Nitta is looking ahead. "I think we're about to find out."

Over by the ruined gates, Ketai has climbed a slab of black stone. One by one, the soldiers take notice and quiet ripples through the square, punctured by the groans of the wounded.

The Hanno Clan Lord stands tall, long robes rippling in the wind. The glow of the new day gilds his outline where he's framed by the maw of the wrecked gates, the fires in the battlefield beyond still trailing smoke. Sweat-slick hair falls over his brow. Splashes of blood paint his skin.

"Warriors!" he calls. "Friends and allies. Look at what we have accomplished! The King's walls have been brought down for the first time in two hundred years!"

While there are cheers, our own group watches with stony faces. From somewhere, a woman's sobs mar the hush.

"And yet," Ketai continues, "for all your bravery, I'm afraid I must ask more of you yet." His eyes pause on Wren and me before continuing to sweep his audience. "The King has gathered all remaining guards in the Inner Courts, where he and the rest of the court are hiding. I know you are tired. I know you have suffered great losses. But we cannot lose momentum now. We must make one final push! See to your injuries, lay the fallen to rest. You have fifteen minutes. Then we charge on! Every death, every wound, every bit of pain you feel right now has led us here. Let us not waste a single drop of it!"

Some of the soldiers punch fists into the air to match the hand Ketai himself is now brandishing.

"We will avenge our fallen!" he cries. "We will tear the court down! Too long have they hurt us, have driven our great land into discord and sickness. Today, we put an end to the Demon King's corruptive rule!" He throws both arms high. "TO *OUR* IKHARA!"

"*OUR IKHARA!*" the army echoes.

Ketai leaps, disappearing into the tide of renewed soldiers.

"Have you noticed," Lova says, "all these speeches start to sound the same after a while? Doesn't matter which clan leader is making them." She lifts a shoulder. "Never been a fan of them, myself."

"No," Nitta says. "You're more one for drunken group singing for clan bonding."

"Drunken *anything*, really." Lova sighs. "I can't wait to get back to my deserts. There's a particularly wonderful blend of spiced rhum I've been infusing for some time now. I think the end of a war is an adequate reason to crack it out, don't you?"

"Let's get *to* the end, first," Wren replies.

I move to her side. "Your father didn't mention the magical blackout," I mutter.

"I don't think he wants to worry the soldiers. I wouldn't."

"Are *you* worried?"

"Of course. Especially because it affects our plans to get to the King."

Wren draws me away from the group so we can't be overheard.

Before Ketai asked me to sacrifice myself, it was going to be me, Wren, Lova, Khuen, Kenzo, and Merrin who went to ambush the King while the rest of our army kept his forces distracted. Shaman enchantments were going to keep us hidden.

"We'll have to move through the palace undetected without the help of magic," Wren says.

I raise a brow. "Kenzo and Merrin are pretty noticeable. And Lova isn't known for her stealth."

"No," Wren agrees. "She isn't."

"But," I say, "a pair of human girls who know the palace by heart and are used to having to make themselves small in the presence of demons..."

Wren hesitates. "Lei—"

"You told me the maps of the palace you studied never showed the internal layout of the King's fortress, specifically to protect him from would-be assassins. I just spent the past few months holed up in that place. I know how to get around. I can help."

Voices rise nearby, the crowd thickening around us—Ketai must be close. I see Kenzo, looking for the most part unhurt. Someone has bandaged his shoulder where the arrow struck.

"Come on," I say, tugging on Wren's arm. "We should go now. You know the others won't let us leave without them."

Wren doesn't shift. "Lei, this is about more than the shamans. *I* lost my magic, too. And if I can't be sure I can fight without my powers, maybe we should talk to my father. Come up with a new plan."

A frustrated growl escapes my throat. "Your father made you believe you're only special because of your magic. Your whole sense of worth has been built on the fact you're the last remaining Xia and Ketai saved you for this one purpose. But, my love—that isn't all you are. Your blood and upbringing aren't everything. *You* make your own power, Wren. You *are* your own strength. You faced the King a hundred times alone when we were Paper Girls. Those nights took far more bravery than any of this. We can face him one more time."

With a rough exhale, Wren pulls me into her arms. "One *last* time," she amends. Together, we look back at our friends.

Blue sits quietly, hugging her legs to her chest. Lova and Nitta chat with a couple of Amala members who've just joined them. They talk breezily, as if we weren't in the midst of a battle that could see us all killed any moment. Nitta even laughs at something one of the cats says, and the sound burrows inside me, warm and precious, a magic all of its own.

Paces away, Ketai and Kenzo head their way. It's clear they're expecting to find us with them.

My eyes water. I want so badly to hug Nitta and Blue before we go—even Lova. To make them promise to look after themselves. Maybe I could even convince Blue to stay behind with the injured. I still can't believe she came. How much she's changed from the petty, vicious girl I first met one year ago.

I have my reasons to hate this place, too, Lei.

I only realize then it's the first time she's called me by my real name.

"Remember what I said about good-byes," Wren says gently.

I swipe my tears away. Before I can doubt our plan, I wind my fingers through hers and we slip through the jostling soldiers. We make for the archway to the northwest of Ceremony Court that'll lead us from our friends and allies and deeper into the heart of the palace—and to the King.

It strikes me that now Wren and I are truly on our own. Yet it feels right in a way. We came to the palace alone, only to find each other. Now, we we'll destroy it on our own.

The two of us. Together.

The whole way.

THIRTY-SEVEN

WREN

G UARDS, TO THE LEFT," LEI HISSED.

The pair of them melted into the shadows of the building they were skirting. There was the sound of a door banging. Heavy footsteps. Gruff voices. Wren caught the words *army* and *Inner Courts* and *hurry*. Her hand strayed to the sword at her waist as a group of demons jogged past. As soon as they were gone, Wren and Lei were back on the move.

They'd been traveling through the palace this way for the past half hour, dodging soldiers on the ground and the eyes of lookouts in watchtowers and circling bird demons. They'd decided it would be too risky to use the passages within the walls, as the girls and Kiroku had done the night of their escape—they could be too easily trapped.

The quiet of the palace after the turmoil of battle was unnerving. But more than that, it was the palace itself. Being back within its walls made Wren claustrophobic. Even if it'd been where she and Lei had fallen in love, a darkness hung over her memories here. A darkness that took the shape and weight of the King's shadow.

A distant scream pierced the air.

Lei faltered.

"They're fighting hard," Wren reassured her. "Otherwise the King wouldn't be pulling guards from the rest of the palace. They must be wearing his defenses down."

As another set of royal soldiers ran by, Wren drew Lei into the cover of a nearby maple tree. They skirted the edge of a training ground before passing a final set of deserted barracks to reach Military Court's northern perimeter.

White curls of clematis clung to an archway in the wall. Beyond, a lush green landscape stretched out, a few bridges and shrines with their braziers and golden idols just visible.

"Ghost Court," Lei said, giving Wren a fleeting smile.

Wren knew she was remembering the time they'd gone there together. How they'd sat under the whispering leaves of the paper tree in the Temple of the Hidden as Wren revealed the truth about her background. It was the moment Wren had felt a wall melting between them, something else forming in its place: not a barrier but a connection. Invisible strings, tying them together.

After checking for guards, Wren and Lei dashed through the archway, emerging into Ghost Court.

"Do you think anyone's here?" Lei asked as they crept along the wall, keeping to its shadows.

"Perhaps a few shrine maidens. But if we keep away from the temples, we shouldn't be spotted—"

The words were barely out of her mouth when there was movement to their left.

In a flash, Wren drew her sword.

A stone plinth nearby carried an idol of a snake-headed goddess. Post-storm light glimmered off the statue's golden curves—and the two figures that had stepped out from behind it.

One was unfamiliar. The other was—

"Lill!"

Lei darted forward at the same time the small doe-eared girl broke into a run. Lei fell to her knees, bundling Lill into her arms. The young Steel girl was crying.

"What are you doing here?" Lei gasped. Her voice hardened. "Did someone send you here to find me? Is this..."

A trap, Wren finished in her head.

She moved to block both Lei and Lill, glaring at the Moon demon who'd accompanied Lill. She didn't lower her sword. "Let us pass," Wren said, "and I won't harm you."

The demon was a statuesque panther-woman, so strikingly beautiful Wren would have known she were one of the Night House concubines even if it weren't for the choker at her neck signifying her position.

The panther demon cocked her head, her cool yellow eyes appraising. "Not the politest of welcomes I'd expect from a Clan Lady, Wren Hanno," she said, scratching at the neck of her low-slung magenta robes with a long feline nail. "I was taught to introduce myself to strangers before threatening them. I'm Darya. Mistress Azami entrusted me with Lill's care... among other things."

Where she crouched by Lill, one arm around her shoulder, Lei said, "You were one of her girls. I saw you at the Night Houses once."

"I prefer *woman*, or *exquisite beauty*," Darya quipped. "But yes. I worked with her. Like Zelle."

"You share her humor," Lei remarked.

"Excuse me. That skinny Paper was ten years my junior. She shared *my* humor."

Though her tone was teasing, there was a rough note. It was clear Darya had cared about Zelle and Mistress Azami.

"You're here to help us," Wren said.

Darya nodded. "The small bird flies."

"On the wings of the golden-eyed girl," Lei intoned.

Wren frowned, but Lei seemed to understand what the strange words meant. "You two need to get inside the King's fortress undetected, yes?" Darya asked. As Wren tensed, she explained, "Miss A told me. She said if the palace came under attack, at least one of you two would try to get to the King while both armies were occupied. She also told me I was to help in the case of her...absence."

Lill sniffed, and even Darya couldn't keep a flash of pain from her features.

"She was so nice to me, Mistress," Lill mumbled, blinking up at Lei. "She looked after me, and brought me sweets, and told me I'd see you again soon so I shouldn't cry so much."

Lei hugged her. She looked at Wren. "She was a good woman," she said. "A good friend."

"Come on," Darya said crisply. "The entrance is this way."

"The entrance to what?" Lei asked.

"The tunnel to the King's palace."

Lei shot a look at Wren. "Did you know about this?"

"It wasn't on any of the plans I've seen," Wren replied.

Darya waved a hand, unconcerned. "Miss A told me you'd say that. According to her, the King's father ordered the construction of a series of underground tunnels within the palace grounds before his death, and the current King completed them just a few years ago. He killed the workers to keep their existence quiet from most of the court. It's almost as if he was concerned about his safety," she added wryly.

"He told me once he has ways around the palace even the court doesn't know about," Lei murmured.

After a chilled pause, Wren said, "But even if they were mostly a secret before, he'll certainly have them guarded now."

"Miss A planned for that," Darya said. "Our spies have taken out the guards by the entrance within the King's building the tunnels connect to, and others have already been here to clear the way on this end. Miss A knew this would be the route you'd most likely take—"

She broke off at an abrupt surge in noise from the distant battle. The Hannos' army must have broken through to the Inner Courts.

"We should hurry," Wren announced. "If the King thinks he's in danger of losing the palace, he might use one of the tunnels to escape. We could lose him."

"And the Demon Queen," Lei added. She swapped a dark look with Wren, then bent to hold Lill's shoulders. "Lill," she said, "I'm so happy to see you, but you can't come with us. It's too dangerous."

"I'm not afraid," Lill said, jutting her small chin.

"I know," Lei replied. "*I* am. I've put you in danger too many times. I'm not going to let anything happen to you again."

The doe-girl clutched Lei's hand, her glassy eyes imploring. "Please, Mistress, I don't want you to go again."

"It's only for a short while. I'll find you as soon as things are safe, Lill. I promise. And you'll be with Darya until then. She's been nice to you all this time, hasn't she?"

Though still teary, Lill nodded, and with a relieved look, Lei took the girl's hand. "Where's this tunnel, then?" she asked Darya as they set off into the grounds.

"Oh, just some old temple. No one really goes there, which is why the old King picked it, I suppose. Its name is fitting—the Temple of the Hidden."

"Sounds scary," Lill mumbled.

"I think it sounds perfect," Wren said, and she shared a private glance with Lei.

How fitting that a pathway the King thought himself so clever for creating—in a place where Wren and Lei had fallen in love, right under his nose—would lead to his downfall.

Their footsteps rang out in the empty temple. It was eerily quiet, the noise of the battle shut out by the stone walls and the large banyan that hung over the building. Darya led them to the central courtyard. The room was cast in a green, underwater glow from the banyan's leaves, its hanging roots drooping through the caved-in roof.

"Over here," she said, sweeping aside a clutch of dried leaves in one corner before prizing up a stone to reveal a narrow passageway.

Wren peered in. Roughly hewn steps disappeared down into darkness. "Where does it come out?" she asked.

"A rarely used courtyard on the ground floor of the King's fortress. Only take the first right turn in the tunnel," Darya instructed. "If you come across bodies by the stairs on the far side, it'll be the demons our spies took out. Use our code with the guards. If they don't give you the correct response, you'll know they're not with us."

Despite Wren's earlier conviction, she was growing uneasy. She wished so deeply she had her magic. The world felt wrong without the steady hum of it at her fingertips, waiting—wanting—for her to call it into life. Not to mention, the pain and exhaustion she'd been fighting this whole time had started to burrow up within her once more, filling her body with a ruinous weight.

Lei had said Wren made her own power. Wren wanted so badly to believe her. But after a lifetime of being special because of her Xia blood, to suddenly be stripped of its properties made her feel incomplete.

Lei said her good-byes to a teary Lill. Then she gave Darya a hug. "Thank you," she said. "Please look after her—and yourself."

The panther demon reached down to rub Lill's furred ears. "We'll be safe here, don't worry." As Wren and Lei descended into the murky tunnel, Darya called after them, "Give them hell, girls. For all of us."

"We will," Lei promised.

There was a low, grinding noise over their heads, and then they were plunged into pitch-black.

THIRTY-EIGHT

LEI

WE GRAZE OUR FINGERTIPS ALONG THE rock wall to follow the passageway's curves and sharp bends. The air is stuffy. Our breathing comes loud. Wren's sword clinks at her hip where she walks in front of me, keeping up a fast pace I match despite my aching muscles.

"How much longer?" I ask, wiping a sleeve across my brow.

"It can't be much farther. We should be passing under the upper-west curve of the river about now."

I shudder, feeling the press of the earth over our heads like a giant's palm. Coming from the open plains of Xienzo, being underground has always made me uncomfortable, and the last time I was beneath the palace was in the King's secret torture chamber where I'd killed Caen.

A bolt shoots through me; Wren has no idea I murdered him. That I killed someone who wasn't only her lifelong teacher and her father's lover, but her friend, her *family*. How will she react once I tell her? After the awful things I said to her on the Amala's ship, she'd have every right to throw them back in my face.

Caught up in my thoughts, I bump into her, not noticing she's stopped. The coppery smell of blood hits my throat. I remember Darya's warning. "The guards our spies killed," I breathe. "We're here."

"Take care not to trip," Wren cautions.

We pick our way around the bodies in total darkness—moving quietly, knowing we're right below the palace—until Wren finds the stairs.

"I'll go first," she starts.

A scream escapes my lips before I have time to silence myself.

Claws have clasped my ankle. I kick out, horrified. The demon lets go with a moan. There's the sound of scraping nails; the rustle of something moving in the dark. I fumble for my knife, a shriek rising in my throat as grasping fingers find the hem of my trousers again, tightening with surprising force.

A hand clamps my mouth.

There's a metallic *shing*, and then I'm pulled with Wren as she lances down with her sword.

The guard goes still.

Wren releases me, and I stagger back, bumping against the wall. Though my chest is heaving, I manage to keep quiet as both of us strain to listen for signs we might have been heard—or that any of the other guards might also still be alive.

"I'm sorry for grabbing you like that," Wren says.

"I'm sorry for screaming. Let's get going."

She doesn't move. "Lei, we can't afford something like that happening in the palace. Maybe you should—"

"If you suggest I stay behind one more time," I growl, "I swear to the gods I'll knock you out and go there on my own." Then I start up the steps before Wren can test me on my threat.

At the top, muted noises sink through the stone covering. There are shouted orders, beating boots, the clink of armor and weaponry. Nothing too loud. Our army can't have made it to the building yet.

"Lei," Wren whispers. Her fingertips graze my cheek. "Once we get out, there's not going to be another time to say this—"

I kiss her fiercely. Her hands wind around me, grasping me back just as firmly. Kissing her feels like breathing. Like coming up for air after a long, difficult swim.

When I pull away, I say, "No good-byes, remember?"

"How about I love you's?"

I brush her cheek, my eyes welling. "We're going to have the rest of our lives for those," I say. Then I reach up, and she joins me in pushing aside the slab.

After the darkness of the tunnel, the daylight is blinding. I squint like a newborn as we clamber out. Sounds that were dimmed now blast at full volume, a staccato of activity and that drumlike undercurrent of fighting, not quite so distant-sounding anymore.

"It sounds like they're right outside Royal Court," I murmur.

Wren's eyes roam the courtyard. We're crouched behind a bamboo trellis lining the back of the square. Flowers weave through it to make a colorful tapestry, as well as the perfect hiding spot for the tunnel. Around us, the smooth white marble of the walls stretches high, carved windows dotting their sides.

"Where are the guards?" I say, peering past fluttering petals. "Darya said there'd be some."

"They must have been called to join the battle."

"That's good, isn't it? It means we must be winning."

Wren doesn't reply, and I realize with a cold flush the other reason the King would have sent these guards from such an important post: that our side is so weakened he is sure a few extra soldiers will finish us off.

"Do you know where we are?" Wren asks.

I match the details of the courtyard with my mental map of the palace. "We're in the Moon Annexe, somewhere in the northeast corner, judging by the windows and the angle of the roof. I'll know more once we're in the corridor. Where do you think the King is? His chambers?"

"He'll be in the Ancestral Hall. It's where they bring the King whenever there's a threat to him or the palace. Being at the heart of the building, it's the easiest room to guard. It's where we had our Unveiling Ceremony."

Memories flash through my mind. A black-curtained archway. All the girls in a line. Wren, stunning in her gunmetal cheongsam, telling me, Now *you look ready*. A vast stepped hall surrounded by viewing balconies and the shining waters of a pool at its center. And the King—the first time I saw him, and him me.

I'd tripped on the hem of my dress on my way to him, falling face-first into the pool. His booming laughter echoed so loudly I could still hear it days after.

I'd felt humiliated. Not because I cared that I'd fallen, but because he'd treated me as if I were a joke. The last thing I wanted to be in his eyes was weak.

The King underestimated me then—and today, he'll die at my hands in the place he first set eyes on me, just a clumsy Paper Girl who didn't know how to walk in a cheongsam.

Suddenly, I'm eager to be in that hall once more. To see the look on the King's face as he realizes that despite his best efforts, he didn't break us.

With my knowledge of the building, it only takes me ten minutes to bring us within a couple of corridors of the Ancestral Hall, taking care to avoid busy routes. As a group of maids appear, I usher Wren into a storeroom to hide. Their voices bubble as they pass.

"I can't believe what Jing-yi told us—"

"No one thought they'd make it through the outer wall, either, but they did—"

"Surely they won't be able to get through Royal Court, too. Almost every soldier is out there now—"

"We're sitting ducks!"

"Sangu, don't say that!"

"Well, it's true! We should run, go to the other courts to hide like Madam Reena's girls did—"

"And get ourselves executed once the court finds out we abandoned our duties? The King is going to win. He always does. They've already captured two of their most important warriors, remember? And most of their soldiers are Papers. How much longer can they last?"

Wren watches me as their voices trail away.

"Don't think about it," I say, even as my own mind goes there— *two of their most important warriors*—their faces flashing in front of my eyes: Nitta, Merrin, Kenzo, Lova. "After this corridor, we have two possible routes. If we stay on this floor, we arrive at the hall's main entrance. If we go up a floor, we can enter by one of the viewing galleries."

Wren considers. "The galleries will be easier to access and will draw less attention, but they'll still be guarded. They make good placements for archers to watch over the room."

"The one above the King's throne," I say. "I remember it being smaller than the others. If we can take out the archers there, we'll have the perfect spot to ambush him."

After checking the way is clear, we head down the hall then along another one, before going up a narrow set of servant stairways to the second floor. We're almost there now, the archway of the viewing gallery right at the end of the passage. My nerves buzz as we jog toward it; we're so close I can make out the ripples in the curtain's vermillion silks, the tiny tear in its lower right corner—

"You there! General Naja ordered all Steel soldiers to the battlefield!"

The shout echoes down the corridor.

Everything happens too quickly for me to react.

Wren's hand slams into my back, shoving me forward.

I tumble, rolling into the gallery through the curtain.

From behind, Wren's voice rises up. "I'm no demon! I am Wren Hanno, a Paper Girl, and I have come to kill the King!"

There's a flurry as the soldiers on the balcony run into the hallway, lured by Wren's shout.

I scramble to my hands and knees. From the other side of the curtain, shouts ring out, along with thumps and the clatter of weapons. I draw back the corner of the silks—and come face-to-face with Wren.

She's been wrestled to the floor. Blood trickles from her mouth where she's been hit. Demon guards pin her down. More rush about, some waiting for orders while others dart off in all directions. Wren's name bounds through the corridors, *Wren Hanno, Wren Hanno*, in time with each frantic beat of my heart.

Wren's defiant gaze fixes mine through the blurred legs of demons. *I love you*, she mouths.

Then she's being wrenched up. She disappears within the crowd of guards. There are more thuds, the dull sounds of kicks and punches.

"Is the girl with you?" a demon demands.

"The Moonchosen!" another barks. "Where is she?"

"She's dead," Wren answers.

More hits.

"Where is she?"

"Where is she!"

Wren spits the words between blows. "She. Is. Dead."

"Search the palace!" a gruff voice growls as they drag Wren away. "This one is just a distraction. The Moonchosen must be somewhere. Remember—the King wants her alive!"

I drop the curtain and scoot back against the wall of the deserted balcony. Tears pour down my face. I gulp down breaths, forcing myself to stay quiet even as I'm shaking all over; even as the corridor outside falls silent; even as I know I am alone, truly alone, replaying that last fleeting image of Wren before she was taken away.

Her determined expression. A trail of red painting one cheek. The motion of her lips.

I love you.

Earlier, I'd spoken the same three words to Wren before I drew a knife across my throat. I know what they mean in the midst of a battle. They mean you know you might not make it. That you want to make sure your loved one hears them one last time.

They're just another way to say good-bye.

I clutch my fists so forcefully my nails dig into my palms, my face hot and wet. This wasn't how it was supposed to go. It was meant to be *my* sacrifice, not hers.

In the vast space of the Ancestral Hall, there's a commotion. Through my daze, I hear Wren's name. Voices talk over one another. Then one silences the others.

"Bring her to me."

The sound of it sends a current of hatred down my spine.

I climb to my feet. Staying low—aware the guards on the other galleries are also peering down, intent on what's happening—I peer over the balcony.

The scene below chills me to the bone.

The steps of the hall are mostly empty, save for rows of soldiers standing side by side, lining the walls. The pool at the heart of the room shimmers in the lantern light. Beside it, in the same place it stood the last time I was here, is a large golden throne. Demons cluster around it. Most are familiar from my time at the King's side as the Moonchosen: court advisers, a few guards, and—powerless now—a collection of his most trusted shamans. Then there are more familiar faces.

Some loved.

Others despised.

Naja, dressed in burnished silver armor over red and black robes, her snow-white fur spotless.

Nitta, bloodied and slumped before the white fox, her chair nowhere in sight. Her hands are tied behind her back. A cloth gags her, a heavy collar at her neck, its chain in Naja's hand.

Merrin, flanked by guards, his winged arms drawn behind him and bolted through with a steel bar, blood dripping down his feathers.

The Demon Queen, her belly rounder than when I last saw it. A chain trails from her right wrist to the throne, where, upon it, *he* sits.

The King.

I *burn* at the sight of him. There is no fear. Only hatred, and a dark, deep, searing resolve. He's covered in heavy gold armor—no armor any true warrior would wear for its impracticality—and his face is protected by a matching war-mask, hammered to the shape of his tapered nose and jaw.

And then—

Wren.

Bruised and bloodied and kicked to her knees, she's being dragged to the King by a group of guards. Yet she holds her head high, her gaze unwavering. My heart swells with tender pride. Graceful, always.

Graceful, until the end.

I want nothing more than to leap from the balcony and drive my knife through the King's skull. But I hold myself back. The moment I expose myself, everything will be thrown into chaos. When I come for the King, I need to be sure.

My eyes skim over the demons on the other viewing galleries. None of them notice me, too captivated by the sight of Ketai Hanno's infamous warrior daughter. Most of the demons are archers. The ones in the first line of each gallery have their bows nocked, ready to fire at a second's notice. If I jumped now, I'd be dead before my body hit the ground.

The King stands as Wren is dumped at his cloven feet. A rapt silence grows. There is only the clink of the King's armor and my racing heartbeat, crashing against my rib cage in a feverish rhythm.

I brace for the King to strike Wren. So when he pitches back his head instead and laughs, I'm too stunned to react. Then my rage, already whipped into a violent storm, *explodes.*

My fury almost blinds me, but I force myself to focus, watching as Wren—my beautiful, brave wonder of a girl—waits with exquisite patience for the King's laughter to die.

When it does, he lowers his masked face to hers. "We *will* find her."

"Lei is dead," Wren says. "She died in Military Court as we were making our way here. If you don't believe me, send for her body."

There's a muffled sob: Nitta. She slumps, her cries loud even through the gag. Beside her, Merrin drops his head.

The King assesses Wren through the eyes of his mask. He flicks a hand. "You three—go." As the guards sprint off, the King keeps his stare trained on Wren. "Whatever you are planning," he says quietly, "it won't work. I know that magic has disappeared. It was your only power, the only thing that gave you an advantage over any demon. And now it is gone. You are *nothing*, Wren-zhi."

The use of her Paper Girl title strikes me like a slap, but Wren's expression doesn't change; she won't rise to his taunting.

The King strikes her across the face. The sound is loud in the hush.

Wren spits out the wad of blood in her mouth, then lifts her head.

The King hits her again.

And again.

And again.

And each time, Wren raises her head, meeting his incensed glare, her face the composed mask it was when I first met her, before I knew it was a shield, before I knew the soft, sweet soul it protected. Before she let me see who she was beneath the walls she'd built against the world.

Something I know she will never let the King see, no matter how many times he tries to break through.

A few feet away, Nitta struggles against her bonds, trying to go to Wren. Naja jerks the chain. Nitta's back arches as the collar crushes her throat.

"Wait," the King commands. He pauses in his beating. "We want the cat alive for now. Use the war-horns to get their attention. Tell Ketai Hanno we have two of his warriors and his daughter. Tell him if he calls off his men and conquers me in a duel, he can have everything. His daughter, the palace...all of Ikhara."

Naja hesitates. "But, my King—"

"NOW!"

Naja shoves the chain into the hand of one of the guards nearby, then crosses the hall, disappearing through the sable curtain covering its vaulted entranceway.

Merrin and Nitta's stifled sobs cleave me. They're crying because they think I'm dead, even as I'm right here, barely meters away.

The urge to launch myself over the side of the gallery rises with new fervor. But the royal archers are all still surveying the room, and the Demon Queen is too close to the King. Even if I somehow made it past the archers' arrows, the tiniest misjudgment in my jump and I could hurt the Queen instead. Or I could land badly and break something, rendering myself useless—and offering myself up to the King.

I won't let him have the satisfaction of having captured both of us.

But I won't let him kill Wren.

As my mind whirrs, calculating every possible move, the King returns to his throne.

"My father will kill you in a duel in seconds," Wren declares.

The King laughs. He leans in his throne, dangling a hand over the armrest, his knuckles dark with Wren's blood. "I'm not going to fight him, stupid girl. You see, your father still believes in honor. In tradition. He will come, believing my offer to be true—then, when he thinks for certain he is about to gain everything he has ever dreamed of, I will have my soldiers kill him. Even the mighty Ketai Hanno cannot compete with fifty expert archers. Their arrows will tear him to shreds, and then I'll turn them on you and your friends." His tone is chilling. "You are going to die here tonight, Wren-zhi. If you have any last words you wish to say to me, speak them now."

Hatred pulses off Wren in cold waves, an echo of her lost power.

The tiniest curl tucks the corner of her mouth. "You are small, and pitiful, and weak," she tells the King. "And I am not afraid of you."

He stares, tense. Then he waves a soldier over. "Gag her," he orders.

The demon shoves a roll of fabric into Wren's mouth, tying it roughly behind her head.

Though I can't see his face, I can tell the King is smiling. "You say you are not afraid of me," he whispers. His voice chills me to the bone. "You *should* be."

THIRTY-NINE

LEI

WHEN KETAI ENTERS THE HALL, accompanied by Naja and a flank of royal guards, his arrival startles me. I wasn't sure he would come. Part of me wants to believe it's for Wren, yet the sharper, wiser part knows it is because of the King's offer.

He can have everything.

All of Ikhara.

The King watches, unmoving, as Ketai is led around the pool. His crisp footsteps echo off the marble. Despite the blood splatters on his clothes and skin, and a nasty-looking slash along his jaw, from the way he carries himself you'd never know this is a man who has spent hours fighting. Like his daughter, it's clear Ketai is determined not to show the King a scrap of weakness. Only the burn in his eyes, intent on his opponent, gives away any emotion. He hardly glances at Wren, Merrin, or Nitta—just a flick of his lashes as he registers their presence, no doubt analyzing the best way to play the situation.

When they reach the throne, Naja drives the sheathed jian she's carrying—Ketai's own weapon—into his back, forcing him to his knees. "Bow to your King," she snarls.

He sinks low, though his brow doesn't quite touch the floor.

"Such formalities," the King drawls. "And to think we spent so many banquets and clan meetings together. We shared food, drink, laughter…Looking at us now, Ketai, anyone would imagine us strangers."

Ketai raises his bloodied face. "We *are* strangers. You have never known me, Demon. Though I am unfortunate not to be able to say the same for you."

"You think you know me?" the King asks, quiet, a threat.

A slight smile tugs Ketai's lips. "*Everyone* knows you. There have always been men and demons like you, and there'll be more after your death." His smile sharpens. "It is easy to spot a coward. Shall I teach you how? A coward is the one who uses force when a gentler hand would be more effective. He is the one who lets his nation suffer while he bathes in their blood. The one who hides within walls while sending others to fight for him. Who dresses in armor and masks, thinking it will intimidate his enemies, when it only proves how fearful he really is—"

There's a *crack* as Ketai's cheekbone smacks into the floor.

"Insolent Paper filth!" Naja spits, drawing her arm to strike him again. "You *dare* talk to the Heavenly Master that way—"

"Leave him. He is mine." The King rises. "His weapon."

Naja hands him Ketai's sword. The King draws it free.

Ever since Ketai's arrival, Merrin and Nitta have been struggling against their binds. We all know the King isn't planning to make this a fair fight, and Nitta and Merrin try to send the message to Ketai, shouting incomprehensibly through their gags. As they jerk harder at the sight of the King wielding Ketai's weapon, the guards standing over them restrain them with sharp yanks of their shackles.

When the dog demon guarding Nitta pulls on her collar, it forces her still. But Merrin's bond is a bar bolted through his wing-arms. His bone-gray feathers are stained red. Though the pain must be unbearable, Merrin continues to struggle. The guard's grip on him loosens—and before he can reassert it, Merrin lurches forward.

He crashes headfirst into the King.

Merrin's gag slips. He calls out, "Ketai...!"

There's a flash of silver.

A garnet spray.

Nitta lets out a stifled scream as Merrin's body hits the floor. His head tilts at an unnatural angle, almost completely severed by the King's powerful slash.

His orange eyes stare blankly up. Blood pumps from his neck, spreading fast on the marble. It drips into the pool, blooming beneath the water's surface.

Shock rocks me, waves of horror and grief so strong they almost drop me to my knees.

I'm too stunned for tears. I see everything all too clearly. Nitta's anguish. Ketai and Wren's astonishment, finally unmasked. Naja's victorious smirk. And the King, offering the dripping blade to Ketai.

"My proposal of a duel still stands," he says. "Take it, and no more will die."

Ketai climbs to his feet and accepts the sword.

"You called me a coward," the King says. "And yet it was your warrior who attacked me from behind. It was you and your clan who betrayed me." He spreads his arms. "Come, now, Ketai. Let us settle this once and for all. Demon to man. King to Clan Lord. Or are you scared you'll lose against a so-called *coward?*"

"I win," Ketai says, "and the battle ends."

"*I* win," the King counters, "and I tear down every last one of your traitorous followers."

"I won't let it come to that."

The King beckons a guard. They pass him a long, ornately decorated sword. The King steps back, opening up space between him and Ketai.

Merrin's body is sprawled between them.

"The gods have witnessed your promise," Ketai reminds the King, adopting a fighting stance. "It is their wrath you face if you break it."

For a second, I think I see the King stiffen inside his layers of armor. Then he lowers his head so his bull horns aim forward, two sharp gilded points, weapons of their own. Thrusting his sword high, he bellows, "ARCHERS! ATTACK!"

Ketai has no time to react. The air fills with the whistle of tens of arrows slicing through it—

And the sickening thuds as they meet their mark.

Flesh tears. Arrows shred cleanly through. Others embed in bones, sticking from Ketai's legs, his arms, shoulders, back, skull. Red torrents burst from his opening body.

Nitta screams.

Wren tries to rise. The boar demon guarding her slams his club into her head, and she slumps to his feet, unconscious.

"My King!" Naja cries with a manic laugh. "You did it!"

He ignores her. Tossing the unused sword, he faces Wren and Nitta.

"Kill them," he commands.

I've already climbed over the lip of the balcony, taking advantage of the archers' being distracted. Now, all there is to do is jump.

I fall hard, landing on the seat of the throne. There are shouts; the King is turning; an arrow whirrs past my head, so close it skims my hair. More come, but I'm already diving to the side, though not toward Wren and Nitta.

Toward the Queen.

Her surprised cry cuts off as I clamp a hand over her mouth and press my dagger to her throat.

"Hurt any of us," I yell, "and I *will* kill her!"

"STOP!" the King thunders. *"STOP!"*

The guards that had been racing toward me, the arrows that had been nocked, still quivering in their bows, fall still. A terse hush sweeps over the hall—and that's when we hear it.

The thuds and crashing of fighting.

The rumble of feet and hooves and heavy paws.

War-cries and screams of pain.

All rapidly approaching.

My heart soars. Our army has made it into the palace. Kenzo, Lova, whoever Ketai placed in control of our soldiers before he left didn't trust the King to keep to his word. They fought on.

As a stream of rushing bodies bursts through the archway, its black curtain torn down to disappear beneath pounding boots, the Ancestral Hall erupts into mayhem.

Guards that had been aiming for me now charge to meet the oncoming army. Fresh arrows rain down—only for cries to sound from the galleries where more of our soldiers have appeared. Flailing bodies are pushed over the balconies. The room reverberates with bone-crunch and sword-slash.

The Demon Queen thrashes against my grip. I come around so

she can see me. "It's me!" I say, taking my hand from her mouth. "The King brought me to your bedside to show me you were pregnant. I'm not here to hurt you. I want to get you out."

Her bovine eyes flash with recognition. "Lei-zhi," she says. "The Moonchosen."

"Please. Just Lei."

She nods. "My name is Shala."

"Can you stand?" I reach an arm around to help her. As she climbs to her feet, I grab the chain tying her to the throne and tug. It doesn't shift.

"Let me help," Shala says.

The chain goes taut in her strong grasp. The two of us strain, groaning with effort—until, with a sudden jolt, the fastenings give way, the chain snapping free. I stumble, Shala catching me before I can fall.

"Thank you," I say, already spinning, looking for Wren.

I spot Nitta instead. She's dragging herself along the blood-slick floor toward the King's discarded sword. Her own chain trails behind her. She grasps the weapon just in time to defend herself as the guard she slipped from in the turmoil bears down on her. Nitta parries his blows, then spears him through with the King's blade.

His twitching body falls on top of her.

Shala and I run over. We haul the dead demon off her. I pull the sword free and hand it to Nitta, helping her sit.

"Lei!" she gasps, disbelieving. "You—you're *alive!*"

"I am," I say, giving her a fleeting smile. I turn to Shala. "Can you carry her? Nitta can't walk."

Shala crouches. "You'll be able to defend yourself better on my back."

As I help her up, Nitta tells me urgently, "Wren was only

pretending to be unconscious when the guard hit her. When our soldiers arrived, she went after the King. She's injured, Lei, she's weak, and I don't know where they've gone——"

"I do," I say, already moving.

I weave through the battling figures, heading for the back of the room. There is a new frenzy to the fight, as if everyone can sense it's come down to this, this one room and these final swings of weapons and claws. I duck a staff as its wielder aims for a Paper close by, then skirt a fistfight between two demons, blood flecking my face from their blows.

I make it to the wall below the balcony I jumped from earlier. As I expected, the King's armored chest plate and leg shields lie discarded below. The gallery is just low enough for demons to help one another reach, but too high for a human. I try to launch myself up the wall, but I slide down, the stone too polished to grip. I spin, looking for something that might help me——

A spear rushes past my face.

Its metal tip impales the wall an inch from my nose.

I hear the steps of a heavy demon behind me. I throw myself aside. The demon's fist misses me by an inch. I swerve as he comes for me again, his blow cuffing my right shoulder. I roll and exit in a jump, thrusting out my dagger. It catches the thick-set tiger-man across the cheek.

He swings a meaty fist at my face. I skate out of reach, then jab my knife into his thigh.

As the demon lists, I jump onto his hunched back and spring off him, leaping for the spear embedded in the wall.

My body judders as I slam into the stone—but my feet have found purchase on the spear's sturdy handle. Before I can topple, I propel myself toward the balcony—

The breath shoots out of me as I crash into it.

My fingers snap around the ledge. Teeth gritted, muscles screaming in protest, I pull myself up. Just when it seems impossible, that my fingers will lose their grip, I bring myself high enough to hook an arm over the balcony and drag myself over.

I fall to the gallery floor, panting. But I don't have time to waste. Still gasping for breath, I haul myself to my feet and stumble out.

The palace beyond is deserted. The roar of battle fades as I sprint down empty corridors, tracking back the way Wren and I came. Even if I didn't know the way, I'd be able to follow the smudged patches of blood on the floor.

When I reach the courtyard where the secret tunnel is hidden, I find Wren and Naja locked in combat.

The white fox lets out a high-pitched laugh when she sees me. Her fur, previously spotless, is now splattered with red. In the daylight, it looks lurid, almost unreal—but the cuts and bruises on Wren's face say otherwise. "Look who it is, Paper whore," Naja sneers, dancing out of reach of Wren's sword. "Your little lover has come to die with you. How romantic."

Wren swipes out again. Naja defends with a slash of her claws.

"Gods," I growl at the white fox, readjusting the grip on my knife, "I am not going to miss you one bit."

And I join Wren's side. There's nothing elegant about the way we fight. Wren's movements are sloppy from exhaustion. Her right eye is so swollen I doubt she can barely see out of it. It throws off her balance—but I'm there to deflect Naja's claws. I'm there to double down on an attack she started but is too slow to finish. We fight together, and even if it is messy, we don't give up, wearing Naja down.

All it takes is one mistake.

Wren and I have pushed Naja against the wall. Wren aims a low, sweeping cut at her legs. Naja can't move back, so she veers sideways instead—

Right into the path of my blade.

I only nick her skin; it's hardly more than a papercut. Yet whether due to surprise or complacency, it makes Naja hesitate—giving Wren time to use the momentum of her previous thrust to swing her sword.

It digs deep into Naja's side.

With a howl, the white fox topples to her knees. Her hand grasps uselessly at her opened flesh as blood spills out, a flood of shining red.

I drive my knife into her chest.

Naja's silver eyes flicker. Then they glaze over. I move back, sliding my knife from between her ribs, and she falls facedown onto the tiles, finally limp.

My heart is racing. "She's dead," I say. "She's really dead."

"Lei." Wren seizes my hand. She's wheezing, almost doubled over. "The King."

I help her to the passage entrance. Its cover has been shoved aside. A trail of blood leads down the steps.

"He's injured," I say.

"I got him," Wren explains between rasping breaths, swaying in place. "As we were leaving the hall. But I don't know..."

She pitches forward.

I grab her, easing her down. I stroke back the sticky hair from her bruised face, seeing her properly for the first time since the Ancestral Hall. She looks terrible. Her skin is mottled and bloodied, its usually tan color gray. Her right eye is a bulbous mess, and beneath it, marking her lovely cheek as clearly as a tattoo, are the imprints of the King's knuckles.

She tries to sit but I push her gently back. Her cracked lips part. "The King..."

I press a kiss to her brow. "I'll get him," I say. "If he's hurt, he can't have gotten far. You've done your part, Wren. It's time for me to do mine."

"Lei," she croaks as I move to the tunnel.

I'm poised to rebuff her protests. Instead, she fixes me with a dark, fervent look.

"Finish it," she whispers.

I find him at the bottom of the staircase amid the corpses of his guards.

In the darkness, the King is nothing more than a sunken form slumped against the wall. But I'd recognize that silhouette anywhere. Symmetrical horns, their gold patterning glinting dully in the dust motes filtering down from above. Rounded shoulders, unusually slim for a bull demon. A long nose and jutting jaw, with its mouth that once claimed my body when it was never his to take. Even in pitch-black I would know it's him, because it is more than physical. I sense his presence with every part of me. Just as how Wren is a song I can't help but answer, the Demon King is a pained, off-chord shriek that repels me from him with each note.

Blood drips from the blade, coating my fist red.

How fitting I am to kill the King dressed in his own colors.

His breathing is labored. A strange whistling accompanies each exhale. As usual, Wren didn't give herself enough credit. She didn't just hurt him; she injured him so badly he barely made it down the stairs before collapsing.

The King's war-mask has fallen off, or maybe he discarded it in his need for air. It lies at his feet, sneering up at us. He'd looked so commanding when I first saw him in his layers of armor. Now, the mask is powerless—along with the demon it failed to protect.

He doesn't move until I'm standing right above him, my shadow falling over him the way his fell over me so many times.

Slowly, with effort, the King lifts his chin.

A single arctic-blue eye meets my stare.

I've never felt calm in the King's presence, but I feel calm now. My gaze tracks down to where his hands are pressed to his side. I kneel down, and, unafraid, ungently, prize them away.

Wren's sword has run deep. Blood pulses out, drenching his clothes and turning his chestnut fur black.

The King's rasping grows more erratic as I lift my knife to his chest, touching the tip to the space between his ribs where Kenzo once showed me.

This is where you aim tomorrow.

Push the blade deep, and do not stop.

Shaky and weak, the King tries to grasp my arm, but I push him away, not breaking eye contact. I want to see it: the fear. The unique kind that only exists when you understand something irreplaceable is about to be taken from you.

I see it, and smile.

I could leave the King to die. It wouldn't take long, and no shamans are coming to save him this time. No magic will knit close his wounds. But as we look at each other, my heart beats with a calm clarity that this is the way it's supposed to be. It is the way *I want it* to be. A power the King always had—to force his desires on others—is now my turn to wield.

Things I could say run through my mind. There is so much. All the words born from my pain and his cruelty, and the lives he wrecked, the bodies and hearts and hopes he broke, the scars he carved. Yet sharing them, giving them to him, feels wrong.

He doesn't deserve them. He deserves nothing more from me—except this.

"We beat you," I tell him simply. Then I slide my knife into the King's chest.

I press it deep.

I do not stop.

FORTY

WREN

THEY EMERGED INTO A CHANGED WORLD.

Or perhaps it wasn't so changed, at least not quite yet. But it felt so to Wren, and she knew Lei felt it, too. A weight had been lifted. Gravity altered. And unlike magic, this was a burdening weight, an unwelcome one that had crushed her for a year without her realizing quite how much until it was gone.

They'd thought the King dead once before. This time, there was no doubt.

After Lei climbed from the passage, hollow-eyed and bloody, yet miraculously calm, she'd helped Wren to her feet and together they had gone to get help. They found their soldiers in the halls of the King's fortress. They'd won. The battle was over. The Ancestral Hall was now a terrible morgue, but they'd done it, they'd taken the King's demons down.

Lei told the first soldiers they came across where to find the King. Neither of them wanted anything more to do with him. Wren knew Lei would have preferred to leave his body there, let him rot in darkness the way he'd made *them* feel, like ruined things, too stained for the light. But ... that wasn't quite true.

There were moments when that was all there was. In the deep of night, when she recalled with painful physicality the mass of the King's body atop hers. And at random, when she wasn't prepared for the sudden rush of memories, and she'd be stopped in her tracks, gasping and trying to calm her wildly beating heart. Wren had had a lifetime of crafting poise and confidence and power, but that could be all it'd take to unravel her: the recollection of the way the King smelled, or moved, or touched, or licked, or *claimed*. And when she thought how he'd done the same to Lei and the other girls—how many more girls?—it would blow the breath right out of her.

Yet sometimes, when her fingers brushed through Lei's hair, or she'd hear Nitta's laugh, or take a deep lungful of sunlit air, the King didn't intrude. He didn't have all of her. He never had, and never would. Wren hoped in time he'd have less and less of her, and less of Lei and the other girls, and everyone else he had branded, until the memories that now felt like freshly made tattoos—still stinging and raw—would, like tattoos, fade.

With magic, Wren had learned how to heal wounds. Perhaps there was a way to heal these kinds of wounds, too, with a different kind of power. One everyone could access. A normal, everyday magic, so simple but so potent a blend: of friendship, patience, kindness, mercy, perseverance, respect, and of course, love.

The magic Lei had taught her. That Nitta and Bo and Hiro and Lova and Kenzo and Shifu Caen and Ahma Goh and the other Paper Girls and even Merrin and her father had each taught her in some way.

At least, if she never got back her Xia powers, she would always have these.

Wren thought she could live with that.

She would be so lucky to live with that.

*   *   *

There were things to do after a battle. With her father dead, authority seemed to have passed to Kenzo and Lova, though when they were reunited outside the King's fortress, after hugs and tears and words shared in voices not quite like their usual ones, both of them deferred to Wren. She was the new clan leader of the Hannos, after all. The new leader of... whatever *this* was.

Ikhara. Not exactly a kingdom, anymore. But not yet something else.

As exhausted and battered as she was, and wanting nothing but to lie down somewhere quiet with Lei, Wren couldn't shirk her responsibilities. Still, she was in no fit state to do much. She told Kenzo and Lova to keep on, trusting them fully, while a team of doctors swarmed upon her and Lei, seeing to their wounds.

There were more reunions. They were fleeting. There was so much to do, and the real conversations would happen later. Still, Nitta passed by, helped by Khuen, since Naja had destroyed her chair when she'd been captured. She'd fought in the Ancestral Hall on the back of the Demon Queen—another visitor who came to thank Lei for freeing her.

The Demon Queen—Shala, as Lei introduced her—was quiet and wary, perhaps unsure of how the others would perceive her. Wren ordered her clan members to work on removing her collar and to find her a quiet space to rest.

Royal Court was a hive of activity, the surviving Hannos and their allied clans using it as a base to tend to the wounded and pass out supplies. They still had to secure the palace, and there were hiding soldiers and councilors, maids and workers to round up.

Not to kill. Gods, no. But their allegiances were murky, and so for now they'd be kept in the barracks of Military Court, guarded by

Hanno soldiers. Wren had given them strict orders to provide the palace's residents with everything they needed to be comfortable. It wasn't perfect, but until they could figure out who they could trust, it was the best she could do.

Some palace residents didn't need to be detained.

The Night House panther demon Darya brought Lill to visit Lei, and they stayed, Lill curled in Lei's lap, Darya tipping her head back to the wall they were propped against, removing the ribbon at her neck, the necklace that marked her as a concubine with a long, slow sigh. The other courtesans were also freed, many of them going to help with the cleanup effort.

After the reunions came the thing Wren had been dreading: those they were too late to save.

Wren and Lei heard the news from various sources. Commander Chang had perished outside the palace walls, crushed under one of the stone pecalang. Kiroku, one of their bravest allies, who'd suffered through so many years tending to Naja's whims, had been killed when the fight reached the Inner Courts. A Hanno soldier told a crying Lei and a shell-shocked Wren he'd seen Kiroku fighting bravely against the King's forces before she fell.

Then there were the shamans.

Lova explained how, after Lei and Wren had left them in Ceremony Court, she'd led a bunch of her cats into the walls of Temple Court. They'd found royal soldiers slaughtering the shamans. With magic gone, the King had ordered them dead. Wren suspected he'd probably been fearful they'd turn upon him given his treatment of them. Lova and her cats stopped the massacre, though not before hundreds of shamans had already been killed. Now, Kenzo was overseeing their liberation with orders to send news if Ruza was found, the shaman boy who'd helped Lei and the girls escape. It was a mammoth task. There were *tens upon thousands* of shamans chained within Temple Court, and with no magic, each collar had to be broken manually.

But it was getting done. They would be freed.

For the first time in two hundred years, the palace walls would lie empty. They wouldn't be a prison anymore. Wren made a vow to herself that whatever they decided to do with the Hidden Palace, those terrible walls would be torn down so no one would ever have to feel caged by them again.

The sun was setting. Wren had drifted into a half sleep when a cry made her start.

For one awful moment, she thought they were being attacked. Then she saw Lei jump up, flinging her arms around a petite figure, a familiar face peeking past Lei's shoulder.

Blue.

Blood-splattered, injured, dazed, and exhausted—but still Blue.

She'd made it.

"Don't get used to this, Nine," the girl said. Her arms wound slowly around Lei's back. But they hugged for a long time, only pulling apart at the sound of cheers.

The bustling crowd of Royal Court was parting, making way for a group of soldiers carrying something on their backs.

The King's body.

A pyre had been erected in the center of the square. The soldiers threw the King onto it amid jeers and stamping feet. Everyone apart from the grievously injured stood to get a good look. Lei took hold of Wren's hand while keeping hold of Blue's in her other. Lei's face shone with tears. Blue looked angrier than Wren had ever seen her, her features scrunched, mouth wobbling as if on the verge of crying or screaming out. Perhaps both. Together, they faced the pyre as a soldier held up a blazing torch.

The square was a roar of noise. The soldier seemed to be looking for someone, and Wren's stomach lurched when she thought they'd want her or Lei to do the supposed honors. Then an elegant figure cut through the throng.

Shala. The Demon Queen.

She walked regally, one hand cupping her swollen belly. Whispers slunk in her wake; most of the crowd didn't know who she was. Wren wondered if she should have made some sort of official announcement—her father would have, to claim her loyalty. But Wren felt it should be down to Shala to decide what role she played in the shaping of the new world. Maybe she wouldn't want anything to do with it.

Wren could understand that.

Shala took the torch. It limned her chestnut fur, picking out its lovely russet accents. Her horns were wrapped in cobalt fabric, as if to mark her allegiance to the Hannos, though maybe they were always worn that way. Wren wondered who she was, this mysterious demon who'd been kept alone all this time, just for the King. She felt a twist of revulsion, chased by fierce relief.

The King could never come for Shala again.

Shala surveyed the King's corpse. Then she brought the torch to the pyre.

It lit slowly, then all at once. The blaze churned out heat, played molten shadows across the faces of those watching, who'd finally fallen silent, the gravity of the moment sinking in.

The Demon King, terrorizer of Ikhara, enemy of Papers, thief of dreams and girls and lives and hopes and peace, was dead.

Lei pressed her head into Wren's shoulder, and Wren curled her arm around her, looking over the top of her head at Blue, who was still holding Lei's other hand.

"We're free," Blue whispered, as if she still didn't quite believe it.

Lei sobbed, and Wren clutched her tighter.

Yes, they were free.

They were free.

FORTY-ONE

LEI

T HERE ARE JUST TWO PLACES IN the palace I want to visit before I leave it for what I hope will be the last time.

Wren, I've gathered from the endless meetings over the past week, will have to come back fairly often to check on how Darya is getting on with overseeing the palace's remodeling. The destruction of the exterior walls has already begun, a process Lova and her cats seem to be having a lot of fun with. Then there's all the damage from the battle that'll need to be repaired before its buildings can be adapted for their new purpose.

Wren and I decided early on what we want the Hidden Palace to become: a sanctuary for women. Papers, Steels, *and* Moons. Anyone who identifies as a woman and who's seeking shelter, whether temporary or permanent. It doesn't matter if they're fleeing violence or simply seeking a quiet space to be. The Free Palace, as we've renamed it, will be open to all.

It wasn't a popular decision with the new council. But Wren and I wouldn't budge, and with Kenzo and Lova's support, we managed to get them on board.

The last morning in the palace, I tell Wren where I want to go.

The first location doesn't surprise her. I can tell the second does, but she assents all the same.

Ghost Court isn't as empty as the last time we were here. All week, funerals have been taking place in its hushed gardens, humans and demons from both sides of the war lighting pyres for their loved ones or setting their bodies into the soil. We've attended funerals ourselves—for Merrin, and Kiroku, and of course, for Ketai. Though she doesn't cry at her father's funeral, Wren leaves our bedroom that night for a long time, and when she returns her eyes are red and raw, and she holds me a little tighter.

This morning, like usual, everyone bows to us as we pass. Many grasp our hands or thank us profusely, and while I'm touched by their sentiment, it's wearying, too.

I don't feel like anyone's savior.

Luckily, the Temple of the Hidden is deserted. We make our way to the little garden and its rustling paper tree.

"Wait," I tell Wren when she brings out the sheaths of paper from the fold in her robes. I draw her down with me beneath the tree's low boughs, sunlight winking through the paper leaves. I tip my head back. "Let's just sit here a while."

I close my eyes, relishing the peace. Wren kisses my brow, and my heart flushes with something both sweet and bitter. There are so many things we've yet to discuss. We've been too busy with the new council, organizing the mess of the King's broken legacy while grieving those we lost in the war. Even though we've spent every night together, wrapped in each other's arms in our rooms in the Night Houses Darya kindly offered us, our comfort and closeness hasn't progressed to anything more. It's not just that we're still reeling from the battle; there are deeper issues, too. Wounds we opened in each other.

We'll have to face them sometime. Just not quite yet.

I push out a shaky breath. "I'm ready," I say.

Wren hands me a small curl of paper and a brush. I smooth the paper open on my knees and dip the brush in the ink pot she holds out. I write a name on it, my eyes already welling.

Chenna

We never managed to find her body. I assume the King had it burned, or thrown somewhere after his failed execution that night. Perhaps someone will come across it one day. I hope so. Chenna was strong in her beliefs. She deserves to be buried in her customs.

I set the paper leaf down, and Wren hands me another.

Mistress Azami

Like Chenna, we haven't discovered her body. Tears fall into my lap, but I keep on, Wren's steadying hand on my leg.

Zelle
Nor
Danna
Mariko
Mistress Eira
Madam Himura

"Are you sure?" Wren asks at the last name.

"Whatever else she was," I say, "she was a lost woman, too. Isn't that who this place is for?"

Wren smiles gently. "It is."

We tie them to the boughs of the tree. Without the enchantments that had lain over the temple, the paper leaves have begun to droop. Some have already shed. I feel a pang as I imagine Chenna and Mistress Azami and the others' leaves falling. Still, even if this ritual is meaningful, it's only that—a ritual. A small tradition to honor these treasured women. Their true legacy is something we'll carry with us in our hearts, where they can never be tarnished.

Wren gathers me into her arms when we're done. "Are you sure?" she asks again, this time meaning where I want to go next.

I nod into her chest, her robes wet from my tears. "I'm sure."

Women's Court is untouched by the battle, though it's changed in a different way. It bustles with activity as Papers and demons of all kinds go about their various tasks in the post-battle cleanup, or snatch a few moments of rest in the lush gardens. All the spare rooms have been assigned to our warriors and the palace shamans, many to one room given the sudden swell in numbers. But no one complains, and the smiles cast our way are friendly as Wren and I head to Paper House.

Like a few of the palace buildings, it's been converted into a makeshift sick ward. Supplies are rushed down the corridors, doctors and soldiers and residents who have offered to help hurrying between rooms.

I could make the walk to our old quarters blindfolded.

The hallway where our bedrooms branch off is narrower than I remember. The paper screens are drawn for the privacy of the patients they now belong to. My heart lurches with each step, thinking of the girls who once occupied them. One of them lost to us forever. Another lost to me in a different way.

My room is the only one that's empty. A patient must have recently left.

I stare in from the doorway. Even though the furnishings are the same, it looks foreign somehow.

"Do you want to go in?" Wren asks.

I shake my head and draw her away.

The bathing courtyard has retained its purpose, its tubs standing full and steaming. We've lucked upon a quiet time; the tubs are empty. The bamboo trees lining the walls rustle in the breeze. The air is honeyed and warm. The fragrance of the courtyard brings back so many memories, and I let them flow over me as we wander through. The girls' laughter. Lill's grin as she told me stories while washing me. The bite of Blue's voice when she insulted my mother, and Wren's firm grip when she stopped me from retaliating. It was the very first time we touched.

Like our quarters, the courtyard seems smaller than I remember. I wonder whether it's some trick of the mind. When a place holds power over you, it looms large, and once that power is stripped away it appears how it really is. Just a room, or a courtyard, or a house, or a palace. Walls and floorboards and gates and archways. Building blocks. Pieces of a place—but not the heart of them.

"There's something I want to do before we leave," I tell Wren.

She lifts a brow. "Oh?"

We've come to my tub. It's half hidden by the overgrown bamboo, the summer light through their leaves painting dancing patterns on the water. I slip my arms around Wren's neck, a smile slinking across my lips.

"Let's take a bath," I say. "You *really* smell."

She returns my smile, sweet and tentative and hopeful, and as our lips touch I feel something warm swell through me, just as sweet and tentative and hopeful.

A place is just building parts brought together. Its true heart—a home—is the people who inhabit it.

THREE MONTHS LATER

FORTY-TWO

LEI

"S TOP PUSHING!"

"I'm *trying* to get a better look!"

"So are the rest of us!"

"Well, if you'd just move your ginormous head—"

"What are you implying?"

"Oh, come on, Zhin, I saw you going back for seconds at every meal at the Jade Fort—"

"Lei's auntie is an excellent cook!"

"As your giant head proves!"

"You're ridiculous. Heads can't get *fat*, Zhen—"

"Tell that to yours—"

"We're here," Blue interrupts hastily, shoving the twins aside to get to the carriage door.

I scramble after her, relieved to be out of the cramped quarters the five of us have been sharing for the past week. I help the twins out, then hold out my hand to the last girl.

Lill takes it with a sheepish grin, leaping to the cobbles. "Your home, Lei!" she exclaims, her doe ears fluttering. "I can't believe you've been away for one whole year! How does it look? Is it just like how you remembered?"

It *is* just as I remembered.

The shop front with its tall shuttered windows, half drawn against the last of the summer heat. The weathered wooden facade. The way it seems to lean out slightly over the road, and how cramped it is by the houses next to it, the whole street a row of old, peeling buildings clustered together as though huddled for safety—which, in a way, we always were.

Zhen and Zhin have already disappeared inside. Blue hovers by the open doorway. She holds something up. "Tien is demanding we wear these ridiculous slippers. If this is what all you poor villagers are subjected to, it's no wonder you're the way you are."

"The way Lei is is *awesome*," Lill says.

I laugh, ruffling her hair. My eyes are warm from the sight of my old shop-house, but my tears don't fall until Tien's barking voice comes from inside.

"Aiyah, what's taking so long?"

I can practically hear my father's sigh from here. "Give them a moment, Tien. They've had a long journey."

"The same journey we made two days ago, and I was still unpacked and cooking *you* dinner not five minutes after we arrived."

I enter my house, beaming so widely it hurts.

Tien tuts at me from where she's bustling behind the counter, selecting herbs from the boxes lining the walls for tea, while Baba rushes to greet me, opening his arms wide.

"Happy tears?" he asks, with a touch of concern as he draws back my hair to dry my wet cheeks.

"*Very* happy tears."

We embrace again. When I finally let go, he smiles in welcome at the others before muttering into my ear, "I have a surprise for you." He leads me by the hand to the back of the shop. "Hurry," he says in a carrying whisper. "Before the old demon changes her mind."

"Change how?" Tien grumbles. "I never approved of it in the first place."

"Approved of what?" I ask.

Baba only winks. We move through the small rooms and corridors of my house. My eyes drink in every detail. I feel off-kilter, as though I've slanted through some crevice in time, finding myself in a pre-palace world—maybe even a pre-*raid* world, when Mama was still around and my father's smile was always this wide, and these walls and the people within it were all I needed to feel safe.

The door leading to the garden lets through a slither of light. As my father goes to slide it fully open, a tiny wet nose appears in the gap.

There's a high-pitched *yap*—then the door opens to reveal a furry black face, bright sable eyes, and floppy ears, with a patch of white on its snout. The little dog bounds inside, waggling so hard I can barely hold on to it. I drop to the floor, bundling it up in my arms.

"We've been calling her Kuih," Baba says as I'm ravaged by puppy licks. "Thought we could keep your mother's tradition of food names going. But we can change it if you don't like it—"

"It's perfect," I say, struggling to speak through my tears.

That's twice now I've been gifted kuih by someone I love.

"Keep her outside! She's not yet toilet trained!"

Tien's voice bounds from the kitchen, along with Lill's confused response.

"Who's not toilet trained? Lei?"

Baba and I laugh. We lead little Kuih onto the veranda, our beautiful garden spreading out before me. Afternoon sun beams down on the overgrown grass and herb plot. The old fig tree is heavy with fruit.

"The girls are going to love her," I say, tickling a spot behind Kuih's ear, one Bao used to love, too.

"Shala and Aoki already do," Baba says.

I hesitate. "Are they doing all right?"

"As well as you could expect," he replies. He smiles. "I'm glad you decided to come home, Lei."

Home.

Though I smile back at him, an ache rises in my chest, remembering what I understood that last day in the palace. I *am* home—and it feels even more special to have the girls with me. But I'm also far from another home.

Once more, after all this time fighting to get back to each other, I am half a world away from Wren.

Life in my house has never been noisier.

Even outside shop hours, when the front room bustles with people clamoring to get a look at me, the Moonchosen, the girl who slayed the King, our once-quiet walls are filled with activity. Tien pretends to hate it, while not-so-secretly thriving at the opportunity to boss so many new people about. Baba is renewed, more energetic than I've ever seen him since Mama's death. Though he told me it almost killed him and Tien not to join the battle at the palace, they stayed at the camp like I'd asked, and they've been making up for it by being as useful as possible ever since. Still, Tien eventually declared she'd had enough of kowtowing to clan lords and ladies who *clearly* didn't appreciate her cooking enough, so she and Baba came back here to reopen the shop. Baba made me promise I'd join them soon.

I wasn't surprised when Shala and Aoki decided to leave with them. Shala told me she wanted a more peaceful place to give birth, though I sense it also had to do with getting away from the political hub the Jade Fort had become. I think she was afraid someone would try and hurt her baby once it was born. After the battle, Wren and I decided to keep Shala's identity quiet for the same reason—as well as to protect her from questions and knowing stares. And even if many suspected who she might be, no one dared ask.

As for Aoki, I know it pained her each moment she stayed at the Hannos' home. Wren told her about her family a couple of days before we left the Free Palace, so she could choose whether to come to the Jade Fort with us and the other girls. Aoki was inconsolable at the news. The thought of the pain she was in broke my heart. I wanted to go to her so badly, but we still hadn't spoken since the night before the battle.

In the end, I think Aoki only agreed to come with us to the Jade Fort because Zhen, Zhin, and Blue were going, and she was scared to be apart from them.

At the Jade Fort, Wren made sure the Hannos' best doctors and maids tended to Aoki. For their part, the other girls didn't harbor what had happened too strongly against Wren. It wasn't as though they were overly friendly to her, but when they saw us together in the hallways or grounds they'd stop to talk, and though their expressions were a little hard, I could tell they were trying.

We were all trying.

It was all we could do.

Then we received news of the twins' family. Their parents and their brother, Allum, had thankfully escaped the battle Wren led at Marazi unharmed, but they'd lost their home. Though it had been destroyed by a stray cannon from Marazi's side, Zhen and Zhin's parents refused to have anything to do with the Hannos. They'd fled Marazi after the Hanno occupation, fearful of repercussions for having close ties with the court. They came to the Jade Fort to collect the twins, planning to relocate to the Black Port where they had distant family connections.

But the twins refused to leave Aoki until she was fully healed, and confessed they didn't like the thought of leaving Blue alone, either, who was also without a home now, much less a family—or rather, her family had become *us*. That's when the twins suggested we might all stay together for a while. Just until... well, none of us were sure of what *until* really meant, but we were sure it wasn't here yet.

I knew without needing to ask that my father and Tien would love having the girls stay. So after sending a messenger ahead to alert them to our arrival, the four of us set out a month later, once the Hannos' doctors were satisfied with Aoki's recovery.

And at the last minute, four became five. Lill's family had stayed on at the Free Palace to work; Wren declared that any palace residents who wanted to remain were welcome to, in whatever capacity they chose. I'd given Lill an open invitation to visit me, and her parents seemed happy to let Lill take some time to be a child for perhaps the first true time in her life. Just a normal young demon on a trip to her Paper friend's home.

There was one condition to her coming: she could not call me Mistress ever again.

FORTY-THREE

WREN

WREN SIGHED, SWEEPING BACK HER sweat-slicked hair, half still draping her shoulders in dark waves. She padded down the hallway to her bedroom. The last rays of light—nights were drawing in earlier with autumn's arrival—slanted in through the latticed windows. Wren rolled her shoulders, pushed out a breath against the pain in her hip.

Another long day of meetings. They were always draining, but today's were particularly difficult. Each province had appointed a temporary governor after the war, but it was getting into the gritty decisions of how best to choose the official representatives. Some clans who'd initially agreed to their restructuring weren't so sure anymore. It had led to some heated meetings.

Wren couldn't tell if she was managing everything well. She was the youngest member of the New Council—the term was official now—but she was Wren Xia Hanno, and she had her father's legacy to uphold, and it was she who sat in his place at the head of the table. Kenzo assured her often she was doing a good job. But that was Kenzo. He'd always reassure her.

Wren wanted the truth.

She wanted Lei.

She paused outside her door. For three precious months, she and Lei had shared Wren's room. No matter how tough a day she'd had, she knew how each one would end: with Lei in her bed, her lithe body curling into her, Wren pressing her nose into the long reams of her hair, the two of them falling asleep—or not.

She wished so deeply she'd find Lei behind her door now.

Instead, she found someone else.

"Evening, honey."

Lova was perched on the windowsill, the sunset gleaming through the shutters at her back, painting tiger stripes on her blond lion's coat.

Wren moved to the table in the corner where maids had set out tea and snacks. "You should be careful," she said, pouring two glasses. "Surprising a girl like that could end in serious injury."

Lova winked. "Sounds like my kind of foreplay."

"Lo," Wren said. "Please, not now."

Not ever, was what she meant, but she didn't have the energy for this to become an argument.

Lova knelt beside her, her tail swishing to brush Wren's side. "Wasn't the best of days, was it? Oh—how hard did you want to punch Lord Muay when he suggested demons are more *efficient, productive* members of society because of our *natural gods-given capabilities*."

Wren let out a gruff laugh. "I should have known things wouldn't change so easily. Prejudice runs so deeply in these lands."

"The Demon Kings had two hundred years to make it so. It's going to take much longer than one war and a few meetings to undo all of that."

"Do you think we ever will?"

"No," Lova said bluntly. "But," she added, "we *can* make it better."

She reached out and clasped Wren's hand. Wren clasped it back. Then she drew it back.

The echo of Lei hovered between them.

Lova finished her tea, then stood. "This came for you." She plucked a scroll from the folds of her wrap shirt. "Something nice to end a long day on, at least?" When she reached the door, she paused. "Let me know how the girls are getting on tomorrow. You know, to keep updated. They were here a long time, using up our resources. There was that girl—the one who fought in the battle. What was her name? With the hair…"

"Blue?" Wren said with a knowing smirk.

Lova waved a hand. "Whatever. I just wondered…she'd make a good warrior. It seemed like she was getting on well here." She rolled her eyes as Wren's smirk grew and left before Wren could tease her more.

Wren hadn't failed to notice the way Lova and Blue had begun to look at each other during their time here. It was the same look she'd seen worn by Merrin and Bo once, and now Khuen and Samira, and Kenzo and the many, *many* handsome warriors that passed through the fort.

Wren was happy for them. Shifu Caen once taught her how to bloom a flower from the tiniest seedling in seconds with her magic. She thought that if magic never came back, at least they would always have this: affection, attraction, *love*, blooming like brightly colored flowers nudged by soft footsteps.

Though gods, she hoped magic would come back.

That was a problem Ruza was working on. The young shaman had volunteered to help in their efforts to understand the Sickness, and if magic might be coaxed back into their world. Ruza was infamous among the ex-royal shamans for his part in freeing them, so

Wren had offered him a position on the New Council as representative of Ikhara's shamans.

She didn't want to make any more decisions on their behalf. They should have a say in how magic is used.

In how *they* are used.

She smoothed out the letter Lova had passed her. Every word shone with Lei's voice.

> Wren,
>
> It's a stupid hour in the morning but I had to write to you as soon as I got the chance, and I know I'll be called back to help soon. You know what Tien is like when she's kept waiting. Well, now there's Blue, too.
>
> Come save me! Help!
>
> Anyway.
>
> Shala has given birth! Two days ago, on the eighth day of the month (I'm hoping no one will read too much into that — you know how I feel about good-luck signs). She and the baby are being well looked after considering they live in an herb shop and Baba and Tien have been preparing for the birth ever since Shala asked if she could come home with them.
>
> The baby is <u>so</u> cute, Wren. Once we got the goo off of him, at least. He's healthy, a Moon, with tiny horns Lill is obsessed with. Kuih is jealous of the attention we're

lathering on him, though she sniffed his feet yesterday and gave them what I'm sure was an approving lick.

Please tell Kenzo and Lova and Nitta for me, and anyone else you trust. We have a little Prince in our midst.

Not that he'll know that. Shala is determined he does not know about his legacy. Not yet, anyway. She wants to bring him up quietly, here in Xienzo. He'll grow up under the care of many adoring aunties — oh, gods, I'm an <u>auntie</u> now — far away from the world that shaped his father. We're all glad about that. I guess there'll always be ways corruption can reach a child, but they'll have to battle through us, first. And we're a pretty strong group.

His name is Ai. Blue hates it, obviously. Says calling him after love is sentimental. But I adore it.

I guess I'm sentimental.

I miss you, Wren. Like you wouldn't believe.

All right — Ai is crying and I can hear Tien stomping along the hall. He's calmed by my arms more than anyone else's, so my arms and I are getting called on a lot recently. I'm not complaining. It's a pleasure to help, even in this small way. Both for Shala and Ai.

Oh. Without magic we weren't sure at first what to do about the Birth-blessing ceremony. We debated it a lot, *but we landed on something perfect. You were actually the inspiration. I'll tell you about it when we next see each other.*

Or come visit and see for yourself.

Stay strong, Wren. Go shape our world into something worthy of a little demon boy named after the most powerful, precious thing in the world.

> *All my love,*
> *Lei*

They held a small celebration the next evening in Shala and Ai's honor. Wren told Lova, Nitta, Kenzo, Khuen, Samira, and Ruza, and they'd all been delighted. Lova had been the one to suggest a party—not that it took much for her to do so. Throwing parties was her specialty. Better if it included explosives and a little fighting.

Luckily, this one did not.

They set up a fire and some cushions outside, near the edge of the forest where they likely wouldn't be disturbed. Wren raided her father's sake collection. Nitta made sweets. She'd been spending a lot of time in the kitchens since the war, and had learned a few things under Tien's strict tutelage. Kenzo dug out an old double-stringed lute that was hideously out of tune, but after a few hours and many drinks, it didn't seem to matter.

Nitta and Wren sat close. Even with the fire's warmth, the night was chilly, and they had a blanket around their shoulders. Past the dancing embers, Lova swung her hips as she warbled along to Kenzo's lute. Kenzo roared with laughter at her lewd lyrics. Khuen and Samira were kissing. Slightly off to the side, Ruza watched them with curiosity. Perhaps it was because they were a Paper and a Steel—or, perhaps it was simply because they were kissing with such...enthusiasm.

Wren watched them, too, not with curiosity but jealousy. Her chest ached. Lei would have loved this. *She* would have loved Lei to be here to love it with her.

Samira withdrew long enough from Khuen's mouth to notice Ruza's and Wren's stares. With a roll of her scarlet hawk eyes, she fluffed her wing-arms and swept them in front of her and Khuen, hiding their faces from view.

Everyone laughed.

Nitta rubbed her arm. "Missing her?" she asked.

Wren smiled. "Always."

"Reminds me of our travels at the beginning of the year," Nitta said, nodding at their party. "That was a good time."

"We were on the run for our lives for most of it."

Nitta beamed. "Exactly. A good time." She gave a little shimmy in her chair. "What do you think?"

Wren eyed it. "Well," she said, "Battlechair's got more weapons—"

"—Which I do love—"

"—And it's more intimidating-looking—"

"—I do like to be intimidating—"

"—But Lazychair *does* look more comfortable."

"Right? It's *so* comfortable! Lova put in lumbar support and extra padding for my bony behind. All it's missing is a cupholder. I should ask her to make one."

"Maybe wait until tomorrow," Wren suggested. "If you ask now, I'm not sure she'll remember."

"No," Nitta agreed, watching affectionately as Lova spun in

circles with Kenzo and Ruza, the lute abandoned, Khuen and Samira still kissing behind the shield of Samira's wings. "I doubt she would."

Wren recollected something then: a heated conversation she'd overheard between Nitta and Lova when Merrin—her heart still pinched at the thought of him, his death vivid in her mind—had first brought Nitta back to the fort.

"You've been getting along well," she said.

"Hmm?"

"You and Lova. You've stopped fighting."

Snatches from that first argument came back to her, jumbled after so long, but Wren had a sharp memory—she'd been trained to notice everything, after all—and she knew what she'd heard, even if she didn't understand it.

We never told her—

I know that! Do you think she'd still be talking to me if she knew? . . . What I don't understand is why.

If you still don't understand, Lova, you never will.

You owe me no allegiance, Nitta. Neither you nor Bo.

Do you think we ever stopped being Amala?

Lova had exiled Nitta and Bo from the Cat Clan a couple of years ago—over something it seemed she was afraid of Wren discovering.

Nitta's face turned serious under Wren's scrutiny. "I told her she'd have to tell you eventually," she sighed.

"Why did she exile you?" Wren asked. "What does it have to do with me?"

"Everything," the leopard-girl said sadly.

As Wren looked back at Lova—who was now in a pile on the floor with Kenzo and Ruza, the three of them laughing—a dark curl of unease rippled through the warm atmosphere.

Nitta clasped her arm. "Not now," she said. "Let her have this moment, Wren."

"You make it sound as though I won't look at her the same way once she tells me."

"You won't," Nitta replied solemnly. "I didn't, either, not for a long time. But none of our hands are free of blood, Wren. We've all made awful decisions for the sake of the ones we love."

"You haven't," Wren pointed out.

Nitta brightened. "Well, not everyone can be as exceptional as me. Shame. The world would be a much better place if it was."

"Yes," Wren said sincerely, smiling. "It would."

She didn't have to wait long to discover the truth. Lova came to her with it the next morning. Nitta had warned Lova about her conversation with Wren, and so Lova told Wren everything, and Wren listened in silent fury.

When Lova left her room, Wren heard murmuring outside. Then there was a knock.

Nitta came in before Wren had time to respond. "I'm here for damage control," she said lightly. "I know magic's gone, so you're not about to blast half the room apart, but I thought you might be a little angry, and I didn't think you should be alone in it."

Wren struggled to breathe. "A *little angry*?"

"Unless you *want* to be alone. I don't want to impose. If it's what you need, I'll leave. But I've learned anger isn't always best left to its own devices. It has a tendency to . . . flourish."

"She had my mother killed," Wren seethed, her hands fisted at her sides. "Of course my anger is *flourishing*. Lova had her killed, and pinned it on the King to provoke my father into starting a war. A war that led to thousands of deaths. That stole away so much from so many. That took—took people I love. Hurt people I love. *Broke* people I love."

"That's all true," Nitta started, "and it's terrible, but—"

"No, Nitta. There's no excusing this!" Wren wished she still had her Xia powers so she could release some of the wrath Lova's revelation had left her with. "So—what? Lo didn't want my father to take the King's place because she didn't think he'd be a good ruler, either? She didn't really believe the King's control could be destroyed from the inside the way my father planned? She wanted a bit of death and drama before it was all over? Is that it?"

"And," Nitta said patiently, evidently ignoring the part about death and drama.

Wren's jaw ticked. "And. What."

"She knew you wouldn't get away with his assassination unpunished. And she couldn't bear to lose you."

Wren jerked away, exhaling sharply. All her life she'd been taught to channel her emotions into her fighting. But now the war was over, what options did that leave her with? How did anyone handle their rage if they couldn't slice it into shreds?

Wren flinched when Nitta touched her. The leopard-girl prized open Wren's fist and slotted her hand inside.

"Remember what I said last night," Nitta told her quietly. "None of our hands are free of blood. We've all made terrible decisions to protect those we love—*and* the things we love. For better or for worse, Lova loves you, and she loves Ikhara, and she thought a war was the only way she could save you both."

Wren could have laughed. "A war is the last thing that would protect me from death."

"I don't think death was the only thing she was trying to protect you from."

Wren stilled at that. Then, slowly, she sank to her knees. She stared out through the windows over the grounds of the fort, the forest and grasses tinted pink from the early sun. Nitta looped an arm around her shoulders.

"That's why you and Bo were exiled," Wren said.

Nitta sighed. "We were thieves of secrets, and we stumbled upon one of our General's own. We were young and stupid and greedy. Bo thought it would be some sort of power move that would force Lova to promote us within the clan if we came to her with it and made sure she knew we could use the information against her. But she knew better. Bo and I had been raised by our fellow clan members since our parents died in a ground-ship accident not long after we were born. We'd never do anything to hurt them. They were our family. *Are* my family." Her lashes dipped. "Still, a challenge against our General couldn't go unpunished. Lova exiled us—and, I suppose, imagined her secret would be exiled with us. She hadn't decided yet whether to act on her plans or not. You know, it was just after the two of you met when she learned Ketai was going to plant you in the palace as one of the Paper Girls. She'd been unsure of him before, but that's what solidified it for her, I think. Knowing he would do that to his own daughter."

Heat pricked Wren's eyes. "He—it was—there was a purpose..."

"Of course there was a purpose, Wren," Nitta said sorrowfully. "There always is. It's whether you can support it or not. Whether you think it justifies the means. I might not condone Lova's actions, but I can stand by her reasoning. Can you stand by your father's?"

The horror of what Nitta was really asking filled the room.

Her father had sent her off to the King to be raped. That was the simple, brutal truth of it. Wren had been trying to run from it for years.

Nitta pressed her cheek to her arm. They were silent for a long while.

Eventually, Wren said, "You truly forgive Lo for all this? Even Bo?"

Nitta answered firmly. "Nothing will bring my brother back. The kingdom was burning long before Lova struck the match. We all know it."

Nitta had told Wren last night that Wren would never look at Lova the same after learning the truth, and she was right. Wren knew it deep in her bones. But it wasn't because she didn't understand why Lova had done what she did. Nor because she'd kept it from her, and for so long. It was because Lova's actions reminded Wren she had done abysmal things herself for a similar reason— and she didn't know whether the girl *she* loved would ever truly forgive her for them.

As if sensing her thoughts, Nitta squeezed Wren's shoulder. "Talk with her, Wren. Properly." She gave her a fortifying smile. "It'll be all right. And if it isn't—come back and bed Kenzo. Seems to be what everyone is doing now when they need to feel better."

Despite herself, Wren laughed. "I'd noticed. He's not my type, I'm afraid."

"No," Nitta sighed. "Nor mine."

Wren hesitated. "What *is* your type?"

"I don't have one." Nitta shrugged. "You know, I'm not sure all that's for me. It's fun to joke about, and it was always easy to pretend about that kind of stuff because I'd heard enough of Bo's stories. But...the flirting part is what I like. I'm not sure about the rest of it."

"And love?"

The leopard-girl's expression was soft and warm. "*That* I have enough of to keep me going for a few good lifetimes."

Wren pressed a kiss to her brow.

"Careful," Nitta said. "Lei might find out. And I've seen what that girl can do with a knife."

Wren laughed. After a pause, she said gruffly, "When I'm gone, keep an eye on Lo for me."

She didn't add that what Nitta had said was right: anger *did* flourish in solitude. But, as Wren had learned the hard way, so did many other destructive things—including perhaps the most destructive of all.

Guilt.

FORTY-FOUR

LEI

THE AUTUMN BREEZE RUFFLES MY CLOTHES where I'm lying on the grass, Kuih napping in the crook of my waist. Apart from the birds and the insects and the sounds of our neighbors going about their business, the afternoon is quiet.

It's the one day of the week we shut the shop. Tien is out at a meeting. Baba has gone for a walk with Shala, Ai, and Blue. Without the twins, who left a few days after Shala gave birth to join their parents and brother at their new home in a nearby village, and Lill, who returned to the Free Palace, it's just me and Aoki in the house. It's the first peaceful moment I've had in a long time. I relish it, enjoying the freshness of the breeze and the fragrance of our herb plot, and Kuih's gentle snoring. She's grown so much already. Her little puppy belly is rounder than it probably should be, and I suspect my father is the culprit.

Like Bao, Kuih is a fan of dried mango.

I'm half dozing when a shadow falls over me.

"You got another letter."

I sit up quickly, startling Kuih. She grumbles at me before going to sniff Aoki's legs. Aoki smiles at her, bending to tickle her ears. She passes me the scroll without meeting my eyes.

I thank her and wait for her to go. It seems as if she's about to, when she stops.

"I'm sorry," she says suddenly.

Then—deepening my surprise—she sits down by my side. Kuih cuddles up to her, and Aoki strokes her absentmindedly, her mouth twisting in a way I know means she's trying not to cry.

"Aoki," I start, "you don't have to apologize—"

"I do." She takes a shaky breath. "Shala and I have been talking a lot. She's...explained things to me. Things I knew already, I think, but needed to hear. Or at least, in the way she told them. Zhen and Zhin, and—and Ch-Chenna..." She wobbles on the name of our friend, the name that brings a fresh snap of pain each time I hear it. "And you. You've always tried to shield me from the reality of our lives at the palace." She pauses. "Blue, not so much."

I huff a laugh.

"But I couldn't take it in back then," Aoki says. "I don't know why."

Her fingers pause. Kuih licks them to encourage her to continue, but Aoki is still now, wet tracks shimmering on her round cheeks; Tien's food has refilled them, and it suits her. She looks almost like her normal self again. And when she turns to me, I almost reel back, feeling seen by her, *really seen*, for what seems to be the first time in an eternity. Her lovely opal-green eyes fix mine, and I feel the weight of that eternity—a time when we were both kind and cruel to each other, patient and cutting—shift slightly, as though it's made just enough space for a new one to begin.

We throw our arms around each other at the same time. Kuih yaps and shuffles about, and it makes me laugh harder, love and relief and affection welling up so strongly in me it makes me weep.

"I've missed you so much!" Aoki sobs.

"I've missed you more." She starts to apologize again, and I shush her, thumbing her tears away. "You have *nothing* to apologize for. Do you understand me? Nothing."

"What he did to you all—"

"To *us*," I correct.

She nods. "It wasn't right. I should have seen that. I should have been there to comfort you. Instead, I blamed you, when really it was—it was all *him*."

"It's all right," I say softly. "You were dealing with it your own way."

She whispers, "I loved him, Lei."

I hold her, my tears leaking into her hair. "I know."

"I—I thought he loved me."

"I think he did. As much as he knew how to love anyone, anyway. But he didn't deserve it. Not your love. Not you."

"What if—what if no one will ever love me again?"

"Oh, Aoki," I breathe. "So many people love you already. As for that kind of love...you'll find it again. I have no doubt."

"How?"

"How do I know?" I clutch her tight. "Because I know you, Aoki. I've seen you in your hardest moments. And even then, *you*...you are astonishing."

We cry and whisper and hold each other until we're both spent. Then we lie back on the grass. The sky above is a clear, ocean blue. A bird darts through it, and there's no jealous pang as I watch it, no reminder of how its freedom taunts my lack of.

After all this time, I can finally spread *my* wings, too.

Aoki cants her head to smile at me. Though her eyes are puffy, the green of her irises looks fresher than before, as though her tears have washed them clean. That's what tears are for, I suppose. Washing things clean. Helping us shed the burdens we carry.

"Thank you," I tell her.

"For what?"

"For being my friend."

Aoki beams. And just then, she's the girl I met last summer, wide-eyed and stunned at finding herself, a farmer's daughter from the remote plains of Shomu, in the royal palace. Not yet hurt. Not yet a survivor. Not yet scarred by *him*. It gives me hope that, even in the darkest of times, optimism and kindness can prevail.

At the sound of footsteps in the house, Kuih dashes off; the others are back. I hear baby Ai's little squeal. Blue's melodic laughter, still such a sweet surprise after all these months. Baba and Shala's voices. A distant door slam that is probably Tien returning from her meeting.

The sounds of home.

No—*half* a home.

Because Wren isn't here. And as long as we're apart, I know I'll never feel whole. Even if, right now, holding Aoki's hand and lying in my garden on an early autumn day, listening to the bustle of my family in the house, I feel more whole than I have in a long, long time.

The slam of the porch door interrupts the peace.

"Little nuisance!" Tien barks. "Get in here, now!"

I roll my eyes at Aoki and hand her the letter. "Hold on to this for me?" Then I brush down my clothes and walk over to Tien. "Is it Ai? I don't hear him crying."

My lynx-aunt clicks her tongue impatiently. "No, though gods know that tiny troublemaker will be complaining soon enough. I think he's taking after you."

"I'll take that as a compliment," I say.

"You shouldn't." But there's a cheeky glint in her eyes. She waves a hand at my disorderly state. "Make yourself presentable. You have a visitor, and this isn't how we greet guests in our house."

My heart leaps.

Sensing my hope, Tien says quickly, "It isn't her. It's the pretty hawk-girl who carries on with that weedy Paper boy."

"Samira," I say, having to steady myself against the kick of disappointment. "I'll see what she wants."

"I suppose she'll stay for dinner," Tien grumbles. "With the state of cooking at that place, they're all bound to jump ship sooner or later."

We have dinner on the veranda, blankets draped over our legs as the nighttime chill sets in. Though the food is delicious as always—pork rib soup and syrupy sago gula melaka for dessert—and we talk easily, regaling Samira with stories of shop-house life, I'm anxious to speak to her alone. I know she hasn't flown hallway across Ikhara just for a dinner and a chat.

Shala and Aoki are the first to leave the table, to put baby Ai to bed. Shala brushes my shoulder before she goes, and I clasp her hand, grateful. In her arms, Ai cooes at me. He has his mother's gentle features, her softly turned eyes. If there's anyone else in his face, I don't see it.

Baba goes next, clearing some of the bowls. Blue tries to make herself small, but Tien drags her to her feet, summoning her to tidy the rest of the table. Though Samira and I offer to help, Tien waves us away.

"It's impolite to allow a guest to help," she snaps, "and quite as impolite to leave her alone at a dining table. Show her to her room when you're done. And don't forget to bring in the last of the things."

"Yes, Tien," I sing.

Samira raises her feathered brow. "She's even scarier than I remember," she says when it's just the two of us.

I laugh. "I think she's getting worse with age."

"The fort isn't the same without her." The hawk-girl's expression softens. "Or you."

"How is she?" I ask, strangely nervous all of a sudden.

The night is dark. Mosquitoes flit around the lantern hanging overhead. Cicadas sing in the grasses; in a few days it'll be too cold and they'll fall silent.

"She's well," Samira answers. "Busy. You saw what it was like. It's not getting easier. The high of winning the war is wearing off, and without magic, it's even harder for Wren to prove herself. Knowledge of her true identity is spreading, and while many clans have respect for her Xia heritage, there are also those who challenge her legitimacy to the Hanno throne."

"Blood isn't everything," I say.

"It is to some."

"Any news of your clan?" I ask carefully. After abandoning the Hannos, Lady Dunya and the White Wing loyalists returned to the Cloud Palace. No one has heard from them, though reports from clans in the region suggest they have yet to leave the immediate vicinity of their homestead.

Samira's feathered face tightens. "Not yet. I think I'll leave it a while longer."

"But you plan to go?"

"Of course. They're my clan. I miss them."

I can tell the subject is making her uncomfortable, so I change tack, giving her a sly look to lighten the mood. "Anyone else you're missing, hmm?" She breaks a smile. "How is Khuen? When we left, you two could barely separate long enough to say your good-byes."

"Oh, trust me," Samira says. "If it weren't for this, I'd still be attached to him now." We laugh, then she goes on, "But when Wren asked me to come get you, of course I agreed."

"Come get me? To bring me back to the Jade Fort?" My pulse spikes. "Is something wrong? She didn't say anything in her last message—"

"Not the Jade Fort. Don't worry, Lei, nothing's wrong. Actually, I think you're going to like this place a lot."

"You've been there?" I say. "Where we're going to?"

Samira nods. "It's a beautiful place. I'm happy to be going back there. I'd love to bring K, but I'm still not so good with passengers. One is my limit."

"Neither of us are big," I point out, then immediately groan as Samira's tone turns gloating, her smile sharpening into a knowing smirk.

"Speak for yourself."

Later that evening, I've just settled on my sleeping mat, rolling open the letter from Wren, when footsteps approach my door.

I start tiredly to my feet. "My arms and I are coming, Tien," I sigh. But when the door slides open, it's Aoki and Blue who appear.

Aoki is carrying a tray of pineapple tarts Tien baked this morning. Blue only carries her usual scowl, though, like everything about her recently, it is tempered. Her edges haven't disappeared completely, but they have smoothed out, like pebbles on a shore kissed into softness by the insistence of waves.

"Fancy a snack?" Aoki asks.

I grin. "Has the answer ever been no?"

They settle beside me, Blue leaning against the wall as Aoki and I immediately dig into the delicious sweets.

"You two are disgusting," Blue says. Then she gestures at the letter. "So? How are things back at the fort? That ridiculous cat demon still prowling around as if she owns the place?"

Aoki and I swap a look. I struggle to keep the smile from my face.

"You mean General Lova? Clan Leader of the Amala? Attractive lioness you spent a lot of time staring at when you thought no one was watching?"

Blue shoots me a death stare as Aoki bursts into giggles. "Gods," she hisses. "Forget it."

I smooth the letter open. "No," I say, "I won't." I hesitate, casting Aoki a sideways glance. "Would this—is this all right?"

Wren's unspoken name hovers in the room. I hate that just as Aoki's finally starting to understand and process what happened in the palace, she has these fresher wounds to deal with. The loss of her family is a trauma of a whole other kind, and I know it's going to be a long time before she starts to feel better about it, let alone Wren and the Hannos' involvement.

But to her credit, Aoki gives me a brittle smile. "It's all right. She's who you love, and I love you."

I squeeze her arm, thankful. Then I turn back to the letter—and my eyes widen. "It isn't from Wren."

The girls lean in as I flip the scroll to see the wax seal I opened in my haste, finding not the Hannos' midnight blue but instead a pale plum shade. We scan the first few lines of the letter together.

"Oh, my gods," Aoki whispers.

Blue stiffens. "Chenna's parents."

"The poor things," Aoki breathes. "You should be the one to read it, Lei. It's addressed to you."

"We all loved her." I spread it out so we can all see it. "We'll read it together—like Chenna would have wanted."

Dear Lei,

We apologize for not addressing you more formally. We
do not know your family name. A friend of ours told us
family names are not common in the more rural parts of
provinces like Xienzo. We hope we have not caused offense.

We are Chenna Munsi's parents, Ramir and Vita
Munsi. We have wanted to contact you for a long time,
but it has taken us a while to gather the strength. Please
forgive us. Losing our only daughter has been difficult.

We appreciate the letter you sent. If we had to be told by
anyone, we are glad the news came from one of her closest
friends. Someone who was there with her, from beginning
to end. Your kind words about Chenna have been a great
comfort to us. We read your letter often to remember her
as you knew her. It sounds as if she grew tremendously
during her time at the palace.

Vita and I would like to thank you for all you did to look
after Chenna. From what you told us about the other
Paper Girls, they were important to Chenna as well. We
would love the opportunity to meet you all one day and
thank you in person.

That brings us to the purpose behind us writing to you. If
it would not be too much of an imposition, we were hoping
we could come visit you to do just that — meet and thank
you in person. We assure you we would not take up too

much of your time, and we would obtain lodgings in an inn, of course, and procure all our own meals. Still, we understand if you are not comfortable with this and will respect whatever decision you make.

Thank you for your time.

We wish you and your family well.

Gods' blessings,
Ramir and Vita Munsi

Aoki's face is wet. I wrap an arm around her. Across from us, Blue sits rigidly, her mouth pressed thin. Then she seems to resolve herself.

"Her parents sound rather pompous," she says.

"Blue!" Aoki cries.

"Well, it's true. No wonder Chenna was so standoffish."

"She wasn't standoffish," I snap, "and you know it."

"She wasn't too bad, I suppose," Blue concedes.

I raise my brows. "A high compliment, coming from you."

Aoki scrubs a sleeve across her cheeks. "Well? What will you tell them?"

"That they can come as soon as I'm back from my trip, of course." As she smiles, I squeeze her to my side. "And that they'll be able to meet four more of the girls who meant so much to their daughter."

Aoki's eyes brighten. "Zhen and Zhin will have so many good stories to tell them! They always tell the best stories."

I shoot Blue a pointed look.

She throws up her hands. "Fine. Maybe they'll take a liking to me and offer to take me back with them to Uazu. If their posh writing style is anything to go by, their home must be far fancier than this one."

"I'd take Lei's house over a fancy one any day," Aoki says, and the three of us fall quiet at her words' significance.

Our last home was the most luxurious in all of Ikhara—and now here we are, living in my rundown shop-house in a nowhere village in Xienzo. Like Aoki, I'd take this over somewhere more opulent any day. And though she mutters a noncommittal response, taking a pineapple tart to avoid further scrutiny, I know Blue would, too.

FORTY-FIVE

LEI

FROM THE MOMENT WE LAND, I know Samira was right. I am going to like this place. A lot.

Even if I hadn't just spent an arduous three days on Samira's back—who, unlike dear Merrin, definitely needs more practice flying with passengers—I'd still be overcome upon our arrival. This is the Southern Sanctuary, one of four secret rest places for shamans and travelers throughout the Ghoa-Zhen mountains, and the place Wren learned about her Xia family during the war. *Sanctuary* is exactly the right word for it. Everything feels warm and safe and comforting, from the amber tint of the morning light to the bubbling stream to the prayers rising from the shrines.

I take a few wobbly steps, patting down my windswept hair. The hum of something familiar runs beneath my feet. Before I can place it, we're greeted by a group of shamans. More move around the settlement, shooting us curious glances before returning to their chores and conversations.

"Samira!" A tiny, ancient-looking shaman embraces the hawk-girl warmly. "It's so wonderful to see you again." She beams a gap-toothed grin, her cloudy black eyes sparkling. She turns them on me. "You must be Lei. I am Ahma Goh."

When I go to bow, she stops me.

"No formalities here, child. We are all one and the same. Besides, my poor back couldn't take it!" She clasps my hands in her wrinkled ones. "I've been waiting a long time to meet you."

"You have?" I say. "We came as fast as we could..."

She chuckles. "I mean since young Samira here and the others first stayed with us. That lover of yours is not much of a talker, is she? But I still knew about you. There are some things we don't need words to convey." My throat swells, and Ahma Goh's face shines. "Come. She's putting away breakfast."

Leaving Samira with the others, the old shaman leads me to an open-sided pavilion at the heart of the site. Its half hidden by a cluster of maples, their leaves the sea green of approaching autumn. Shadowed figures move inside.

That's when I hear her laugh.

I stop dead. Ahma Goh waits, smiling patiently, one arm wrapped around my waist.

That sound.

Wren. *Laughing.*

It splits me right down the middle—in the best possible way. In the way sunlight shears through heavy clouds, or a flower pushes up through a field of ashen soil. Not a breaking but an opening, a bloom of light and color, because it's Wren, *laughing*, here in this warm, magical place.

I race into the pavilion, past the others who cry out in surprise, and Wren is half turning when I launch myself at her with such force she staggers back, the two of us almost crashing to the ground.

But she is Wren, and she is strong again, and she is *happy*, so she regains her balance effortlessly, crushing me to her chest where my head is curled, one ear to her fiercely beating heart.

"Lei," she breathes, fingers knotting in my hair.

"Wren," I breathe back.

She presses a kiss to the top of my head, and I draw free just enough to tip my face, so her lips can find mine.

There are kisses of ours that felt like beginnings, and kisses that felt so awfully like endings. This one falls somewhere in between. Not new exactly, nor something coming to a close, but...a renewal. A promise of more to come.

"What's with everyone kissing all over the place?"

"Ruza!" I exclaim, untangling myself from Wren to give the shaman boy a hug.

He laughs, stumbling. "Easy there. I'm still working on my muscles."

"They're looking great," I tell him, and it's true. His form has filled out. Even the angry scar at his neck where the collar the royal shamans wore has faded to a faint mark. My eyes travel over him. "Really. You look great."

"I'm right here," Wren says.

I'm frowning now. "No, I mean..."

Then I go still, sensing properly the familiar warm hum beneath my boots: faint, but definite.

"Magic," I choke out, my eyes flying wide. "There's—is that—this place—*magic!*"

Ruza looks at Wren. "I think we broke her."

But Wren's smile, like her laugh, is more open and truer than I've seen it in months, and I know then that I'm right.

I gape at her. Joy and awe and disbelief and a dark twinge of fear compete in my chest. "You're—magic is—what have you done?!"

Ahma Goh approaches us, tittering. "Calm down, child. It's just a bit of magic."

We all know it's not *just a bit of magic*, but her words disarm me. I press my hands to Wren's chest. "It's really back?"

"Only here," she says. "And it's not nearly as strong as before. But it's a start."

"How do you feel?" I whisper.

She smiles. "Like I'm home."

Ahma Goh waves a tattoo-scrawled hand. "That's got nothing to do with magic, child. It's because you *are* home."

I clutch Wren's waist, looking around in awe. "Wren, it's *so* beautiful."

"*You're* so beautiful," she replies huskily, drawing me back to her lips.

"And that's my cue to leave," Ruza announces, as Ahma Goh claps us gleefully on.

It's almost midnight by the time we are finally alone. I feel giddy and the kind of bone-deep happy that comes from spending a blissful day somewhere as idyllic as the sanctuary.

"I could live here," I say as I swish my legs in the water.

Wren and I are sitting on the grassy bank of the bathing pool. The night is quiet. An owl hoots in the forest. The stream tumbles by, lustrous under the starlight. Though trees gather close, their boughs don't close over the sky, and reams of silver fall over everything: the rocks pushing up between the mossy carpet; Wren's dark waves of hair; the tawny skin of her thighs, our robes pulled aside to dip our legs into the pool. The water is unnaturally warm. Like the rest of the settlement, it glimmers with magic. I hadn't realized how accustomed I'd grown to the feel of it during my time in the palace, or even on our travels before the war, Wren and Hiro always weaving protection daos over our camps. If it was strange for me after magic disappeared from the world, after a short time of living closely with it, I can't imagine how it felt to Wren.

"We could," Wren says, gazing at my face. "Live here."

"There's plenty of herbs for me to work with in the forests," I say. "And I'll regain my magic."

"You'll use to it to heal the injured and tired who pass through."

"We can sleep under the stars in summer."

"And go on snowy walks in winter."

"Baba and Tien and the others would come visit."

"We could grow old like Ahma Goh," Wren says.

"I don't think anyone in the history of Ikhara has ever been that old," I reply, and we laugh, though not for long.

Because we both know what we're talking about isn't real.

Maybe we could do these things, if we were different people. But we're not. Wren has a nation to fix, and I have a new family to love and care for. They've lost so much already. It wouldn't be fair to disappear on them, too.

Wren draws my right hand into her lap. Her fingertips brush over where my enchanted bangle had been.

Wren had her best smith remove the bracelets from mine and Aoki's arms as soon as we arrived at the fort. Without magic to bolster them, they broke easily. The scars they left, however, have taken longer to fade—particularly for Aoki. Back in Xienzo, Baba has been tending to her half crushed wrist, doing his best for the old wound. She has problems picking things up sometimes, and I know it still hurts her to move it, but she's brave, and never complains.

I'm so proud of her.

"All that much magic used to harm," Wren murmurs, tracing the paling mark. "And all the pain caused to create it."

I twine my fingers through hers. "It doesn't have to be that way."

"Magic is going to be restored, whether we help it to or not. It's already starting here. It's bound to spread with time."

"That's a good thing. We *should* restore it."

She tips her head. "Should we?"

"It's our way of life, Wren. It's integral to so many of our cultures, so much of how we do things."

"How we do *terrible* things," she says.

"And how we do brilliant things." I hesitate. "Wren, what I said to you on Lova's ship. I'm so sorry. I didn't mean any of it."

"I wouldn't blame you if you did."

"No. You should. It wasn't fair—and you had to live with it for months afterward, thinking that's what I thought of you. I'm so, so sorry, my love." I push out a breath. "I'm not saying what you did was right. But I understand better, now. I—I've done horrible things, too. Like killing Caen. And watching others suffer without stepping in to stop it. And all the demons I hurt. I broke families, too, Wren."

She shakes her head. "You were only doing what you could given the circumstances—"

"Just like you."

"Lei, I've grown up like this, I was made to kill—"

"*Exactly.* Ketai forged you into his perfect weapon. He made vindication your whole world. It was all you knew, and he was all you had. Of course you did everything he asked of you."

"I did things of my own accord, too," Wren says, looking away. Her words come out hard as stones. "At the White Wing's palace. I didn't have to kill Eolah. I got scared when it seemed she might disrupt our alliance with them."

"And you knew it's what Ketai would have asked of you. Just because he wasn't there doesn't mean his voice wasn't in your ear, whispering. Look at Aoki," I say. "When someone gets into your mind, they don't just go away like that. They live there. They put down roots."

Wren grimaces. "How is she?"

I recall the conversation we had in the garden a few days ago. "She's getting better."

I loved him, Lei. I thought he loved me.

It's the first time I've heard her speak about him in the past tense. That's got to be progress.

"She'll never forgive me," Wren says.

"Maybe not. But you have to forgive yourself." I lift my hands to her cheeks, cradling her face. "I believe in you, Wren. I'll help you, and you'll help me. We'll work on forgiving ourselves, together."

She closes her eyes, tears welling at their corners, and whispers, "Can *you* forgive *me*?"

With a sob, I pull her close. "Oh, love," I say. "I already have."

When both of us have spent our tears, we sit side by side, my head on her shoulder, warm water swirling over our legs. Our wet cheeks shimmer. With one finger, I trace a word on the muscle of Wren's thigh.

"What are you writing?" she asks.

"Your name. I know he isn't here to ask, but...I think I know why Ketai chose it for you."

Wren waits for me to go on.

"It's written the same way as *endurance*," I explain, a little rushed, knowing what I'm saying is only a theory. "The character is made up of two symbols." I draw them with my fingertips. "A blade, and a heart." I give her a tentative smile. "That's you, Wren. Ketai might have chosen it for its literal meaning, seeing as you're what has endured of the Xia, and your endurance is one of the things that makes you so strong. But look at the way it's written. A pair of symbols. Balanced. Two parts of a whole. You've been made to believe your strength is all about the way you fight, but it's about your heart, too. The way you care. The way you love."

Wren looks so touched by my words it aches my own heart. I can tell she doesn't believe it yet. But I'll help her see.

For as long as it takes. I'll be here.

"Speaking of names," I say, "how do you like Ai's?"

Wren smiles. "It's perfect. You were going to tell me about his Birth-blessing pendant?"

"Not pendant. But yes. Want me to show you?"

She's frowning now, curious. "Show me?"

"You'll have to come to the house to see it properly," I say, reaching into my robes where I've tucked a folded piece of paper for safe-keeping. "But Blue drew this to give you an idea. Turns out, she's quite an artist. Who knew? She's been painting all sorts of things. Portraits of us, and Ai, and Kuih, and she does these hilarious cartoons. We have to hide those from Tien, though—they're mostly about her."

Wren opens the paper I've handed her. The picture is of a tree—but not a normal tree. There are paper leaves tied to its crooked branches, and on each of them are words.

Wren's fingertips move over each one. "This is…you made…"

"It isn't anything like the one in the Temple of the Hidden," I say, suddenly embarrassed, unsure if what we've done is somehow offensive. "But there's this little bonsai tree we've always had. It was Mama's pride and joy. She looked after it so well, and I was in her and Baba's room one day before Ai was born after we'd been discussing what to do about his Birth-blessing, and I saw it, and it reminded me of the paper tree in the temple, how safe and blessed that made me feel, so I wondered what if instead of names, we wrote the things we wished for Ai's future..."

I stop my rambling. I'm scanning Wren's face, worried about how tense she's gone. But when her eyes flick up to mine, her gaze is bright, incandescent—the same look she's given me countless times. A look that is fierce, and pure, and true.

A look that never fails to set my heart alight.

"I love it," she breathes. Then, setting the paper aside, she brings her hands to my face and beams at me, a smile so wondrous it makes my stomach swoop. "I love *you*."

She kisses me with the same force of her look, and my blissful day turns into a long, sweet, blissful night. And with it, the promise of—just perhaps, if I am lucky enough—a long, sweet, blissful life.

THERE IS A TRADITION IN OUR lands, one all castes of demon and human follow. We call it the Birth-blessing. It is such an old, deep-rooted custom that it's said even our gods themselves practiced it when they bore our race onto the earth. Once, we used magic to perform the custom, shamans crafting the small golden pendants that held our fates. A single character that would reveal a person's true destiny; whether our lives would be blessed, or whether our fates were something far darker, cursed years to be played out in fire and shadow.

Since the war, magic is hard to come by. The earth has slowly begun to recover from the Sickness, and over the past few years the faint thrum of magic has started to well up again in pockets all over Ikhara. A few of the shaman clans not decimated by the old rule have started practicing magic again. Still, it'll be a long time yet until enchantments are once again the norm.

Without magic, parents have been practicing Birth-blessing ceremonies in their own ways. I hear some write prayers on stones they plant in their gardens, a seed they hope will grow its own kind of power. Some cast little wooden boats onto rivers, watching their prayers take sail. Some make their own charms and trinkets, placing a lock of hair inside, so their children will never be without some piece of them, even after they are gone. Others hide words within—sometimes one, sometimes many, as we did with Ai's Birth-blessing paper tree—capturing their wishes in ink and sweeping calligraphy, sealed in anything from boxes and lockets to coiled shells picked from sandy shores.

I might be biased, but I prefer these forms of the tradition to the old one. In the end, what fate could be more precious than the one your parents dreamed for you when you were still barely a dream yourself? What words could guide you more gently through life?

No child should ever have to burden the weight of a Birth-blessing word like Wren's again.

As for Wren, she—like me—now carries a new word with her wherever she goes. We threw her old pendant away shortly after our trip to the Southern Sanctuary, on one of my visits to the Jade Fort. My own pendant was never recovered from the palace, and though I initially missed it, I've come to think it fitting it was lost. The fate it held for me all those years has been freed, after all. I have grown my wings. I have learned to fly.

Oh, how I fly.

A new necklace rests on my neck now, identical to the one around Wren's. We performed the ceremony ourselves, writing our hopes for each other on leaves of paper before sealing them within. We don't need to wait for the pendants to open. We don't need to see what's inside to know it's something beautiful, something full of love and promise, because isn't that all we truly wish for the ones we love?

When I initially suggested we redo our Birth-blessings, Wren wasn't sure, since neither of us are newborns and we already know the fates first given to us. But I managed to convince her. After all, that was a lifetime ago, and if all we've been through has taught us anything, it's that it is never too late to start over.

It is never too late for new dreams.

AUTHOR'S NOTE

I'VE TALKED IN THE FIRST TWO books about how personal this trilogy is to me—and how much it means to me that it's become personal to so many of you. I feel endlessly privileged to hear your stories of drawing courage and kinship from me and the girls. I hope I've represented us well in this book, too.

While continuing to explore issues of sexual abuse, physical and emotional trauma, post-traumatic stress disorder, unhealthy coping mechanisms, racism, sexuality, and misogyny, in *Girls of Fate and Fury* there's another matter highly personal to me: disability.

As with those other topics, I can only write from my own experience, which is as a disabled person with an incurable degenerative genetic condition, Ehlers-Danlos syndrome. Having always lived with pain and illness, my perspective is different from Nitta's and Wren's, Blue's and Aoki's, and Naja's and the King's sudden injuries, but the sense of having lost something, of dealing with a diminishing of one's ability and self, is painfully familiar to me. EDS is a cruel condition that robs more from me with each passing day. I didn't want to minimize the bitterness and torment this can bring, but I also wanted to show that disability is not all defining. Yes, I am my illness, but I am so much more besides. I hope this came through, especially with Nitta's character (oh, how I love her).

A final message about the main themes of *Girls*. So much of this trilogy is about reclaiming oneself: after abuse; after manipulation; after toxic relationships; after others have imposed their expectations and demands upon you. That's what my experience with sexual and emotional violence has ultimately come down to. How to define myself confidently once others have forced their own definitions upon me—or taken others away. How to come back to myself in the aftermath of trauma.

That's the journey the Paper Girls have to take now. It's one I'll continue making myself. I hope that those of you undertaking it have an abundance of love, patience, kindness, strength, and support.

And wings. I think we could all do with some of those.

If you are the victim of sexual, emotional, or physical abuse, please consider speaking to a trusted adult, or contacting one of the following resources if you need to seek help anonymously.

Crisis Text Line
Text: HOME to 741741
Info and chat: crisistextline.org

Substance Abuse and Mental Health Services Administration (SAMHSA) National Helpline
Call: 1-900-622-HELP
Info: samhsa.gov/find-help/national-helpline

RAINN (Rape, Abuse & Incest National Network)
Call: 1-800-656-HOPE
Chat: online.rainn.org
Info: rainn.org

Love Is Respect—National Dating Abuse Hotline for Teens
Call: 1-866-331-9474
Text: LOVEIS to 22522
Info and chat: loveisrespect.org

National Domestic Violence Hotline
Call: 1-800-799-SAFE
Text: START to 88788
Info and chat: thehotline.org

ACKNOWLEDGMENTS

WHEW. THIS TRILOGY HAS BEEN A *journey*. Though not nearly as grueling as Lei and Wren's, it has still been an epic few years, with physical and mental battles fought, friendships forged, teams built and broken, loves gained and lost, triumphs and failures, new homes and new dreams, a literal Sickness sweeping the globe, and my own share of life-threatening moments. But like Wren and Lei, I survived. And like them, I have so many to thank.

My new team at Little, Brown Books for Young Readers, for welcoming these books with warmth and passion, especially Alexandra Hightower. We turned this book around in mere weeks, and it was only possible due to your sharp editorial eye, fortitude, and hustle. My UK team at Hodder, for also getting these books through difficult circumstances. Molly Powell: thank you for taking the reins so adeptly. To everyone at Hachette on both sides of the Atlantic for all you've done for these books: every good thing that's happened with them is because of you. And, always, my original Jimmy crew, for championing *Girls* from the start. I owe so much to you all. Jenny Bak: your vision and belief is what got us here. I'll forever be thankful.

Taylor: for being endlessly patient and fierce and wise and kind. Every author deserves an agent like you. Love to you and everyone at Root Literary. And to Heather, for helping find *Girls* wonderful homes across the globe.

A huge, heartfelt thank-you to the health-care professionals who helped keep me going these past few years. Hospital trips and oper-ations and medical tests are never fun, but I'm so grateful to the wonderful doctors, nurses, cleaners, carers, and so many more who make hospitals as comfortable as possible for not just me but all patients—especially during such heavy times.

Friends and family and fellow writers who've buoyed me through this adventure: I love and appreciate and admire you all. Mum and Dad: thank you for the long-distance support. I feel it always. James: knowing you is a privilege. Callum: Lei's belief in the power of kindness has always been inspired by your sweet heart. Fab: I wish all men were like you. Chris: I'm so sorry I forgot you in book one's acknowledgments. Here you are! (And deservedly so.) And Sara: for simply being the best.

Last, but never, in no ways, least, my eternal gratitude to you, the readers who stayed with me and the girls all this time. I write words. It's you who make them come alive. Every letter, DM, post, tweet, review, share, article, list, display, book club, sale, library loan, panel, and podcast; just all and any instance in which you have talked about this trilogy: this is what has created a space for these books in the world. A space I was told by many couldn't—and shouldn't—exist. I get so many messages of thanks from readers who feel seen by my and the girls' stories, but it's each of you who deserves the credit.

Thank you, eight thousand times over.

ABOUT THE AUTHOR

NATASHA NGAN is a writer and yoga teacher. She grew up between Malaysia, where the Chinese side of her family is from, and the UK. This multicultural upbringing continues to influence her writing, and she is passionate about bringing diverse stories to teens. Ngan studied geography at the University of Cambridge before working as a social media consultant and fashion blogger. She and her partner live in France, where they recently moved from Paris to be closer to the sea. Her novel *Girls of Paper and Fire* was a *New York Times* bestseller. She invites you to visit her online at natashangan.com or on Twitter and Instagram @girlinthelens.